Woman's Book Club

The Mistletoe and Sword · The Suckling

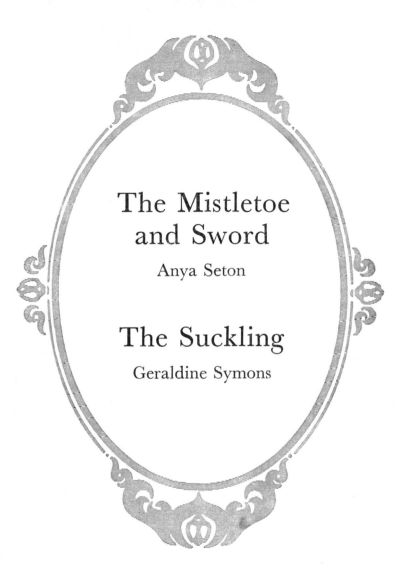

The Mistletoe and Sword

Anya Seton

The Suckling

Geraldine Symons

Odhams Books London

WOMAN'S BOOK CLUB, LONDON

The Mistletoe and Sword (copyright Anya Seton)
is reproduced by special arrangement with Hodder and
Stoughton Ltd. *The Suckling* (© Geraldine Symons 1969) is published by
special arrangement with Macmillan and Co. Ltd.
This compilation © 1972 The Hamlyn
Publishing Group Limited.

Printed in Great Britain by C. Tinling & Co. Ltd,
London and Prescot

600797015.
R.1. 972

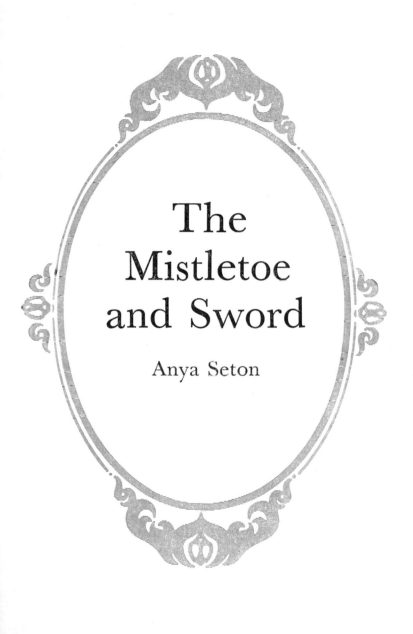

The
Mistletoe
and Sword

Anya Seton

About the Author

The author of our novel 'The Mistletoe and Sword' is Anya Seton, well-known writer of many books including 'Dragonwyck', 'Foxfire', and 'Katherine' – a fictional biography of Katherine Swynford, who eventually married John of Gaunt. Anya Seton was born in New York and grew up on her father's estate in Cos Cob and Greenwich, Connecticut, where visiting Indians taught her dancing and woodcraft. One Sioux Chief called her Anuthia, meaning 'cloud grey eyes' and this was shortened by the family to Anya. She came to Europe, first to England and then France, to study medicine, but married at eighteen, and with the arrival of her first child, she gave up her medical studies. In 1938 the urge to be a writer finally caught up with her when she sold a short story to a newspaper syndicate, and her first book, an historical novel called 'My Theodosia' was published in 1941.

FOREWORD

THIS STORY happened in England in A.D. 60–61. It is entirely based on history and follows in every particular the only contemporary sources that we have, *The Annals of Tacitus* and the *Roman History* of Dio Cassius. Dozens of authors have since speculated on the facts offered by these two sources; I have consulted most of these and found that *Boadicea; Warrior Queen of the Britons* by Lewis Spence (London, 1937) is the most detailed and convincing.

Boadicea, her daughters, the evil Procurator, the Governor, Suetonius Paulinus, Seneca, and General Petillius Cerealis are all historical characters; so was Postumus Poenius, prefect of the Second Legion, who actually behaved in the mysterious way I have shown, though I have used my own interpretation of why he did so.

It may be interesting to know that General Petillius Cerealis of the Ninth Legion became governor of Britain ten years after this story ends—a very good governor.

There is much uncertainty as to the extent of Druidism during this period, but most authorities agree that Stonehenge was used, though not built, by the Druids.

For the sake of simplicity and ease in locating I have used the modern names for Roman places in Britain. And for the same reasons I have followed one consistent system in the naming of characters because Roman nomenclature is confusing. Also 'Boadicea' is the fairly modern name for what was originally 'Boudicca'.

A complete list of my source books on Roman Britain would be tedious, but the works of R. G. Collingwood and Jacquetta Hawkes were perhaps the most useful.

A.S.

CONTENTS

[continued overleaf

CHAPTER I

The quest—Quintus the standard-bearer—a Druid's warning—
sparkling gold on the sacred oak—Navin the interpreter—
violence planned

QUINTUS, standing in the prow of the Roman war galley, was eagerly peering through swirling fog ahead, towards a glimpse of high white cliffs.

That was Britain at last! The savage misty island that he had dreamed about all his nineteen years, or at least it seemed that long. For Quintus could not remember the time when he had not known the strange story of his great-grandfather Gaius Tullius' weird and horrible death.

I'll find it, he thought with growing excitement. I'll find that place of the golden tree and the stone circle if I have to search through every inch of this barbarian land!

He lurched on the heaving deck as a great wave hit the galley. He grabbed at the painted eagle on the prow and lost his footing. Green water sloshed over him, and he collapsed with a clatter of shield, sword, and armour on the wet deck. The galley slaves, though straining at their oars to keep the boat headed for shore in this rising wind, nevertheless sniggered.

Quintus heard them, flushed, and ignored them, while he pulled himself up. It was beneath the dignity of a Roman soldier to act as though galley slaves existed. But he glanced nervously towards the stern, where his officer and ten other cavalrymen were huddled. Fortunately his officer, the centurion Flaccus, was seasick, and the others, having, unlike Quintus, no private reason for desiring duty in the wild half-conquered island, were grumpily huddled in their cloaks.

The wind blew harder, the waves mounted, and Quintus began to wonder if they were to be blown back across the channel to Gaul. Though it was autumn and not sultry, lightning suddenly zigzagged across the sky, and the galley slaves set up a wail. 'Neptune! Neptune! Deliver us!'

Quintus muttered a few prayers himself, but chiefly to Mars, the god of war, for whom he felt affection. He promised Mars a sacrifice if they landed safely, but it was not for his own safety he was so much concerned as for that of the transport which immediately followed them. That vessel contained the horses, including Quintus' horse, Ferox, of whom he was much fonder than anything in the world except his mother and his little blind sister back in Rome.

Ferox was a huge, intelligent, black stallion and as fond of fighting as his name implied, or indeed as Quintus was himself, though Quintus had had little opportunity to fight yet. He had entered the Roman army only last year, when he was eighteen, and there hadn't been anything but dull guard duty in Rome. It was a distant cousin on his mother's side who had finally wangled Quintus' transfer to these troops that were being sent to Britain. The cousin had influence. He had even sent a petition to the Emperor Nero about it.

Thunder crashed over their heads, torrents of rain drenched them. Quintus set his jaw and let the icy trickles stream off his bronze helmet and down his back beneath the leather cuirass. The galley slaves might groan and curse at discomforts, but a Roman soldier must take what came, stoically.

Fortunately the rain flattened the waves, and in a little while the galley's keel grated on a pebbly beach, not at all where they had meant to land, but it *was* land. And the horse transport soon loomed out of the murk and beached near them.

Quintus ran down the shingle to help the horses. Ferox whinnied and snorted when he saw his master, and floundered obediently through the shallows, where Quintus received the black stallion with a relieved pat and low word of greeting, 'So there, old boy—thanks be to the horse goddess that you're safe!'

Two of the other horses were not. They had broken their legs by falling on the heaving deck, and Quintus turned away his head, ashamed of the rush of moisture to his eyes, as a soldier cut the injured beasts' throats. There was certainly no time for tentiment. Flaccus, the centurion, was ramping up and down she beach, barking orders to his men, and cursing the climate and everything about this miserable island, where he had already served several years, before a trip back to Italy for recruits. It was penetratingly cold and dripping wet, quite unlike anything these southern-born troops had ever felt, but they saddled their horses, mounted, and fell into ranks, with the ease of long discipline. They climbed a steep cliff and made their way inland to a camping place.

Nobody bothered them. The silent forest seemed as uninhabited as the heaving ocean beneath the white cliffs. There was no sound but the rain, and as they made camp, Quintus was disappointed. He mentioned this to his friend, Lucius Claudius Drusus, who was Roman-born and young like himself but far more aristocratic, since he was distantly connected with the late Emperor Claudius.

'I thought we might see some action when we landed,' said Quintus morosely, settling himself on the ground beneath the partial shelter of his shield, and stretching his steaming leather sandals towards the little camp fire. 'I thought the natives were hostile—that's why they sent for us to build up the Ninth Legion.'

Lucius shrugged, thrust his sword into the simmering pot, and speared himself a hunk of mutton, 'I wish I was back in Rome,' he said, shivering. 'The sun'd be shining, there'd be the smell of flowers, we'd be all going to the games in the Circus Maximus, there'd be beautiful girls with gilt curls and sweet smiles. Jupiter! Even Nero's fat head up in the royal box'd look good to me right now. The gods, of course, preserve our august Emperor-god,' he added hastily.

Flaccus thrust his long, glum face over the fire and said, 'You two elegant young Romans make me sick. This tribe here in Kent is friendly, but if you *got* this action you've been wanting, Quintus Tullius Pertinax, I bet you wouldn't like it so much neither. One of these blue-painted savages come screaming at you in a war chariot, and you'd be bawling for your mamma and your cosy little white-marble villa, and your rose-water baths, *that* you'd be!'

Quintus' temper flared; he thought of a dozen scathing remarks to hurl back at his officer, but managed to swallow them. He contented himself with muttering to Lucius, 'That dog of a Spaniard, nothing but a colonial himself!' For the Roman army consisted of men drawn from all the conquered countries in the vast empire, and this Ninth or 'Hispana' Legion, which they were on their way to join, contained many Spaniards, to whom the young Romans from Rome felt quite superior.

As Flaccus disappeared to administer some reproof at the other side of the camp, Lucius said to Quintus, 'Why you ever moved heaven and earth to get sent out here to Britain, I'll never understand! Now *me*, I couldn't help it. My father thought it'd be good experience and discipline for me. By Mars, I'll count the days till I get home again!'

Quintus was silent. He had told nobody, not even Lucius, of

the story that had so fired all his childhood, of the queer feeling that in Britain his fate awaited him, or of the impetuous vow he had made long ago. Not a practical vow, his mother had said, too dangerous, and virtually impossible to fulfil. And she had added gentle words of warning designed to curb her son's impulsive tendencies. So he had stopped talking about the quest for the golden tree and the stone circle, but he had not been able to stop thinking about it at times.

Quintus munched on some mutton and shivered a little in the cold rain as he stared out into the silent, pressing forest. Suddenly a thrill went through him. It must have been quite near here, he thought—that long-ago battle when Gaius Tullius was captured.

'What's the matter with you, Quintus?' asked Lucius, yawning and putting down the jug of wine he had been drinking from. 'All you do is gawk at those trees!'

Quintus started. 'I was wondering where that first battle of Julius Cæsar's happened. I had a great-grandfather there too, and——'

'Oh Jupiter,' interrupted Lucius, yawning again. 'Can't you find something better to wonder about? What's it matter *what* happened in this wretched place over a hundred years ago! I wish Cæsar'd stayed in Italy, where he belonged; then *I* might be there too.'

Quintus laughed. 'Hardly a patriotic sentiment. Rome wouldn't be mistress of the earth today if Julius Cæsar'd stayed at home.'

'Maybe she wouldn't,' agreed Lucius, without interest. 'Here, move over; you're hogging most of the fire.'

This was not true, but Quintus was used to Lucius' grumbles and was fond of him, partly because they were the only two in this company who had actually come from the city of Rome itself.

Quintus obligingly moved over and soon both young men were asleep.

When Quintus awoke the next morning the rain had stopped, and by the time he was astride Ferox and riding next to Lucius on the road through the forest he felt eager for excitement. This was a good road they were marching on, twenty feet wide, and made of paving-blocks topped with gravel. Straight as a spear it led towards London through the land of the Cantii, a peaceful Kentish tribe. The Roman legions had built this road and many others like it since the second and successful invasion of Britain seventeen years ago, when the Emperor Claudius had actually come here himself and made a triumphal march to Colchester.

'Imagine!' said Quintus to his friend, 'Claudius' elephants plodding along here—didn't he have camels too?—miserable natives like those over there must've been terrified.' He jerked his chin towards a village he had just discovered to the right of them There were several round mud houses huddled inside a circular palisade made of sticks. A woman was squatting by the opening in the palisade pounding something in a stone bowl. She wore a shapeless garment that had once been striped and squared with colour, but it was very dirty. A naked little boy stood beside her. He was very dirty too, and as the legionaries passed on the road, both the woman and the boy raised their heads and stared narrowly, unsmiling.

'What a funny colour their hair is,' said Quintus, gazing back at his first native Britons. 'Red like brick dust. And shouldn't they salute us or something? After all, they're our subjects.' He spoke with the instinctive arrogance of Rome, and the woman's cool, level stare annoyed him.

Lucius shrugged. 'Too stupid,' he said languidly. 'I've always heard that these red-headed Celtic savages are very stupid. O Roma Dea—how I wish I was back in civilization! It isn't even as though we'd have anything to do here except police some dismal outpost in one of these everlasting forests. The Britons are perfectly quiet now and glad enough to enjoy Roman comforts, and good government, and the security we bring them. The interesting times of Julius Cæsar and Emperor Claudius are all over.'

Quintus nodded and sighed, 'Yes, I guess so, though Flaccus says there might be trouble up north.'

'Oh, Flaccus,' said Lucius with contempt, glancing ahead at their officer. 'He's as jumpy as a chicken; all those Spaniards are.'

The two young Romans rode on in silence behind Flaccus, but ahead of the rest of their company of eighty-two men, called a 'century', because, in the old days, it had always consisted of one hundred men. Lucius and Quintus both held minor office and had a limited amount of authority. Lucius was an Optio; Quintus a standard-bearer, carrying a tall staff topped with the Ninth Legion's number and emblems. It rested in a socket fastened to his saddle. Sunlight twinkled on their embossed bronze armour, on their helmets with arching crests of clipped red horsehair, on their oblong shields, and the scabbards of their short, deadly swords. Quintus and Lucius rode without stirrups, like all the cavalry, and were both excellent horsemen. When a white figure suddenly appeared from behind a large tree and waved its arms in front of them, the horses shied without disturbing the young men's balance in the saddles, though Flaccus nearly fell off his horse.

'By Hades, what's the meaning of this!' cried the centurion furiously, recovering himself and glaring at the apparition in the road. 'Hey, you, old man, get out of the way!'

The old man shook his head and said something in a heavy, guttural language, while he stood squarely in the middle of the road, his skinny arms outstretched. He wore a long greyish-white robe, and he had a grey beard through which gleamed a golden necklace with a dangling, mottled stone shaped like an egg. There was a crown of oak leaves around his partly bald head, and Quintus started to laugh. 'Here's the funniest sight I've seen since our Saturnalian games,' he chuckled to Lucius.

'Keep quiet!' shouted Flaccus angrily over his shoulder to Quintus. Then he beckoned for the interpreter, who came up and saluted.

'Find out what the old goat wants,' said Flaccus, 'and be quick about it or I'll ride him down.'

The interpreter saluted again and addressed the white-robed man. This interpreter was a British hostage, who had been captured in the Claudian campaign seventeen years before and taken to Rome, where he had spent the intervening years and learned excellent Latin. He was tall, raw-boned, and sandy-haired; a middle-aged man. His name was something unpronounceable like Neamhuainn, so the Romans called him Navin.

'This old man,' said Navin, at last turning back to Flaccus, 'is our Arch——' he checked himself, went on quickly, that is, I mean he's one of the British priests, sir. A Druid. His name is Conn Lear; he is a very important man.' Navin paused, and Quintus, watching, had a sudden impression that the old man somehow understood the Latin the interpreter was using, and was listening intently. Navin went on after a moment: 'Conn Lear wishes to warn you not to go farther up-country with your troops, sir. He says you must return at once to Gaul while there is still time. That his people want no more Romans in this land.'

'*What!*' shouted Flaccus between fury and astonishment. 'You

dare to tell me this impudent drivel! Navin, you're crazy, and
most certainly this old man is.'

'Possibly, sir,' said Navin tonelessly. His light blue eyes gazed
up into the officer's dark ones. 'But that is what he said.'

The priest suddenly put his hand on the interpreter's arm and
murmured something else rapidly and earnestly. Navin listened,
then turned to Flaccus. 'He says that *he* means no harm to the
Romans, but that all the omens and auguries point to fearful
trouble. The sacred hare has run its course through Stonehenge,
the great stone circle in the west. The mistletoe has been found on
three oaks near the Holy Well of Mabon, and the sea has turned
red as blood near Colchester. The British gods have spoken. *Turn
back!*'

'Phuaw,' Flaccus spat on to the road at the priest's feet. 'Scize
him!' he cried to Quintus. 'Bind him and haul him along with us.
We'll get to the bottom of this nonsense when we get to headquarters.'

Quintus jumped off his horse, eager to obey. So *this* was a
Druid! he thought, with angry excitement. It was white-robed
priests like this one that had killed his great-grandfather. All that
stuff about stone circles and mistletoe made it certain. 'Here,
greybeard,' he cried, striding up to the quiet Druid and holding
out a leather thong to bind the man's wrists, 'come along now.'

'NEGO!' said the old man sternly in Latin, and added Celtic
words which Navin, who stood by impassively, interpreted. 'He
says you have no right to bind or coerce him. He came only to
warn.'

Quintus hesitated in spite of himself. There was power in the
old man's steady, glittering eyes.

'Hurry *up*, Quintus Tullius!' shouted Flaccus, snapping the
bridle. 'Haul him off to the rear; you're delaying our march.'

Quintus thrust out his hands with the thong, and at once
something happened. It was as though his hands hit an invisible
wall. Quintus' vision blurred for a moment too; all he could see
was the Druid's fierce eyes. Then there was a whirl of white, and
he heard Flaccus' furious voice. 'By all the gods, you fool—you've
let him go! Run after him!'

''Twould be no use, sir,' said Navin calmly. 'These Druids have
magic tricks and many hiding-places in the forest.'

Quintus blinked and reddened. 'I'm s-sorry, sir. I don't know
what happened—it was his eyes——'

Flaccus, most surprisingly, did not burst into the torrent of

abuse with which he usually disciplined his subordinates. Instead
he bit his lips and cast an uneasy glance towards the thick grove
where the Druid had vanished. 'This infernal country,' he said
beneath his breath; 'there's many strange things . . . well, no
matter. The old man was crazy.' He kicked his horse while
raising his sword high as a marching signal to the ranks behind.

All that day and part of the next, until they reached London,
Quintus continued to feel perplexed and embarrassed at the way
the old Druid had somehow made a fool of him. He tried to talk
about it to Lucius, but that young man soon grew bored and
took to humming Roman love-songs to himself, especially one
that the Emperor Nero had written which celebrated the charms
of a lady called Acte. Lucius substituted the name of a pretty
Greek dancer he had yearned for back home, and managed to
forget the rain, which had started up again.

But Quintus still thought about the meeting with the Druid
which had made the old story come even more vivid than it ever
had in Rome, and as they plodded on, he went over again all that
he had heard from his father and tried to remember new details.

The tragedy to Quintus' great-grandfather, Gaius Tullius, had
happened a hundred and fourteen years ago, when Julius Cæsar
had tried to conquer Britain.

Gaius was an officer in the Roman army of those days, a
centurion, or captain, of the Seventh Legion. And in 54 B.C. his
legion was ordered to Gaul, where Cæsar was making preparations for invading Britain.

Cæsar had made a quick reconnoitring trip into Britain the
year before, but the great general had had bad luck, or even, it
was whispered in Rome, had shown poor strategy. The Romans
had never seen tides like those of the northern seas, nor such
quick, violent storms, and several disasters overtook their fleet.
Moreover, the Britons turned out to be fierce, strange fighters
who hotly resisted the Roman invasion. Cæsar tamely returned
to Gaul and decided to try again the following year. This time
Cæsar took with him eight hundred vessels of all classes and five
legions and cavalry, some thirty-two thousand men in all, so that
the British look-outs who guarded the great white cliffs by Dover
were dismayed at the sight of the huge force and withdrew into
their secret forests while they decided on the best resistance.

Gaius Tullius was a tough, brave soldier, and his Seventh
Legion was a crack one. He was delighted when Cæsar ordered

it forward to take a stockaded hill fort that the barbarians had built a few miles inland. The Seventh Legion took the fort easily, but no sooner did they plant their flaunting eagle standards along the stockade than a panting runner brought word of new disaster back on the landing beach.

Again, like the year before, Cæsar had under-estimated the force of wind and water. The tides had risen, a fearful storm had blown up, and the entire fleet had been smashed to bits.

Gaius had been standing near the general when this news came. He had seen the bald head redden, the flash of the eyes, and the sharp thinning of the lips, as Cæsar grimly gave the order to retreat—back to the beach-head. It was very humiliating, especially as there were jeers and taunts from the British captives they had taken—big, fair-haired men with blue tattooings on their faces, who wore helmets horned like bulls and long, gaudy, plaid trousers that the Romans thought ridiculous. But there was nothing ridiculous about British fighting. This Gaius discovered for himself ten days later when new boats had been built and Cæsar marched forward again into the interior. The British had profited by the interval. They had summoned a great force from all their near-by tribes, not only the Cantii of Kent, in whose territory Cæsar now was, but the Atrebates from farther west, the Trinovantes from Essex, even the Iceni who lived in Norfolk. And the British had chosen a general of their own, Cassivellaunus, King of the Catuvellauni tribe, who had a capital north of the little village of London at a place called St Albans.

This British army encountered Cæsar's in Kent about twenty miles from the coast, and the Romans did very badly and lost many men—a temporary set-back which Cæsar barely mentioned in the account he later wrote of this campaign. The heavily armed Romans were confused by the darting agility of the Britons, and particularly by their extraordinary methods of fighting in low war-chariots, which were furnished with whirling scythes on the wheel-hubs, and which could be manœuvred as deftly as the shaggy little ponies that pulled them.

Cæsar soon worked out a better defence and tactics. He crossed the Thames River and eventually made his way to King Cassivellaunus' capital, which he subdued, but for Gaius the war was finished in that first defeat.

He and a friend of his called Titus, another centurion of the legion, somehow got cut off from the main body of their cohort, and were captured by some little dark warriors from the mountains in the west of Britain. These little men, delighted to exhibit as prizes two Roman officers, thereupon carried the bound Gaius and Titus in a wagon back towards the west.

Titus survived to tell the grim story and its sequel to Gaius' son in Rome—the same story that Quintus had heard so many times from his father as it was handed down the years. Now, remembering it in the very land where it had happened, Quintus felt the shiver that had always chilled his back as his father had gone on with the tale.

As Titus told it, he and Gaius had suffered much from shame at their capture and from hidden fear of what would be done to them. The wagon bumped day after day through the wild, black forests. Their captors did not harm them, in fact they fed and treated them too well, and Titus, who understood some Celtic, told his friend that amongst the fierce, little blue-faced men there was constant talk about 'the place of the great stones, the place of sacrifice', and that they talked of the sun-god, of sacred oaks and mistletoe, of Druid priests. And when they mentioned these, the British warriors cast uneasy glances about them and seemed afraid.

At last one day their captors came to a giant oak on the edge of a great open plain. On this plain there were circles of strangely formed stones, standing as tall as houses. The Britons stopped near the giant oak and threw their captives on the ground so roughly that one of Gaius' rawhide bonds loosened, but this he did not notice at first because of his amazement.

The oak-tree sparkled with gold. Its branches were hung with golden bracelets thick as a finger, and a sharp golden sickle rested in a low crotch of a branch beneath a great ball of mistletoe.

The British tribesmen threw themselves on hands and knees and seemed to be worshipping the oak-tree. Then they pointed to the distant circle of great stones standing on the plain, and they ran off towards it, leaving only one man on guard. This guard took several long pulls of the honeyed mead he carried in a drinking-horn and squatted down quite near Gaius and drowsed.

'May the gods of our fathers be merciful,' Titus had whispered to Gaius. 'I heard what they said—they mean to sacrifice us over there in that circle of stones, to cut us into bits for an offering to their god. They've gone to fetch their priests.'

'No,' Gaius whispered, while he worked one hand loose from the bond. 'We'll not be minced up yet.' Suddenly with his freed hand he hit the unsuspecting guard so mighty a blow on the head that the man crumpled silently on the ground.

Gaius seized the Briton's knife, cut his own bonds and Titus', but there was no time to escape, for the tribesmen came running back, and with them a dozen white-robed, long-bearded Druids, shouting and waving golden spears.

Titus did not remember exactly what happened then, except that as they were surrounded, Gaius reached into the tree for a better weapon than the knife and pulled down the golden sickle, which caught on a trailing frond of the mistletoe ball, dislodging the plant which fell to the ground.

At this the Druids and tribesmen let out a wail of horror. They stared at Gaius with glittering snake eyes and began to move forward slowly in an ever-narrowing circle round their sacred tree and the Roman who stood backed against it.

'Run, Titus,' said Gaius in swift Latin; 'they've forgotten *you!*' He brandished the golden sickle. Again the gasp came from the advancing Britons, and then, at a sharp command, the Druid priests drew their arms back as one man and hurled their golden spears. Gaius fell, quivered once and was still, while the Britons crowded around murmuring, staring with shuddering awe at the trampled mistletoe and the sickle in the Roman's hand. Titus did escape then, running back into the forest. Nobody noticed him, but as he went he heard a Druid cry in a great voice, 'Do not touch the dead Roman. He must never be touched. He has profaned our gods. He shall lie here as he is, forever more, in sacrifice!'

This was the end of the story Titus told when, after incredible luck and difficulties, he got back to Rome. But little Quintus had always asked one earnest, fearing question. Would, then, his great-grandfather's bones still be lying there in the heart of Britain under an oak-tree? And Quintus' father had solemnly answered that perhaps it was so. Here Julia, his mother, would weep and say that it was because of this that bad luck had come to the Tullius family, that it offended all the spirits of their ancestors to have one of them lie unavenged, and that this had brought a curse on them all.

In truth, matters had gone badly with the family since Gaius' death. It had lost favour with the emperors and become impoverished. There was much ill-health and many early deaths. Quintus' father died young of fever, the four brothers before Quintus died one by one, his little sister, Livia, was born blind.

'Some day, when I am big, I shall go to the dark island of mists,' Quintus, as a child, had boasted to his mother, 'and find the golden tree and poor Gaius Tullius beneath it. *I* shall see that he has the proper burial rites at last, and I'll take some of that gold and bring it back to you.'

Julia always smiled sadly, reminding him of how much time had passed since those days, that the tree might be no longer standing, and that it was cruel to trouble her heavy heart with foolish talk about the impossible.

And yet, mused Quintus, riding along the Roman road towards London, I always had a feeling that I'd get here some day, and I still have a feeling that the quest will succeed, but how? and where? and when?

This he could not guess, but his curiosity about this strange new land was keen, and some miles before they reached London, he summoned Navin, the British interpreter, to come and ride beside him.

'It must feel queer to be coming home after all these years in Italy,' said Quintus thoughtfully. 'Where did you live here?'

A faint, grim twinkle appeared in Navin's blue gaze. This was the first Roman soldier who had spoken to him as a human being, instead of as a barbarian captive or a useful piece of machinery. 'I was once a chief—the nephew of King Cymbeline,' he said quietly. 'I am a Trinovante, from the country north of the Thames, where Colchester, your capital, is.' He paused a moment, then added, 'It *is* strange to be coming home. To be here'—he glanced at the dull, dripping skies, at some rough mud huts glimpsed through a grove of birches—'after Rome.'

Lucius suddenly stopped humming and leaned over. 'By Venus, I should think so indeed! I vow you'll be in as great a hurry to get back as the rest of us. When I think of the glorious warm sunlight, and the delicious joys of the baths, and our food, our wine and music—yes, even our orators! The beautiful bustle of the Forum, the splashing of our fountains—O Roma Dea, Roma Dea,' groaned Lucius, invoking the spirit of his beloved city.

'Rome for me was not quite like that,' said Navin, while a shut look came over his big-boned face. 'This,' he added with a peculiar emphasis, 'is *my* country.'

Lucius shrugged and went on humming to himself, but Quintus noted the Briton's intonation, and for the first time a prick of doubt pierced his Roman superiority. Good old Navin had been travelling with this company ever since he was assigned to it in Rome. A quiet, courteous man, thoroughly romanized in clothes and speech, and grateful, one naturally assumed, for the fine treatment he had received. Indeed, all the British captives had been positively pampered; everyone knew that. And look at the royal reception the captured British King Caractacus had got from the Emperor in Rome too. It was no wonder the British had settled down so peacefully under the enlightened Roman rule.

As for that Druid's—Conn Lear's—warning yesterday, well, that was surely superstitious nonsense. But I wish I'd understood exactly what he was saying, Quintus thought.

He turned round and called back Navin, who had dropped behind. The interpreter brought his horse up level with Ferox again.

'I'd like to learn some British words,' said Quintus. 'Teach me.'

Navin looked startled; again the twinkle appeared, and he gave the attractive eagle-nosed young face a quizzical glance. 'It is seldom indeed that a Roman concerns himself with the language of his subjects, O Quintus Tullius.'

'Well, I think it might be useful, I like to know what's going on. For instance, what's "horse"?' He patted Ferox's sleek neck.

'We have several dialects,' said Navin, 'but I will give you words that can be understood by most Britons.'

By the time they had crossed the long wooden bridge over the Thames and entered the straggling little town of London, Quintus had memorized about twenty common Celtic words and was quite ready for some other distraction. But he did not find it in London, which was a dull place, except for the water traffic. The river was full of round, woven fishing-coracles and some trading vessels from Gaul, and there was a hubbub of sailors on the water-front. The town itself was mean and ugly. The houses were one-storeyed and mostly made of wattle and daub thatched with reeds; even the military and government buildings were of unadorned wood. Here and there on the outskirts one of the retired Roman soldiers had built himself a villa, but though many thousands of people lived and did business here, it seemed to be only an overgrown village.

'No decent forum,' moaned Lucius, as they passed the open market-place of trampled earth, 'no public baths, no circus—not even a temple.'

They drew up before the military headquarters, and Flaccus went inside to report the arrival of his company. He came out again almost at once.

'We're to proceed immediately to Colchester,' he said. 'Seems the Governor's there.'

'I thought, sir,' said Quintus, 'we were to stop in London, then go north to Lincoln to reinforce the Ninth?'

'Since when do you question orders?' snapped Flaccus. 'They've changed. That's all. One of these native kings has died, and there's a commotion about it.'

He turned his back, flicked his horse, and gave the signal to march.

'So much for London,' said Lucius, shrugging and easing himself in the saddle. 'Not that I'm tempted to linger. . . . Ah, more forest ahead, I see,' he added, as they headed east. 'The charming variety of the scenery here intoxicates me, and the climate——' for it began to rain harder.

'O'h, quit grumbling,' said Quintus good-humouredly. 'After all, they're sending us to the capital, and they say it's really quite a place. Maybe there'll be lovely British maidens, and even some fun.'

'Ha!' said Lucius morosely, expressing profound disbelief.

But actually Colchester was a fair provincial city. It had been the capital of that part of Britain under King Cymbeline, and the Emperor Claudius, on his visit, had given orders to turn it into a Roman capital.

The young men's spirits rose as they saw paved streets, stone villas, corner wineshops like those at home. The government buildings, and basilica and palace stood on the edges of the forum, which was properly furnished with a rostrum for orators to stand on, a mammoth statue of a winged Victory, and little altars to Jupiter, Mars, Minerva, and other gods. But one scarcely noticed those because the centre of the forum was occupied by an enormous building, big enough to shelter a thousand people, and obviously a temple with its dozens of white-and-gold columns, its elaborate carved cornices.

'Now WHAT is that?' cried Quintus, amazed at this unexpected magnificence, and Navin, who had remained near him and taught him more Celtic words during the boring three days' march from London, answered dryly:

'That is the Temple of Claudius, dedicated to our divine and late lamented Emperor who is now, of course, a god.'

'Not bad,' said Lucius grudgingly, preening himself a little, for he was proud of his relationship to Claudius and hoped that it could be used towards future promotion, and eventually towards speedy return home.

Quintus had a less personal reaction to the gorgeous temple. 'And do the British really worship here the spirit of their conqueror?' he asked slowly of Navin.

A muscle flickered in the corner of the Briton's mouth. 'Undoubtedly,' he said, in an odd tone, 'but you forget, sir, that I have not been home for a long time.'

This man knows something we don't know, Quintus thought, or am I imagining it?

As they continued to march along the edge of the forum towards headquarters, Quintus cast curious looks at the townsfolk. There were Roman citizens in thick white wool togas, slaves in short tunics, well-to-do Britons in gaudy tartan trousers and capes held with bronze brooches, and poor Britons huddled in mangy goatskins. But all of them, even the Romans, shrank to the wall as the legionaries marched by and gave the proper arm's-length salute, crying, 'Welcome, Eagles of Rome, welcome!' Evidently, the populace was well trained.

Flaccus went off to report, while his two subordinates accompanied their men to the barracks. Quintus saw at once to the stabling and grooming of Ferox, and when he rejoined Lucius he learned that they were summoned to appear before the Governor at once.

The 'imperial' palace was warm and comfortable, the chilled young Romans discovered gratefully. The shivery dankness outside had increased with the incredibly early nightfall of this southern climate. The palace was solidly built of marble and snug brick. The atrium—the great central hall—was roofed over as it would never have been at home, and the mosaic floors were well heated by hot-air flues from below.

A slave ushered Quintus and Lucius into the frescoed hall, which was lit by six torches and a bevy of little oil lamps. They clearly illumined a portentous group gathered round a parchment-littered table.

'The High Command!' whispered Quintus, staring up the hall at two throne-like chairs. One was occupied by a bull-necked, red-faced man in elaborate gilt armour who could only be Governor Suetonius Paulinus, the military ruler of Britain. The other throne contained a small, fat man with hunched shoulders and the domed head and hooded eyes of a frog. His white toga was embroidered in gold and so banded with purple that it was not hard to identify him either—he was Decianus Catus, the Emperor Nero's procurator for Britain, in charge of all its civil affairs, and only slightly less powerful than the Governor. Or perhaps he did not consider himself less important at all, for he talked continuously in a shrill, insistent voice, which quite drowned out Suetonius' occasional gruff interjections.

'I wonder what they wanted *us* for,' murmured Lucius after twenty minutes of unrecognized waiting by the entrance. Flaccus was there too, half-way down the room, and several other centurions, as well as senior officers—tribunes and prefects.

Four legionary generals, or legates, were milling around the Governor and the Procurator, and some other patricians in togas, but it was difficult to hear what was going on, until Catus suddenly stood up, banging his puffy white hand on the table, and shouting, 'I tell you, this is the chance I've been waiting for! We'll show these chuckle-headed savages we mean business. We'll call in the loans and help ourselves to all that ripe, juicy treasure the Icenians have been traitorously hoarding. The huge tribute we'll send back to Nero—the gods keep His Imperial Majesty in health and grace—*that*'ll startle him!' Catus' pursed pink lips drew back in a smile. 'The Emperor will be pleased with all of us,' he added quite softly, staring—as though he dared him to deny it—at the Governor, who rose also, while his gold-hilted sword clattered against the table.

'If—Decanius Catus—you will stop talking long enough to listen to me,' cried Suetonius, his heavy jowls quivering, 'you might learn that I am in complete agreement with you, and have no intention of interfering with your little plans for the Icenian nation. My interests are elsewhere—in the west. I am going to stamp out this disgusting Druidism once and for all, if I have to chase each one of the scurvy priesthood into the Irish Sea.'

Ah, thought Quintus, that's interesting. So we're to fight the Druids, are we? He had edged unobtrusively along the wall to a nearer viewpoint where he could hear and see much better.

And the talk went on. There was a tall old man in a toga who was called Seneca and made occasional comments which the others listened to respectfully. This Seneca was a philosopher and author—Quintus had read some of his books at school—and it also appeared from the conversation that he was, rather surprisingly, a money-lender as well. Then there were the generals who commanded the four legions in Britain—the Second, the Ninth, the Fourteenth, the Twentieth. Quintus recognized the legion each general was in command of by the badges, but he looked hardest at the legate of the Ninth, the 'Hispana' Legion

THE MISTLETOE AND SWORD

from Lincoln. For this was the post to which his company was assigned, and this man, Petillius Cerealis, would be his own commanding officer. He looks all right, Quintus thought, with relief. The General seemed very young for so much rank. He had keen hazel eyes and was slightly built, but he gave a pleasant impression of competence and strength.

After a while Quintus began to understand what it was all about. There was a large country north of here in East Anglia that belonged to a wealthy tribe called the Iceni. They had had a King, Prasutagus, who had died a week before, leaving no heirs but his Queen, Boadicca, and two young daughters. To be sure, the Icenians had a peace treaty with Nero and had been co-operative in the matter of paying tribute and giving up all their weapons in observance of a Roman decree. Also the King had named Nero co-heir with his wife and children, as a gesture of confidence. But Catus, the frog-like procurator, saw no reason for these facts to bother anyone now the King was dead. Prasutagus had reigned over a prosperous kingdom and was reputed to have amassed a huge fortune in gold. It was idiocy to let a weak woman and a couple of girls stand in the way of acquiring all of it.

'Well, that's settled,' said Governor Suetonius at length to Catus. 'Your own guard here should be ample to handle the business. But I'll give you a special detachment—a vexillation of picked men, besides. After all, the Icenians have no weapons and won't dispute you, anyway. As for me, I'm off tomorrow into Wales with the main army.'

General Petillius of the Ninth suddenly put out his hand. 'Your Excellency,' he said to the Governor, 'I fear that the Icenians may resent this plan more than you think. I've heard that the Queen Boadicea is a proud and passionate woman. Besides, this course seems to me hardly—hardly just.'

The Governor, who had been gathering up some parchments, turned and stared. His red face grew more purple, but he had reason to trust Petillius, and he spoke with restraint. 'Do you suggest that my administration of Britain is lacking in justice?'

The young General smiled apologetically. 'I suggest that these measures against the Icenians may damage Roman prestige.'

'What utter bosh!' interrupted Catus in his shrill, high voice. 'The whole country wants a lesson taught it; there've been mutterings and disobedience lately. We must show who's master!'

Suetonius glanced at the fat Procurator with some distaste, but he spoke with courteous finality to Petillius. 'I understand your objections, my friend, but I agree with Catus. Besides, this Icenian matter is unimportant—it's these slippery Druids who're causing the trouble—— That reminds me——' He looked down the room towards Flaccus. 'O Centurion of the Ninth, where is the young standard-bearer who had the encounter with the Druid priest?'

Flaccus saluted, turned around, and spying Quintus, said, 'Go to the Governor—and, Your Excellency, my Optio there, Lucius Claudius, was also a witness.'

Lucius stepped forward eagerly.

Both young men walked down the room and stood by the table. After a few questions, Lucius, to his mortification, was dismissed before he even had a chance to insinuate his relationship to the Emperor Claudius, but Quintus was kept much longer.

'Do you think,' asked Suetonius, frowning, 'that the Druid cast an evil spell on you, so your hands were paralysed?'

'Not exactly, Your Excellency; it was more the power in his eyes. I—I felt like a fool.'

Suetonius nodded while inspecting the young standard-bearer. A fine specimen of Roman manhood, big, well-spoken, and well-educated. The quality of recruit they're sending us is improving, he thought. 'I don't know who this straggler was,' he said, reverting to the Druid priest. 'I thought we'd got them all combed out and bottled up on their "sacred" island of Anglesey, off Wales, where I'll finish them off once and for all. But we'll take care of *him*. Tertius Julian!'

An officer of the Governor's own guard stepped forward.

'Yes sir.'

'Take a detail of men down into Kent, find this priest, and execute him, then rejoin me in Wales.'

Again General Petillius intervened. 'But, Your Excellency, from the accounts, the Druid said he was friendly to the Romans and came only to warn.'

'Well, imprison him, then,' said the Governor impatiently. 'Put him in that dungeon below the guardhouse in London, but be careful he doesn't work any tricks on *you*,' he said to his officer.

'Not on me, sir,' said Tertius Julian, throwing Quintus a look of patronizing amusement.

The Governor shrugged dismissal, Quintus stepped back, but the Procurator suddenly spoke up in his wheezy whine and demanded the vexillation the Governor had promised for disciplining the Icenians. 'And I'll take that one to begin with,' he said, pointing a stumpy finger at Quintus, as though he were a cut of beef to be purchased. 'He looks like a good man.'

Quintus' heart sank. He had not the slightest desire to find favour in the Procurator's eyes, nor to take part in what sounded like a messy and inglorious bullying of women and children.

But there was no help for it. Quintus remained in Colchester as a temporary member of Catus' new guard, while the Ninth was on the march towards Lincoln next morning, including most of the newly landed cohort and Flaccus and Lucius—to the latter's unbounded annoyance. For he had been given no time to taste the pleasures of Colchester and was frankly jealous of what he considered Quintus' preferment.

'Well then,' said Quintus, as the friends said good-bye, 'we're neither of us pleased. I'd *like* serving under General Petillius, and I don't like that Catus. I'll be glad when this business in Norfolk is over and I can get to my proper legion. By the Furies though —why didn't I get sent with the Governor to fight the Druids? That's what I *really* wanted to do!'

'Because,' said Lucius, irritably flicking a blob of mud off his elegant bronze breastplate, 'the army never by any chance lets you do what you want to do. *Quod est demonstrandum.*'

Nor, thought Quintus glumly, do I have the slightest chance of finding that huge stone circle in the land of the small dark men to the west, either. Already he had discovered that this country was much larger than he had realized, and he perforce put all thoughts of his quest out of his mind for the present.

Quintus lived at the Colchester barracks for some days, and kept fit when off duty by throwing the discus with fellow soldiers, or galloping Ferox along the hard-frozen tracks outside of town. He flirted mildly with a Gallic wine merchant's daughter and drank a moderate amount of her father's wares. And he awaited without enthusiasm Catus' orders to accompany the Procurator into the country of the Iceni.

These orders actually came on a cold winter's morning when a sifting of snow fell from the grey sky. And Quintus found himself starting north as one in a company of two hundred of the roughest, most brutalized men he had ever seen—the Procurator's hand-picked mounted guard.

CHAPTER II

Queen Boadicea's palace—a gesture of friendship—humiliation
of a proud queen—a British maid rescued from Roman savagery—
the cry of foxes

IT TOOK THEM three days to cover the sixty miles between Colchester and Caistor-by-Norwich in Norfolk, the land of the Iceni,
because though the guard were all mounted they must not go
faster than Catus' slave-borne litter. The Procurator lolled in a
sort of cushioned bed on poles, gilded and ornamented with
imperial eagles. It was warmed, too, by a charcoal brazier, while
Catus reclined in a nest of fox-skin robes from which he called
constant orders to the harassed slaves who ran alongside, especially Hector, a beady-eyed Sicilian, who by cunning flattery
had become Catus' steward and confidant.

The guard was commanded by a gigantic Belgian centurion
called Otho, who had the look and temper of a wild boar. He
mistreated his horse and bullied his men, but with Catus he had
a smooth, deferential manner, and the Procurator showed him
high favour. Though the guard were all technically Romans,
most were auxiliaries of different nationalities who came from
many parts of the far-flung empire, and were fierce fighting
machines, as stupid, most of them, as the gladiators who pum-
melled each other in the Roman circuses. Quintus found them
thoroughly uncongenial and, whenever they struck camp in the
dark night forests, hunted out Navin, who had come along as
interpreter.

On the third afternoon they emerged from the forest and saw
a haze of smoke from a thousand fires, and a huge circular mound
of earthworks, high as a tree, that surrounded the city of the
Iceni.

'Ha!' cried Catus, leaning from the litter, his eyes sparkling
with greed. 'They look prosperous. That's the finest native town
I've seen!'

A good many of the buildings were of stone, and in the middle
of them rose a large two-storey edifice. It had many windows
curtained by deer-hides and a large bright golden shield fastened
to the stone wall above a great portal.

'Obviously the palace,' said Catus. 'And where did they get enough gold to make a thing like that?'

The cavalcade drew up at the gate in the earthworks, and Otho, the centurion, banged on it with his sword, shouting, 'Decianus Catus, imperial Procurator of Rome, desires to enter!'

At once the gate swung back and an old man came forward bowing and crying a Celtic greeting.

Navin stepped up. 'He says the Queen has been eagerly awaiting you, O Procurator. Welcome and enter!'

Catus smiled and winked slowly at Otho. The guard and Catus and his servants moved through the narrow, crowded little streets. Shy faces peered at them from doorways, then disappeared. A giggling, nervous little girl ran out from a round stone house, thrust a pottery cup of amber liquid into the Procurator's hand, then ran back again.

'They are honouring you, Excellency,' explained the interpreter. 'That is their precious heather ale.'

'Pah,' said Catus, sniffing it, and he dumped it on the ground.

There were several wooden steps leading up to the palace portal, and on these steps stood four women. The central figure was so astonishing that a gasp came from the advancing Roman guard, and Quintus stared astounded.

Queen Boadicea was a majestic, full-bosomed woman, as tall as Quintus. She was over forty, but her hair, which cascaded down to her knees, was still the colour of ripe wheat, or of the golden gorget that hung like a half-moon on her breast. She wore a plaid robe of red and violet, belted by a golden circlet. Her face was broad, with high cheekbones; above them her eyes glinted a proud ice-blue.

As the Procurator's litter drew up before her, she inclined her stately head and said in accented but correct Latin, 'You are welcome, Romans. I knew that you would come to comfort me for the loss of my beloved husband and help me govern my people in his stead.'

She smiled and, descending the steps, held out to the Procurator a branch of white-berried mistletoe.

'What's this?' mumbled Catus, staring at the mistletoe.

'It is our most sacred totem,' said the Queen solemnly. 'I give it to you in token of the friendship between Rome and the Iceni.'

'You'll give a lot more than a hunk of vegetable before you're through,' said Catus below his breath, as he hopped out of the litter and contemptuously waved to a slave to take the mistletoe branch.

The Queen's eyes narrowed at this rudeness, but she bowed slightly, and said, pointing to two of the girls on the steps, 'These are my daughters.'

The Princesses were large, red-headed girls of about eighteen. They looked as forceful and regal as their mother, but they had not quite the beauty she must have had in her younger days. The buxom, fair-haired Princesses produced a chorus of lip-smacking and whistles from the rest of the guard, and several coarse jokes, but Quintus' eye was caught by the third girl who had been hidden behind the Princesses, for she was much shorter than they. Her hair was not flamboyant like the other women's; it was a soft, bright chestnut with gleams of light in the curly tendrils that fell below her waist. She wore no jewellery except an enamelled bronze brooch that fastened her plaid robe. She had a small, delicate face and a pair of very large blue-grey eyes, which were surveying the Romans with curiosity and some distrust.

The Queen turned with her daughters and ushered Catus through the portal; the other girl turned too and her eyes met Quintus' frankly approving stare.

At the moment when their glances crossed, Quintus felt a shock of interest. More than interest, a peculiar sensation of sympathy, and a sudden desire to touch that soft curly hair. His expression must have changed, for she gave him a faint, startled smile and then turned and ran through the portal after the others.

Nothing unusual happened that night. Catus remained in the palace with Otho, his captain, and all his slaves, and Queen Boadicea entertained them most hospitably. Quintus and the rest of the guard encamped outside the town, to await orders, which Quintus felt would not come.

The Icenians had received them graciously and trustingly, and surely even Catus would not make too outrageous demands. Romans did not war on women, or without provocation. To-morrow no doubt they'd all march back to Colchester again with whatever booty the old skinflint had prised out of the poor Queen, and that would be that. Except for a slight regret that he would not see the unknown girl again, Quintus was relieved.

He was also quite wrong in all his expectations.

The next morning the Roman guard was summoned back to the palace and ordered to come on foot while leaving the horses outside the town. Otho met them in the courtyard. 'Fun's going to begin pretty soon, boys!' he shouted. 'Procurator says to have some swigs of the good Roman wine these buzzards had hidden. There it is!' He jerked his chin towards two huge amphoræ that had been hauled out to the courtyard. Red wine trickled down their curved sides. It was obvious that Otho had had a head start on the wine, and his men, with roars of appreciation, began at once to catch up. Quintus did not join them. He was not thirsty, and he was disgusted. These wine-bibbing rowdies were totally unlike the disciplined Roman soldiery he had trained with. Of course, he thought with contempt, Catus was not a general, nothing but a civilian.

He glanced towards the portal of the palace as a ringing, angry woman's voice inside cried out in Latin, 'Never! Never shall these things be done. It is not *possible* that the Emperor Nero would so abuse his faithful allies!'

Quintus glanced at Otho and the guard, who were milling round the wine-jars, and he pushed open the heavy wooden door.

It was dark in the low, long hall, and smoky from a great central fire, but in a moment he could see the tense group around Catus and Queen Boadicea. They were both standing near the fire; Boadicea towered over the Procurator, who was surrounded by his crouching slaves. Behind the Queen stood a dozen of her Icenian nobles and kinsmen. They were tall, gold-bearded men in horned helmets and they were unarmed, as Roman law had decreed. They looked uncertain, anxious, straining to follow the Latin language, which their Queen had learned so well.

There were women too, huddled in the corner by a great loom filled with half-woven cloth. Quintus saw amongst them the two princesses, and the small girl with chestnut hair.

'Am I to understand,' said Catus softly, darting his bald head towards the Queen, 'that you refuse our glorious Emperor's commands . . . ?'

Boadicea quivered, her face grew pale, her eyes flashed, and she cried with furious scorn, 'Commands that I abdicate . . . ? That I turn my kingdom and people over to *you*, that I give you my children's *inheritance* . . . and bow down as abject slave to Rome . . . ? Yes, O Procurator. I *refuse*!'

'Ah . . .' said Catus, smiling on a long, satisfied note. He turned and barked a command to his chief slave, Hector, the Sicilian, who jumped up and darted for the door where he saw Quintus.

'Back to your post,' Hector hissed, 'the time has come.'

Quintus frowned, but he went to the courtyard where the slave was relaying Catus' order to Otho.

The Belgian centurion's little pig eyes gleamed, he shook his head to clear it of the wine-fumes. 'Form ranks,' he shouted. 'Into the palace! Let no Icenian escape, but do not kill unless you must!'

The two hundred men drew their swords and rushed forward, Quintus with them obeying automatically. They stormed into the hall and so quickly had it happened that the Icenians were motionless at first. Then they fought with fists and teeth and stools and flagons, whatever they could lay their hands on, but the Romans thwacked fierce blows with the flat of the sword. They jabbed and slashed too, while Catus' slaves joined in. The Procurator himself, safe on a table out of the brawl, capered with glee.

The Icenians were soon tied up and stacked like wood in the corner of the hall, while Otho seized and bound the Queen herself and threw her to the ground.

'Stand her up,' shrilled Catus, 'Boadicea shall feel how Rome punishes those who defy her might!' He gestured to Hector, who ran up with a huge black three-tailed whip. Otho jerked the Queen to her feet and held her at arm's length while the slave, giggling, plied the great whip. It hissed and snapped through the air, the long snake-like scourges wrapped again and again round Boadicea's body. Her plaid robe tore to ribbons, blood trickled down her shoulders and matted the golden hair. She uttered no sound, but stood stone quiet under the lash, her face as grey as ashes, her eyes sunken and terrible as those of a corpse.

It was her daughters who screamed, and Quintus, angry and sickened at these sights, whirled to see that two of the burliest soldiers had grabbed up the red-haired Princesses and were carrying them from the hall.

Catus turned too and laughed. 'Let them go,' he said. 'My soldiers have led a dull life of late; they deserve a little fun. . . . Cease,' he said impatiently to the slave, who dropped the whip. 'No doubt the Queen has learned her lesson. Put her over there out of the way and ransack the palace—here, we'll start with that chest!'

While Catus spoke, Quintus had suddenly caught sight of the girl who interested him. She had tried to hide behind the loom and a squat Frankish soldier was lunging for her.

Quintus reached the Frank with one bound and knocked him

spinning on the floor. 'Here, quick!' he said to the girl, and as
she only stared at him with dumb horror, he picked her up and
rushed with her through the door which led on to a side court.
As the chill air hit her, she gasped and began to struggle frantically, hitting him in the face, trying to scratch his eyes.

'No, no—don't!' cried Quintus. 'I won't hurt you.' He dared
not put her down because the Frank was clattering through the
door after him. 'You little idiot,' he said angrily, as he ran with
her across the court; 'I'm trying to help you!'

She understood little of his actual words, but the sense of them
reached her. She quietened and suddenly whispered something
and pointed to a round building raised on high piles. It was a
granary, and Quintus saw what she meant. He flung her up
through the open door, climbed up himself, and pulled the six-
foot ladder after him, as the Frank arrived shouting furiously.

'It's no use, my friend,' said Quintus, peering sardonically
down at him. 'You can't get up here. Go find yourself another
girl.'

The Frank looked up at Quintus' drawn sword poised for
action, at the young Roman's cold, watchful eyes, then he
shrugged and walked away.

Quintus sheathed his sword and turned into the granary. The
girl lay crumpled, sobbing, on a heap of grain. He sat down
beside her and awkwardly patted her shoulder. 'I think you'd
better stay here a while until I think of some way to get you far
off from—from what's going on in that palace.'

She spoke some Latin and understood most of what he said
this time. She shuddered, covering her face with her hands, and
whispered something in her own language. Then she translated
it slowly. 'I *hate* you, Roman,' she said through her teeth. 'I shall
hate you till I die.'

'I know,' said Quintus. 'I don't blame you. That was a rotten
business in there. You mustn't believe all Romans are like that.'

She raised her head and gazed at him with her huge grey eyes.
'Romans are beasts—like wolves—they betray, devour—you
too.'

'I don't think so,' said Quintus gently, 'but never mind that.
What's your name, by the way?'

She had ceased crying and looked at him steadily in the darkness of the granary. He saw that for all her fear and smallness, she
had a thoroughbred control. After a moment she pronounced a
Celtic name.

'Regan?' he tried to repeat the difficult sound. 'Is that your name?'

'Near enough,' she answered. 'I am Queen Boadicea's foster-child. My parents are dead. She has been a mother to me. Never shall I forget what has been done to her this day—and to my foster-sisters, the Princesses.'

Quintus said nothing. On impulse he put out his hand and touched the soft dishevelled hair that rippled down her back. She jumped as though he'd struck her, throwing her hands out to ward him off.

'Listen, Regan,' said Quintus stiffly, folding his arms across his breastplate. 'I like you, and mean you no harm. You mustn't be scared of me. Now where can I take you that you'll be safe? Think!'

She relaxed gradually, sitting up straight on the pile of grain and examining him through the thick lashes of her half-closed eyes. His helmet with its arching crest of red and its engraved eagle gleamed in the half darkness—the odious panoply of Rome. But above the leather chin-strap, the lean, weather-tanned face and the steady, dark eyes were attractive.

Her look softened, she started to speak, when from somewhere outside there came a long, sobbing wail, anguished cries to Celtic gods for help, and a shout of drunken laughter.

She whitened, fear came back into her face. She started to tremble though she tried to control it. I must go to Boadicea—I must help——'

'No, you don't,' said Quintus. 'If you go back in there, I certainly couldn't protect you against all Catus' rabble. But we can't stay here either. You must know some house in town where you can hide. A poor one,' he added grimly, 'that Catus won't bother with.'

Her breathing slowed and she bowed her head, knowing that he was right. 'Pendoc,' she whispered after a moment. 'The potter. He has always protected me. His hut is down there by the river.'

Quintus nodded and, going to the granary door, peered out cautiously. Nobody was in sight except three of Catus' slaves squatting by a wall and squabbling over a pouchful of Icenian coins they had found. Quintus did not bother with the little ladder. He jumped down and held up his arms for Regan. 'I'll carry you,' he said, speaking very distinctly so she would understand. 'You must lie across my shoulder and pretend you have fainted.'

She nodded with a frightened little smile. While he pulled her down from the granary and adjusted her light body over his left shoulder, he thought with sudden warmth, she trusts me now, poor child. Though she was about sixteen and he not quite twenty, the protection he was giving her made him feel infinitely older. In some ways she reminded him of his little sister, Livia; in some ways only, for as he carried her according to her whispered directions, through a maze of littered alleys down a slope towards a thatched hut, he felt a new, strange tenderness that even his sister had never aroused.

They were challenged once. Three of the Roman guard were busy ransacking a stone house that belonged to one of the wealthier Icenians. They were piling up shields, bracelets, household goods on the doorstep for the later inspection of Catus. 'Halt, Quintus Tullius!' cried the soldier in charge. 'Centurion's been looking for you. Get up to the palace!'

'That's where I'm going,' called Quintus gaily, trusting that the maze of alleys had confused the man's direction.

'With *that*?' cried the soldier, pointing to Regan's limp body.

'I thought Otho might be interested,' answered Quintus, and added a rough bit of army slang.

The man guffawed and started walking towards Quintus, who moved fast, turned a corner, and started to run.

'Here,' whispered Regan. 'Here!' She slid down from his shoulder and pulled him after her through a door that was curtained by a cowhide.

Inside the small round hut it smelled of wet clay and pigs, who were snuffling after garbage on the packed, earthen floor. The potter was a big, scar-faced man with long, sandy-red hair. He jumped back from his wheel with an astonished grunt as Regan and the tall Roman legionary burst in.

The girl explained in a string of urgent Celtic. The potter answered, drawing himself up and staring at Quintus with narrowed, hostile eyes.

'It's all right,' said Regan. 'Pendoc says he'll take care of me. But he knew nothing of what's been going on. He's—he's very angry.'

Quintus sighed. The potter, indeed any Briton, had a right to be angry, but Pendoc's continuing harsh, excited speech to Regan was destroying the girl's fleeting trust. Quintus could see it. She turned and would not look at Quintus. Her small, pretty face hardened to a stony mask. Quintus caught the word 'trap'—one that Navin had taught him—and understood. There was no use protesting that he had no sinister purpose in rescuing Regan, that he deplored this whole shocking treatment of the Iceni. It was obvious Pendoc would not believe him, and that Regan no longer did.

'Farewell,' he said to the girl. 'May Jupiter and Fortuna both have you in their keeping, Regan.'

She looked at him then. 'ROMAN gods——' she said with blistering contempt, and turned her back.

Regan's contempt bolstered Quintus during the following three days that he spent in the Icenian city. After all, he was a legionary under oath to the Emperor to obey orders without question. And it was not fitting for a Roman to go sentimental and soft or fraternize with natives who were, on the whole, being civilized for their own good. He almost managed to forget Regan and the peculiar, new feelings she had roused in him.

And after all, thought Quintus sardonically, as they started on the march back to Colchester, the Icenian incident was finished to the satisfaction of Catus, anyway.

The Procurator was extremely pleased with himself. Quintus, who rode near the slave-borne litter, could hear his jubilant comments. Accompanying their cavalcade were twelve carts full of booty—bronzes and beautiful British enamels, gold gorgets, torques and brooches, coffers full of Icenian coins, and the huge golden shield that had hung over the palace door. There were six new slaves too, or hostages, as Catus, with unusual delicacy, preferred to call them. These were some of the Icenian noblemen who had been surprised in the palace. Around their necks they now wore heavy iron collars attached to chains which bound them to each other between two Roman soldiers who held the ends.

'It'll do the Trinovantes good to see these,' said Catus repeatedly to Hector. 'Object lesson. I've noticed them in Colchester lately—very lax in worshipping our divine Claudius in the temple.'

'Shockingly lax, O Beloved Master,' agreed Hector, bowing as he trotted along beside the litter. 'Yes, it will do the Trinovantes good to hear how you have broken the spirit of the Iceni.'

Catus tugged at his ear-lobe. 'That Boadicea—she never uttered a sound when we flogged her, or afterwards when I so considerately allowed her to retire to her own apartments with those stupid, screaming girls of hers. You'd think they'd all been *seriously* injured.'

Quintus jerked Ferox's bridle and to his own amazement heard himself saying to the Procurator, 'Would *you* not consider it serious injury, Your Excellency, if your home were sacked and your kinsmen enslaved, if you were publicly whipped, and your daughters dishonoured?'

Catus jerked round, staring up at the young man on the big black horse. 'You speak like a fool! These barbarians don't have feelings like Romans do.' His eyes narrowed and he said, 'You've been a disappointment to me, Quintus Tullius Pertinax. I've been watching you. Half-hearted soldiering, lazy—now insolent. I had thought to get you promoted, maybe command my personal guard. As it is, I shall see that you return at once to your legion, where I trust your General Petillius Cerealis will beat you into shape.'

'Yes, sir,' said Quintus, respectfully, reining in Ferox and dropping back to the rear, where he had trouble hiding his satisfaction from the other soldiers, who were pleased by the Roman newcomer's fall from favour.

They camped that night at a ford on the river Stour, which was the boundary between the Icenians and the Trinovantes. Here there was a rough Roman fort containing a cabin where Catus decided to spend the night rather than endure the few remaining miles to Colchester. His slaves at once set about the usual routine. They heated water and scented oils for the Procurator's bath. They arranged his cushioned couch for him to recline on while he ate the delicacies he demanded even in the wilderness—jellied eels, larks stewed in honey, poppy-seed cakes, all washed down with a flagon of imported Gaulish wine.

Quintus observed the dishes being rushed into the Procurator's cabin. May Hygeia send him indigestion, thought Quintus maliciously, invoking the goddess of health. The guard had to be satisfied with the usual marching ration of hard wheat cake and dried fish, supplemented tonight by boiled mutton from an Icenian sheep. Quintus made a tour of the fort and glanced at the six prisoners, who had collapsed in a heap on the ground, hollow-eyed, silent. Their big blond heads slumped forward on their chests. Blood trickled from sores in their necks made by the iron collars. 'What've THEY had to eat?' asked Quintus of the captives' guard.

'Nothing,' said the guard, gnawing on a chop. 'Procurator gave no orders to feed 'em.'

'Well, *I* do,' said Quintus. 'Give them some of our rations, and if I weren't still serving under Decianus Catus I'd say the man is an utter imbecile. If he wants his captives dead, he should kill them. If he wants them to be useful slaves, he's got to keep 'em alive.'

'True enough,' said the guard, shrugging. He gathered up a handful of wheat cakes and took them to the Icenians. Otho had been left behind in the Icenian city with a dozen men to maintain order and also to hunt around in case any valuable booty had been overlooked. In his absence another officer and Quintus had been given temporary command.

It had been one of those promising late-winter days, when the sun was warm and the air smelled of spring. There were patches of snow still, beneath the holly-bushes and towering oaks in the forests, but through the brown earth pushed green spikes o. cuckoo-pint. Thrushes and blackbirds sang at their nestings, while deep in the greening wilderness on each side of the Roman road the wild things were mating.

Quintus too felt the restlessness and yearning of spring. In the twilight he wandered outside the fort and quite a way along the river-bank, which was margined with reeds where moorhens and coots were paddling. He thought how different spring was here from the sudden lush flowering back home. He pictured his mother and Livia sitting in their frescoed atrium, listening to the splash of their fountain. The sun would be hot, his mother's Persian lilies would be in full scented bloom. He sent them both a homesick greeting, and then suddenly he thought of Regan.

On the eve of their departure from the Icenian city he had gone back to Pendoc the potter's little hut to say good-bye to her, to try—though he did not quite admit it—to wipe that last contemptuous look she had given him from his memory. The hut was completely deserted. The potter's wheel and the pigs, too, were gone.

It was reasonable that Pendoc should take the girl away— doubtless to one of the many caves and hiding-places in the forest where the other Icenians had fled. For the Roman destruction had continued. Wanton fires had been lit, many of the buildings destroyed. In a short time the Icenian capital had become a city of the dead, hushed, empty. Except for the Queen and her daughters, who were barricaded in a wing of the ruined palace.

But I'd like to see Regan again, Quintus thought. To tell her —to make her understand—what? He was a Roman and she was a Briton. The Romans were conquering and subduing the Britons. What more was there to explain?

Impatient with himself, he shied a pebble amongst the water-fowl and idly watched them scolding and fluttering off.

A twig cracked behind him and he jumped round, his hand on his sword.

It was Navin who stood behind him in the shadows, watching with a sardonic lift to his bushy red eyebrows. 'You're far from camp alone, Quintus Tullius,' Navin said quietly. 'There are wild boar and wolves in the forest. And there may be other enemies too—for a Roman.'

Quintus smiled. He had developed considerable liking for the interpreter and he knew that it was returned, and yet he had not the faintest idea what Navin really thought or felt. Navin had kept to himself during the days of sacking the Icenian city, except when Catus called on him to interpret. He had made it clear that the fate of the Icenians was a matter of indifference to him. He was a Trinovante, and the two nations had not been friendly with each other.

'I was wandering along and doing some thinking,' said Quintus, laughing ruefully, 'about a girl, as a matter of fact. A little Icenian named Regan that I—I, well, took care of, back in that disgraceful brawl Catus produced.'

'Yes,' said Navin. 'I heard that you rescued the Queen's foster-child. Regan is not an Icenian.'

'She isn't?' said Quintus, startled.

'No. Regan comes from a different part of Britain, though she is distantly connected with Boadicea. When her parents died, her grandfather——' Navin paused and it seemed as though he changed his mind about something he was going to say. He went on quickly, 'Regan's grandfather brought her here six years ago to be raised by the Queen.'

'Oh?' said Quintus. 'Then isn't that Pendoc an Icenian either?'

'No. Quintus, you ask a great many questions and think too much. Until you give it up you'll never make a good Roman soldier.'

Quintus flushed. 'I *am* a good soldier,' he said hotly. 'Just because I don't lick the sandals of that fat civilian fool of a Procurator——'

'And you've not yet learned to hold your tongue and hide your thoughts,' continued Navin imperturbably. 'But you will have to.'

Whatever Quintus was going to reply he forgot as something

about the Briton startled him. He stared through the waning light. 'Navin! You're in native dress!'

The belted tunic, the high military sandals, the brass badge of the hostage all were gone. Instead Navin wore tight plaid trousers. A tartan cape was thrown over his shoulders and fastened by a huge brooch of Celtic scrollwork. His chin and upper lip were covered with reddish stubble where before they had been carefully shaven like the Romans. And on his forehead was a circular patch of blue, the woad sign of the warrior chief.

'Even so,' said Navin, nodding and watching Quintus.

'But what does it *mean*?'

'That I have found things not to my liking in Colchester or in London, and throughout the country of the Trinovantes which once my father ruled. That in Rome I was lulled into believing that my people benefited by Roman progress, that they were contented. It is not true. I find them thrown out of their homes in favour of Roman veterans who bully and despise them. I find them crippled by debts. And now Seneca, that philosophical moneylender, has suddenly called in all the debts—without reason. My people can't pay.'

'Well, that's bad,' said Quintus unhappily. 'The Icenian incident was shocking, I know, I know, but——'

Navin held up his hand. 'The Icenians today. The Trinovantes tomorrow—and soon all the other tribes. That's enough, Quintus. I too have said more than I should.'

There was silence. Quintus was dismayed, and yet he thought: they can't really do much. The tribes aren't even friendly with each other. This poor Navin will be caught and brought back. Then an unpleasant realization struck Quintus. It was his duty to seize now, this instant, what was, after all, an escaping and defiant hostage. His hand moved slowly to his sword hilt.

'No, my Quintus,' said Navin, quietly watching. 'You are very far from camp—and listen . . .'

All through this conversation Quintus had been half conscious of the yelping of foxes. As Navin motioned for silence, there was a short, sharp bark near-by from a thicket. It was answered by others to the right, the left, and farther off, and others fainter yet in the distance. They were surrounded by the harsh, strange barks.

'Foxes——' said Quintus quickly. 'They always make a noise like that when they're mating. . . .' But cold ran down his spine, for Navin's eyes had changed as much as his clothes had. They were now wary, sardonic.

'Those are not foxes,' said Navin. 'Quintus, this is the last time we meet as friends. Go back now to the fort. You won't be molested. The time isn't yet ripe. . . . Go——'

Quintus turned and obeyed. As he walked glumly along the river-bank he felt the impact of a hundred watching hidden eyes. There were rustlings and movements in the blackness of the forest just beyond eyesight. And Navin stood where Quintus had left him, stern, implacable. Quintus reached the fort and reluctantly went to report this threatening incident to the Procurator.

Catus was lolling on his couch listening to Hector strum a little lyre. When Quintus approached saying, 'O Procurator—I'm sorry, but something's just happened I think you should know,' Catus impatiently wiped some cake-crumbs from his chin and, turning on his elbow, frowned.

'Well, well. What is it? You KNOW I'm not to be bothered at this hour. Jupiter! I *never* get any peace and quiet!'

Quintus briefly related the encounter with Navin, and the Procurator, who was drowsy, full of wine, and completely unwilling to bother with anything, said pettishly, 'And you consider this stupid story important enough to disturb me with! I never liked that Navin, anyway. Let him dress in anything he wants to and flounder around in the wilderness. He'll come back when he gets hungry, all right.'

'But, sir, you don't understand. Navin means trouble. There's resistance getting under way, and those fox-barks——'

'Those *fox-barks!*' cut in the Procurator with scorn. 'You're always imagining things, like that Druid in Kent. I suppose you think they were ghost foxes.'

Quintus reddened, but he said as quietly as he could, 'No, sir. I'm quite sure they were made by Trinovantes, by Navin's own clan, which, I know, has the fox for its totem.'

'Well, let 'em all bark in the woods then—sounds just like the Britons.' Catus rolled over and poked in a red pottery dish for a candied fig. 'Go away,' he ordered, turning his back on Quintus, and said to his slave, 'Go on playing.' Hector picked up the lyre.

So what in Hades can *I* do? thought Quintus angrily, as he walked out.

The next noon they reached Colchester again, and Quintus thankfully received orders to depart next day for the north, for Lincoln, where General Petillius and the Ninth Legion were stationed. He was to travel with a squad of auxiliaries who were bound farther north into Yorkshire, where the Romans had a fort in the wild country of the Brigantes.

Quintus enjoyed himself that night in Colchester. He went first to the great public baths and had a thorough steaming and soaking and rubbing down. Then he went to see a gladiator fight a bear in the circus. The gladiator got badly mangled, but in the end he killed the animal with his bare hands. It wasn't like the wonderful spectacles at home, but it was exciting. And there were dances afterwards, performed by some Spanish slave-girls who belonged to a wealthy Roman merchant of the town.

Nor did Quintus neglect his religious duties. He entered the magnificent Temple of Claudius and bowed down before the statue of that Emperor-god, as everyone was expected to. In the vast, shadowy temple there were other little altars, and he duly lit some incense on that of the soldier's god—Mars. He paused by the altar of Venus, the goddess of love, and thought suddenly of Regan, which was of course utterly ridiculous. He was annoyed with himself, passed on quickly, and went out into the forum, where the colossal winged statue of Victory shone white against the sky. In the forum there was the usual bustle of togaed Romans and town-dwelling Britons, and Quintus, back in a city atmosphere as normal as home, began to think that perhaps he *had* been foolish to give so much importance to Navin and his fox-barks. Or indeed to that whole time he had spent with the Icenians. Well, anyway, he thought, he'd soon be seeing Lucius and other friends in his own cohort—even Flaccus seemed worthy after Catus' ruffians. He bought himself some wine at the corner shop, teased the admiring and very pretty winemonger's daughter, and altogether passed an agreeable evening.

During the night a peculiar thing happened. Quintus' barracks were close to the forum, and it seemed to him afterwards that mixed up with his dreams he had heard a loud noise at some point, a sort of shattering crash outside, but it had not really awakened him. He was, however, awakened at sunrise by the murmur of many voices and the shuffling of feet.

Quintus rubbed his eyes, yawned, and went out just as he was, in his undertunic, to see what was going on. It was a hushed crowd that thronged the edges of the forum, all staring down at something on the marble pavement below. As Quintus edged through to look, a woman's voice cried out on a long quavering wail, 'It is an omen! A dreadful omen!'

What is? thought Quintus, and then he saw. The colossal statue of Victory had fallen off its pedestal. It lay broken into a dozen pieces on the pavement of the forum.

'An omen! An omen!' The frightened whisper ran like wind through all the crowd. 'Victory has deserted the Romans.'

What utter nonsense, Quintus said to himself, and at that moment the old philosopher, Seneca, suddenly appeared on a balcony and put Quintus' thoughts into sensible words.

'Fellow citizens and Britons!' Seneca shouted, waving his arms. 'There is no omen of any kind connected with this unfortunate accident. There was wind in the night and the statue was top-heavy, no doubt. We will at once erect another one!'

The crowd listened respectfully to the grave and portly Roman, but Quintus heard some hissing words behind him. They were in Celtic, but he caught their meaning—venomous hatred of Seneca. He turned instinctively and caught two more words hissed in a sneering voice. Something about a rope, and the wind. He stared behind him. Yes, quite near there were Trinovantes, for all that they wore Roman clothes. Their type was unmistakable, the height, the light hair. But he could not tell who had spoken. There were a dozen of them, and their big, raw-boned faces were all expressionless, turned up towards Seneca.

Quintus walked back to his barracks to prepare for the march north. 'Rope . . . wind,' he thought, puzzled, and in a moment the solution came. Without a doubt it was not the wind but a stout rawhide Trinovante rope that had pulled down the statue of Victory in the night, had shattered the hateful symbol of Roman dominance.

He wondered if Catus would believe this if Quintus told him, but he knew that it was hopeless. Well, if they stop at *symbols* it'll be all right, Quintus thought. But again later, when the sun was warm and he set out west with the auxiliaries on Stane Street, his apprehension seemed silly. It was market day, the entire town hummed cheerfully. British peasants from the country had set up little stalls and hawked their produce in deep Celtic voices. Some of them sold lengths of woven cloth or bronze trinkets ornamented with ruby enamel, some sold the red glossy Samian ware they had learned how to make from the Romans. Some sold beaver skins and capes of woven kingfisher feathers. A trading-ship from Gaul had anchored in the river Colne, and its crew mingled cheerfully with the crowd. There was music and laughter; even the Britons seemed to be enjoying themselves, while above the whole scene rose the majestic gold and white Temple of Claudius, as solid and permanent as Roman power, no matter how many statues tumbled down.

'I'm really sorry to leave Colchester, after all,' Quintus observed to one of the auxiliaries as they rode out of town. 'It's a nice little city.' Nor did he have the faintest intuition that the next time he came here there would be no Colchester at all.

CHAPTER III

The march to Lincoln—Boadicea seeks vengeance—Colchester sacked, the Romans defeated—Quintus saved from death by Regan —his escape on Ferox into the summer night

THOUGH THE FIRST PART of the journey to Lincoln ran through Trinovante country, nothing unusual happened; in fact until they turned north on the highway called Ermine Street, Quintus saw hardly anyone at all. There were no sounds except those made by themselves and the birds.

The third day, they passed along the edge of the fens. Quintus gazed out over the distant tangle of green marshes and wondered if there were fever mists in them like the Pontine marshes outside Rome. At any rate, fever or no, these fens were a treacherous, secret maze of islands and twisting waterways always avoided by the legions and indeed by the Coritani tribe, who dwelt on the western border of the marshes. There were quite a few villages now that they were out of dense forest land, and there was a peaceful feeling, because the sun stayed out for two whole days and shone on the backs of grazing sheep and shaggy little British cows. The Coritani tribesmen, who were very tall like the Iceni to whom they were related, seemed friendly. There were actually smiling faces as the auxiliaries marched by, and sometimes children ran out from the round wattle-and-daub huts to offer the soldiers bunches of anemones and buttercups.

The foreboding of trouble and disaster which Quintus had felt back in Icenian country now vanished completely. Though he was partly relieved, he was also faintly disappointed, as he resigned himself to the prospect of routine barracks life in Lincoln, and decided to concentrate on earning a promotion and finding some way to get sent to the west, where he might start on the quest for Gaius' remains.

After so many hours of marching through the flattest country Quintus could have imagined, it was a welcome change to see Lincoln's sudden high hill jutting up against the sky. At last the company trudged up the steep road to the top and entered the oblong fort at Lincoln, station of the Ninth Legion.

Quintus was received with enthusiasm. Not only had he been popular with the men, but he was a welcome distraction. The Spanish centurion, Flaccus, ordered that broiled fish from the river Whitham be added to the evening rations, and issued an extra amphora of red wine as well.

'Flaccus isn't such a bad fellow, after all,' said Lucius languidly, as they all lounged in the barracks hall after dinner. 'He's as bored as the rest of us, up here on this hill, so we all go hunting when we're off duty, and we've had horse-races and discus-throwing. The baths aren't badly fixed up either for a piddling little outpost like this. Good steam-room, and a dice game always going on round the massage table.'

Quintus laughed, looking at his friend with affectionate amusement. 'Anybody ever do any work up here?'

'Oh sure,' answered Lucius, wrinkling his nose. 'Roads. Miles of 'em. We're pushing north to the Humber. And patrols. Besides the usual drills and parade, *you* know.'

'Patrols . . . ?' repeated Quintus thoughtfully. 'Any trouble with the natives?'

'Oh Jove, no—our Parisii tribe here are as gentle as rabbits. They love us, they palm off all sorts of worthless junk on us, and their girls . . .' Lucius' sleepy eyes brightened suddenly. 'Big, strapping blondes, they——'

Quintus sat up straight and interrupted sharply, 'You'd better not fool around with their girls, Lucius. These Britons all have a strict code of honour——'

'Oh twaddle!' said Lucius rudely. 'What in the world's come over you down there in the south? You come back clucking like an old hen. Bet you're out of condition too, all this pampering by the Procurator.' He suddenly delivered a fierce, half-playful punch at Quintus' stomach. Quintus gasped, doubled his fists, and retaliated. They threw off their tunics.

Soon with the ease of long practice they were in the thick of a fairly scientific wrestling match; rolling, scuffling, grunting, and thoroughly enjoying themselves.

The other men gathered round and laid bets. Flaccus watched with an indulgent and slightly envious eye. For all that these two were the patrician young Romans that he sneered at, they were tough and fit. Their strong-muscled bodies scarcely reddened beneath the pummelling they gave each other and they were well matched, though Lucius was slightly stockier and slower. Quintus had nearly knocked the wind out of Lucius, when the fight was abruptly ended by a messenger from the General who announced that Standard-bearer Quintus Tullius Pertinax was to report at once.

The young men disentangled themselves and got up. 'Continued later,' said Quintus, panting and grinning at Lucius. 'I almost had you.'

'Like Hades, you did!' wheezed Lucius. He growled some extremely vulgar taunts with what breath he had, and everyone laughed. Quintus did too. He was never angry with his friend, no matter how hard they scuffled, or who won, though Lucius was of more uncertain temper, and hated to be beaten.

Quintus washed his face, buckled his breastplate and shin-greaves, put on his helmet, picked up his shield and the cohort's standard, then presented himself to the General.

Petillius Cerealis sat at a camp-table in a bare, white-washed room, frowning at a map. He raised his alert, young-looking head as Quintus came in, and said, 'Good evening, Standard-bearer.' Quintus responded and waited. The General was in no hurry. His sharp eyes inspected Quintus from helmet crest to sandals. When he had finished, he said sternly, 'Your sword-hilt needs polishing, and your left sandal thong is frayed. Your whole appearance is slipshod. See that these matters are fixed by morning.'

'Yes, sir,' said Quintus.

'I know you've been on the road for days,' continued the General, 'but I have pride in my legion. We've a hard job to do here and an example to set. No detail is too small to count.'

'Yes, sir,' repeated Quintus, and despite the reproof, felt a liking for the man, as he had in Colchester, especially when the hazel eyes suddenly twinkled, as they did now.

'The report on you sent by the Procurator, Decianus Catus, is not particularly flattering.' Petillius shoved the map aside and fished a small piece of parchment out from a pile of dispatches. 'Let's see now—uhmm—"slack, insolent, at one time actually insubordinate, given to association with the enemy. . . ." '

'The ENEMY!' cried Quintus, forgetting himself. 'By the spirit of my father, sir, how anyone could call those wretched Icenians the ENEMY—and the way we treated them, the Procurator . . . by Mars, I guess they're enemies *now*, all right—but——' He clamped his lips together as the General raised his eyebrows. 'Sorry, sir.'

'I gather,' said Petillius, leaning back in his chair, 'that the Procurator's disappointment in you was also vice versa,' and to Quintus' great relief, there issued from his General's throat an unmistakable chuckle. 'Now what really happened in the country of the Icenians?'

The spring passed pleasantly enough in the fort, on top of Lincoln's high hill. Quintus' duties were not hard. Frequently, under one of the tribunes or senior officers, he supervised the road-building, and though this bored Lucius, Quintus had an aptitude for engineering and took an interest in the continual problems to be met. He learned the routine of clearing the way, while leaving brush and trees ranged alongside as fences. He learned to choose and lay the paving-stones, to see that the gravel was packed properly, to build bridges and fords, and drive the new highway straight as an arrow's flight through every obstacle, as they penetrated farther and farther into the northern wilderness.

The legionaries were well housed and fed; the baths—as Lucius had said—made a fine club-house and recreation centre. They even had music, for two of the foot-soldiers played the lyre and flute. It was not a bad life at all. Quintus was too busy to think much about Regan or the Icenians. And he had a gratifying prospect to hope for. Flaccus one day had said that the General was soon intending to send some dispatches to the Second Legion headquarters in the far west at Gloucester. Quintus was interested by any mention of the west, where Gaius Tullius' remains were, and he wondered if he might be chosen as one of the official messenger's escorts. 'You apply for the job and I think you'll get it,' said Flaccus one night in the baths, as they came from the steam-room. 'It's certain that nobody else wants it. Too much devilish magic goes on in the wild country between here and Gloucester. People turned into stones and stood up in a circle to shriek every night; animals that talk and cast spells on you—little black gnomes that burn you up in wicker baskets!'

'Oh come, Flaccus,' said Quintus, grinning; 'where'd you get all that stuff?'

The Spaniard shook his head darkly. 'Oh, I've heard. . . .
That's Druid country *that* is in the west. Our Governor Suetonius
may think he's got 'em all chased to Anglesey, but I've heard
there's plenty left.'

'I wonder how our revered Governor is getting on with his
campaign,' drawled Lucius. 'We might as well be on the moon
for all the news that ever comes up here. . . . Jupiter, that's *cold*!'
he cried, as he suddenly plunged into the small swimming-
pool.

'You should've waited longer to cool off, idiot,' said Quintus
from the edge of the pool. 'What's your big hurry tonight,
anyway?'

Lucius dived under the water and swam the length of the pool
without answering.

So it was those blonde girls in the British village at the foot of
the hill, Quintus thought. He gave an uneasy sigh. If the General
ever found out how Lucius sneaked out of the fort almost every
night and what he was up to—but there was no holding Lucius
when it came to girls, even though the whole garrison had been
given strictest orders not to enter the village. But Quintus had no
intention of being told again that he clucked warnings like an old
hen. So when Lucius clambered out and made for the dressing-
room, giving Quintus a wink behind Flaccus' back, Quintus
waved to him cheerfully, saying 'See you later—I hope.'

To his great surprise he saw Lucius in half an hour, the time
it had taken him to run down to the village and climb up
again.

Quintus was throwing dice with a couple of standard-bearers
from other cohorts, and his teasing greeting died on his lips
when he saw Lucius' face. 'What's happened——?' he began, and
stopped as Lucius shook his head and jerked it sideways towards
the corner of the hall. Quintus followed. 'Trouble?' he asked
briefly, restraining himself from an 'I told you so.'

'Not what you think,' said Lucius. All his languid airs were
gone, his face was pale and his round eyes worried. 'Quintus,
there's nobody down there in the village. It's deserted. Not a
soul, even a dog.'

'Well, that's not so strange. They've gone off hunting or on
some religious expedition; they do that——'

'No, no,' said Lucius impatiently. 'You don't understand.
Their furnishings are gone, everything, the ashes scraped out of
the fire-holes, their supplies. It looks as though they've gone for

good, and yet they and their ancestors've lived there since long before Julius Cæsar came to Britain. That isn't all'—he went on as Quintus was about to speak—'look at this!' He drew a large clay tablet from under his cloak and held it out gingerly. Quintus peered at it and made a horrified sound. Rows of little figures had been crudely carved on the tablet, figures with crested helmets and breastplates. One figure held a standard with an emblem that was unmistakable. The standard of the Ninth Legion. Something else was unmistakable, too; spears were shown piercing each of the little figures' breasts, and the whole clay tablet was sticky with fresh red blood.

The young men looked sombrely at each other. 'Where did you find this?' said Quintus at last.

'In the centre of their village courtyard, on a stone they use for an altar to that victory goddess of theirs. They'd been burning the—the insides of some animal on it.'

'Well . . .' said Quintus, on a long breath, putting down the bloody tablet, 'the message seems clear enough. Charming little thing. We'll have to take it straight to the General.'

Lucius bit his lips and stared down at the tile floor. 'How are we going to say that we—uh—happened to find it?'

Quintus was silent a moment while he felt a distinct shock and almost contempt, quickly mastered. 'You want me to say *I* found it, Luce?' he asked evenly.

His friend's eyes shifted and he spoke very fast. 'Well, but you're a favourite of the general's. He wouldn't really punish *you*. The old boy can be mighty unpleasant when his orders are disobeyed. I—well, I didn t tell you, but I was in a lot of trouble with him before you came.

'All right,' Quintus cut in. 'I'll lie about finding the tablet, but I'm not so noble that I'm going to take the blame for *all* the monkey business you've been up to. Come on!'

The young men walked silently to the General's quarters, while Quintus held the sinister tablet by one corner. When they were admitted, Quintus said, 'General Petillius, here is something we feel you'd want to see at once. It comes from the altar in the British village, but the Parisii have cleared out. Entirely. No trace of them.'

The General examined the sticky red tablet long and carefully, but his face showed nothing. His eyes were frigid when he looked up at Quintus. 'How did you happen to visit the village? You know my orders.'

Here goes, thought Quintus with distaste. 'I was on the ramparts and heard some strange noises from below, sir. I decided to investigate.'

'You must have exceptionally sharp ears, since the village is over a mile away and the wind in the wrong direction. Did it occur to you to report these remarkable noises to a superior officer before taking independent action?'

'No, sir,' said Quintus, staring at the wall above Petillius' head.

The General's stern eyes moved from Quintus' face to the flushed and subtly defiant one of Lucius.

'Our Britons here have always been extremely friendly until recently,' said the General, 'but there has been a change, and this'—he indicated the tablet—'is a declaration of war. I should like to know the reason.'

Both young men were silent.

'Can you think of any reason why the Parisii should become suddenly hostile to us, Quintus Tullius?' said the General, each word dropping like a stone.

'No, sir,' said Quintus, his eyes on the wall.

'Can *you*, Lucius Claudius?' continued the implacable voice.

'Oh no, sir,' said Lucius quickly. 'None at all.'

There was another silence, and the General sighed. Then he stood up with decision and called a sentry. 'You,' he said to Quintus, 'will accompany this sentry to the guardhouse to await my decision on your disobedience. . . . You,' he turned to Lucius, 'report at once to your centurion. The whole legion will now be alerted. An attack on the fort seems likely.'

Quintus followed the sentry with a sore and heavy heart. As he crossed the parade-ground, Lucius ran up to him and whispered, 'I'm sorry, Quintus, I—I'll get you out soon. You'll see.'

Quintus did not answer.

The guard-house was an underground prison below the west gate tower. It contained six cells, very small and pitch black, with ventilation holes, and stone floors, nothing else. Quintus was shoved into one of them and given a jug of water. His sword and armour were taken from him. The thick oaken door banged shut, the iron bolt clanged through the sockets. He was alone.

It was afternoon of the next day before there was a sound on the other side of the cell door. The bolt shot back and Quintus, blinking in the sudden light of a little lamp that someone carried, finally recognized Lucius.

'It's all fixed now, Quintus,' cried Lucius in an excited voice. 'You're to come out!—General's orders.'

Quintus made a harsh sound. 'So you finally told him the truth. . . .'

'Shut up!' whispered Lucius, quickly glancing at the guard who stood in the corridor. 'No, it isn't that—I didn't have a chance yet—but something's happened. Come on—hurry up!'

Quintus' resentment towards Lucius and his relief at being released were both forgotten in amazement when he saw the parade-ground. The entire legion of six thousand men was there in full battle dress, and forming into cohorts under the shouts of the centurions. The cavalry, already mounted, were quietening their prancing horses in a square near the stables.

'Jupiter Maximus! What's up?' Quintus cried. 'Have we been attacked?'

'No,' Lucius answered. 'We're on the move. A messenger came. The Iceni have risen. We're going to the relief of Colchester. It's besieged.'

During the desperate forced marches of the next three days, Quintus learned what had happened. An exhausted Roman messenger had tumbled into the Lincoln garrison at noon of the day Quintus spent in jail. He brought a frantic summons for help from the Procurator, Catus, who was in London. The Iceni and the Trinovantes both had risen, with Queen Boadicca as their leader. She had turned into an avenging fury. Her forces marching down from Norfolk had killed on the way not only every Roman but every Briton friendly to the Romans. And they had marched on to Colchester. There were thousands of them—nobody knew exactly how many, but there were women amongst them. Warrior women like the Queen. Something terrible was happening in Colchester. The Procurator wasn't sure what yet —he had only been able to send a few of his guard to its relief. He had sent a messenger to the Governor, who was in Wales with most of the army, but the gods only knew when Suetonius could get back. Petillius and his Ninth Legion must come at once and put down the insurrection.

'By the divine spirit of our august Emperor, I implore you to hasten,' the Procurator had written. 'I hear some of the other tribes have joined the rebellion, the Coritani, your own Parisii.'

The General had read this message aloud to the assembled legion. It was obvious why Quintus had been released from jail, quite apart from the fact that he was needed to fight with his men. The General had realized that the Parisii flight and defiant tablet were part of the great concerted rebellion and doubtless had little to do with any action of Lincoln's garrison. Lucius had not had to confess. The minor incident had been forgotten in the crisis.

All the same, Quintus thought, as he rode down Ermine Street on Ferox, my name hasn't been cleared. And he could not help wondering if Lucius ever would have told the truth about the visit to the village. There was no outward difference in the relationship between the two young men. They shared their scanty marching rations together, snatched sleep side by side in each night's camp, but Quintus' trust was shaken. It was painful, but fortunately there was scant time to brood on personal matters. They were constantly on the watch for attack. But there was none. The Coritani villages beside the fens were deserted too. They could see marks of the broad British wagon-wheels on the road ahead of them, so that some force must have passed that way, but until they reached Braughing, where Ermine Street joined the Essex Stane Street, there was no sign of trouble. At Braughing there had been a small permanent stockade for the accommodation of passing troops; Quintus had stopped there on the way up. A time-expired Roman veteran had lived within the stockade with his wife and children, and acted as quartermaster.

Now there was nothing left of the stockade or its cluster of wooden buildings, nothing but a heap of ashes, while from the branches of a great oak tree, outside the ramparts, dangled four hacked corpses, the bodies of the Roman veteran and his family.

At this sight, the legionaries became silent, though before they had been light-hearted—pleased by the break in the monotony of garrison life, joking about how quickly they were going to subdue a yapping pack of natives led by a *woman*.

'Imagine fighting with women!' Lucius had laughed earlier on the way down. 'We'll spank all the little dears and send them home to their pots and pans.'

Lucius' jokes no longer amused Quintus and he merely said, 'You didn't see Queen Boadicea. She's as strong and proud as any man. So for that matter,' he added, 'are many of our Roman matrons.'

Braughing's fate was sobering, but still did not prepare them for the sight of Colchester, which they reached next day. The smell of smoke had met them two hours before they got there, and as they came near it became intolerable, suffocating.

Quintus' whole concentration for some minutes had to be given to Ferox, who plunged and trembled and finally bolted sideways up a little hill.

Here Quintus managed to soothe the horse and incidentally to get a good look at Colchester. Except that it simply wasn't there. The forum, the government buildings and basilica, the neat streets of villas and shops, the theatre had all become heaps of smoking rubble. Quintus blinked and looked again. The enormous, magnificent white-and-gold Temple of Claudius wasn't there either. In its place was fire, a vast bonfire with flames leaping high enough to touch the clouds.

'Merciful gods——' Quintus whispered. Suddenly, as he realized the incredible extent of the destruction and thought of the concentrated hatred that had prompted it, he felt a thrill of fear. But where *were* the Britons? Where had they gone after destroying Colchester?

This was the problem which also occupied General Petillius. Nor was it answered for some hours. The General drew up his legion beside the river Colne, away from the city, while he sent men to search amongst the ruins for any sign of life. They came back with tales of frightful death. Every inhabitant of Colchester had apparently been slaughtered and the place was full of bones and half-burned corpses. At length they found an old Roman shopkeeper, who crawled trembling out of a cellar near the river when he saw the legionaries. They took him to the General, who conferred with him beneath a tree on the river-bank. Presently, Quintus, to his amazement, received another summons from his General, who greeted him without preamble, or apparent memory of Quintus' disgrace, and said, 'This old man thinks the British forces have withdrawn to the north, where they are making plans to march next to London. You are the only one of my legion who has recently covered that road to Iceni country. Can you remember a likely encampment for their forces?'

Quintus thought a moment and said hesitatingly, 'Well, sir, there were some earthworks and a hill up past the river Stour. The British use that sort of thing for a fort.'

The General nodded. 'We'll go after them at dawn. Take them by surprise, I hope.'

That night was a tense one for the Ninth Legion as they listened to the measured footsteps of the sentries or snatched what sleep they could. Even the war-scarred veterans of many a battle were keyed up and jumpy, more so than Quintus, who had never seen actual warfare, or Lucius, who got thoroughly drunk even under Flaccus' watchful eye. Whatever the circumstances, thought Quintus, Lucius always managed by devious means to gratify his own desires. Flaccus grew more and more gloomy, his long Spanish face set in grim furrows. He pointed out that the waters of the Colne had suddenly turned blood-red as the legion camped beside it. Nobody else had noticed, but Flaccus said it was so, and he went to pray to Mars once again at the little altar which they had set up in the camp. And Flaccus said he heard the shriek of spirits issuing from the burning Temple of Claudius, where some of the doomed inhabitants of Colchester had held out for two days against the Britons.

Quintus did not hear the ghostly shrieks, but as he forced himself to shut his eyes and relax his body as Roman soldiers were taught, he heard something else—something from the dark woods across the Colne: the sharp yelping of foxes, and more distant answers. And he thought that there was little chance of surprising the British forces, for there were unseen eyes watching every Roman move.

The Ninth Legion marched at dawn, heading north for the Stour. They marched in close formation ten abreast with the cavalry at the sides, as usual in times of danger, though they did not expect to find the British forces for many miles. It was a gentle summer dawn. There was no sound but the rustling of the trees. It seemed impossible that the peaceful day could hide any threat. I don't believe they're up this way at all, Quintus thought, looking at the blue sky—and as he thought it, the quiet air exploded with blood-curdling war cries. They heard before they saw, for the pandemonium of hideous sound came from all around them.

The legion had marched into a pocket encircled by slopes, and over the brow of these slopes, on every side, poured masses of yelling, frenzied Britons—thousands of them. The legion's shields clanked together, forming the solid battle fence they were trained to make, but the attack was so sudden and they were so grossly outnumbered that the whirling chariots, the shaggy British war-ponies, the hate-driven, howling warriors mowed them down in the first minutes. While the cavalry galloped to protect the infantry's flanks, General Petillius shouted the order to charge. They could not charge. The Britons with their blue-painted faces and flying gaudy tartans were on top of them, while from a war

chariot high on the hillside a woman yelled hoarse orders—
Queen Boadicea, a spear in her hand, her long golden hair flying
as she shouted encouragement to her army. Behind her were
clustered other women and her two daughters.

Quintus fought as in a nightmare, slashing with his sword,
seeing blood flow, yanking Ferox away from the darting British
chariots, dodging spears, protecting, as long as he could, the
standard of his cohort until it was knocked from his hand.
Unbelieving, dazed, Quintus saw the main body of the legion,
the foot-soldiers, fall. The little valley was a sea of thrashing
bodies that grew quiet, and a sea of Roman blood. Through the
roaring in his ears, and the spine-chilling whoops of the victorious
Britons, Quintus heard the command of his own General.
Retreat! retreat!—Make south for London.'

Quintus turned blindly to obey, but his forehead was gashed
so that blood and sweat ran into his eyes. He did not see a huge
Icenian sneak up behind him. His sword was flung from him.
The Icenian seized Ferox's bridle, and the horse plunged and
snorted, unseating Quintus, who fell to the ground on one knee.
He knuckled the blood from his eyes and saw the Icenian pick up
the sword and turn to raise it high with the point towards
Quintus' throat. Quintus floundered frantically and could not
rise, for his leg had twisted under him. Helpless, he looked up
into the murderous eyes.

But the gleaming sword did not descend. Someone had
grabbed the Icenian's arm, someone gave a sharp command and
then ran back towards the sloping hillside. The huge British
warrior threw down the sword and suddenly scooped Quintus up,
flinging him over his shoulder like a sack of grain. He strode out
of the mêlée and dumped Quintus on the ground beside the
chariot of the warrior Queen.

Boadicea did not see Quintus as she leaned far over her chariot
and called in a great harsh voice to her men below, 'Kill! kill!'

'We *have* killed, Your Majesty!' came a mighty roar in answer
from the multitude of Britons, 'Look how *well* we have killed!'

'Andraste! Andraste!' shouted the Queen exultantly. 'The
sacred hare prophesied this when it ran towards the sun! Oh
goddess of victory, we thank thee!' She raised her powerful arms
towards the sky. Her body trembled. Her face was white and
glistening with triumphant tears.

Quintus, too dazed to think or speculate why he himself was
not yet dead, tried to ease his leg and struggle to his feet. The

Queen's exaltation died. She lowered her head and saw the wounded Roman beside her chariot. 'Why do you suffer this hell spawn to live?' she cried angrily to the warrior nearest her. Suddenly she peered hard at Quintus. 'I remember him! This is one that came to my palace with the Procurator. He watched them scourge me!' Her face convulsed. 'Roman, Roman—it is well you are not yet dead. By Lugh, the sun god, and his life sap, the holy mistletoe, I swear you shall suffer the tortures of——'

'No! no!' cried a terrified girl's voice. 'My gracious Queen, do you not remember? This is the Roman I told you of. This is the one I stopped Murdoch from killing just now!'

Quintus turned and stared blankly at Regan's tense, imploring face.

'Ah . . .' said the Queen. Her blue eyes lost their frenzied fire, they became cold. 'Then I shall spare you for now, Roman,' she said in Latin. 'As you spared Regan here. Because *Icenians* pay their debts . . . and I shall pay my debt to Rome too, never fear——' Her eyes glinted with implacable meaning. 'We will rid this country of you, every one of you. Do you see my people——?' She waved her arm towards the plain below. 'A few are dead, but there are still fifty thousand of them—Icenians and their allies—Trinovantes, Coritani, Parisii—soon *all* the tribes of Britain will be with us—and do you see *your* proud legion, Roman?'

Quintus looked down at the acres of mangled Roman bodies, the blood-encrusted shields, helmets, eagles glinting in the sunlight. His throat choked.

'Aye,' went on the Queen, with a terrible laugh, 'there *is* no more Ninth Legion, is there? And now you see how it will fare with all Romans everywhere.' She turned from him contemptuously. 'The Roman does not speak. Bind him, Murdoch. *He* shall see what it feels like to be a slave.'

The huge Icenian yanked off Quintus' helmet and threw it away. It rolled and bumped down to the hollow below, where it stopped near all the other useless helmets of the dead. He bound Quintus' wrists behind his back with leather thongs. He snapped an iron collar round Quintus' neck, jerked him to his feet, and hauled him along by a chain. The twisted ligaments in his leg throbbed violently, but Quintus did not feel them. He tried to calm the panic in his head, to think collectedly, as he stumbled along amongst all the triumphant Britons who were heading back to their fort. They passed the edge of the battlefield, and Quintus, whose forehead wound had stopped trickling, suddenly saw a familiar breastplate amongst a heap of corpses. Beneath a battered centurion's helmet he saw Flaccus' pallid face, the eyes wide open as though they still could see the blue sky above. Bitter fluid rose in Quintus' mouth; his stomach heaved; he turned away. May Charon give easy passage across the river Styx to poor Flaccus, he prayed, and to all these others.

But the General had got away, and some of the cavalry. Quintus had seen that, though in all the turmoil and confusion the Britons had not noticed.

I must think coolly, repeated Quintus to himself. I must make a plan for escape. Just think of that, nothing else.

Yet there was no possible escape for a chained Roman amongst fifty thousand enemies. Except Regan. She had saved his life, it was true, but after pleading with the Queen, she had not looked at Quintus. She had gone back to the Princesses and other women, and they had all disappeared, riding on ahead in their chariots.

Regan has paid her debt, he thought. There will certainly be no more help from her. He clenched his jaw and tried not to give way to fear.

They marched two days before they reached the great ring of earthworks that circled the Icenian fort. The Britons started at once on a victory feast. They lay on the ground guzzling great skinfuls of their heather mead. There were whole oxen roasting at several fires. Murdoch wished to be rid of his captive. He chained Quintus to a small oak tree outside the earthworks and there left him. Night began to fall and Quintus grew faint from hunger and thirst. Nobody came near him. He groped on the ground behind his back until he found a sharp stone and tried to rub the thongs that bound his wrists against it. But the stone slipped away. He crouched on the ground beneath the tree, and his chin fell forward on the iron collar. He thought of his mother and Livia at home. He thought of Gaius, his ancestor, and of the quest which had seemed to promise nothing but adventure. Gaius himself had been captured like this and got free, for a moment, anyway. Ah, but Gaius had not been put in chains. The Britons had learned much from the Romans in a hundred years. From inside the earthworks the sound of revelry grew louder. They were chanting triumphal songs, wild, barbaric chants. The lights of their bonfires turned the sky red.

An hour passed. Quintus dozed from exhaustion and jumped as he felt a touch on his arm.

'Sh . . .' whispered a voice in his ear. 'Don't speak!'

A strand of silky hair blew against his cheek as he looked dully up into Regan's shadowy eyes. The warning pressure on his arm increased, and she shrank behind him. He saw then that where she was looking—on top of the earthworks—a tall man's figure was dimly outlined. The man peered down for a few seconds towards the oak tree. Then the tall figure disappeared.

'It's Navin, chief of the Trinovantes,' Regan whispered. 'I heard him arguing with our Queen. She wants to torture you to-morrow for a sacrifice, the torture of the——' She used a Celtic word he could not understand, and shuddered. 'It's horrible,' she whispered.

Quintus swallowed hard. 'What did Navin say?' he whispered back.

'He said that because you had once befriended him, you should not be tortured, only killed quickly. She would not agree.'

'I shall try to die as a Roman soldier should,' said Quintus grimly. 'But then why did you save me today, Regan? I'd rather have died with my men.'

'I know,' she whispered. 'I did not think the Queen would be so—so cruel. I too hate Rome—I have tried—but I cannot—quite hate *you*. I've brought a knife,' she added very low. 'Lean over so I can cut the wrist thongs.'

'May the divine gods bless you!' he muttered through his teeth, as Regan sawed away behind his back. The thongs fell apart and without thought he raised his freed hands and, pulling her face to his, kissed her fervently. She stiffened and pushed him back, but for a moment he fancied he had felt her soft lips yield.

'Fool!' she whispered breathlessly. 'I do this only out of justice, and you're not free yet.' She fumbled with the clasp of his iron collar. 'Here, like this,' she said, guiding his fingers behind his neck; 'it's too stiff for me.'

They struggled for agonizing seconds until the clasp loosened. 'Now go——' she whispered, while he eased the collar and chain soundlessly to the ground. They uprooted a small bush to place it by the tree so it might look, from the ramparts, like Quintus' crouching figure.

He took a step and limped so badly that she gave a smothered exclamation. 'Wait,' she said. 'They've put your horse alone over by the grove of our goddess Andraste, for the sacrifice tomorrow. I think I can get it.' She disappeared while he waited feverishly. The instant he saw her appear between the trees with Ferox he whistled very low, and the horse responded at once, trotting to him. Ferox was still saddled. Quintus mounted and leaned over. 'Regan—some day we'll meet again. I know it, and I'll tell you —tell you——'

'Hurry——' she said. 'Go quickly, quickly—may the gods of my people forgive me for what I've done this night.' She ran, light and silent as a moth, back towards the fort.

CHAPTER IV

Quintus' flight to London—Regan forced to seek his protection— retreat to the south—Quintus volunteers to fetch help—and sets out in disguise with Regan

IF QUINTUS HAD any remnants of softness, he lost them on the desperate flight from Boadicea's camp. He had no weapon with which to kill game, no means of making fire. He lived on berries and a tiny raw fish which he caught with his hands by great good luck, as he forded the river Lea. Ferox did better, for he could crop the sweet wild grasses, but Quintus dared give the horse little time to graze. He followed the road only at night; by day he slept in snatches or pushed his way through the forests, listening every moment for unusual sounds, and wondering— whenever he heard a badger call, or the scream of a wildcat, or the bark of foxes.

At times he thought about Regan with warm gratitude. But then he would think of Colchester's destruction, of the slaughter of the Ninth, of Flaccus' dead eyes staring up into the sky, of the hideous torture Boadicea had decreed for himself. And he hardened his heart against all memory of Regan, who had paid her debt to him, but who was still an enemy.

On the third night he staggered into London and found it a city of dread. Knots of white-faced Roman citizens were gathered on the street corners, whispering to each other. The shop windows were barred. A hush of uncertainty hung over the town—which Quintus did not understand, for as the poor lathered Ferox dragged him haltingly towards the centre of town by the Wal Brook, Quintus saw that Governor Suetonius must have arrived. The royal eagle flag was flying from the Government House, and in the encampment by the Thames he saw a crowd of pitched tents, with emblems of the Fourteenth and Twentieth Legions. Thanks be to Mars! Quintus thought hazily; we'll be all right now. He managed to reach headquarters and give his name to the startled sentry at the gate, but then, to his humiliation, his brain began to swim, the sentry's face wavered in sickening circles.

Quintus stumbled off Ferox, tried to speak again, and slumped instead to the pavement.

When the black mists cleared, he knew he was lying on a couch. He felt the pressure of a cup to his lips and found that he was swallowing strong wine with a stimulating herb in it. He opened his eyes and saw who was holding the cup. Petillius Cerealis, his General. But the General was dreadfully changed, so haggard and drawn had his face become. And the hazel eyes looked down at Quintus with a terrible sadness.

'He's coming round,' said Petillius quietly to someone behind him. 'Here, Quintus, drink—don't try to talk yet.'

As Quintus drank, he saw another face swim up next to Petillius'. A square, florid one above a bull neck. Crisp, greying curls beneath the elaborately embossed helmet of the Governor. The gilded helmet was dazzling, and Quintus shut his eyes.

'This lad's in pretty bad shape—loss of blood—exhaustion,' he heard his General say in a tone of bitterness, 'but at least *he's* alive.'

'You were a madman, Petillius,' said the harsh voice of Governor Suetonius. 'A dangerous fool. Pushing up into enemy country, letting yourself be ambushed. May the gods forgive you, for you've cost us a legion.'

'By all the spirits of my ancestors, Excellency——' cried the General violently. 'Don't you think I am tortured by that night and day? The shame will never leave me. I did not guess Boadicea's numbers, nor judge their fury. I've resigned to you my command—the disposition of my life—or death, is in your hands, yours and our august Emperor's.'

There was a heavy silence, while Quintus felt a stinging behind his closed lids. Petillius had said 'or death . . .' with unmistakable emphasis. Yes, as every lowliest auxiliary knew, death was the most honourable course open to a Roman soldier who had bungled. The quick, self-driven sword-thrust was the end of shame to a Roman general who had lost his legion.

'You know I would have joined in death my legionaries who lie rotting up there to the north—before this, Excellency,' went on the sad, bitter voice, 'except that you have said you need me and commanded me to stay with you.'

Again there was silence and the sound of the two men's breathing. Then Suetonius said, 'Aye, it is so. I need you and every help I can find. You've been a fine general, Petillius, and will redeem yourself. You shall continue to command the remnants of the Ninth and help me with the other legions.'

Suddenly Quintus heard the sharp slap of sandals on the pavement as Suetonius began to pace the floor. 'But *where* is the Second Legion?' the Governor said as though to himself, '*Where*, where? I sent to Gloucester for them ten days ago. Why haven't they come?' Then with a change of tone, as though he had remembered the unhappy General beside him, 'Oh, I understand the fatal error that you made, but by the GODS, Petillius —there must be no more errors! Everything must be sacrificed —*everything*—to one aim.' His voice trumpeted out, 'We must vanquish that she-devil of a Queen!'

Later, when he had eaten and recovered some strength, Quintus told to Petillius the story of his capture and escape from Boadicea, and learned that a couple of hundred of their cavalry had indeed managed to get back to London and had now been quartered amongst the two legions Suetonius had brought from Wales.

And it was then that Quintus finally nerved himself to ask the question which had been occupying his mind for days. 'What happened to the Optio, Lucius Claudius Drusus, my—my friend, sir? Did he get away?'

'He did,' said the General grimly. 'In fact he got away some time before I gave the order to retreat.'

Quintus reddened slowly as he took in the meaning of this. 'You mean, sir——'

'I mean that Lucius Claudius turned tail and fled in that first moment when the Britons leaped upon the infantry. I saw him gallop off.' He added quietly, looking at Quintus' shocked face, 'Yes, panic is a fearful thing to some men—those who haven't learned to control themselves.'

Quintus moistened his lips and said, 'Where did he go, sir?'

The General shrugged wearily. 'I don't know. We've not seen him here. It may be that he escaped to Gaul by ship, as has the Procurator, Decianus Catus. Ah, trust the Procurator to save his worthless skin and leave us to the terror he brought on us!'

Quintus bowed his head and stared down at the mosaic floor.

C

So the Procurator had fled to safety across the water. That was not surprising, but——

'I don't think Lucius has done that too, sir,' he said unhappily. 'He wouldn't really desert you and our legion.'

'Yes, you are loyal, Quintus. Foolishly so, I think. As I also think it was not *you* who visited the Parisii village that night back in Lincoln. I want the truth this time. Was it you?'

'No, sir,' murmured Quintus. 'But Lucius would have confessed, he——'

The General raised his hand and let it fall as though he cut something in two. 'In the light of what came after, and what is still to come, that incident is trivial—forgotten. Lucius Claudius is not the first young aristocrat I've had sent to me for schooling, nor the first to break under discipline and fear. We've no time to waste on such weaklings now. Go to the barracks and get some rest. The next days will be gruelling if Boadicea's forces get here before our plans are complete.'

The next days were gruelling not because of battle but because of uncertainty. The Governor had made a terrible but inevitable decision. He would not try to defend unfortified London. He explained this to a hushed populace from the rostrum before Government House. Until the Second Legion from Gloucester joined him, his entire army consisted only of the Fourteenth and part of the Twentieth. Less than nine thousand men. He must play for time until the Second came, and a few cohorts of raw auxiliaries who had been sent for from the north—if indeed these could get through the enemy lines, or did not turn traitor to Rome themselves and join the British forces.

He was therefore, said the Governor, abandoning London, and fast. Such refugees as could keep up with the army would be taken along. They would march south to Chichester in Sussex, where the Regni tribe was still loyal to Rome. But he warned them that there was little surplus food for them. The army provisions must be hoarded, not wasted on non-combatants. And he was leaving at once. That night. After the army had crossed the Thames, the bridge would be burned.

The Londoners received this ultimatum with weeping and protestations. Some of them made ready to leave, and it was the duty of Quintus and other junior officers to shepherd these evacuees across the river and start them on the road south to Chichester. But many more begged for time to secure their property first, to find means of transporting those too small or old or sick to keep up with fast marches. While many others simply did not believe that there was danger: they preferred to stay in their own homes and take a chance. Surely, they said, Boadicea would not bother with women and children and sick people. She would pursue the Roman army, if indeed her greed for vengeance had not already been satisfied by the havoc she had wreaked in Essex.

Suetonius was unmoved by any arguments. That night the legions marched across the Thames and the last men of the last cohort fired the city-side end of the bridge as they passed over it. Soon the whole wooden bridge was burning, while dimly through its flames the legionaries could see the anxious faces of those who had remained in London.

May Vesta, goddess of the hearth, somehow preserve the poor things and their homes, Quintus thought. But he had seen the ruins of Colchester, while the Londoners had not. Yet Suetonius was undoubtedly right; it was better to abandon one town rather than risk the certain loss of a province.

The Romans marched some miles to a great open heath. Here they could camp in comparative safety, since there were no trees near them to harbour enemies, and a loop of the wide river protected them on two sides. Suetonius' forces had had no proper rest for days, and the General decreed a six-hour respite.

Quintus wolfed down his scanty ration of food—he had still not made up for the days of hunger—tethered Ferox to a bush, lay down on the ground, and instantly went to sleep.

He was roused by a commotion near him, and shouts of 'We've got him! We've *got* him—the filthy Icenian!'

Quintus jumped up and, drawing his sword, ran towards a group of struggling figures. 'What's going on?' he cried, seeing two Roman sentries dragging a man's figure between them.

'It's a Briton, sir, an Icenian by his tartan. He was sneaking around the edge of the camp. In broad daylight too, the stupid fool; he might know he'd be caught!' answered the excited sentry.

A spy? Quintus thought, puzzled by something familiar in the big, red-haired Briton's sulky, scarred face. The Briton let loose a flood of expostulation in Celtic, seemed to be explaining something, then suddenly came Latin words, 'Quintus Tullius—I look for Quintus Tullius.'

The sentries tightened their grasp on the man's arms and cried sneeringly, 'Well, you're *looking* at him, you pig of a Briton. Though how'd you know his name?'

'Quintus Tullius——' repeated the captive with a sort of angry despair.

'I——' began Quintus, peering harder at the scarred face, when suddenly he recognized it. 'Pendoc, the potter!' he cried, remembering the little hut he had taken Regan to, after the outrage on Boadicea.

Pendoc nodded with relief and nodded again as Quintus finished by saying, '*I* am Quintus Tullius.' Pendoc had not known him. During the excited moment he had seen Quintus before, he had not examined the face of the helmeted young Roman.

'Amicus!—friend!' said Pendoc, pointing to himself, and frowning over the Latin. 'I have—message—Quintus Tullius.' He fished around in a deerskin bag he carried slung on his belt and held something out on his palm. Quintus stared and flushed brick red. On the great calloused palm lay a lock of soft, curly chestnut hair. 'Regan,' said Pendoc, 'wants—you.'

The sentries gaped at Quintus' astonished red face.

'Where *is* Regan?' said Quintus, recovering and watching Pendoc closely. This might well be a trap, and this villainous-looking Briton did not inspire much confidence.

Pendoc jerked his head backwards towards the river. 'Hidden in a coracle. Come,' he said in Celtic which Quintus understood.

Quintus thought for a moment, then turned to the sentries. 'I'm going to see what this is all about.'

'Not *alone*, sir!' cried one of them.

'No. That'd be foolish. You continue patrolling. I'll take some men with me.' He roused three foot soldiers and explained briefly. With swords drawn and tense watchfulness they followed Pendoc down to a little bay in the river where reeds grew high.

Pendoc gave a high, whistling cry, like a curlew, which was answered by the same sound from the reeds, which quivered and parted.

Regan stepped up on to the bank and looked at Quintus with anxious uncertainty. Her small face was pale and bruised. Her lovely hair was tangled. Her violet tartan was torn and dirty.

Before Quintus could speak, she shook her head, signifying her understanding of the three other soldiers and the wary looks they gave her. 'No—no,' she said. 'There's only *us*, Pendoc and me. I—I have come to you—for protection.' Tears filled her grey eyes and the trembling of her proud little mouth showed the effort it cost her to say this.

'You've run away from Boadicea?' Quintus asked in amazement. 'You want *Rome's* protection?'

She bowed her head, while a long sigh that was half a sob shook her. 'Quintus, could I speak with you—alone?'

He hesitated yet a minute, then said to his three men, 'Stand over there—keep a sharp look-out.' As they obeyed, he turned back to Regan. 'Tell me,' he said gently, 'what's happened to change you like this?'

She found it very hard because she was frightened and ashamed. She spoke in a mixture of Latin and Celtic, but as he helped her with questions he began to understand.

Regan's part in his escape from the British camp had been discovered. Suspecting something was amiss, Navin had not gone back to the victory feasting after they had seen him on the ramparts that night. He had crept down behind them and watched.

'But why didn't he stop me from escaping?' Quintus cried.

'Because he thinks you are a good man, though a Roman. He did not want you to be tortured.'

'But then why did he tell Boadicea what you had done? Why did he capture *you*?'

'Ah,' she said with a bitter sigh, 'that is different. I'm a Briton. I was betraying my people and disobeying my Queen. He felt I must be punished, though not——' Her voice sank, and terror thickened it as she went on very low, 'Navin did not want me to suffer in the way Boadicea commanded I should.'

He saw how painful all this was to her, but he felt he had to know exactly what had happened. As they stood there by the river reeds, the three soldiers watched curiously. Pendoc squatted on the ground and chipped at a flint spear-point, while Quintus continued his questions. He was appalled at her answers.

When Boadicea had heard from Navin how the girl had managed Quintus' escape, the Queen's anger had been fiendish. All the maternal kindness she had previously shown to Regan had vanished in an instant. She had called the girl dreadful names, of which 'hypocrite' and 'traitress' were the least. With arms upstretched to the skies she had cursed Regan, and she had decreed that since Andraste, the goddess of victory, had been defrauded of her rightful sacrifice, Regan should take Quintus' place in the sacred grove. There would be first the torture of the hooks, and then of fire. Andraste's victims were enclosed in wicker baskets and slowly burned alive on her altar.

Quintus stopped the girl violently when he heard this.

'That's enough,' he cried. 'It's past; you're safe now. Don't think about it! But how did you get away?'

She moistened her lips and said, 'Navin. He's not quite like the Icenians, not so fierce and cruel. Boadicea put me in his charge, and he called Pendoc, who was my father's friend. Navin found us a coracle and let us go. He didn't care where we went, or even if we drowned, but he gave me a chance to live. I couldn't think where to go—we came down to the Thames seeking you, for I have no other friend now. From the river we saw the legions camping. I sent Pendoc to try and find you.'

Quintus was silent, thinking of the girl's extraordinary story, the days of sailing down the coast in the coracle, of the horror she had escaped, and of Navin, and his savage code of retribution, which was tempered and civilized by the years he had spent in Rome. And yet Quintus knew that in actual battle Navin would show no mercy. Then a new thought struck him. 'What will happen to Navin, since Boadicea must suspect he let you go?'

'Nothing, I'm sure,' she answered. 'Navin will give some excuse that she won't dare question. Navin is chief of the Trinovantes and commands many thousand fighters. She needs his support.'

'Ah,' assented Quintus, 'I see. Is Boadicea still planning to march on London?'

'Her forces must be nearly there now,' said the girl, with a frightened glance down the Thames. 'They were to start right after the—the sacrifice to Andraste.' She had been answering him steadily, but now she swayed and gave a little gasp.

'Poor girl—you're exhausted,' said Quintus remorsefully, steadying her. 'Come, we'll go up to the camp. I'll take care of you, Regan. You need fear nothing any more.' A brave promise that he prayed he could fulfil.

During the next days, while the legions in full retreat marched south, Quintus caught only occasional glimpses of Regan. She and Pendoc had been put amongst the London refugees, and everyone's private emotions were swamped in the physical strains and necessities of reaching the fertile lands and friendlier people along the Sussex coast. The Regni tribe under their King Cogidumnus was a small, peaceful one, close-knit with Gaul across the water, and more Romanized than any of the other tribes. The Regni welcomed the legions as best they could and provided them with grain and fruit and flocks. But obviously this

situation could not last indefinitely and the army was cut off
from all its usual supplies by Boadicea's forces to the north.

There were two small trading-ships in Portsmouth, the harbour.
Some of the refugees sailed for Gaul on them, and the Governor
sent desperate messages asking for reinforcements to be sent him.
But he knew it must be weeks before help could possibly arrive.

In the meantime Boadicea and her growing army could—and
doubtless intended to—massacre them all.

The morning after the Romans arrived on the coast, the sun
rose broiling hot in a hazy, coppery sky. The men were restless,
anxious, reflecting the uncertainty felt by their superiors. Quintus
spent some time with Ferox, currying him and removing a stone
from his hoof; then, there being no orders or special duties to stop
him for the moment, he yielded to a desire he had been suppres-
sing on the march.

He walked from the camp to some little bark-and-leaf shelters
that the remaining civilians had set up in a corner of the ramparts. Here he found Regan on her knees by a large mortar,
pounding wheat with a stone pestle. Pendoc was near her,
shaping flint into spearheads. She looked up as the young Roman
approached and smiled politely, though her eyes were shadowed
and heavy from weariness.

'It's hot, isn't it?' said Quintus inanely, suddenly embarrassed.
He had thought a lot about her. His heart swelled at the thought
of how she had fled to him for help. As he looked at her now, she
seemed grateful, but ashamed and unhappy too—probably torn
by a feeling of disloyalty to her own people. Despite her smallness
and softness there was always a shell of reserve.

'It is hot,' she agreed, continuing to pound the grain. She was
flushed; damp tendrils of hair stuck to her forehead, but she
looked extremely pretty. Were it not for the watchful Pendoc,
Quintus would have taken the heavy pestle and crushed the
stubborn grain for himself. But a Roman standard-bearer would
look ridiculous doing menial woman's work, and Regan probably
would not admire such softness—although it was hard to know
what she thought. And the more he looked at her, the more he
wanted to know.

'Can't you stop that, for a moment?' he said imploringly.
'Walk down to the beach with me—there's a breeze, and——'
Quintus broke off as a trumpet blast resounded through the
fort.

He jerked round and listened carefully to the call. 'That's

assembly,' he explained to Regan. 'The Governor's going to make some announcement, I guess. I'll have to go.' He heaved a sigh, as the realization of the Romans' grave predicament returned. 'I'll see you later?' he asked with unmistakable longing. She gave him only a dark, unencouraging look, and bent to her pounding.

So she *doesn't* like me! Quintus thought hotly, as he walked away. Well, what of it? She had had a right to his protection and she was safe enough now, as safe as any of them in this menacing country. He certainly was not going to force unwelcome attentions on her, attentions, moreover, that were forbidden by Roman law. She is nothing but an ignorant little barbarian, after all, remember that, Quintus told himself, and stalked on to the parade-ground.

The officers were assembling; the prefects, the tribunes, the centurions; the lowlier standard-bearers and Optios. They formed a semicircle in front of the striped tent that was topped with a gilded eagle. The Governor stepped out. Behind him were the generals of the Twentieth and Fourteenth Legions, and Petillius Cerealis, who no longer had a legion.

Suetonius climbed into a chariot and began to talk earnestly. Beneath the glittering helmet, his heavy red face was drawn with fatigue and worry.

'Roman officers,' he began to the tense listeners, 'I shall speak frankly. We are in a tight and shameful situation. We've retreated as far as we can without quitting the island completely, which is, of course, unthinkable. Rome has never tasted total defeat, nor will she now. But we are not yet nearly ready to engage the British forces.' He paused. 'I have just received terrible news. The spy I left on the southern bank of the Thames has just come to me.' He stopped again and wiped the sweat from his forehead. 'Boadicea has totally destroyed London,' he said in a harsh, dragging voice. 'She massacred all those we left behind. When the spy left, the Queen was apparently bound for the town of St. Albans, where she will doubtless do likewise.'

Suetonius shut his eyes for a second and clenched the rim of the chariot. A choked murmur came from the ring of officers.

Suddenly Suetonius raised his head and shouted as though to the sky, 'By Mars, by all the sacred gods of Rome—WHERE is the Second Legion? *Why* does it not come?'

The hot sun beat down on the silent group in the fort. A bee hummed lazily and winged off over the ramparts.

The Governor continued on a lower note, 'When in Wales I

first heard of the revolt, I sent a trusted messenger straight down to Gloucester. I sent another before we left London. And we've heard nothing. It's true the legion *may* be on its way. I propose to march north cautiously and try to intercept it. And yet I feel there's something wrong. I've called you together because I need a volunteer. No, wait—' he added sharply as several hands went up. 'This will be a mission of great danger. The man must travel secretly direct from here over a hundred miles of unknown country. We've built no roads through that land, and the Belgic tribes there have never been tamed. It will mean traversing the sacred places of the Druids. True, I've exterminated most of that filthy priesthood on the island of Anglesey, but not all, I fear. I think some may still lurk near the monstrous ring of stones to the west. This mission is one of almost certain death—I know a Roman will not cringe from this, but I need other qualifications as well as sheer courage, or it will be the waste of a man. . . . Who volunteers . . . ?'

Hands were raised again, more slowly, but Quintus broke and stepped forward eagerly. '*I* do, sir. Quintus Tullius Pertinax, standard-bearer, third cohort of—of the Ninth!'

The Governor's heavy-lidded eyes roamed over the faces of the other volunteers, then returned to Quintus. Suetonius leaned over and whispered something to General Petillius, who nodded and sent a quiet smile of recognition to Quintus.

'And why,' said the Governor, 'are you so eager to undertake this mission?'

Quintus could not say that he was hurt by Regan and eager for any action, nor explain at this inappropriate moment about his quest—his heart had jumped when he realized that this mission might take him through the very place he had longed all his life to reach. But there were other reasons, and he told them.

'I've seen something of the Britons, sir, and have plenty of personal reasons for hating them—besides wishing to avenge the Ninth. I speak and understand some Celtic, and I think I could get through to Gloucester——'

He saw from the Governor's face that he was not convinced. The pondering gaze turned again towards an older man, a tribune, whose hand was raised.

Suddenly a girl's clear voice rang out. 'O Roman Governor, may I speak?'

The astonished officers made way, as Regan walked through with perfect composure and stood before the Governor's chariot.

'What's this?' growled Suetonius, frowning at Regan. 'One of the refugees?'

Again General Petillius explained in a quick aside, for Quintus had earlier reported Regan and Pendoc's arrival to his General.

'Oh,' said Suetonius with heightened interest, 'you're the girl who fled from Boadicea? Well, what is it, maiden?'

'I have understood most of what you said, O Governor,' said Regan carefully. 'But not Quintus Tullius, nor anyone, will ever get to Gloucester in the way you ordered.'

'Why not?' said the Governor sharply. 'How do you know?'

'Because no Roman could. There are trackless forests—there are strange things that happen——' she broke off suddenly. 'It was once my country—I was born in the sacred plain to the west —so I know.'

So that's where she came from! Quintus thought, amazed, and was more astonished as her quiet little voice went on:

'But we will help. Pendoc and I. Quintus shall dress as a native. He is dark, so we will say he comes from the land of the Silures across the mountains in Wales. We will speak for him. And we will'—she hesitated—'we will set him on his way. I will not harm my own people, but I will do *this* much for Rome.'

'Well, I'll be——' murmured the Governor, looking down at the small, resolute figure with a certain admiration. Regan's clear grey eyes looked back at him steadily. 'If she weren't a Briton, I might—it almost seems like a sensible plan. . . .'

'Yes, Suetonius, I think so,' said General Petillius gravely. 'Our need is too desperate for quibbling. Quintus Tullius, come here.' When Quintus had obeyed, Petillius said in a low voice, 'Do you trust this girl completely?'

Quintus answered from deepest instinct. 'Yes, sir. There's much she doesn't say, but what she does say is true.'

Petillius nodded. 'These Britons keep the most extraordinary exact moral balance-sheets. They pay back precisely each good or evil done to them. You rescued the girl in the Icenian city, so she saves you from Boadicea. You sheltered her from Boadicea, so she will guide you to Gloucester. They're all like that—and if' —his face darkened—'that thrice-cursed fool of a Procurator had not committed those outrages on the Icenians, we wouldn't be in this fix now.'

'No, sir,' agreed Quintus, and he glanced towards Regan, who was conversing with the Governor.

Petillius saw the look and said half sharply, half smiling, 'Here now—you haven't got any unduly tender feelings towards that little British savage, have you?'

'If I had, sir, you may be sure they'd not be returned. She operates only, as you say, from a strict sense of justice.'

'Quintus,' said his General, laying a stern hand on his arm, 'I needn't tell you that the success of your mission is of supreme importance, that the whole fate of Rome here may depend on it —that no sentimentality must be allowed to intrude for a second. . . .'

'No, sir,' said Quintus, solemnly tightening his square young jaw. 'You needn't tell me.'

An hour later, a party of three nondescript Britons trotted out of the fort on shaggy little native ponies—Pendoc first, his gangling feet almost touching the ground beneath his shaggy, plaid trousers, his coarse, sandy-red hair blowing round his shoulders in the sea-breeze that had cut the heat; then Regan in her violet tunic, her head and lovely hair all hidden by a rough linen scarf; and Quintus last. If the situation had not been so grave, Quintus would have been laughing wryly at himself, and there had been a momentary twinkle in his General's eye as he gave Quintus a folded, sealed parchment, the official message from the Governor to General Valerianus of the Second Legion, and then rehearsed last instructions.

Regan had done a thorough job of metamorphosing Quintus from a Roman officer, by commandeering a few garments from the Regni village outside the fort. Quintus now wore long, dirty wool trousers, fastened at waist and ankle by thongs, and a plaid cloth tunic so faded and soiled that the pattern was unidentifiable. A point Regan insisted on. Most Britons could recognize many tartans as belonging to this or that tribe, and Quintus, posing as a Silure from far-distant Wales, must provoke no doubts. She finished his costume with an ancient cloak of mangy otter-skins, held at the neck by a spiral iron brooch. His weapon was a clumsy spear tipped with one of Pendoc's flint heads. Regan spent several concentrated moments on the problem of his short hair and clean-shaven face, which were so unmistakably Roman, and solved it by means of a horned British helmet to which she stuck wisps of black horsehair. 'That is all right,' she said critically, surveying her achievement. 'The Silures have strange customs which no one quite knows. But your *face*! All Britons have beards.' She frowned a moment, then seized a charred log from the hearth fire. She rubbed the charcoal on his chin and upper lip. 'That's better, as though you were growing it, which you must. Try to keep your face hidden in your cloak.'

'Don't worry,' Quintus had said dryly, staring at himself in a polished shield. 'You've done a perfect job. My own mother wouldn't know me.'

'Your mother?' said the girl quickly, as though startled from the business-like efficiency she had been showing.

'Yes,' said Quintus with faint irony, 'I have a mother—in Rome—a very dear and good one. Also a little sister, Livia.'

'Is it so . . .?' said Regan with sudden gentleness. 'I had not thought of you as—as—of your life before you came here. *My* mother died when I was ten, just before I went to Boadicea— sometimes I have so longed—I thought Queen Boadicea . . .'

She snapped the sentence off, the soft look left her eyes. She turned briskly to speak to Pendoc, who had gathered in the ponies.

Poor little thing, thought Quintus, this time understanding her cool abruptness, she's had a hard time. But in pursuance of his promise to Petillius and also of a vow he had made to Mars, Quintus resolutely shut his mind to tender thoughts of Regan. He would treat her like a boy, on this wild mission to the west.

CHAPTER V

A moonlit camp—the story of the sacred mistletoe—arrival
at Stonehenge—secret ritual of the Druids—threats of death—
welcome at last from Conn Lear, the Arch-Druid

WHEN THEY HAD LEFT THE COAST and the pastures of the Regni, they plunged into a great forest, and Quintus soon realized how impossible it would have been for him to make any time at all without Pendoc's and Regan's help. Pendoc, who lost most of his sulkiness once they were away from the Roman fort, was particularly helpful, and by means of an occasional grunt, or the twist of his scarred lip that passed for a smile, even showed pleasure at being back in his own country, which he had not seen since he had been sent to the Icenians with Regan six years before.

The trails through the forest seemed absolutely invisible to

Quintus, but Pendoc knew what to look for—a tiny spot of blue woad on the directional side of an oak trunk, or three pebbles arranged like the huge stone dolmens they sometimes passed. These dolmens consisted of flat table-stones supported by upright stones, and Quintus asked Regan about them.

'I don't know,' she answered, hesitatingly. 'They were of the old, old time, longer back than memory.'

'*Druid* stones . . .?' he persisted. 'Like the great circle at Stonehenge—is that what you call it?'

The girl turned round on her pony and looked at him. 'Romans understand nothing about the Druids,' she said quietly. 'Your Governor, Suetonius, has tried to kill them all . . .' She started to say something else, but seemed to change her mind. 'Quintus, why are you interested in the Druids?'

Following Pendoc, they jogged along in silence amongst the great trees while Quintus considered. The feeling between them was more natural, less tense and, now that he was no longer garbed like a Roman soldier, Regan had lost much of her defensiveness. They seemed very close, and he decided to tell her of the quest later, when they stopped to eat and rest.

That evening just before moonrise they camped by a brook, under an enormous ash. Pendoc lit a small fire and they heated a stone for a griddle. They had ground wheat in their leather pouches, which Regan mixed with water and baked in cakes on the stone. Pendoc disappeared downstream to spear a fish. And Regan suddenly repeated her question. 'Why do you ask about the Druids?'

'It is because of my great-grandfather, Gaius Tullius,' Quintus began slowly. 'I can't manage the Celtic words for such a long story . . .' he added thoughtfully.

'No,' she said with a faint smile, 'Though we are each learning the other's language fast. Tell it in Latin, I think I can understand.'

'It was in Julius Cæsar's day,' he began. 'You know who he was?'

He heard her sigh. 'Yes, the *first* Roman general who came here to conquer us. Oh, *why* can't we all live in peace? Why did Rome want our island too, when it has all the world besides?'

Quintus was taken aback. For a moment he could not think of the answers to that, so natural did it seem to him that Rome must rule everywhere. Then he took a deep breath and explained to her the benefits the Roman Empire brought to conquered nations, the more advanced education, the prosperity that came from increased trade with other countries, the better health everyone would have because of Roman cleanliness and sanitation, the social justice meted out by wise Roman law, and the advantage of a strong over-rule in keeping the tribes from warring amongst themselves.

She listened patiently awhile, not quite understanding the complicated words he had to use to explain these things; then she said with a small, rueful laugh, 'Yes, well—I suppose there must be fighting, because men have always fought. It's true our tribes here fight each other. I see that you believe in what you grew up to believe. It is so with us all. Tell me of your great-grandfather, Quintus. . . .' She put her arm round her legs, rested her chin on her knees, and gazed up into his face while the firelight flickered over them.

He began the story which had always so fascinated him, and she listened quietly until he came to the place where Gaius tore down the mistletoe, and trampled on it. Then she gave a gasp and cried, 'Ah, it's no wonder the Druid priests killed him! Oh, Quintus, don't you see—I don't know your Roman gods, but they are sacred to *you*—if someone profaned them, trampled on them—wouldn't you be afraid and want revenge to appease the angry god?'

'But a plant is not a *god*,' objected Quintus.

Regan frowned and wrestled with the problem of expressing her belief. 'No, but the mistletoe is sent from heaven to rest high in the great oaks which make our temples. The mistletoe berries are the life-sap of our great god, the sun. Lugh is his name, and without him we should all die.'

For an instant Quintus smiled at what seemed to him such foolishness; yet Romans too had a god of the sun, Apollo, and the thrill of conviction in her low voice touched him.

'We may not agree on that,' he said gently. 'Yet Britons believe in proper funeral rites, as Romans do. You must see why my family is sure that Gaius' fate has given us bad luck for years and why I'd like to find the spot where he lies.'

'Yes,' she said after a moment, 'I see that. It would be the same for us. And wherever this sacred oak is on the plain ahead, you may be sure he will be there still—the Druids would not touch him.'

He glanced at her curiously. 'You seem to know a lot about the Druids, Regan. I mean, you speak with such certainty.'

The moon suddenly topped the trees and shone down on them. It dappled her face with silver as she turned and answered, not in the reserved way she usually did, but in a rush, mixing Celtic and Latin words together. 'I want to tell you something! This trip Pendoc and I are guiding you on, it isn't only because I—I wanted to help you. You will not be harmed—I gave you my word on that. And I will show you how to get to Gloucester, if you really wish it. But first——' She stopped and began pleating the folds of her tunic, back and forth. 'First you must go to my grandfather.'

'Your grandfather! But, Regan, I thought you had no people left now in the world.'

'None but my grandfather. He will be at this time in the Great Temple of the Stones. In Stonehenge.'

'WHY?' asked Quintus, astounded. I don't understand at all.'

'Because my grandfather is the Arch-Druid of Britain,' she said solemnly. 'He will be at Stonehenge for these days of Lugh's festival.'

'Jupiter Maximus . . ' whispered Quintus, gaping at her. 'You really are the most extraordinary girl. Just as I begin to think I know you, I find out something new and startling.'

As though telling him her secret had relieved her, Regan gave a sudden smile, cocked her head and—as nearly as he could be sure in the moonlight—looked at him mischievously.

'I have heard,' said Regan in a demure voice, 'that a little mystery makes a woman more attractive.'

Quintus, with a shock, rearranged all his thoughts and burst out laughing. That little flash of feminine coquetry startled him as much as her previous revelation, and it delighted him. Too much so, he realized at once, remembering his vow to Petillius and Mars. Sitting in the secluded forest moonlight with a girl like this was dangerous. He discovered that he had quite unconsciously moved nearer to her, and it was with relief that he heard Pendoc crunching through the bracken behind them. The potter dangled three fish from his spear and threw them down triumphantly on the moss beside Regan.

Regan pulled her reserve over her at once like a cloak and with her little iron knife set about cleaning, scaling, and then broiling the fish.

They ate in hungry silence. After a while Quintus, throwing the fish-spine over his shoulder into the forest, said, 'Regan, why do you insist upon taking me to this Arch-Druid? It'll delay me, and——' He did not like to seem to doubt her word that he would not be harmed, but she might very well be over-estimating her influence with her grandfather.

'Because,' she answered, 'he is very wise and powerful. And because'—she hesitated—'we do not know the way farther north towards Gloucester.' Again there was the curious pause before she said slowly, 'Conn Lear must tell you how to go.'

'Who——?' cried Quintus. 'Conn Lear—that was the name of the Druid priest we met on the road the first day in Britain. Is *that* your grandfather? But Suetonius ordered him captured; he sent one of his tribunes!'

'Nobody can capture Conn Lear,' said Regan, wiping her knife and putting it in her pouch. 'He is a magician, he can see things —and do things that others cannot.'

Quintus thought of the strange power of Conn Lear's eyes, of the numbed, helpless way he had let the old man escape, and he fell silent trying to rally his courage. He tried to remember what the Arch-Druid had said that day—that the omens and auguries were bad for the Romans, that he came only to warn. Well, the omens were right, so far—Quintus thought of the slaughtered Ninth Legion, of the massacre in Colchester and London. While he had been talking with Regan, the seriousness of his mission to Gloucester had been submerged in other thoughts, but now it stabbed him with fierce reality again. His mind darted here and there, exploring the possibilities of stealing off from Pendoc and Regan; beating his way to Gloucester alone somehow. And he knew that it would be foolish. He trusted Regan and had committed himself to her guidance. He must continue to do so. But when the three of them had wrapped themselves in their cloaks and curled up beneath the tree, Quintus' brief doze was an uneasy one.

They left the camping place while the dawn-light was still grey. The shadows were weird and wavering beneath the great overhanging branches, and as they emerged into a clearing they heard the long-drawn howl of a wolf. Quintus' shaggy pony snorted and trembled, its ears pricked forward. He soothed it as he would have Ferox, whom he greatly missed. Pendoc made a queer sign with his fingers to ward off evil, and Regan said, 'The wolf howls with joy that he won't be sacrificed on this day, as he would have been in the old times.'

'Sacrifice of wolves?' asked Quintus, glad enough to talk, for the uneasiness was still with him.

She nodded. 'Once many beasts were burned in wicker baskets —and not only beasts but humans too, like—like——' She stopped and shut her eyes.

Quintus knew she was thinking of Boadicea and the terrible rites for Andraste.

Then Regan went on with her usual composure: 'My grandfather does not believe as Boadicea does, though he put me in her care because she has much learning and was a cousin of my father's. The Icenians are not of the true religion—nor were those wild Druid folk that your Governor, Suetonius, killed on the far isle of Anglesey. Conn Lear is merciful.'

'Well, I'm glad to hear it,' said Quintus as lightly as he could, and would have asked more questions, but Pendoc suddenly reined in his pony and said 'H-sst!'

The three of them grew very quiet—listening. There was a confusion of guttural voices ahead. Pendoc's eyes narrowed and he indicated by a gesture that they should move cautiously to the right and slip by unobserved. Quintus nudged his pony with his knee, but unfortunately the little beast scented a mare in the group ahead and let out a loud whinny of greeting.

Instantly the voices were stilled. 'Hide your face,' whispered Regan to Quintus, who pulled up his cloak. And the next moment a dozen British warriors galloped through the trees with spears drawn.

Quintus wheeled his horse in front of Regan and clumsily drew his own spear, wishing passionately that he had his familiar sword. 'Wait!' called Regan in Celtic to the warriors. 'Wait! We are friends, we go like you to the Feast of Lugh. Lugh, god of light!' This was a shot at random, since this Belgic tribe, which she recognized by the tattooings, might be only a band of wandering marauders, in which case nothing would stop them from stealing the ponies at least. The leader of the band had a swarthy, vicious face, with blue stripes on his cheeks, and he held his spear aimed at Pendoc.

'We *kill* strangers who seek to spy upon our sacred feast . . .' growled the leader, but his spear arm dropped. His little redrimmed eyes shifted from Regan to the two men. 'You are not of our tribes. Your clothes are strange!' he said uncertainly.

'But we are not strangers!' cried Regan. 'Look at this brooch! Look well——' She pointed to the bronze and enamel pin that held her mantle. 'What do you see?'

The little eyes peered warily, then the horn-helmeted head

jerked up. 'I see the mark of the ruby serpent,' muttered the man with a touch of awe. 'It is a Druid sign.' He bowed his head in a gesture of reverence. His companions crowded round, gaping at Regan. Then suddenly the leader raised his spear again.

'But how did you get this?' he cried. 'Perhaps you've stolen it! And this man . . .' Quick as light his spear darted out and tore the folds of cloth down from Quintus' chin. In the same stroke he tipped the British helmet off Quintus' head. It rolled on the ground, the long tresses of horsehair trailing.

'Sure, this is no *Briton!*' shouted the warrior, staring at the clean-shaven face and short curly black hair. 'By the sacred fires of Beltane I think it is a——'

'A Silure from Wales,' cried Quintus, feigning outraged dignity, and praying that his Celtic was recognizable. 'You have insulted a Silure!'

'Yes,' cried Regan quickly. 'Is this the hospitality Conn Lear teaches you? You should be ashamed to mistreat those who come in peace to worship at the Feast of Lugh.'

Above the long dangling moustaches and wisps of matted beard, the tattooed face looked perplexed. Regan gave him no time to think, but said, 'We go straight to Conn Lear now. Follow if you like,' and dug her heels into her pony's flanks. The three started forward. The band of Belgics let them go, then closed in behind them, muttering to themselves.

'Whew,' breathed Quintus, 'that was close.' And still is, he thought.

It was hard to act confidently when there was the continual mumbling behind them, and the spot between his shoulder-blades tingled with awareness that a whistling spear might land there any minute.

'Don't speak,' said Regan through the side of her mouth.

He nodded. All these Britons had ears as keen as bats, and a knowledge of woodcraft like the wild things. Pendoc, don't get lost! Quintus implored silently, for the Belgics just behind watched the potter's every move as he led the two others. It was obvious that this was a test. No stranger could have found his way through the forest towards the great plain. If Pendoc hesitated, it seemed certain that Quintus would end up in this country in much the same way that Gaius had. And that, thought Quintus grimly, was definitely not my plan.

At last, and suddenly, they emerged from the forest and looked down a slope towards a winding blue river. 'Avon,' grunted

Pendoc, pointing. 'The river.' His scarred lip lifted, and he turned squarely on his pony to face the Belgic leader. He pointed again across the river. 'Beyond that hill is a ditch,' he said, 'and a village called Og, and many long earth tombs made by the people of the past, and farther towards the west there stands the Great Temple of the Stones.'

The Britons consulted sourly amongst themselves, then the leader spoke. 'It is so. *You* at least are not a stranger.' He darted one more suspicious look at Quintus, ignored the girl, and signalling to his band, trotted down the slope towards the river.

'That's the last of them, I hope,' observed Quintus as Pendoc led them on upstream towards the ford.

'I think so,' Regan sighed, her tense fingers relaxing on the bridle. She glanced back across her shoulder at the sun which had climbed half-way up the eastern sky. 'Hurry,' she said. 'We must reach Conn Lear before the ceremony starts at midday.'

They had not many miles to cover, and it was easy riding over the rolling, fertile chalk plains where tracks were plainly marked. They passed earthwork forts, villages, and dozens of turf-covered mounds, which contained ancient burials. Soon after they crossed the river, they entered an avenue of single stones mounted on high banks on either side of them. And now they were no longer alone. Increasing hordes of people were trudging or riding along this processional way that led to their temple. Each man, woman, and child held in his hand an offering of growing corn or wheat or flax. Their mood was quiet and reverential. There were a few curious glances, but nobody molested the three who rode on silently until they topped a hill and looked down to the plain below, then Quintus let out a cry of wonder. He had expected a few crude stones, dotted helter-skelter like some rings he had seen in the north. He had expected to be much amused at the contrast between this savage temple and the magnificent buildings he had known in Rome.

But there was nothing amusing about Stonehenge. It was awe-inspiring in sheer monstrous bulk. Thirty stone megaliths stood in the outer circle, Quintus could see other rows of stone, tons of them—a forest of stone—but more massive, and even in the full noon light, more sinister and brooding, than ever a tree forest grew.

'But how *could* those enormous things be up-ended and then made to support others?' Quintus cried. And where could they have come from?' he added, staring round the barren, grassy plain.

'Ah, I don't know,' said Regan, smiling, though her eyes were misty from the joy of seeing again the temple of her childhood memory. 'This place has always been here—always. No doubt in the beginning of the world, Lugh built it for himself—with magic. That is what Conn Lear used to say. I only know that the ancient folk worshipped here as we do now.'

It must certainly be some sort of magic that set these great stones here, Quintus thought as they approached. He tried to count the silent, looming megaliths—ninety, a hundred—two hundred? His eyes swam, and not entirely from the sun. There was a strange sensation that flowed out from the forest of stones.

'Yes,' said Regan, watching him, 'You feel the enchantment. It is always so here. We must walk now,' she added on a brisker note. They had reached a fence of wooden posts set across an opening north of the great ditch that surrounded Stonehenge. Regan and Quintus dismounted, tethering the ponies by a pen full of small, sacred white bulls. They returned to join the people who were, one by one, filing through a gate, and passing a flat stone within the posts, which they touched. They began to chant.

'Lugh!' the people chanted on two notes, 'Lugh—give blessing!' They raised their faces to the bright sky and walked thus with arms outstretched amongst the great stones.

A tall young man dressed in a leaf-green robe stood by the entrance, watching the crowds go in. He held a silvery birch wand in one hand, and a small harp was slung over his shoulder.

'Ah, that's a Bard,' said Regan, with glad recognition. 'I must speak to him.'

The Bard, who belonged to a minor class of Druid, smiled and touched Regan's hand in greeting, as she showed him her brooch. Timidly she asked for the Arch-Druid and the Bard frowned a little.

'Conn Lear,' answered the Bard, bowing at the name, 'is in his secret retreat, preparing for the ceremony. You cannot disturb him now, nor until sunset when the rites will be over.' He spoke a very pure and solemn Celtic, because, like all Bards, he had been trained for recitation.

Quintus followed the Bard's words anxiously and was so dismayed that he cried without thinking, 'But, Regan, I can't wait that long; you know I've got to get on my——' He bit off the last word, while fiery heat rushed over him in a wave of shame. For he had spoken in Latin. And the young Bard had turned lithely like a cat and was surveying him with a detached, chill gaze.

'This is a strange language to hear at our temple gate,' the Bard said quietly. 'We do not welcome Romans here—no matter how—artfully—disguised.'

You fool, you *blasted*, impulsive fool! thought Quintus to himself. He knew there was no use pretending he was a Silure now. This Bard was obviously highly intelligent and in a subtle way more threatening than any band of savage Belgics. The Bard turned his cold, considering eyes on Regan, who was also flushed and frightened. 'You, maiden,' said the Bard, 'I find it most peculiar that you should bring a disguised Roman here—that you should ask for Conn Lear—I'm not unmindful of what has been done to Druids throughout the land—by Romans—nor that there has been treachery and spying——' His suddenly menacing glance swung on Pendoc, who was standing a little way off, then moved to a group of fully armed men who were clustered outside the gate. Quintus with a sinking heart saw that the Belgics had arrived and were amongst them.

'You are wrong, O Bard—in your suspicions!' Regan cried at last in a shaking voice. 'Take me at once to Conn Lear, for I am his granddaughter.'

The young Bard's lips thinned; he looked at Regan's Icenian tartan. 'I have never heard that the Arch-Druid had a granddaughter,' he said imperturbably. 'Nobody can disturb Conn Lear now. I think it safer that you never see Conn Lear at all. I think——' He glanced again towards the party of warriors and raised his wand.

He's going to put us under guard or worse! thought Quintus, while Regan, realizing the same thing, suddenly grabbed his hand. 'Run, Quintus!' she cried. 'Run—INTO the temple!'

Before the startled Bard could stop them they darted past him, and Regan, dragging herself and Quintus to the 'Heel' stone that guarded the temple gate, cried 'I claim protection! The protection of Lugh!'

The Bard ran up to them, and stopped.

'You can't touch us!' cried Regan, panting.

'I see you know the ancient law,' answered the Bard, frowning. 'Go then to the stone of safety and stay there without moving—or—you know the penalty?'

She bowed her head and silently walked forward a little way with Quintus, until they entered the edge of the great outer ring of megaliths. Here there was a boulder, different from the others in shape and colour. And a branch of mistletoe lay on it. 'We must stay here,' she said to Quintus, sinking down on the stone. 'We're safe for as long as the ceremony lasts.'

'And then?' said Quintus.

'And then we MUST get to Conn Lear.'

Quintus tightened his lips and glanced back through the posts where he saw Pendoc's sandy-red head towering amongst the horned helmets of the Belgics. They've got Pendoc under guard, he thought.

'Regan—there's no use saying it—but when I think how I've run you into danger—why I didn't keep my cursed mouth shut —how I could forget—I'm always acting first and thinking afterwards——' He pounded his clenched fist on the stone.

'Never mind,' she whispered gently. 'It's done. It'll be all right—as—as soon as we can get to Conn Lear.'

Quintus thought a moment. 'The Arch-Druid must be going to officiate, isn't he? When you see him in there'—he indicated the dim place of the altar through the concentric rows of megaliths—'can't you run to him, tell him who you are?'

She shook her head and gave a quivering sigh. 'Look over behind that stone, and *that* one.'

Then he saw that half hidden by the shadows stood two figures in white robes, silently watchful—and beside each figure there was the gleam of a golden spear. 'They'd not let me run far,' said Regan grimly. 'Those are Druids-of-Justice. This stone of safety where we are sitting used to be called the Slaughter Stone. It might become so again.'

The gods be merciful to us, Quintus thought. He did not invoke either Roman gods or Celtic gods; it was a general, fervent prayer for help. The sun beat down on them. From inside the stone circle, where the people were all crowded, there came the rhythmic chant to Lugh. The Bard in green walked by without looking at them, while he strummed harsh, monotonous notes on his little harp. He passed into the temple. The Belgic warriors filed in, all but those who had remained to guard Pendoc outside. Then Quintus and Regan were alone except for the white figures in the shadows. If it had not been for them, Quintus would have taken her hand and held it close in his. He could no longer deny tenderness for her, mingled as it was with shame that his own stupidity had brought them to this. She seemed very small and helpless as she sat there beside him on the stone, her head drooped, while the sunlight struck gleams in her soft, curly hair. Despite all the dangers they had passed through, he had never seen her lose courage, but he could tell from the strained look round her lovely eyes and the tightness of her red mouth that she was trying to hide fear now.

'*Cara*——' He whispered the little Latin word for 'darling', but so low she did not hear. 'You mustn't be frightened,' he said more loudly. 'We've both got out of far worse troubles than this.'

'I know,' she said, trying to smile, 'but it's so frightening not to be able to get to him——you see, *he* is merciful, but the Druids-of-Justice are not. I think they won't touch me, because of this brooch, unless I try to leave the stone, but *you*—the minute the ceremony is over——' She twisted her hands together and was silent.

Yes, Quintus thought, they'll finish me off. Roman eyes would certainly not be allowed to see the sacred rites and live. A fine secret agent *you* turned out to be! said Quintus to himself. The mission to Gloucester! He had been so confident of success when they left Chichester—when?—less than two days ago. It seemed like months. And he was only half-way now—if indeed there was ever to be any more journeying for him.

At a stir in the temple, he roused himself from his black thoughts. Wild and strident music burst out, the clamour of bagpipes, and harps, and voices.

'Look!' whispered Regan, straining forward. 'There is Conn Lear!'

Quintus followed her gaze and saw between the stones, far on the other side of the temple, that a procession was filing in through the sacred Druid entrance. There were bare-foot, white-robed priests waving branches of mistletoe and oak leaves. There was a white bull with a garland of wheat round its neck, its horns tipped with gold. And at the end there walked a strange, impressive figure, also in white. On his head there was a golden crown set between grey feathers like wings.

The Arch-Druid's arms were raised in invocation, his face was turned up to the sky while he marched steadily towards the centre of the temple and the altar stone.

The music grew louder, as the Arch-Druid passed amongst the stones. The people near-by fell to their knees crying, 'Lugh—shine on us. Lugh! Lugh!' The sun beat down upon the altar where had been placed corn and wheat for blessing. The white bull was led beside the altar, and two of the Druids held it by the horns.

The ancient ceremony began, solemnly. And it went on a long time with complicated ritual, of which Regan and Quintus could see little from their stone. But there was one moment when Quintus saw the flash of a golden sickle in the Arch-Druid's hand, and saw it descend swiftly towards the bull. The bull fell without a sound. The blood from its neck dripped on the altar, and the people cried out in ecstasy. This was not very different from the sacrifices to the gods in Rome, and Quintus recognized the rites of blood to purify the land and make it fertile for the coming year. But there were other parts of the ceremony he did not understand. Strange dances with mistletoe and with oak leaves, and hooded women in black who circled the altar and gave forth wailing cries.

The ceremonies went on until the sun had slanted towards the west and touched a stone which had been in shadow before. Then the Arch-Druid stepped up on to this stone and began to speak to the hushed people. Quintus could hear his deep, resonant voice, but not what he was saying, yet the voice seemed to exert a heavy thrall. Quintus grew drowsy, almost lulled. He ceased to fear the watching figures; he ceased to thrash and plan and worry over his chances of getting away. He glanced at Regan, and saw that she too was calmed, the strain had left her listening face. It was exalted.

The hours passed until sunset, and Quintus, suddenly awakening from his dream, saw that the time of their safety was nearly over. The red light was dying and only a half circle of sun showed above the hill to the west.

The Arch-Druid ceased talking and pointed towards the sun. At once the thousand voices renewed their frenzied chant and fear came back to Quintus. He saw that the procession was beginning to form, and that it would take the Arch-Druid back the way he had come, far away from them. He saw the Bard in green suddenly appear between the nearest stones and look at them with steely eyes. He saw the white Druids-of-Justice move their golden spears from the left hand to the right.

Regan saw all these things too, and she saw Conn Lear turn his back to go, but the fear and confusion which had paralyzed her melted away. Just as the sun dipped out of sight, she seized the sprig of mistletoe from off their stone of safety and, standing on the stone, raised the mistletoe high above her head, so that the waxy, white berries and pale green leaves caught the last ray of sun. And she cried out with all her might, 'Conn Lear! Conn Lear! Come to me! It is Regan, daughter of your daughter, who calls!'

The Druids-of-Justice lifted their spears, while Quintus held his breath. It seemed the girl's voice could not reach that distance through the chanting. For one moment the Arch-Druid did not move, then he turned slightly in their direction. Regan stood with her arms held out to him.

Quintus' heart thundered in his chest, and he took a deep breath. For slowly, slowly, with ponderous steps, the Arch-Druid walked from the sanctuary and came towards them.

Conn Lear moved through the maze of megaliths towards the stone of safety, and the people made way for him on either side. At last he stood and looked at Regan, then he smiled a little. His piercing, hypnotic eyes softened.

'You have been frightened, poor child,' he said in a deep, tender voice. 'You did not trust my powers? Yet you have been protected in all your journeying. I knew that you were here, and no harm could have come to you—or'—he turned his wise old face towards Quintus—'or the Roman you have brought—a young man I have met before.'

Regan knelt down at the Arch-Druid's feet and placed her cheek against his hand. 'I was frightened,' she whispered, 'for we seemed surrounded by enemies, and I could not get to you.'

'It was written that way in the omens and in the stars,' said Conn Lear solemnly. 'Through fear and evils you must win to safety. As,' he added, 'much else is written for the future too, which will in time come to pass.'

The Bard crept up behind, afraid to speak, but listening intently. The two Druids-of-Justice also had come near them, and one now spoke, saying 'Great Master of Wisdom, this Roman —he has watched the sacred rites, he must not be allowed to go from here—alive. Great Master, do you not remember the dream? That a traitor would come to us in disguise—a Roman soldier who is on his way to summon other Romans to be our enemies!'

The Arch-Druid held up his hand, while his face grew sad and his eyes looked towards the sunset as though seeing something in the sky. 'I remember the dream, and the prophecies too, Druid-of-Justice. Nevertheless, I say this Roman shall live, and *shall continue on his way untouched*—Enough!' he cried in a voice of absolute command, as the Druid-of-Justice seemed about to protest. 'I have spoken.'

Under the impact of the fierce, burning gaze, the man turned pale, and bowing, slunk away.

'Release my granddaughter's man, Pendoc,' said Conn Lear to the Bard, then turning to Regan added, 'Come, I will now talk to you—and the Roman.'

CHAPTER VI

Regan learns of Quintus' love—the herb of forgetfulness—
all memory gone—the Celtic brooch—Quintus' departure with
Bran, a tongueless guide

THE ARCH-DRUID lived in a circular stone house in a large grove of ancient oaks to the north of Stonehenge. There were other buildings in the sacred grove which contained a sort of college where Druid priests lived and instructed those who aspired to join the order. There was a school for the green-robed Bards, where they were taught the poetic branches of Druidic lore, while another school taught more practical learning to a different rank of Druids called Ovates.

While Quintus and Regan followed Conn Lear, they saw various members of the priesthood walking back and forth conversing earnestly. There was a hushed feeling in the grove, where twilight made mysterious shadows amongst the darkening oak leaves. The dread of violence fell away from Quintus. When they actually entered the Arch-Druid's strange home, all turbulence gave place to awed quietness.

Quintus found himself in a large round room hung with woven cloth on which were painted trees and symbols. There were five-pointed stars, the sun, the crescent moon, a cup that glowed as red as rubies, and balls of mistletoe. These symbols and many others were so artfully painted that the great room really seemed to be in the open amongst the trees; while the stars, the mistletoe, and all the other objects on the branches seemed as real as the bright fire that sparkled on a little hearth near the door. And the room smelled of incense, a pungent, woody perfume that drifted in blue smoke from a bronze brazier. There were a few wooden benches and a table and couch, dimly visible by the light of flickering lamps, but it certainly was not these, nor even the tapestries, that gave the room such an odd feeling. It was the huge column in the centre, and it took Quintus several moments to realize that the column was a living tree. An enormous oak that grew through the Arch-Druid's house and spread its leaves high above the thatched roof.

'O Conn Lear,' cried Regan, clasping her hands. 'I remember this room of the sacred tree and this lovely smell, though it was so long ago—and the painted forest too!' She walked to the tapestries and touched them softly with child-like pleasure.

The Arch-Druid's austere face relaxed as he looked at her. 'Aye, little one,' he said, 'you have been a long time in the fierce land of the Icenians—it was necessary—it was your destiny. But now you shall stay with me awhile.'

Quintus felt an unjustified pang as he saw the leap of delight in the girl's eyes. What better provision than this could there be for Regan? And what right had he to feel bleak disappoointment that he must leave her now and go on with a Roman soldier's mission, alone?

'Sit down, Quintus Tullius,' said Conn Lear suddenly, in Latin. 'Indeed,' he smiled, seeing Quintus' surprise, 'I can speak your language when I *wish* to, and I remember your name from our meeting last autumn upon the Kentish road.'

'I'm sorry, sir,' said Quintus uncomfortably, as he thought of his futile attempt to capture this same priest then, 'I was but following orders.'

'Even so,' agreed Conn Lear calmly.

The Arch-Druid had removed his gold and feathered crown to reveal his head half shaven in the Druid's tonsure. Beneath his grey beard, Quintus could see hanging the mottled stone like a serpent skin, suspended on gold wire—but Quintus felt no impulse towards ridicule as he had on their first meeting.

Conn Lear—even seated on a simple wooden bench, in this queer stone house in the wilds of Britain—was the most majestic figure that Quintus had ever seen. Far more so than Governor Suetonius—or, thought Quintus, startled, than the *Emperor*, than the great Augustus Nero, whose plump, dissipated young face rose in his mind. At once Quintus checked this treasonable thought. He rose and, slightly ashamed of having been led into such an unpatriotic comparison, cried sharply, 'I can't stay here, Conn Lear. I must be on my way. Your granddaughter has promised.'

He stopped as Regan gave a little moan and running to the Arch-Druid, knelt at his feet. 'Yes, it's true,' she cried, 'my worshipful grandfather. And forgive me that I brought the

Roman here. But *you* will know how to persuade him and turn him from his purpose! You have arts, Conn Lear, that will make him see that what he's going to do is terribly wrong.'

Quintus gasped. And then he frowned. '*Regan!* You promised me! I trusted you. Because you speak so fast in Celtic, do you think I don't understand what you're saying? You promised that you'd set me on the way to Gloucester!'

She raised her head and stared at him. Her face had gone as white as the Arch-Druid's robe, her lips trembled as she answered fiercely, 'Yes, I promised—IF you *wished* to go on.'

'But you thought I wouldn't *wish* to? You meant all along to get Conn Lear to—to hypnotize me—I suppose, as he did on the Kent road—to change my mind! Regan, now I see that, coming of different races, you and I, we think differently. I've been a fool to trust you.' He gulped and turned his angry gaze from Regan to the Arch-Druid, whose mouth curved and who stood up, separating the two excited young people, and said, 'Peace!— Quintus Tullius, you shall go to Gloucester, as my daughter's daughter has promised!'

'But Conn Lear——' cried Regan desperately, turning on him. 'You don't know—Quintus goes to summon a legion, he goes to add to this killing—this torrent of violence and blood. Conn Lear, make him see that Romans have no right in our land. Make him see they must go back to their own place. Don't let him add yet more to the misery that's come to us—and that has turned—my foster-mother, Boadicea—into a—devil!'

She crumpled suddenly and, hiding her face in her grand-father's robe, burst into tears.

Conn Lear bent down. His long wrinkled hand stroked her head gently. 'Poor child,' he said. His old face became very sad, the piercing eyes were veiled, as though they looked inward and had forgotten Quintus, who stood by uncomfortably while his anger ebbed. Yet Quintus refused to let himself feel pity for Regan, as he held sharply and firmly to his purpose. He watched the Arch-Druid warily, guarding against any magical spell.

After a moment Conn Lear sighed and straightened up; stern-ness tinged the sadness of his features and he spoke in the chanting voice he had used in the stone temple—the voice of prophecy.

'It will be as it will be, Regan,' he said solemnly. 'I have consulted all the sacred oracles. They have spoken. There will be blood and yet more blood—there will be anguish—for our people—and in the end . . .' He shut his eyes, and when he opened them, looking directly at Quintus, he did not finish in the same voice, but in a lower, more normal tone. 'And you— young Roman soldier—you will go to summon the Second Legion from Gloucester, as it is your destiny to do, *but*——' He shook his head, a peculiar smile flitting across his eyes. 'No matter,' he said, 'you will find out for yourself.'

Quintus' relief almost made him dizzy. 'Then I'd like to leave at once—Conn Lear,' he cried. He heard Regan give a stifled gasp and he kept himself from looking at her.

'You shall leave when you have eaten,' said the Arch-Druid. 'My own servant will guide you. There is but one stipulation. Your way for some miles west will pass through a land of holy wells and groves where the sacred plant is. There are things there you may not see, nor do I wish you to remember what you have already seen this day. I am going to give you the herb of forgetfulness.'

'No!' cried Quintus, starting back, all his fears aroused again. 'So after all, you'd trick me into forgetting my mission!'

Conn Lear's mouth tightened. 'You are stupid, Quintus Tullius! Do you think I could not make you forget your mission without warning you? Do you dare think I lie when I say you will get to Gloucester? This drug will dim your memory of only this *one* day. No more.'

'And if I refuse to take the drug?'

'Then you will remain here until you do.'

Quintus set his teeth. He had no alternative except to trust the old Druid, and indeed he instinctively did so. But Jupiter Maximus, Quintus thought, the weird and unpredictable things that kept happening to him in this country! And with the thought came remembrance of the quest that had first brought him to this land.

'Conn Lear,' said Quintus suddenly, 'perhaps I've taken the drug of forgetfulness already, for all this day I've not thought of the reason I so wished to see your Great Temple of the Stones.'

'And what *is* that reason?' asked the Arch-Druid rather absently, leaning his head on his hand.

'A hundred years ago, my great-grandfather, one Gaius Tullius, a Roman who came with Julius Cæsar, was killed near here by——'

'STOP!' thundered Conn Lear. He rose and drew himself to his full great height. His eyes flashed blue fire at the astounded Quintus. '*Say no more*, or I shall forget my mercy and my kindness!

So it was YOUR ancestor who first invaded our peaceful plain here, whose filthy bones did desecrate our holiest place! By Lugh himself, had I known this——' His hand moved to the magic stone on his breast, a dreadful stillness flowing over his tall white figure.

'Conn Lear!' cried Regan in fear, as she watched the change in her grandfather. 'It's not Quintus' fault! He only seeks the bones of his ancestor to give them proper burial.'

'And shall *never* find them!' The fierce voice resounded through the room. 'That Roman brought a curse upon us. A curse——' he repeated. His long old body shuddered, as though he suppressed the violence of his thoughts. But his hand slowly dropped from the serpent stone. Then he clapped his palms sharply together. At once a lad in a red tunic ran in carrying dishes of smoking meat and a jug of mead.

'Eat,' said Conn Lear coldly to Quintus. 'And drink!' As he said this he pulled from under his robe a little bag made from the grey, furry skin of the sacred hare. He opened the pouch and took out a pinch of greenish, powdered herb, which he dropped in Quintus' cup. Then he poured the mead in. 'Drink!' He held the cup to Quintus' lips.

Quintus drew back. 'A moment ago you had hatred in your eyes, Conn Lear. Can I believe this is some simple herb of forgetfulness?'

'Grandfather——' whispered Regan, putting her hand on his arm. 'I too am afraid—don't harm him for I—I——'

What was it she whispered lower yet so that Quintus could not hear? Anger gradually left the Arch-Druid's face and was replaced by the sadness. 'Sorrow, sorrow,' he murmured as though to himself. 'Always *He* lurks in waiting, the dark god of the shadows—whose name must not be uttered.'

He roused himself and turned impatiently to Quintus. 'Drink the mead in safety—O Unbelieving Roman—the dark god will not come for you through me—and you know in your heart that the Arch-Druid of all the Britons does not speak with double tongue.'

Quintus looked at Regan suddenly and caught on her unguarded face a look of yearning directed at him. Her lips formed the word 'Please. . . .'

Quintus bowed his head and quietly began to drink. The mead was sweet and cool, faintly aromatic. He finished the cup and waited for some strange sensation. But there was none. He heard Regan give a little sigh of relief. She walked over and smiled down at him. 'Now, eat,' she said matter-of-factly, 'and I will too. We've had no food since dawn.' She took her dish of meat, and sat down by Quintus on a bench.

The Arch-Druid glanced once towards them, then moved abstractedly to the other side of the great round room to a window cut between the tapestries. For some moments he sat at a table and seemed to be writing. Then he went to the window. He opened it and stood gazing out towards the stars, murmuring some brooding incantation. The huge oak trunk in the centre nearly hid his white figure from Quintus and Regan, and while they ate, a new intimacy came to them. They sat very close together on the bench. Quintus was intensely conscious of the warmth of her slender body, and of the silken feel of her long hair as it brushed his arm. He wanted to put his arm round her. He felt a tightness in his throat as she looked up at him sideways through her lashes. A dimple he had never noticed appeared near her mouth, and she said, 'But *Quintus*, you're not eating! Don't you like the flavouring of this roast lamb? Conn Lear's cooks are supposed to be so good!'

'I think you know very well why I've stopped eating, Regan,' said Quintus, looking steadily into her face.

She coloured and dropped her eyes, but the dimple was still there as she said, 'Oh, I *do* hope it isn't the herb of forgetfulness that's spoiled your appetite! But truly, if Conn Lear says it's not harmful it isn't.'

'No,' he answered, very low, on a harsh breath, 'it's not the herb—*Cara*.'

She had put her dish down and now her hands clenched on a fold of her robe. The dimple vanished. 'Why do you call me that?' she whispered, and he felt her shoulder tremble.

'Because it means "beloved". I love you, Regan.'

Her own breathing quickened. She held herself still and tight, but he could see the shaking of her heart beneath the thin woollen bodice.

'You must not,' she whispered at last. 'It is forbidden. . . .' Her shadowed eyes moved to the distant figure of the Arch-Druid. 'There can never be love between us, never——'

'But there *is*!'

She made a sharp sound in her throat, and slowly, as though against her will, she raised her face.

He kissed her, not in the quick and grateful way he had done when she rescued him from Boadicea's camp, but warmly, passionately. The hard kiss of a man, and she responded as a woman. To them their kiss lasted an eternity or a second, it had no dimension—except beauty; then realization crept in, and pain.

His arms fell from her, she turned away her face, which was wet with sudden tears. The Arch-Druid had not moved, he still gazed out towards the stars.

'*Cara*—my Regan—I'll come back to you. Wait for me here —I'll come back. I don't know how or where—but after——'

'After . . .' she repeated in a despairing, lifeless voice. 'After you've done your duty as a Roman soldier—after your people and mine have slaughtered each other. It's no use, Quintus. Yes, I love you, but there can never be a future for us.'

'How CAN you say that?' he cried. 'When now we both admit the love that's between us, when we both knew as we kissed that we belong to each other! That's changed everything.'

She shook her head, tears slipped down her cheeks, but she gave a weary little smile. 'You won't remember what we've said, Quintus. Nor o ur kiss. Otherwise, I couldn't have let it happen.'

'Not remember! You mean the drug? Why, that's impossible!'

'Conn Lear is never wrong,' she whispered, 'and yet—oh, may all our gods forgive me—I *want* you to remember some day. Remember a little.' Her hand went to the brooch that clasped her mantle; the bronze brooch decorated with Celtic scrolls and the ruby enamel Druidic emblem of a tiny snake. 'Quick, take it —and keep it hidden.' She fastened it inside his woollen tunic next to his heart, while she glanced quickly towards Conn Lear's back. 'At least it will help to keep you safe. And I'll pray—pray to Lugh for you.'

'Regan——!' He seized her hands, so overcome with emotion that he could not command his voice. Nor did he ever say the things to her he wished to, because the Arch-Druid turned from the window and walked towards them round the great tree-trunk. Quintus dropped Regan's hands and was silent.

'The Star of the North has mounted high in the sky above the Sign of the Warrior, Quintus Tullius,' said Conn Lear, looking sombrely down at the young people. 'It is time for you to go.' He raised his voice and called 'Bran!'

A strange creature shambled into the room and, kneeling at the Arch-Druid's feet, made gobbling noises. In Rome Quintus had seen big apes that had come in the galleys from Africa. This creature was like an ape with its short body clothed in otter skins, long, powerful arms and a round head covered with matted, rusty-black hair. But between the flattened nose and the low jutting forehead the eyes were bright and intelligent. Conn Lear drew the creature to one side, handed him a large deerskin bag, and seemed to be giving instructions, though he spoke in a swift dialect Quintus could not follow, and was answered by inhuman gobbling noises.

'This is Bran,' said the Arch-Druid, walking back to Quintus. 'My servant. He belongs to the little people of the west who were here in the old, old days, even before my own race, the Celts, came to this land. He will guide you to Gloucester.'

Quintus bowed. 'Thank you, Conn Lear.' Through the desolation in his heart and his consciousness of Regan beside him still, he tried to examine his peculiar guide. 'Doesn't he speak?'

The Arch-Druid frowned. 'He does *not* speak—because he has no tongue.' He gestured, and Bran came to Quintus and opened his mouth to disclose a scarred and pulpy stump where the tongue had been.

Quintus drew in his breath, and the Arch-Druid went on coldly. 'It was necessary, for once Bran talked too much. Those who know some of our secrets cannot be allowed to tell of them.'

Quintus swallowed. Would this have been his fate too, if it had not been for Regan?

'Now GO!' said the Arch-Druid. He raised his arm and pointed towards the door, and as Quintus turned instinctively towards the girl, Conn Lear stepped between them, blotting her from Quintus' sight. 'There is nothing for you to say to her, Roman!' added the grim voice. 'Go!' The piercing blue gaze fastened itself with power on Quintus as it had on the Kentish road. But Quintus did not this time yield to the Arch-Druid, he yielded to reason. He dared not risk subjecting Regan to her grandfather's anger.

'*Vale*,' he said in a dragging voice, 'farewell,' and turned quickly.

But I will come back to her some day, somehow, he vowed, as he preceded Bran from the round stone room of the living tree.

Quintus slept a short time that night beneath a hazel bush and opened his eyes into a fine mist, through which the new-risen sun could not penetrate. An extraordinary-looking man, like an ape, was squatting beside him, gnawing at a chicken drumstick.

'What in Hades are *you*?' cried Quintus, reaching for his spear, which lay beside him. The man put down the drumstick and made a chuckling noise. His hairy hand pawed into a deerskin bag, and bringing out a large oak leaf he handed it to Quintus. There was some Latin writing crudely scratched on the leaf. Quintus scowled at it until he made it out. The writing said, 'This is Bran who will guide you to Gloucester. Trust him.'

'Bran?' said Quintus, frowning harder, for he was exceedingly puzzled. The man nodded, pounded his chest, grinned amiably, and began to gnaw the drumstick.

'Where did you come from? Where are we?' said Quintus in painstaking Celtic.

Bran shrugged, opened his mouth to show Quintus he had no tongue and could not answer.

This happened before in a dream, Quintus thought; where did I dream it? He rubbed his eyes and stared again at Bran. But where is Pendoc, he thought, and the camp-fire we were sitting by in the forest last night when we broiled the fish? WHERE IS REGAN?

At this he was overwhelmed with a feeling of pain and loss, far greater than he could understand. For amidst the dream-like confusion, he had a certainty that there was nothing wrong with her. She was in no danger. Then she and Pendoc must have slipped away in the night, leaving him this extraordinary guide and the message? Could Regan write Latin? That was strange, and yet the only explanation.

But then, had Regan deceived him all along? Had she never intended to take him to Stonehenge and her grandfather at all? This thought hurt him, even while a part of him denied it utterly. He knew that Regan was trustworthy. And yet so many things were strange; faint dream memories slipped in and out of his mind, bright sun and huge, sinister stones, angry voices, a room of mysterious shadows, many trees. And something lost. Something beautiful and very precious. I've had a fever, that's what it is, he thought. He touched his cheek and found it cool. Well, he was all right now, whatever had happened, and on his way to Gloucester. That was the important thing. His military mission. How long had he been delayed?

He read again the message on the leaf, then tore it into tiny bits. 'Well, come on then, Bran! Hurry—on to Gloucester!' He reinforced his Celtic with gestures.

The man nodded and threw away the drumstick. He pointed towards two ponies Quintus had not yet noticed, though one was his own—the shaggy native pony on which he had left the Regni fort. At least he was certain of *that*, Quintus thought, slightly reassured. They mounted and Bran set off in the lead, as the mists lifted and merged into a grey sky.

They were in a fertile land of pastures, brooks, and fields of ripening grain, with here and there a prosperous-looking native farmhouse. It's queer, thought Quintus, as the rough little ponies trotted along tirelessly. I wonder why we don't ever get to the great plain of the stone temple? The country isn't all what I expected.

Despite a maze of criss-cross tracks, Bran, never hesitating, went as fast as even Quintus could desire. After a while they came in sight of some foothills and a ridge beyond, where Bran turned north along a river, which they followed for a long time until they struck off to the left up a hill. When they reached the top, Bran drew in his pony and, grunting, pointed down below.

Quintus peered into the cup-like valley and was startled. There was a large cluster of houses on the bank of a river, not the round British huts, but substantial stone houses and a white edifice that looked very much like a Roman temple. A cloud of steam rose into the air from near the temple.

Surely those were hot springs down there, Quintus thought, and remembered that poor Flaccus had once mentioned hearing of healing springs in the west country. Could this possibly be Gloucester, though there was no sign of a fort?

He said the word for 'Gloucester' questioningly to Bran, who shook his head vigorously and pointed farther north. Then, by gestures of sleeping and eating, conveyed to Quintus that they would spend the night down below.

Quintus nodded reluctantly, anxious to press onwards to the end of this difficult journey. But he was aware of badly needing sleep and food, for they had finished the meat provided by the deerskin bag as they rode. During the last hour he had hardly been able to keep his eyes open, and his drowsiness extinguished curiosity as they entered the little town on a paved stone street which was lined with tiny shops and comfortable villas. Bran rode straight towards the temple, which, seen close, did not look quite as Roman, though it had rude columns built of whitish stone, and on the pediment above the entrance was a large sculptured face of an ugly woman, obviously some goddess, but none that Quintus recognized.

They dismounted and made for a sort of wooden shed from

which clouds of steam were rising. Suddenly Quintus was jolted from his sleepiness by the sight of a Roman toga. In fact two of them! They were worn by very old men who were sitting on a bench beside the shed talking to an elderly woman in the draped blue palla and under-stola of a Roman matron. Quintus stared at her tiara of tightly curled grey hair, done in the fashion worn by his mother when he was a child.

'Why does that filthy Briton stare at us so, I wonder?' said the woman loudly to her companions. 'And look at that ape man. Ugh! The most extraordinary people come to Bath. If it weren't for my rheumatism——'

It took Quintus a moment to realize that he was the 'filthy Briton', and another to decide whether to disclose his true nationality. But after all there was nothing to be lost, and much to be gained by finding out what these Romans were doing in this remote spot and what they knew of the revolution that was shaking the east.

They knew nothing at all, Quintus soon discovered after he had addressed them in Latin, endured their incredulity, given explanations, and received theirs.

The old men were time-expired veterans of the Claudian conquest, seventeen years ago. They explained that there were about a dozen others like them living here because the climate was gentle and the healing hot springs, called 'Aquæ Sulis', in which they bathed daily, kept them healthy. The Roman lady was a wife who had been sent for from Italy, during the peaceful years.

'Why, no,' said the matron, still eyeing Quintus suspiciously, 'we've heard of no particular trouble. But the natives, you know, Standard-bearer—if you really *are* one—well, one has to really *understand* the natives. They don't bother us when they come here to the springs—and we let them keep their silly temple.'

She pointed to the sculptured face. 'That's their goddess Sulis, but we call her Minerva, and it doesn't matter.'

A lot of things will matter to you, my dear lady, thought Quintus, exasperated—if Boadicea decides to include *you* in her plans. But he didn't say it. These people were old and incapable of understanding the situation. One could only hope, for their sakes, that their smug isolation would continue.

'Have you any knowledge at all about the Second Legion at Gloucester?' he asked.

But the old people shook their heads, without interest. 'The prefect of the legion, Poenius Postumus—an enormous German

he is—came here only last year to take the waters,' answered one
of the old men, 'but he was a dull dog. Never spoke to anyone
—ate too much—had some sort of stomach trouble.'

'Oh no, Marcus,' said his wife impatiently, 'it was boils he had.
You never remember anything right.'

'My dear Octavia, I believe my memory is quite as good as
yours, and am certain it was stomach trouble the prefect suffered
from.'

Quintus murmured hasty farewells and escaped, totally un-
interested in whatever ailments had afflicted the Second Legion's
prefect.

He found that there were rooms for travellers provided near
the bath-shed and, after gulping some food, fell sound asleep.

CHAPTER VII

*Roman luxury at Bath—journey to the Second Legion at
Gloucester—a baffling mystery—escape with two companions*

QUINTUS AWOKE in the town of Bath to a familiar though long-
unheard sound—the clatter and a creak of a chariot on flag-
stones, like the sounds that had awakened him many a morning
in his own frescoed cubiculum at his mother's villa in Rome. He
jumped up and peered through the door of the wooden shelter to
see the Roman couple, Marcus and Octavia, sedately rattling
along towards the baths. Their large old horse—obviously a
cavalry veteran—their bronze-studded chariot, the precise drap-
ings of his toga and her stola, all looked so thoroughly respectable
and commonplace that Quintus suddenly laughed.

Bran, who had slept on the floor, looked up alertly. 'They
might be my own aunt and uncle driving over from Ostia to
spend the day with poor Mother, and scold her for household
extravagance, or for spoiling Livia and me!' said Quintus
whimsically to Bran, who naturally did not understand but
grinned, then made gestures indicating that they should go.

'Yes, I know,' said Quintus, sobering at once. 'Get the ponies,
buy food—here.' He gave him some coins. 'I'll be ready when
you are.'

While Bran nodded and went off to obey, Quintus ran to the
baths. He had not washed properly for many days and was

delighted to find in this unlikely spot a fair example of Roman comfort and progress. The hot springs had been visited by Britons for centuries, and it had always been for them a sacred place of healing, under the protection of their goddess Sulis. But the few elderly Romans who had so far discovered the virtues of the spa had naturally not been satisfied with a lot of steam and a muddy pool. They had begun at once to transform these into acceptable baths. Quintus, after he had soaked himself in the steam and heat of the shed which enclosed the springs, encountered Marcus and some other Roman gentlemen breakfasting on the edge of a great rectangular swimming-pool made of stone bedded in 'puddle' clay.

'Ah,' said Marcus, who was sipping a cup of wine, 'greeting, Standard-bearer. I must say you look more like a Roman without those ridiculous native clothes on! You see what we're doing here? Though it's slow work and we're extremely short of slaves. Every inch of lead for these pipes has to be dragged out of the Mendip hills, and we haven't even a decent tepidarium yet—fearfully hard getting anything done in the wilderness.'

'Yes—I see,' said Quintus politely, hurrying towards the stone step at the corner of the cold plunge, 'but I think you've already done wonders.'

'Did you get your massage?' called the old man. 'We do have a slave who's good at oiling and scraping the skin with strigils.'

'Haven't time, thanks,' answered Quintus, diving into the chilly water. When he clambered out at the other end, Marcus was waiting for him on the brink.

'Have some of those wild eastern tribes really revolted?' the old man asked, frowning. 'You young people all exaggerate so.'

'They *have* revolted, sir,' answered Quintus shortly.

'Oh well . . .' Marcus said comfortably, as he wrapped a woollen robe round his skinny, hunched shoulders. 'Our legions'll soon deal with the trouble. Probably all over already. By the way, if the Prefect, Postumus, *is* still at Gloucester, you might just find out if it was stomach trouble he came here for last year. I'm positive'—he glanced towards a small arcade at the end of the pool where Octavia's tiara of grey curls was bent towards that of another old lady—'POSITIVE it was not boils.'

'I'll try to find out, sir,' said Quintus with control. He made a hasty farewell and ran towards the vestibule, where he had left his clothes. He threw them on and hurried out to the court where Bran was just riding up with the ponies.

The dew was still on the grass when Bran and Quintus climbed out of the quiet, cup-like valley where Bath lay; and the last part of their journey was slower going than even the great forests had been because here they were in hill country. These Cotswolds were most lovely wooded hills through which the native track woiund and climbed and dipped suddenly down to little brooks whch the ponies stumbled and splashed through.

Though his anxiety mounted with each hour that brought them nearer to the goal at last, Quintus was aware of the special beauty of the country. Once when they paused to let the horses drink, Quintus looked down a small ravine that opened on to a view of hazy, purplish hills beyond and thought that it would be a wonderful site for a country villa. There was ample water, shade, and lush meadows to turn into farmlands. And he discovered that in picturing his villa, which would be spacious, built of brick, well warmed, and decorated with fine mosaics, he was also picturing Regan there as the mistress of it. He had an image of her charming little face thoughtfully bent over the home fire, between two altars, one for household gods, the Lares and Penates, and the other for the gentle hearth goddess, Vesta.

A very silly picture, he realized impatiently. Regan had certainly emphasized her indifference when she had changed her mind about taking him to her grandfather, and instead had deserted him in the forest and gone off with Pendoc. Also, if a young Roman soldier were to do anything as ridiculous as to build dream villas in the wilderness, and dream a wife to fit into them, let him at least dream the latter in the shape of a beautiful Roman girl, with neatly curled black hair, large melting eyes, lush olive skin. Like Pomponia, he thought, remembering the daughter of one of his mother's friends who had given him definitely languishing looks last year at a banquet.

But Pomponia did not seem in the least attractive now.

Quintus jerked his pony's bridle, and they started forward up the next hill. This time with Regan it's finished for good! Quintus thought in sudden anger, exasperated by the sick yearning and sense of loss that came to him when he remembered her, and which he could not seem to control—a baffling feeling, as though something had happened that part of him knew, but that was hidden where he could not find it.

They rode and rode, and then they walked; for even the British ponies began to tire. It rained gently at times, at others the sun came out warm on their backs. But finally it set, sinking in a blaze of rose and violet beyond a broad estuary that they could see shining far below.

They trudged on through the long northern twilight, until the moon rose like a golden plate, above the distant Welsh mountains.

At long last they descended to an open plain, and Bran gave a grunt of satisfaction. By the brilliant moon's light, Quintus saw rearing up ahead the unmistakable ramparts and turrets of a large Roman fortress.

At *last*! thought Quintus exultantly. And as the fort seemed so quiet, he thought, They've gone, thanks be to Mars! He did not even feel disappointment that his long journey was for nothing, in relief that the Second Legion must now be united with Suetonius' forces. It might even be that the smug old Marcus in Bath was right, and the revolt put down by now. This gave him a pang, that the great final battle should happen without him, but he decided stoically that he would have to take what comfort he could from having faithfully fulfilled his mission.

As they got nearer he saw the dark shape of a sentry walking along the ramparts from turret to turret. Perhaps this was not surprising since they *might* leave some guard at the fort, though they shouldn't. Suetonius had ordered complete abandonment because he needed every fighting arm to help him. But then Quintus noticed something else.

The legionary flag was flying! It suddenly flapped and billowed in a gust of wind, and below the eagle on the pole Quintus saw plainly the curious capricorn badge—half goat, half fish—that denoted the proud royal 'Augusta', the Second Legion.

So, after all, they were still there! A standard moved with the legion.

Quintus' heart began to beat fast. 'Hold the ponies. Stay here! I'll arrange for you later,' he cried to Bran, throwing him his horse's bridle. But the little dark man shook his ape head and gobbled something vehemently, at the same time pointing south the way they had come.

'You mean you won't wait?' Quintus asked, astonished. 'But you must have food and rest.'

Bran shook his head again and made it clear that he was leaving with the two horses.

'Well, I can't stop you,' said Quintus ruefully, 'and I thank you for your guidance, but I wish I knew where you came from and where you're going.'

Bran made the hoarse sound in his throat that meant a laugh, and even in the moonlight Quintus could see that the alert eyes were looking at him with a peculiar expression, as though he could have told some strange things if he could speak. Bran raised his arm in salute and, jumping on his pony, led the other pony rapidly off into the night.

Quintus had no time for conjecture. He called 'Farewell, Bran,' then ran towards one of the four portals to the great rectangular fortress.

The sentry had seen the shapes moving below and heard the voice. He leaned over, poised his spear, and called out a sharp challenge.

Quintus started to shout back his name and rank and legion, but before he could get it all out, the startled sentry at the gate rushed forward waving his sword and crying, 'Silure! Silure!' as he lunged at Quintus.

'I'm not a Silure—you fool!' cried Quintus, jumping sideways and barely escaping the sword-point. 'I've a message from the Governor!'

He yanked off his native helmet and shouted the universal Roman army password, 'In the name of Cæsar Augustus Nero!' at the sentry, who slowly lowered his sword, while the sentry from the ramparts ran down to join him, crying, 'What is it, Titus? What've we caught?'

'You haven't "caught" anything, my friends,' said Quintus impatiently. 'I'm as Roman as you are, a standard-bearer of the Ninth. Take me at once to General Valerianus!'

'Another one. . . .' said Titus slowly and cryptically to his fellow sentry. 'I wonder what the Prefect'll make of THIS one.'

'Never mind the Prefect!' said Quintus sharply. 'Take me to the General. . . . Look men, here I have a message from His Excellency, Governor Suetonius Paulinus——' He held out the piece of parchment that he had been given at Chichester. 'It's of desperate importance—desperate.'

'Well,' said Titus, shrugging, 'desperate or not, you'll have to take it to the Prefect, Poenius Postumus, and I dare say you won't like the result.'

'Why?' cried Quintus, ignoring the last words, which he did not understand. 'Why to the *Prefect*?'

'Because he's in command of the legion just now, that's why.'

'But where's the General, Valerianus?'

'That,' answered the sentry, with a puzzling blend of rudeness and hesitation, 'is a matter for guessing, and not with outsiders neither, my lad.' He made a quick sign with his fingers as protection against the evil eye, and added on a sharper note, 'The General's gone away.'

Quintus frowned, thinking—what's happening here?—something queer. Though the sentries did not meet his eyes, they seemed not so much unfriendly, as ashamed, or anxious.

'Then take me to the Prefect,' said Quintus grimly.

The sentry called Titus nodded and started in the army's formal quickstep along the Via Principalis, or Principal Street, which bisected the vast enclosure inside the walls.

As he followed, Quintus noted unconsciously the usual layout of a legionary fortress: the acres of barracks built in blocks, and the granaries, kitchens, stables, baths, parade grounds—everything for the care of six or seven thousand men. Ahead loomed larger stone buildings, which were of a type always built as the headquarters of a fortress, to house the staff, the treasure chamber, and administrative offices.

It was very late. There was no sound from the sleeping men; only a dog barked over by the north portal, and a whinny came from the stables.

As they drew near the heavy wooden door that led to staff quarters, Titus suddenly turned and said, 'There you are! Old Jumbo Postumus is in there. Good luck and good-bye. I don't suppose I'll be seeing *you* again.'

'Why not?' snapped Quintus, staring.

'Because nobody's seen the other two, since we took 'em in here.'

'Other two *what*?'

'Messengers from the Governor. Leastways, they said they were. I wouldn't know.'

Quintus whirled and put a firm hand on Titus' arm. 'Listen, sentry! I can't make head or tail of this. If you've had two messengers, they came to summon the legion, as I do. And why hasn't it gone? What in the name of all the divine gods is the matter here?'

'I expect you'll find out,' answered the sentry, with a tinge of sympathy. 'Us, we're not here to speculate. We do our duty and obey orders.' He banged the heavy iron knocker and called out a password.

After a moment the door swung open, a sleepy guard held up a torch and, peering at the sentry, said, 'What's up, Titus?'

The sentry jerked his chin towards Quintus. 'Messenger. Wants to see the Prefect right now.'

'Oh,' said the guard without expression, inspecting the stubble of black beard on Quintus' chin, the tattered native clothes. 'Pass in.'

Quintus entered the sparsely furnished vestibule of the post commander's quarters and was faintly relieved to see the usual little altar to Mars in the corner. So peculiar had been his reception, that anything which indicated normal legionary life was reassuring.

The guard, who was a middle-aged man with shrewd grey eyes, put the torch in a bracket and said without interest as though he knew the answer, 'You have credentials and identification?'

Quintus held out the letter. 'This is the Governor's dispatch, under his personal seal. Arouse the Prefect, Postumus, at once!'

The guard did not look at the seal; his eyes flickered over Quintus with the same mixture of embarrassment and what seemed like hidden sympathy that Titus had shown. 'The Prefect's not asleep,' he said tonelessly. 'It is seldom that he sleeps these days. Come with me.'

In the next hall they passed the great iron-barred door to the strong-room which was marked with a large 'Il Augusta' to show that there the legion's treasure was kept and its standards and emblems also, when they were not in use.

'Aren't there any guards in here by the strong-room?' asked Quintus, in surprise.

'I—Balbo—am the guard,' answered the man quietly. 'The Prefect doesn't want others around.' He raised his hand to pull aside a heavy leather curtain that screened the commandant's private room from the hall and paused involuntarily as they both heard a strange sound. It was like laughter, peals of it, mirthless, high-pitched as a woman's and yet somehow masculine. It came from somewhere to the left and ended abruptly, as a heavy voice from behind the leather curtain shouted, 'Stop it! *Stop!*'

Quintus' breath was cut short; he stiffened against the shiver caused by that uncanny laughter, but Balbo gave him no time to think. He pulled the curtain roughly aside and said, 'Poenius Postumus, O Exalted Prefect, here is a messenger!' Balbo dropped the curtain and disappeared.

A man sat at a table, alone in the room.

Quintus by now was prepared to be confronted with almost

any peculiarity in the Prefect. But he had not expected what he actually saw. An enormous man with a shock of flaxen hair was sitting at a completely bare table with his head bowed on his clenched fists. He raised towards Quintus a stolid peasant face from which round blue eyes stared out with an expression of ox-like misery.

'Messenger?' said the Prefect in the thick, guttural accent of the Rhineland troops. 'I want no more messengers. Leave me alone!'

'Impossible, sir!' cried Quintus. 'The whole east of Britain is in revolt, the Governor is fearfully outnumbered by the native forces. He commands that your legion march this instant to his aid. Here is his dispatch.' He put the parchment on the table in front of the Prefect.

'It is perhaps a trap,' said the Prefect dully. 'How do I know that it is not a trap?'

'By Jupiter Maximus, sir—READ IT!' Quintus cried. 'And that is the Governor's own private seal.'

The big flaxen head wagged uneasily from side to side. 'I do not know the Governor's private seal. I will not read it—it is addressed to General Valerianus. So I must not read it. You see, it's addressed to my General?'

This is incredible, thought Quintus, feeling as though he were fighting shadows in a nightmare. 'By Mars, of course it is! But since you are in command, *you* must read it and act, now!' The big man hunched his massive shoulders, as though to shut out the voice of Quintus which cried out suddenly, 'Where *is* General Valerianus? I demand to know!'

Quintus knew that his tone was highly improper coming from a lowly standard-bearer to the commander of a legion, but he did not care what discipline might be given him if he could only penetrate this baffling fog.

There was a silence. The Prefect stared at the dispatch with unseeing eyes. He seemed to have forgotten Quintus when suddenly there came a sound from the left—a snatch of song and a high, laughing wail.

Quintus whirled round and gazed at a door covered by another leather curtain. 'What's that?'

The Prefect lumbered clumsily to his feet; a colossus, six and a half feet tall, whose tow head grazed the low ceiling. He thrust his underlip out and made a gesture to Quintus with a ham-like hand. He trod heavily to the curtain and raised it. 'There,' he said in a hoarse, dragging voice, 'is General Valerianus.'

Quintus looked into a small room that was lit only by a tiny wall lamp. He saw a man in a white shirt crouching on a pallet. The man was pulling straw out of the pallet and arranging it on the floor in six neat little piles. He was emaciated; his cropped hair was grizzled on a knobby skull head. His hand, like a yellow eagle's claw, carefully placed the straw now on this pile, now on that.

Quintus' mouth went dry, for, in the second that he took in the scene, the man began to snicker. He flattened out a whole pile of straw and burst into a peal of metallic laughter.

'The gods take pity on him, he's mad,' whispered Quintus, starting back.

The Prefect dropped the curtain. 'Not always,' he said dully. 'Only sometimes. The legion doesn't know. I tell them he's gone off to visit the western fort at Cærleon.'

'They know, all right,' said Quintus in a hushed voice. 'Or at least they suspect. It's a terrible thing, and now I understand what was so puzzling—but Poenius Postumus, this tragedy does not affect *this*!'

He picked up the Governor's message and thrust it at the Prefect. 'Don't you understand? Our whole army's in fearful danger. You've got about seven thousand men here, nearly as many as Suetonius' whole force, since my legion—the Ninth—was wiped out by Queen Boadicea. Your legion must start to-night, straight east, and pray we're not too late!'

He spoke vehemently but distinctly straight up into the huge, ox-like face, trying to reach through the barrier of doubt and indecision.

It was no use. Apparently Postumus took in only one sentence, for he said, 'Your whole legion was wiped out?—yes. You see? If this should happen to *us*—what could I tell my General when he is himself again? No, messenger, we stay here at Gloucester, as my General has ordered.'

Quintus gasped. 'But he ordered it before he knew this—and he's mad——' he began, and stopped. The round, blue eyes were as blank as pebbles. There was no reasoning with the stubborn, closed, and obviously frightened mind behind them.

The tribunes! Quintus thought. The six ranking officers of a legion must be quartered somewhere near. Surely if he could get to them with the message, they would dare to override this dangerous fool with his misguided loyalty to a madman. Get myself out of here, somehow, find the tribunes, Quintus thought.

'No, no,' grunted the big man, shaking his head as though Quintus had voiced his plan. '*I* am commander of this post. I know what to do. I will not be bothered all the time, worried, badgered . . . I have decided . . . Balbo!' he called suddenly.

The guard rushed in with his sword drawn, as though he had been waiting for this. 'Yes, sir.'

'Put him with the others.'

'No!' cried Quintus. 'I've imperial protection from the Governor! You can't touch me!' and cursed inwardly that he had no sword, nothing but the native spear which he could not use at close quarters. It was hopeless. The giant German strode across the room and picked Quintus up as though he'd been a child. He pinioned his arms, tossed the spear in a corner, and carried him out to the hall.

Balbo pulled the bolt on the great oaken door of the strong-room, and Postumus threw Quintus inside. The bolt grated back into place.

Quintus lay dazed for some moments on the stone floor. When his wits returned, he found that there was a light burning, and two men's faces were peering down at him curiously. Both were young, both were dressed in army fatigues, their leather jerkins bearing the number and emblem of the Fourteenth Legion. One was dark, short, and snub-nosed, with merry brown eyes; the other, who looked older—about twenty-six—had freckles, crisp, reddish hair, and a determined chin, also a deep, half-healed cut across his cheek.

'I see you're coming to, after the Prefect's truly hospitable reception,' said the small, dark one to Quintus. 'Welcome to our select company. Have some wine.' He held out a cup. Quintus drank thirstily and sat up, rubbing his head where a bump as big as a large egg was forming.

'Messenger from Suetonius Paulinus, no doubt?' stated the grave, freckled young man. As Quintus nodded, he added, 'So are we. Dio here arrived first, about two weeks ago. The Governor sent him off from Wales as soon as we got news of the rebellion. I was sent later when we arrived in London and there was still no sign of the Second. I had a spot of trouble getting through the Atrebate country—somebody's spear did this.' He fingered the wound on his cheek. 'But I made it. Five days ago. We've kept count.' He indicated a row of scratches on the wall. 'And here we are. Where'd you get sent from, and what's happened since we've been here?'

'Let him eat first,' said Dio. 'He's still groggy, and the gods know we have plenty of time.' He held out a handful of hard wheat cakes to Quintus, who murmured thanks and started to eat.

'You from Rome?' continued Dio cheerfully. 'I thought so— could tell from the classical way you muttered "thank you", though you certainly aren't a very trim-looking citizen of the imperial city at the moment.'

Quintus smiled faintly. He sensed that Dio was rattling on to give him a chance to recover, and he was soon to learn that a great deal of judgment lay beneath the young man's light manner.

'I'm from Naples,' continued Dio. 'I've got a lot of Greek blood. While Fabian'—he punched the other messenger affectionately in the ribs—'he's a blasted Gaul—but not a bad fellow, for all that. We've come to know each other quite well.'

'I should think so,' said Quintus dryly. Looking round their prison, he noticed several iron-bound, triple-locked coffers. Dio was sitting on one of them. As Quintus went over to examine them, Dio explained that they contained the legion's money, the imperial coins which paid the troops. The sacred emblems, flags, and standards were neatly stacked in a corner. There was nothing else in the way of furnishing in the small, stone room, and no window. But fortunately there was a tiny, grilled, fresh-air shaft to prevent the accumulation of dampness. And there was a lamp beside the wheat cakes and wine.

'Balbo sees that we get light and enough food; as far as prisons go it's not so bad,' Dio added. 'We might have been thrown in the dungeon.'

'Postumus couldn't do that without exposing the whole situation to a lot of other people, I guess,' said Quintus slowly. 'I think in his own way he's as crazy as that poor General.'

'No,' said Fabian, his lean, freckled face growing thoughtful. 'The Prefect's not crazy, but he's scared, scared of responsibility. It'a a certain type of German mind. I've fought beside lots of them and seen it before—splendid at obeying orders *and* giving them, as long as there's someone over them to tell 'em what to do.'

'Governor Suetonius *is* telling him what to do,' protested Quintus.

'Yes, but Postumus has never seen the Governor and has no more imagination than a bull. All he really knows and cares about is his own General and his own legion. He loves and is protecting Valerianus, who, I have heard, grew up in the same Rhineland village with him.'

Quintus considered this and nodded. 'That's all very well, and I think from the look in the Prefect's eyes he's suffering in that stupid, gnat-sized mind of his—but what are *we* going to do now —and, more important, what will Suetonius be able to do without this legion?'

'That,' said Dio, curling his legs up under him on the coffer, and quirking one eyebrow, 'is precisely what Fabian and I've been wondering. But I'd suggest, before you join our fascinating and so far quite useless discussion, that you get some sleep, my friend!' He indicated a strip of stone flooring next to the pile of standards. 'That elegant accommodation is—so far—unreserved. I say "so far" because we never know, of course, when some other messenger from the Governor may not arrive and be ushered into Posthumus' unique hotel! Here,' he said, interrupting himself with brisk practicality, 'put my cloak under your head, which I see from the wince you just gave is still aching.'

'And might stop aching if you'd stop babbling, you little southern wag-tongue,' interrupted Fabian, grinning at Quintus. 'I'm not the talkative type myself. . . .'

But you're both mighty good fellows, thought Quintus thankfully. This fact was the one ray of light in a decidedly grim blackness. For a moment before he fell asleep he pondered on the irony of his position. After all the dangers that he had already escaped —from the Britons, from Boadicea, from these last days of perilous journeying through enemy country—how dismal it was to end up now with a banged head, imprisoned in the very heart of what should have been about the safest place in Britain for him—the Roman fortress of the famous 'Augusta' Second Legion!

It was midday when he awoke, but there was, of course, no light in the strong-room except the lamp. Quintus raised his head, which felt much better, and saw that Dio and Fabian were playing checkers with different-coloured fragments of wheat cake. They had carved the board on the back of a coffer with the little eating-knife which Balbo had allotted them after their weapons had been taken away.

'My game,' said Fabian sternly, picking up and munching one of his men. 'Now you owe me forty thousand sesterces. Mark it up!'

'Oh, but no, Fabian—you cheat yourself,' protested Dio, solemnly scratching a row of M's on the wall. 'It's forty-one thousand, I believe; you forget the wager I lost on our fly race when my fly basely disappeared up the air-shaft. . . . Hullo . . .' he added, catching sight of Quintus. 'You finally wake up?'

'Uhmm,' yawned Quintus, stretching, then gingerly feeling the bump on his head. 'And delighted to find I've such rich companions. I should think you could've bribed Balbo and the whole legion by now.'

'Yes—you'd think so,' answered Dio, chuckling. 'Only I'm afraid they'd not be impressed by airy numbers on a wall. Our actual material wealth amounts to four pennies between us. How about you?'

'A bit more than that. I was given a purse for the journey at Chichester, but I—I don't seem to have used much.'

'Tell us your experience from the beginning,' said Fabian gravely. 'We've just been killing time till you woke up.'

The two earlier messengers naturally knew the grim story of Roman misfortunes up to the time Fabian had been sent from London, and as they listened intently to Quintus' account of the forced march south to Chichester, the Governor's speech to his officers, the massacre in London and Quintus' appointment as messenger to Gloucester, even Dio's cheerful face grew long. 'It sounds very bad,' he said quietly. 'Only the Fates know what's happened to Suetonius' force by now. You say he was going to try and march north to the Thames and wait for the Second to join him? How long ago was it you left?'

'Well,' said Quintus, counting, 'I left Monday noon, and it's been—let's see—two and a half days. Today must be Thursday.'

'But this is Friday,' said Fabian, glancing at the scratches which counted the days.

Quintus stared at him dismayed. He drew his heavy, dark brows together. 'All along I've had the oddest feeling that I've lost a day somewhere. I can't understand it.'

'Probably that bump on your head,' said Dio kindly. 'Makes one dizzy for a while. And it really doesn't matter.'

Quintus knew it was not the bump on the head, but he let it pass. There were far more important things to be decided.

'What do you think the Prefect's plans for us are?' he asked.

'Just keep us here indefinitely until and if Valerianus recovers from this fit of madness?'

Both young men nodded. 'That's my guess,' said Dio.

There was gloomy silence, then Quintus said, 'If we could only get to the tribunes somehow with our messages. . . .'

Fabian shook his head. 'I doubt it would do any good. Most of them are Germans like the majority of his legion. I don't think they'd disobey their commanding officer—not if Postumus told them he thought these messages weren't genuine, which I think in a muddle-headed way he's made himself believe.'

Quintus sighed, depressed by the soundness of this reasoning. There was another silence. Then Quintus roused himself and cried passionately, 'But by Mars and by the spirit of my beloved father, we've *got* to get out of here and get back to Suetonius ourselves! We can't just sit here like toads in a hole when we know what they're up against. Your own legions need you two, and my General Petillius needs what small help I can give. Why, they may be fighting Boadicea this minute!'

'Exactly,' said Dio, smiling a little as he tightened the thong on his sandal. 'Fabian and I some time ago came to the same conclusion.'

'Yes, of course,' said Quintus contritely. He began to pace the tiny cleared space between the coffers. 'What about Balbo?' he said after a moment. 'Couldn't he be overpowered when he puts the provisions in here?'

'We never see the guard,' answered Fabian. 'He shoves our food through that hole down there.' At the bottom of the door there was a square of about eight inches filled with a block of wood which barred it from the outside.

'I see,' said Quintus wearily. 'Yes, of course, most strong-rooms are built so they can be converted to temporary cells.'

'There *is* one, very feeble hope,' said Dio slowly. 'Friday's pay day. They have to get at the money to pay the troops and they wouldn't dare skip now when they don't want them suspecting anything queer. Last Friday, Fabian hadn't arrived yet, and I was here alone when Balbo and Postumus rushed in here and counted out the coins they needed. They bound me, and you can imagine that with my size and being unarmed, I could scarcely fight off that tow-headed elephant . . . but with three of us . . . and you, Quintus, are pretty big yourself . . .'

'Not *that* big,' said Quintus ruefully, but his eyes suddenly shone. 'Yet that's a great idea, wonderful, at least it has a chance . . .'

Fabian nodded, less impetuous than the two young men, but no less excited in his quiet way. 'We must plan this very carefully,' he said. 'Think of every possibility and try to be ready for it.'

The hours dragged by. They had no idea what time it was, but could at least tell that it was day by a faint glimmer in the airshaft. Dio thought it had been about sundown when they had come for the army pay before, and, as the glimmer grew fainter, the three of them grew tense and silent. They had made what preparations they could, which consisted chiefly in transforming Quintus back into something like a Roman, as the Silure costume could only be an embarrassment in a Roman fortress—though indeed none of them dared think how they would get out of the fortress even if, by a miracle, they got out of the strong-room. They had hacked off Quintus' long, native trousers, so that his knees were again bare, and covered his tartan tunic with Dio's mantle. It was during this process that Quintus had been puzzled to feel something hard in the breast of his tunic and discovered Regan's brooch. He held it in the palm of his hand, and in spite of his tenseness, a feeling of extraordinary sweetness flowed over him—sweetness and reassurance. It was as though a shutter half opened, and, in the crack, he could see her face looking at him with love, and hear a low, tender voice saying, 'Yet—I want you to remember some day—this will keep you safe.'

'Quintus, Quintus,' said Dio, craning over to see what Quintus was staring at, 'surely not a lady's brooch . . . ? And a British lady's brooch at that . . . ? Though now I remember you made some offhand mention of a girl who guided you . . . surely our little blind god, Cupid, has not loosed a careless arrow?'

'Oh Pax, Dio—hush up!' said Quintus, with an embarrassed grin, closing his hand over the brooch. 'I'm mighty glad to have this brooch, for I've a feeling it'll bring us luck,' and he pinned it back inside his tunic.

'Well, we need it,' said Fabian sombrely. 'Nothing but the most extraordinary favour from Fortuna is going to get us out of this fix, and I hereby vow to build an altar to her if she protects us.'

Quintus and Dio murmured agreement and fell silent. They waited.

Quite a while went by before their sharp ears heard a noise in the vestibule, then the slow grating of the bolt as it was drawn back.

The three young men instantly flattened themselves against the wall behind the door. Surprise was their only hope.

The first part of the plan worked perfectly. The door opened wide. Balbo walked in carrying a bunch of keys for the coffers. He was dressed in helmet and full armour, his sword gleaming. The Prefect followed, his mammoth body also armoured in ceremonial gilded bronze with red epaulettes, for he was to review the troops later. He wore no helmet, nor indeed would his head have cleared the ceiling if he had, and he had not bothered with a weapon, having perfect faith in the strength of his enormous hands.

'Now, where are they?' he said to Balbo. The three had known that they could go undiscovered no more than a second, but it was that second which they counted on. They sprang round the door. Fabian, flourishing the little knife, leaped out sideways at Balbo, while Quintus and Dio made a concerted rush for the Prefect's knees and, grabbing them, exerted all their combined force to jerk the big man off balance.

For an instant Quintus thought they had succeeded. The Prefect tottered and, letting out a sharp grunt, he swayed, while Quintus with desperate strength pounded upwards with his fist against the massive chin. The Prefect's great head wove from side to side, astonishment, rather than Quintus' blows, stunning his slow mind. He tried to raise his arms but could not, because Dio was clinging to them like a monkey, while Quintus went on hitting.

Suddenly the Prefect let out a bellow of rage. He shook Dio off and seized Quintus by the neck. We've lost! thought Quintus. Red mists swam in his eyes as the huge fingers tightened on his windpipe, then he heard a resounding thwack, and the fingers round his throat went limp.

He blinked and staggered back to see with amazement that the Prefect was clutching at the air, reeling. Then he sprawled face down over one of the coffers.

Dio sprang to Quintus' side, and they stared at the fallen giant.

'What happened?' stammered Dio. They both swung round at the same moment, remembering Fabian.

Fabian was standing by the wall gazing open-mouthed, not at the Prefect, but at Balbo, who was in the act of hurriedly sheathing his sword.

'HE did it!' gasped Fabian, pointing at the guard. 'He knocked Postumus on the head from behind with the flat of his sword.'

'Aye,' said Balbo, 'I did it, or you young fools'd have had every bone in your bodies broken. Now be off with you quick, before he rouses.'

The Prefect was already beginning to snort and groan.

'Be off with us?' repeated Quintus. So sudden was this reversal of their expectations that all three young men were having trouble taking it in.

'Back to your legions, back to the Governor! May Jupiter Maximus get you there safely,' and Balbo added on a lower note, 'May the great god also take pity on this legion and commander which have disgraced Rome forever. Go out by the southern portal. Titus is on guard there. Tell him only that you're sent back. No more. And the password today is "Gloria et Dignitas" —glory and dignity are *brave* words for the *brave* "Augusta" Second Legion, are they not?' he said with indescribable bitterness. 'Go! Your weapons are in the corner of the hall!' He bent over the Prefect.

The three young men obeyed, picking up their weapons and walking with controlled speed out of the staff-quarters door. Most of the legionaries were lined up in the forum waiting for their pay. No one noticed the three. They came to the south portal and gave the password as Balbo had told them. Titus, the sentry, let them through without comment, until Quintus, who was last, stepped through the gate. Then Titus whispered, 'I'm glad you fellows are all right. What's been happening up there?' He looked towards headquarters. 'Are we marching soon?'

Quintus dared not answer, but hurried away after Fabian and Dio on a track that led towards the east.

CHAPTER VIII

Three in a cave—the wolves' return—shelter and much to be learnt in a peasant's hut—the horse-dealer's roast pig—bargaining for three ponies

THE YOUNG ROMANS marched for a long time without speaking: Quintus, a cavalryman, had not been as well trained as the two official messengers in the long, easy stride that the legions were taught: a pace designed to cover a steady three miles an hour, no matter the conditions. But he was taller than the other two and had no difficulty in keeping up with them along the hilly trail. Fabian led because he had travelled this very route last week on his way to Gloucester from London.

The moon shone as it had the night before, so that when the sky suddenly clouded over, they had come a long way across several ridges, and through brooks and copses. It had begun to drizzle when they reached a clearing, in the centre of which was an ancient burial-mound, a long barrow surmounted by a cairn of stones. Here Fabian stopped.

'I think we should get some rest,' he said. 'I remember seeing a cave over there on that hillside when I came by before. I'm sure it was up here to the right of this cairn. We could keep dry in the cave.'

They were in a deserted part of the Cotswolds and had seen no native huts at all since leaving the fort. The cairn and the track were evidence that Britons sometimes passed along here, but no Roman road had as yet been built in this direction.

'Well, I'd be pleased to keep dry,' said Quintus, as they struck off the trail and began to climb the hill, 'but I'd be a lot more pleased to have a square meal. Even those wheat cakes would help.'

For some time Quintus had felt nothing but relief at their escape from the fortress, but now it occurred to him that their present situation gave little cause for rejoicing. Ahead there was a four-day march, at best, to find Suetonius' forces which they were not even sure of locating. Also they must traverse Atrebate country. Fabian's encounter with an Atrebate on the way west would indicate that that tribe too had revolted against the Romans. Moreover, their weapons consisted of but two swords, and Quintus' clumsy native spear—hardly the most efficient means of killing game or defending themselves.

'But I've *brought* some food,' said Dio unexpectedly, with his bubbling little chuckle. 'I scooped it up from the table outside the strong-room while we were getting our weapons. Guess what it is?'

'Wheat cakes!' cried Quintus, with resignation, and gratitude.

'Exactly. Our own daily allotment Balbo had ready to bring in to us.'

'And mighty useful to have,' observed Fabian approvingly. 'I was so thunderstruck, when I realized that Balbo not only wasn't fighting me but was watching for a chance to bang Postumus over the head, that I didn't have my wits about me.'

Nor I, Quintus thought ruefully, aware once again of his own lack of forethought as well as his inclination to blunder and blurt things and act on impulse. For an instant, there was again that queer little stab of half memory. Somewhere, lately, he had stupidly blurted out something that had led him into unnecessary danger. Led him and someone else—Regan? But how could it be? Like an image in a pool, he glimpsed the cold, angry face of a man in a green robe, against a background of tremendous, up-ended stones. The image dissolved as Fabian said, 'Look, there's the cave!'

Ahead on the hillside amongst a stand of white birches, they could dimly see a pile of rock and a black opening in the pile which, they found when they got nearer, led into a cave quite large enough to shelter the three of them, crouching. It had an overhanging ledge and was dry.

They settled themselves comfortably against the rocky wall and began to devour the wheat cakes, which Dio produced from beneath his leather jerkin.

The army's standard wheat cakes might be monotonous fare, but they had been designed to be the best hunger-satisfiers for the least bulk. They were made from crushed whole wheat mixed with fat pork and water, then baked into hard, flat biscuits. Three of them apiece took the edge off their hunger but left nothing for next day.

'I wonder,' said Quintus, 'if I could possibly spear a rabbit for us with this thing.' He balanced the spear on his fingers. 'The Britons do, but I can't seem to throw it straight, though I've practised plenty.'

'Beaver maybe,' said Fabian. 'I noticed a dam on the brook below. We'll see if we can't get one somehow when it's light. Beaver's not bad eating, but I admit I don't much fancy it raw.'

The making of fire was a difficult process, so the Romans were accustomed to carrying only dried or cooked provisions with them. In emergencies they commandeered a live ember from some peasant's hearth.

'I watched Pendoc—that was the Briton I told you about—making fire with two sticks,' said Quintus. 'I could try. It seems to me that there are quite a few useful bits of knowledge neither my Roman school nor the army ever taught——' He broke off abruptly. 'Listen, what's that?' he whispered. 'Something's in the back of the cave.'

They all stiffened, turning towards the small, dark tunnel behind them, where there were faint scuffling noises mixed with higher sounds, like mewings or squeaks.

'Oh, bats, of course,' said Fabian, who had had more varied experiences than the others. 'They always live in caves.'

The other two nodded. 'Of course.'

Dio yawned and said, 'Well, I don't need a bat's lullaby to make me sleep. Call me when you've caught AND cooked that beaver, boys—and I'd suggest you add a little wine and truffle sauce to make it tastier!'

'Ha! You lazy lout,' said Fabian sternly. 'Every man to his own breakfast.'

Dio snorted, Quintus laughed. There were good-natured grumbles back and forth as to the use of the cramped space for sleeping; each one of them aware that they were joking so as not to think too much. Finally the three of them curled up on Dio's mantle and spread Fabian's mantle over the top of them.

The white birches near the mouth of the cave cast faint shadows over the sleeping three as the sky greyed into early dawn.

Quintus was sleeping heavily and dreaming of Rome. An extremely pleasant dream in which his mother was laughing with Regan, who was dressed in gorgeous clothes like those of Nero's beloved Poppæa—all peacock satins and cloth of gold, which Quintus had somehow provided for her.

He didn't know what the sound was that woke him, but he sprang up, grabbing his spear. The other two woke at his jump, and without knowing what the trouble was, both backed against the wall and drew their swords in one motion.

For a second, between sleepiness and the uncertain light, they could not see anything, but then the sound which had awakened Quintus came again. A low, snarling growl that raised the hairs on his neck. He had never heard that sound before, yet he knew what it was, even before Dio whispered, 'Wolves.'

Then Quintus saw two huge shapes slinking towards them through the birches.

'Shout!' cried Fabian. 'Make a noise! They'll go away, they can't be hungry this time of year.'

The young men shouted and yelled until the cave reverberated behind them, but the two sinister shapes behind the birches did not retreat. They stopped and watched, their cruel yellow eyes glinting with menace.

'Jupiter Maximus——' groaned Fabian suddenly. 'I know what it is—this is their lair and those were wolf-cubs we heard in the cave. They're going to attack us!'

The great grey wolf and his mate had started to move forward again. They drew slowly nearer, and the horrible, low growling grew louder.

Quintus' hand clenched round his spear. The mouth of the cave was too low. He couldn't straighten up to aim. He began to edge outside, until his head cleared the rock ledge.

'No, don't——' whispered Fabian. 'If you miss him we'll have lost the spear. Get behind us, we've the swords——'

Quintus did not hear. His heart was pounding, but his mind was cool and alert as he carefully counted the distance between him and the larger wolf, who kept advancing. Quintus drew his arm back and waited. He saw the white fangs bared, the slobbering red tongue. He saw the fur on the shoulders stiffen and rise, as the great beast tensed for the spring.

Quintus drew a rasping breath and waited yet another second. The instant the wolf lunged, Quintus hurled the spear straight at the lighter fur on the chest. There was a fountain jet of blood as the spearhead pierced to the wolf's heart. The wolf fell from mid-air into a twitching heap on the ground. And the other wolf, snarling and panting, stopped her stealthy advance and stood irresolute, the yellow eyes glaring at the heaving body of her mate and at the blood that spurted once more—and stopped.

'Bravo, Quintus!' cried Dio. He and Fabian rushed together towards the she-wolf. But she was too quick for them. She doubled back and flattening herself belly-to-ground ran past their drawn swords straight into the cave.

'Whew——!' breathed Quintus, looking down at the dead wolf. 'Thanks be to Diana, to Fortuna, even to the Celtic gods, that I've finally learned how to throw that thing.'

He hauled and tugged until the spear came out, dripping red. He examined the flint head, which was undamaged. Even the rawhide which bound the flint to the shaft had not loosened.

'Here, quick—help me,' grunted Fabian, who was on his knees beside the wolf, expertly carving out a piece of haunch with his small knife. 'Get a stick.'

Quintus found a long, pointed one, and he and Dio skewered the hunk of meat on it. Dio hoisted the stick over his shoulder.

'Interesting change of menu,' he said. 'Wolf instead of beaver, one never knows. . . .'

'And one doesn't know what that she-wolf intends to do either,' interrupted Fabian curtly, with a glance over his shoulder at the cave.

'Won't she stay by her young?' asked Quintus.

'Probably, or by the body of her dead mate, but——'

'We'd better be going,' Quintus finished the sentence.

They started down the hillside with considerable haste, crashing through the thickets and brambles until they reached the barrow with its cairn of stones, and the overgrown, rutted track. They started east again along the track and had gone a few yards when Dio, shifting the heavy hunk of skewered meat from one shoulder to the other, said, 'You know, it suddenly occurs to me that we've left our mantles and helmets behind in the cave, Fabian.'

'Yes, it occurs to me too,' said Fabian grimly.

'Also,' continued Dio, 'that returning for them doesn't appeal to me. Madam Wolf is in full possession, and for all I know has summoned all her relatives by now.'

As if in answer to him they heard a sound floating down from the hillside behind—the long, mournful howl of a wolf.

The three paused and listened, then walked on silently.

'So now we are in the same boat as Quintus,' observed Dio after a while. 'And there's nothing to show definitely that we're Romans, except the Fourteen on our jerkins, which can be hidden.'

'And your swords,' said Quintus a trifle enviously, but not as he would have said it yesterday. He now clasped his spear with confidence.

'And our swords,' agreed Dio. 'Though I hope we'll have no use for them—until the big battle. I find that my adventures of the last fortnight have left me with a—shall we say—disinclination for more excitement right away. I find myself shamefully thinking of a good bed, of sweet Neapolitan sunshine and music, of gentle, smiling girls, and soft living generally.'

'Go ahead and think,' said Fabian dryly, striding ahead and lacing the top of his jerkin, for a cold, wet wind had sprung up.

But Quintus was startled by something reminiscent in Dio's chatter. 'I had a—a friend, in the Ninth, who used to talk like that,' he said hesitantly, though realizing at once how little Dio and Lucius really resembled each other. Dio's rueful complaint had been humorous, unresentful. For all his light manner, Dio had a tremendous loyalty to his job, and a strong sense of duty. While Lucius——

'Something queer happen to the friend?' asked Dio, looking up at Quintus. 'Your voice was funny.'

Quintus wished that he could confide the pain and disillusionment that the thought of Lucius gave him. But he couldn't bring himself to say, 'I was awfully fond of him, and *thought* he was a friend, but he let me down once; and far worse than that, when all our men were being slaughtered around us, he ran away.' So he nodded briefly instead and stared ahead at Fabian's shoulders.

'That's too bad,' said Dio gently, thinking that the friend had been killed in the disaster to the Ninth, and he changed the subject. 'How long are we going to lug this blasted hunk of wolf meat, Fabian? I'm hungry enough to eat it raw.'

The elder messenger turned round. 'I hope we won't have to. There's a native hut there in the valley; perhaps they'll let us use their fire.'

They looked down at an isolated little British farm. Behind a paling there was a round wattle-and-mud hut thatched with reeds.

From the circular vent on top of the roof, smoke was curling upwards. They descended the hill and approached the stockade of saplings that enclosed the barnyard. From inside, a dog barked savagely, a goat bleated, and pigs snorted alarm. The three Romans stopped outside the barred gate.

'I'll try,' said Quintus. 'I speak enough Celtic.' He raised his voice and shouted, 'Greeting! greeting! We are friends; will you talk to us?'

The dog lunged against the gate snapping and growling, but there was no other answer.

'Better get that spear ready, Quintus,' said Dio, chuckling. 'This dog is as fierce as the wolf.'

'I'm sure there's someone in there,' said Fabian. 'Isn't that a baby crying?'

Quintus nodded and tried again. 'Greeting, friend! All we want is a bit of your fire. We can pay.'

At that an old woman stuck her head round the deer hide that served for a door. She had long, tangled, grey hair, and a fat, stupid face. She inspected the three men and spoke to the dog, who stopped his furious barking. 'What is it you want?' she quavered.

Quintus explained again, and the old woman disappeared, but in a moment she waddled out into the yard. 'You can *pay*?'

As Quintus assented, her pendulous lips parted in a silly, gratified grin. She unbarred the gate. 'Where do you come from?' she asked, as they threaded their way between sheep, goats, and pigs, while the dog sniffed suspiciously at Dio and jumped towards the wolf meat.

'From the north,' said Quintus vaguely.

'Oh,' she said, 'that's why your speech is not much like ours. You're off to fight the Roman swine too, I suppose!' She walked into her hut as Quintus grunted something that might be agreement.

'She thinks we're Britons; be careful,' he whispered hastily to his friends before they stepped into the hut.

When their eyes got used to the smoky darkness, they saw pallets of animal skins stretched along the walls, and a huge loom at which a young woman was heaving lumpy grey strands of rough wool, while she nursed a naked baby on her lap. She was a handsome girl with the dark hair and greenish-hazel eyes of the western tribes. She turned her head as the three men came in, and giggled, blushing a little.

'Cook your meat there,' said the old woman, pointing to the fire. 'It's good to see visitors. My daughter and I are lonely since our men all left to join the great Queen of the Icenians.'

The girl sighed and murmured, 'It is so. They've gone far away.'

Quintus, looking at them, realized that they were both simple women without guile, who had probably never travelled three miles from their home. Maybe I can learn something, he thought with sudden hope.

'When was that?' asked Quintus casually, kneeling beside Dio, who was broiling the meat, while Fabian sat down on a pile of skins and watched Quintus, knowing that something important was afoot but unable to understand what they said. 'When did your men go?'

The old woman shrugged. 'Long time. I don't know. Some days——'

'It was the day Mog here got his tooth,' said the young mother eagerly, forgetting her shyness. 'His father felt it with his thumb before he left. This many days——' She held up three fingers.

Not so long, then, Quintus thought, with growing excitement. 'And where were they going to find Queen Boadicea?' he asked. 'We want to be sure we know the way.'

But the two women looked blank. 'Over there somewhere——'
said the old one, pointing towards the east. 'Past the Great
White Horse, then along the ancient road of the little people, and
far—far towards the rising sun.'

Quintus hid his disappointment at this vagueness by poking
an ember under the broiling meat.

'Why don't the *others* speak,' asked the girl suddenly, casting
curious looks from Dio's snub-nosed, merry face to Fabian's
grave, thin, freckled one.

'Well, you see, they come from a far country over the mountains,' said Quintus hastily. 'Their tribe has a different language.'

The women were satisfied by this, and Quintus was astonished
at their naïveté until he realized that they had doubtless never
seen a Roman, certainly not one without the full panoply of
flashing armour. As for him—by now, with a week's stubble of
beard, the spear, and the increasingly dirty tartan tunic, he must
make a fairly convincing Briton.

The girl left the loom and put the baby carefully down near
Fabian, who recoiled from it in dismay. She went to a large
pottery jug and poured its contents into a clay cup. 'We have
goat milk,' she said shyly to Quintus. 'Have some.'

'Not unless they pay,' said the old woman quickly.

Quintus reassured her again, though wondering how much the
greedy old woman would demand. He accepted the milk with
thanks. When they had all drunk and choked down great hunks
of the rank wolf meat, Quintus knew they must be going, but
tried once more for information.

'Have all the Atrebate men left to join the war against the
Romans?' he said, putting his cup down and smiling at the girl.

'The *Atrebates*?' she repeated, with some surprise. 'Perhaps.
We don't know. They live yonder in the country of the Great
White Horse. WE are Dobuni,' she said proudly.

'Oh, I see—' But Quintus was dismayed. So the revolt had
spread to still another nation. How many tribes had Boadicea
amassed by now? Where WERE her forces? Did these women
know anything at all? It seemed unlikely and yet an intuition
told him to keep on.

Dio was staring at him, obviously wondering why they were
delaying, but afraid to ask in Latin. Fabian had risen from the
skins and was waiting by the door.

Quintus made them both a quick, quelling gesture and shook
his head. Both men instantly understood and nodded. They

turned their backs and negligently pushed aside the deerhide curtain as though considering the weather outside, thus leaving Quintus a free hand.

'We have travelled a long way to do battle,' said Quintus with perfect truth. 'So far that we've become fearful that we may have missed the fighting. Do you think that perhaps there has been a great battle already between the Britons and the Roman Governor's army?'

The women looked at him intently, willing to answer, but comprehending neither his thought, nor the way he had expressed himself in his halting Celtic.

He tried again, more carefully. The old woman hunched her shoulders and, losing interest, stirred a mess that bubbled in an iron pot over the fire.

But the girl, who was pleased with this break in her monotonous life, finally got the gist of his meaning and shook her head. 'I think not. The runner who came to call my husband and brothers, he said the great Queen would wait until so many tribes had joined her that the land would be black with warriors as far as the eye could see. And women too will fight,' she added wistfully, 'but my husband would not let me go. 'Tis not the custom of the Dobuni.'

'I should hope not,' Quintus murmured, and was forming another question when the girl picked up her baby and, holding it to her breast, cried, 'Andraste, the glorious goddess, will give us victory, yet I grow a little afraid when I think of the many, many Roman monsters, so many—like pebbles in a brook.'

I wish there were, thought Quintus ruefully.

'I have never seen a Roman,' continued the girl. 'I've heard they have tusks like wild boars, and claws like bears, and heads made all of gold that gleams in the sun. The Icenian runner said that when he passed near their camp on his way here, he saw one watching from a mound who had a red horse's tail growing from his head and who flashed in gold all over.'

Quintus put on an expression of horrified interest and held his breath as he said, 'Where was this camp where the runner saw the Roman in gold? Did he say it was near a river? Near a town?'

She looked puzzled. 'He did not say—except it was a place the Roman beasts had always used, since the first one came.'

'The *first* one? Did he say the name? Was it Julius Cæsar?'

'It might be—yes, I think he used some sound like "Cæsar". Why do you care so much?' she said curiously.

'Simply,' answered Quintus, 'that I and my friends would like to look at the Roman monster too, before we meet it in battle. . . . Good wife, you've been most kind, you and your mother. We thank you and must go.'

'The payment——' whined the old woman, looking up from the pot. 'For the fire—for the goat milk!'

'Yes, yes.' Quintus reached into his pouch. 'Shall we say three pennies?' which was generous recompense. He held out the coins. They were, of course, Roman coins stamped with the head of Nero, but he thought he could invent some story to explain that to these people, if they happened to notice.

'What are *those*?' cried the old woman contemptuously. 'Little thin bits of metal! You promised to *pay*.'

'I *am* paying,' protested Quintus. 'This is good money. It's used all through the land.'

'That's no *payment*!' The old woman's fat face grew suddenly purple. She knocked Quintus' hand viciously, so that the coins scattered on the trampled clay floor. 'You are lying thieves——'

'Here, wait a minute!' cried Quintus, between anger and astonishment, as Dio and Fabian, seeing trouble, came silently to stand beside him. 'I don't understand——'

'Why, Mother wants an iron bar, of course,' said the girl frowning. 'A small one.'

'A large one!' screamed the old woman, shaking her fist.

'Small or large, I don't know what you're talking about,' snapped Quintus, when he felt a tug at his tunic and saw Fabian make a motion of the eyebrows. 'I must speak to my friend a moment.'

By the door Fabian spoke in low, rapid Latin. 'These backward tribes use iron bars for currency—that's the trouble, isn't it? They've never seen coins.'

'What'll we do?' breathed Quintus.

'Talk yourself out of it, somehow.'

Quintus turned back to the women and tried. The girl soon accepted the fact that the tribe these three came from did not have iron bars and that the coins on the floor were ample payment, but the old woman did not. Her bleary eyes were sparked with fury. 'Liars! Thieves!' she kept shouting. 'Pay me! Pay me!' And she hopped up and down angrily.

There was no use arguing. Quintus sent the girl an apologetic look and turned hastily to go with the others, whereupon the old woman, in a frenzy, grabbed the ladle from the iron pot and flung it straight at Quintus. The pot contained some sort of stew and the ladle carried a portion through the air in a boiling spatter. Quintus ran, and the others, with him, pelting ignominiously across the barnyard, while the old woman yelled insults after them, and the dog snapped and bit at their heels.

They vaulted over the gate, thus getting rid of the dog, and ran down the road until they were out of sight, when Dio took a good look at Quintus and burst into a roar of laughter. 'Stop! stop!' he choked. 'Let us take count of our wounds after this shameful defeat. Let us at least cleanse Quintus from beans—and yes'—he reached up and removed something from Quintus' hair—'and pieces of stewed rabbit.'

Quintus scraped beans off the back of his neck in disgust. 'That blasted stew was *hot*!' he said angrily, then suddenly joined Dio in laughter. 'We're a fine dignified credit to the legions! Routed by a pot ladle!' Even Fabian chuckled as he said, 'And a mangy little dog who's made off with some of my sandal.'

'As long as he didn't take part of your ankle too,' said Quintus, who spied a brook and sluiced his head and neck in it until all the old woman's stew was off him. He came back to the others and said, 'No, but listen—I *did* get some information, I'm not sure just how useful. Is there any place that's called "Cæsar's Camp"?'

'But, of course,' said Fabian and Dio together. And Fabian continued, 'It's a British earthwork fort, which Cæsar is said to have used. We camped there with Suetonius on the march down from Wales. It's this side of the Thames and south-west of London. Why?'

'Because I think that's where Suetonius is now,' and he told them what the girl had said.

Fabian nodded. 'That seems very likely. At least we know where to strike for. What else did she say?'

'I tried to find out where all the tribes were convening with Boadicea, but all they knew was something about "beyond the White Horse and then the ancient way of the little people, and far, far towards the rising sun"—doesn't make any sense.'

'Yes, it does,' said Fabian thoughtfully. 'I know their Vale of the White Horse. In fact we'll be there ourselves tomorrow, and the ancient road would be the Icknield Way, which leads north-east from here, though I'm not sure how far. At any rate Boadicea is apparently somewhere near her own East Anglia.'

'I wonder what she's been up to, since you last heard of

her, Quintus?' said Dio, all the laughter gone from his face.

'To no good for us, that's sure,' answered Quintus. 'Boadicea is a terrible woman with the heart of a lion—of a wolf——' he added sombrely, thinking of the wolves that morning, and their fury to protect and avenge their own.

As they strode along, he thought of Regan and the unspeakable torture she would have suffered from Boadicea if she had not escaped. His hand went of itself to feel the outline of the brooch Regan had given him, which he still wore inside his tunic next to his breast. A piece of sentiment he hoped the others hadn't noticed. Perhaps, if he had shown the brooch to the old woman in the hut, she might not have been so furious at not getting her iron bar; the Druid sign on it seemed to work miracles with the Britons—— But wait a minute, he thought, so startled that he stopped dead on the road. How do I know that little red enamel snake is a Druid sign? Did Regan ever say so?

'What's the matter, Quintus?' asked Dio. 'Something bite you?'

'A thought,' said Quintus, starting to walk again.

The little Neapolitan chuckled, and the three of them marched on. But all the rest of that day, as they cautiously skirted the Dobuni capital of Cirencester, which was hardly larger than a mud village, and came down out of the hills to the banks of the infant Thames, Quintus kept mulling over the puzzle. He rehearsed every word that Regan had said to him that night by the camp fire in the forest. There had been no mention of the brooch. Yet he was convinced that he had been present when that brooch had been shown to hostile people, and that they had looked on it with respect. When the three young Romans paused to drink from the river, Quintus suddenly said, 'Do you believe in spells? I mean do you think something could be done to make one forget a day in one's life?'

Dio laughed and said he forgot things all the time, but Fabian answered gravely: 'That depends—I have seen magic things in Gaul. I know it's possible. Why?'

'Because I think it's happened to me. But the memory of that day is coming back a little.'

'Is it important?' asked Fabian. 'Does it affect our mission, or Rome?'

'I don't think so. It feels'—Quintus' tanned skin flushed, and he gave a lop-sided smile—'like a private matter . . . a very strange one.'

If Regan did *not* really desert me, he thought, if after all she was with me on that day I think I've lost—A feeling of exquisiet relief came to him, and a rush of tenderness which was cut short by a cry from Dio.

'Look! Dinner—ahead! Just as I was offering up another vow to Fortuna!'

A hundred yards away on the river-bank a man sat by a roaring fire turning a large pig on a spit.

Quintus sniffed at the intoxicating odour of roast pork, then saw beyond the fire an even more alluring sight.

'Horses!' he breathed, his eyes sparkling. 'That's better than dinner!'

'We will hope to get both,' whispered Fabian, drawing his companions behind a large hazel bush, 'by fair means or foul. But let's be sure he's alone.'

They couldn't see the man very well, because he was sitting on the other side of the camp fire, but he seemed to be large, with a mane of shaggy blond hair, drooping yellow moustaches, and a plaid mantle of a type Quintus had seen on Britons in the towns. Behind him was a native two-wheeled cart with an ox between the shafts. Round the cart were seven rough-coated ponies tethered and grazing on the lush grass.

'He seems to be alone. Let's try our luck. Quintus, let loose your best Celtic again.'

The three walked out from the hazel bush and advanced with their arms high in token of peace while Quintus called out a friendly greeting.

The man gazed at them through the smoke of the fire. 'Oho!' he called in a deep, bass voice. 'And what do you want of a poor unfortunate, who is protected by the gods?'

Now what does he mean by that? Quintus thought, not sure he had understood. But as they walked nearer, he and the others paused in consternation.

In the face the man turned up to them, one eye was gone. Where it had been, there was a shrivelled pit, while the same blow had sliced off half his nose. Nor was this all, for on the ground beside one long tartan-covered leg, there was a stump bound neatly with the rolled-up trouser.

'One leg, one eye——'whispered Quintus. 'He says truly that he's unfortunate.'

The three looked at each other with the same dismayed thought. They needed food and wanted the horses and had planned to help themselves if the man resisted, but this was different. The man was a cripple.

'Who are you and where are you going, friend?' stammered Quintus.

The man flicked off a piece of crackling from the pig, ate it, and licked his fingers. The one eye peered at them sardonically. 'I am Gwyndagh, a trader in horses. I travel where I wish, and no man molests me.'

Which would be as true for Romans as it was for Britons. In both countries cripples such as this were considered to be under direct supervision of the gods who had punished them, gods jealous of their rights, and who would send fearful wrath on a person who mistreated one of their chosen.

'We need to eat, O Gwyndagh,' said Quintus, sighing and glancing hungrily at the roasting pig. 'And we badly need horses to carry us on a journey of great importance. Can you think of any way we can get these things?'

It was hard to be sure, but it seemed that beneath the greasy, yellow moustache there was a smile. The shrewd eye roamed calmly over each of the young men.

'Come here—all three of you,' said the horse-dealer at last. They came slowly and stood close to him. He raised his hand and pointed a finger at Dio. 'Say the words "Cæsar Augustus Nero, Emperor of Rome," ' he commanded. Dio was so astounded to hear this come out in passable Latin that he stifled a gasp and looked for help to Quintus, who did not know what to make of it either.

'*Say those words,*' repeated the cripple sternly, 'or you have no chance of help from me.'

Dio swallowed and said, 'Cæsar Augustus Nero, Emperor of Rome,' very fast, while Gwyndagh listened critically.

'Now you,' he said, turning to Fabian, who hesitantly complied, and then Quintus.

'So,' said Gwyndagh. 'I thought so. You are Romans, though you try to hide it—legionaries too. I see by the shape of the swords.'

'You see a great deal with that lone eye, good Gwyndagh,' said Quintus, still trying to brave it out. 'But how can you be sure? My friends may have stolen the swords.'

'That might be,' agreed Gwyndagh, twirling the spit nonchalantly. 'But there is *no* way to steal the true accent of a Roman when he salutes his Emperor!'

So that was that. And no more use pretending.

'Well . . .' said Quintus, uncertainly for he could not tell how this revelation of their nationality affected the man. 'You are right. But we still need meat and horses. We have some money —Roman money, but not enough to pay you fairly.'

'You are honest,' said Gwyndagh, breaking off another piece of crisp pork skin. 'It is not believed by many of my fellow Britons, but some Romans *are* honest. I might trust you with three of my horses. I might trust you with half my pig, except that you will soon fight the British forces and will certainly be killed. Then I would be quite out of pocket.'

Quintus translated this to Dio and Fabian, while Gwyndagh listened intently. He understood much Latin, having lived in London and purveyed horses to the Roman Government.

'Then there's nothing for it,' said Fabian to Dio and Quintus, 'but to pay for the pig and take three horses, whether he likes it or not.'

'And brave my curse? The curse of the gods? Of the all-powerful Lugh who rules the earth and skies?' cried Gwyndagh in a great solemn voice.

'I'm sorry,' said Quintus, 'but we must chance it. And the curse of Lugh will doubtless not affect a Roman.'

Gwyndagh considered this in silence, then appeared to make up his mind. 'Very well,' he said. 'Give me what money you have, and do as you like. In truth I am pleased to ill-serve the Icenians, since it was an Icenian chariot of the whirling knives that did this,' he pointed to his face, 'some years ago. This'—he pointed to his amputated stump—'came from another cause we won't go into.'

'Many thanks,' said Quintus fervently, and the other two echoed him.

Gwyndagh shrugged. 'If you are not killed—which, I repeat, seems improbable—I'll find you again some day, never fear. And get back my horses.'

'You shall have them!' cried Quintus. 'And a pouch of gold as well. We promise you!'

Fabian made a grimace at this exuberance, but he said nothing. They sat down beside Gwyndagh and, since the pig was roasted, split it carefully. They ate a portion of their half, stowed the rest in their bags, paid Gwyndagh all their coins, and departed with the three likeliest ponies.

The last they saw of the horse-dealer, he was clambering into his cart, managing skilfully on his one leg. He saw them looking after him and raised his arm in a philosophic wave, that showed he bore no resentment.

'I think our luck has turned,' said Dio. 'And now we can really hurry—thanks be to Fortuna!'

CHAPTER IX

A warm welcome—Quintus a Centurion—reunited with Ferox—black rubble and ashes—strategy in Epping Forest

AFTER LEAVING THE HORSE-DEALER, the three Romans had forded the Thames and slept briefly in the Vale of the Great White Horse, within sight of that strange, chalk beast, as big as a village, which the ancient people had long ago carved out of the green hillside.

The white horse with its long, spindly legs and snaky head was worshipped by the Atrebates, and this was the heart of their country. The three young men therefore proceeded with great caution, but they had no further adventures. They climbed to the Ridgeway track, which they followed for some time. It was almost deserted. The natives they did pass occasionally were old or very young, and incurious. It was clear that the vigorous portion of the Atrebate population was not there, and all too easy to guess where they had gone.

Calleva, the Atrebate capital near Silchester, also seemed deserted, a circumstance which Fabian found sinister. He told the others that once there had been a Roman camp adjoining the British town, where, for some years following the Claudian conquest, the Atrebates had lived on friendly enough commercial terms with their conquerors. But now the Roman camp was as abandoned as the town seemed to be, though the three young men dared not investigate closely.

But they found mute testimony of what must have happened as they picked up the road again the other side of town and nearly stumbled over the body of a man in a Roman jerkin. The jerkin was marked with the sign that showed him to be a veteran of the legions. The Roman sprawled face down, as though felled in a frantic rush to escape. The back of his head was crushed in; the blood-stained slingstone which had crushed it lay beside him.

'There were sights like these along the way when I marched down from Lincoln with the Ninth,' said Quintus grimly, turning from the dead Roman. 'And we dare not even take the time to give him burial rites.'

'No,' said Fabian.

Nobody spoke again for a long time. They followed the good road that the Romans had built, and the next noon came upon a milestone that said 'A Londinio XX'. The milestone had been overturned; filth and the half-burned entrails of some animal were scattered on it.

They gazed at this small, senseless expression of hatred, then Fabian said, 'Twenty miles to London, or what was *once* London, but "Cæsar's Camp" is considerably nearer. We'll soon know now if Suetonius is there.'

They kicked the horses' flanks and broke into a rough gallop.

The sun came out from behind clouds. It shone upon the loops and windings of the Thames and it shone—after they had struck through forest and emerged on to a broad heath—upon the sight they had all prayed to see. Above strong circular ramparts made of earth and timber and stone, the eagle standard reared itself proudly, and the imperial flag was flying!

They dismounted by the great ditch which was the outer ring of fortification, and suddenly all three of them looked at each other, and joined hands in a firm, quick clasp. They needed no words to seal their friendship; the recognition of all they had been through together, and of what was still to come, was enough for each of them.

Leading the horses, they strode to the first sentry post. The look-out on the ramparts had already seen them and recognized Dio and Fabian.

Here there was no difficulty, no mystery, as at Gloucester's fortress. Here they were received with shouts of joy, and back-slappings, and a chorus of eager, excited questions. 'Where's the Second? Are they just behind? We've been watching for days!'

The questions were soon repeated by the Governor himself, for they were ushered at once to Suetonius' red-and-white-striped tent in the centre of the fort. He got up to receive them, his heavy-jawed, ruddy face alight with relief. 'Welcome! Welcome, imperial messengers!' he cried. 'You *too*?' he added, recognizing Quintus with a smile. 'So you are all together. Ah, this is good news. Where's General Valerianus and the Second? Are you much ahead of them?'

'Your Excellency,' Fabian dropped to one knee, and, fixing his eyes on the Governor's gilded sandals, continued very low, 'we bring bad news. . . . The Second Legion has not left Gloucester.'

'Not left Gloucester! But this is monstrous. I can't delay battle much longer! It'll take at least five days' march to bring the whole legion. What's the matter with them? When are they starting?'

Fabian grew very pale. He cast one quick glance towards Dio and Quintus, then raised his eyes resolutely to the Governor's empurpling face. 'They are not starting, I'm afraid—Your Excellency.'

The Governor's harsh breath rasped through the tent. 'Have they been slaughtered? Has the fortress fallen? By all the gods, what *has* happened?'

'Nothing has happened to the legion, Excellency, they're all right—I—we——' Fabian looked beyond the Governor to the officers and guards clustered round the back of the tent and the entrance.

'For the honour of Rome, Excellency, it is better that we tell you alone,' he said very low.

It looked as though the Governor's ready and violent temper might get the better of him, but he restrained it and made a signal. The other men left the tent, all but the general of the Fourteenth, and Petillius Cerealis of the Ninth, who had greeted Quintus with a quick look of welcome. These two stood behind the Governor as Fabian explained what had happened to the Second.

'You mean,' roared Suetonius, banging his fist on the table, 'that because Valerianus is a madman, and the Prefect a coward, the Royal "Augusta" Legion refuses to obey my orders? You mean that half of Rome's military force in Britain is bottled up useless on the other side of the island, while the Britons are preparing to massacre us all?'

'It is so, Excellency.'

'Do you two say the same?' said the Governor, looking at Dio and Quintus.

They bowed their heads. 'It is so, Excellency.'

Suetonius slumped heavily on to his chair. Beneath the brilliant gilt of his cuirass, his shoulders sagged. The thick fingers of his right hand drummed slowly on the table-top, while he stared, frowning, at the wooden floor. 'Leave me alone, all of you!' he muttered. 'You'll get your orders later.'

Silently, the two generals and the three messengers filed out of the tent.

General Petillius put his hand on Quintus' shoulder as they started across the parade-ground. 'Come with me—I want to talk to you.'

In Petillius' quarters, Quintus enjoyed the first full meal he had had for days. His General sent for a flask of Gaulish wine and indulgently watched Quintus drink and eat, forbearing as yet to question him.

'You don't eat too, sir?' asked Quintus timidly, after a bit.

'No, I'm not hungry,' said Petillius briefly, though his tired eyes smiled. Quintus saw that there were new grooves in Petillius' thin cheeks; he no longer seemed like a very young general. Suddenly Quintus guessed.

'This is your own supper I'm eating, isn't it, sir?' he said unhappily. 'Food *must* be getting very low in camp.'

'We'll hold out a few more days,' said Petillius. 'Boadicea's forces too are short of provisions. They've descended like a storm of locusts on all the country north of the Thames. And they sowed no crops this spring—so certain were they of victory.'

'I wonder they haven't crossed the Thames and attacked us,' said Quintus, putting down his wine-cup. 'We—Dio, Fabian, and I—were dreadfully afraid of that during these days we were struggling to get here.'

'Boadicea is so confident that she's been in no hurry for the final show-down. These three weeks since the sack of Colchester, and our'—Petillius paused and went on through tight lips—'the disaster to the Ninth, she's been fully occupied, burning and plundering: London, Colchester, St Albans. She's managed to torture and kill about fifty thousand civilians as well. She has—as I say—been busy.'

Petillius' dry understatement awakened Quintus to the immediate gravity of the crisis. He felt a thrill of hatred for the Queen, a thrill intensified by the memory of her behaviour to Regan. And yet in justice he could not help saying, 'Boadicea was terribly wronged, sir, in the beginning. I was there and I saw. I saw her while Catus' slave flogged her. I heard the two Princesses screaming when Catus' men——'

'I know.' Petillius cut him short. 'Rome has made a series of incredibly stupid blunders, of which my own is not the least. We have through our own folly let loose a monster of death and destruction. But this monster must be cut down, so that peace can return to Britain.'

Peace here? Quintus thought—and could not imagine it.

'Sometimes the sword is the only way to peace, Quintus,' said his General quietly. 'Now I want you to tell me in detail exactly what has happened to you during these seven days since I saw you last at Chichester, when you were disguised as a very peculiar Silure, jogging on a native pony between a villainous-looking Briton and an extremely pretty girl!' The twinkle flickered briefly in Petillius' hazel eyes.

'Yes, sir,' said Quintus, colouring a little. 'But, sir—I don't suppose you'd know about it, but I've been worrying a bit about my horse, Ferox. Do you suppose he was brought here from Chichester with the other cavalry horses? He's an awfully good mount, sir,' Quintus finished quickly, loath to have his General suspect sentimental fondness for the horse.

'Your Ferox is here,' said Petillius, smiling. 'I saw to that myself.'

Quintus sent the General a look of passionate gratitude and launched at once into a carefully unemotional report of his journey.

Petillius listened without interrupting, and at the end he nodded. 'Yes, there're some bits of information here which'll be useful, however disquieting. So the Dobuni and Atrebates are also joining Boadicea?—well, at least we've got the Regni with us.'

'As auxiliaries, sir?'

'Yes. The old King Cogidumnus let us have a couple of thousand men. They're not up to our regulars, of course, but they'll fight all right.'

'How many are we altogether, sir?' asked Quintus. He had been speculating anxiously on this question with Dio and Fabian, and was not sure he would be trusted with such an important military secret. But Petillius had throughout this interview been treating him without consciousness of rank and he answered at once.

'Our force consists of the full Fourteenth, six thousand in all, a third of the Twentieth, plus the Regni and a sprinkling of Cantii warriors from Kent. We have altogether a bare ten thousand.'

They were both silent, thinking of Boadicea's forces, which now numbered sixty thousand at least—probably more.

'Yes,' said Petillius, reading Quintus' expression. 'It is not a very bright picture.' He made a sharp, dismissing gesture with his hand and changed the subject. 'All that Druid business you told me is interesting. So you think you have forgotten a day, do you?'

'Yes, sir. I'm sure of it. I'm beginning to think I got to Stonehenge, for I keep remembering little bits. I think I met the Arch-Druid too—he was Regan's—that's the girl—Regan's grandfather.'

'Aha,' said the General thoughtfully. 'I met Conn Lear once—a remarkable man. I don't agree with our Governor that all Druids should be exterminated—but that's neither here nor there. Tell me every single thing you can remember about the Druid stronghold.'

Quintus complied, and the General listened carefully. Then he said, 'Quintus, you had some special reason for volunteering to take that mission to the west, didn't you? I could see that.'

'Yes, sir, to find the bones of my ancestor, Gaius Tullius, who was killed there by the Druids during Cæsar's campaign.'

'And did you find them?'

Quintus shook his head. 'I'm sure I didn't. I seem to remember speaking about it, and that someone—Conn Lear, I think—grew frightfully angry.'

'And was the girl angry too?—ah, never mind, I shouldn't have asked that.' Petillius smiled. He started to say something else, but they both turned as a messenger ran into the tent and, kneeling, murmured to the General. Petillius rose. 'This is what I've been expecting. The Governor has decided on a course of action. He'll speak to the troops at sunset.'

'What course of action, sir?' asked Quintus quietly.

'Do you need to ask?' The General looked into Quintus' earnest face, then glanced towards the pegs where his own magnificent armour hung, the crested helmet with the red horsehair fringe, the ceremonial shield, and gilded sword. 'We fight.'

'Thanks be to Mars,' Quintus murmured, and meant it. Soon now the long-drawn-out suspense would be ended. Yet, deep within him, for the first time he was aware of cowardly shrinking —a hollow feeling. On the plank floor it was as though he saw Flaccus' dead eyes staring up at him. 'I'm young; I don't want to die yet.' The sentence flashed through his mind as though someone else spoke it, but his face showed nothing as he stood respectfully awaiting orders.

'Before we go out to hear the Governor,' said Petillius after a moment's silence, 'there's one—ah—detail—to be attended to.'

'Yes, sir,' said Quintus, and waited. His General walked to the camp table and picked up a square of parchment and a white staff about two feet long.

'For you,' said Petillius, handing the parchment to Quintus, who looked down to see his name jump out at him in heavy black script, '*Quintus Tullius Pertinax*, standard-bearer to the third cohort, Ninth "Hispana" Legion of the imperial troops. . . .' There were a lot more words that Quintus skipped over in a daze, because all he could see were the last ones that seemed to ring out like a shout: '. . . *from this time forth is promoted to* CENTURION'. He read them three times, and his face and neck flamed.

'For *me* . . .' Quintus whispered, staring at the parchment. 'Oh, General Petillius . . .'

'For you, Centurion,' said the General in a carefully light tone. 'You're very young and sometimes foolhardy—but you have courage, intelligence, and leadership, and you've shown a remarkable amount of ability in dealing with the Britons since you landed. I wish you to be one of my officers. Here's your badge of office.' He handed him the centurion's staff. 'Apply at once to the Quartermaster's department for the proper helmet and shield. AND,' he added sternly, cutting across Quintus' excited stammers of thanks, 'I believe my men refer to me as "old fusspot"—nevertheless, I command that you have a shave, a bath, and a haircut before I have to look at *you* again. HURRY UP!'

'Yes, sir,' breathed Quintus gratefully and ran.

It was certainly the sprucest, shiniest young centurion in all the legions who emerged from the barracks just before Governor Suetonius mounted the earth platform to address the troops.

The portions of Quintus' old uniform which he could still wear had been brought from Chichester and cleaned and polished by one of the auxiliaries. The crested helmet and the shield with its great, murderous boss in the centre were issued to him by the Quartermaster. They had belonged to some other centurion whose use for them was over, but Quintus did not let himself dwell on that. His own sword hung again at his belt and he carried the deadly Roman cavalry lance in one hand, his staff of office in the other. There hadn't been time to greet or saddle Ferox before Quintus strode across the parade-ground with the proud, long step of the Roman legionary, his tall figure followed by many approving eyes. Quintus had been popular in the Ninth, and the remnant of that demolished legion, now temporarily merged with the Fourteenth and Twentieth, had spread news of him. Dio and Fabian had been forbidden to tell the true story of their trip, but there were many who knew that, though the dangerous mission to Gloucester had somehow ended in failure, it had been gallantly carried through none-the-less.

Quintus had not yet been told what 'century' would be assigned to his command, so he walked over to join Dio, who was standing near the altar to Mars.

'*Well!*' cried Dio, bowing and saluting with excessive ceremony. 'Will you look at what's happened to our shabby little Silurian friend from the back hills? I tremble with awe. I am blinded by the glory.' And Dio covered his eyes with his hand.

'Oh, don't be an ass,' said Quintus, grinning and striking down Dio's hand. 'I'm the same simple boy at heart, no matter how gorgeous I may appear.'

'Don't you believe it,' Dio snorted. 'There never was born a sweet, simple boy who was also a Roman of Rome. Masters of the Earth, you people are, and now you *look* it too.'

For an instant of dismay, Quintus thought that Dio was jealous of his promotion and was hinting that it had come from the usual preference shown by the High Command for officers actually born in the imperial city.

Dio sensed this and his sparkling eyes softened. He shook his curly black head as he took Quintus' hand in a warm grasp. 'My silly jokes! Quintus, I congratulate you with all my heart, and so will Fabian when he knows. We expected it. And I'll make a prophecy. You'll be a tribune some day, and then a general yourself. A good one!'

Quintus returned the hand-clasp, much moved by this generous extravagance and feeling guilty that he should be eligible for promotion when his two friends were not. Official messengers such as they were attached to a legion's staff and bore no special rank, though they were very well paid.

'I wouldn't have got this,' said Quintus soberly, 'if my legion weren't so short of officers . . . and there weren't considerable doubt as to whether . . .' He did not finish the thought aloud— whether any of us lives long enough for a promotion to matter one way or the other—but Dio understood, nodded quickly, and said, 'Here comes the Governor.'

Suetonius' approach was heralded by solemn horn-blasts. He was a majestic figure as he mounted the platform and stood beneath the huge standard of imperial Rome—a solid silver eagle. Behind him were grouped the smaller standards of the legions represented here tonight: the Twentieth, the Fourteenth, and the Ninth.

A spontaneous cheer broke from the packed troops below as Suetonius looked down on them, and the Governor's heavy face lightened into a smile. He raised his arm slowly in acknowledgment.

When the outbreak had died down, Suetonius leaned forward and began to speak in a strong, confident voice which gave to the troops no inkling of the shock and dismay he had shown earlier in his tent.

They would wait no longer for the Second Legion, said Suetonius. It was unfortunately delayed. But they could manage very well without it! One thoroughly trained Roman soldier was worth a dozen scatter-brained savages. They all knew that. And they had but to remember the many glorious Roman victories in the past when a handful of legionaries had easily vanquished a whole host of the enemy. Besides, it seemed that the British forces included women, and were led by a woman!

'Almost,' cried Suetonius with infinite scorn, 'am I ashamed to command that we do battle with such a weak and miserable foe! Yet too long this silly, painted people, this woman-led rabble, has been allowed to have its head. Yes, there have been unfortunate incidents, it's true. There have been disasters you all know of—to one of our legions—to the towns of Colchester, London, and St Albans—but we must forget these! Nor consider that they represent anything but temporary set-backs!'

'H-mm,' whispered Dio to Quintus. 'Brave words . . .'

'And much needed . . .' nodded Quintus, himself impressed by the powerful, assured voice, and whole-heartedly admiring the Governor as he never had before.

'You must not think of past disasters,' the voice continued, 'EXCEPT as they fill your heart with zeal to fight and avenge Romans who have been slaughtered, and other innocent people who have suffered hideous fates, deaths inflicted by these unruly hordes who are little better than beasts—and here, there's one thing I must warn you of! Like wild beasts these barbarians whom we shall fight make howlings and shriekings and fearful noises when they do battle. To this you will shut your ears, each one of you in grim, determined silence, performing your appointed task—as it shall be allotted to you!'

Then Suetonius spoke to them in some detail, telling them the general plan he had made. They would march in the morning, cross the Thames, and take up a position north of it in Epping Forest, a position which he had chosen after long consultation both with maps and with some of the London refugees who knew the terrain well. He had reason to believe that Boadicea's forces were on the move and would arrive at that spot in about two days; then they would fight. More than that it was unnecessary for the legions to know. Their officers would acquaint them with special orders.

In conclusion, Suetonius suddenly turned, and grabbing the great silver eagle from the chief standard-bearer, held it in the air and cried, 'As our imperial eagle rises high above our heads, so will the winged Victory soar above us! And we shall win through to law and justice, win through to honour, win through to the greater glory of our beloved and eternal Rome!'

'Ave! Ave! Ave!' thundered the troops. 'Salve! Roma! Roma Dea!' Then they cheered the Emperor and the Governor, and clashed swords on shield in their exuberance.

The enthusiastic cries resounded for some time unchecked, while Suetonius, with the two generals and his staff officers, walked back to his tent.

'That was a good speech,' said Quintus on a long, shaky breath. His eyes shone. 'I'd no idea the Governor was such an orator. He managed to remove all the qualms I confess I had. But how do you suppose he knows when Boadicea's apt to turn up at the place he's picked?'

'Cantii spies,' said Dio, who had been talking with his friends during the time Quintus was cleaning up and dressing. 'Several of them have been sneaking around up north, keeping track of Boadicea's forces. They tell me one of our spies got back here just before we came.'

'Oh,' said Quintus thoughtfully. 'And I suppose Boadicea has spies watching *us*?'

Dio nodded. 'It seems they caught two Iceni in that wood over there the other day. One wouldn't tell anything even under torture, but the other admitted Boadicea's forces were almost out of food, and she was on the march preparing to wipe us out and overrun the south, where she must think we've left more food than there is.'

Quintus would have conjectured further as to the exact site Suetonius had chosen and the military tactics involved, but an orderly came up and, saluting, inquired if this were the centurion Quintus Tullius Pertinax? Upon receiving Quintus' rather flustered assent, he announced that the new centurion was to report to headquarters for orders.

The next morning at dawn, when the Roman army marched from camp, Quintus rode on Ferox at the head of the century of ninety men that had been assigned to him. His company was composed of auxiliaries—all of them Regni from Sussex, on their native ponies, except for three men of the regular cavalry who had belonged to the Ninth, part of Quintus' original cohort.

Quintus was proud of his first command. The Regni were a tall, fair, Belgic tribe, much Romanized, as their Sussex coast, like that of the Cantii in Kent, had always been in close touch with Gaul across the water. They were fine horsemen, already well-trained in the use of cavalry weapons, and were pleased to have been assigned to a real Roman who understood much of their language. They showed this by extra smartness and co-operation as the legions marched along the broad road, then forded the Thames at Chelsea.

Ferox leaped up the far bank of the river in one great bound. The horse had had no exercise for days and was, moreover, so glad to see his master that he was prancing with excitement and had to be continually curbed.

'Quiet down, you black imp,' Quintus whispered affectionately. 'I'd like a tearing gallop just as much as you would, but we're not going to get it!' He patted the gleaming, black satin neck, and Ferox slewed a bright eye round and wuffled as though he had understood.

Quintus reined to one side of the bank, carefully watching the remainder of his company splash through the ford, and found himself near one of his men, a stocky little Italian called Rufus, with whom he had played many a ball game in the garrison at Lincoln.

'Ferox is so mettlesome today,' remarked Quintus amiably. 'I'll bet you he could beat your horse by a mile, pig or no pig!' This referred to a race he'd run against Rufus in Lincoln, which had been a standing joke in the garrison because of a pig which had entangled itself amongst the contestants. Rufus had never before failed to defend the merits of his own horse, and Quintus was startled to have him smile politely and say, 'Yes, sir. No doubt.'

Jupiter, thought Quintus, he answers me the way we did Flaccus! A gulf had opened; he had become a thing apart, an officer. It was a rather lonely state, and Rufus had quite rightly reminded him of it. Quintus soberly counted his company, saw that they were all there, and gave the order to proceed.

Ahead and behind Quintus' century, the legions marched, four abreast, like a broad, shining ribbon of gold unrolling under the hot, late August sun.

They advanced along the river road until they came to an island in the Thames on their right, the marshy Isle of Thorns, where there were a couple of native huts raised on piles, with blue curls floating up from the smoke-vents.

Governor Suetonius, with most of the legions, had already marched past the island, to the rhythmic pounding of sandalled feet, and Quintus' company had reached a point near the island when he thought he heard a voice calling his name. He couldn't be sure above the clop-clop of the horses, but he looked around startled.

'Quintus!' cried the voice again—a man's voice—and suddenly out from behind a thicket on the bank there rode a familiar figure. It was a Roman legionary on a drooping, mud-caked horse, a legionary in tarnished armour. The face was half hidden by the helmet and chin-strap, but before the horseman got near him, Quintus recognized the arrogant set of the head, and in the repetition of his name he heard a defiance not unmixed with nervousness.

'So it is you—Lucius Claudius,' said Quintus tonelessly, as the new-comer wheeled his horse into step beside Ferox. 'What do you want?'

'The legions are on the march again?' said Lucius, his handsome face bent down, not quite looking at Quintus. 'I saw Suetonius pass some time ago. I waited until you came along.'

'You saw from where?'

Lucius hitched his shoulder backwards. 'From there, the Isle of Thorns, where I've been—been—staying.'

'You found natives to receive you—Lucius? To keep you in safety, even though Boadicea's forces must have overrun this bank?'

'No—not here. She turned north for St Albans before she got here. I found a British woman, a Catuvellauni, who has given me shelter in her hut.'

A woman, of course, Quintus thought. So that's where he's been this three weeks!

'Then you had better go back to her, Lucius Claudius. You'll have more need of her protection than ever, since we are going to fight, and Boadicea's forces have grown immeasurably since that disaster to the Ninth, *part* of which you may remember.'

Lucius caught his breath, his knuckles whitened on the bridle. 'What's happened to you, Quintus?' he cried sharply. 'You were my friend. Oh, I see they've made you a centurion, and I suppose it's gone to your head. But you've no right to speak to me like this! You *all* retreated. It was every man for himself!'

Not until our General gave the command, Quintus thought, and, as it happened, *I* was captured—but he rode on in silence for a while, somewhat ashamed of the bitterness with which he had spoken, aware of the bond between them, the old friendship Lucius had invoked. And yet unable to really trust again.

'Why have you come out of hiding, Lucius?' he said at last in a cold voice.

'I'm sick of the filthy natives and that mud hut. I want to get back where at least I can hear my own language,' said Lucius flippantly.

'Then gallop up ahead until you find General Petillius. Report to him. He's a just man. He'll decide what he wants you to do.'

Lucius reached over and put his hand on Quintus' arm. His lazy, persuasive voice held all its old, warm charm as he said, 'Why can't I ride along with you, Quintus? The High Command'd never know. You're an officer, you can do what you like. I'll fall behind amongst your men. No one'll notice. By Mercury, I've missed you—my old comrade!'

Quintus felt a sinking in his chest. He remembered the cowardly thoughts he had himself suffered yesterday. He remembered all the loyalty he had once felt for Lucius. He thought that perhaps if Lucius was really ashamed and wanted to make amends, he should be spared further ignominy—until after the battle. But—Quintus forced himself to consider the other side, for he was an officer now with full responsibility—the legions depended on discipline. They were going forth to a great battle in which no individual's private feelings should count. And Lucius was—quite simply—a deserter. The decision could not be Quintus'.

'I'm sorry,' he said at last. 'You can't hide here with me. If you want to rejoin the legions, you must report to our General.'

'He hates me, Quintus, he always has—he'll put me in irons—he'll have me flogged—I won't——'

'Then go back to the Isle of Thorns—where you can skulk the rest of your days. I'll not give you away.'

Lucius gave him a strange look. There was hatred in it, and yet there was appeal. The slack-mouthed young patrician face for a moment showed a sort of confused despair. Quintus set his jaw and turned his head.

Lucius slowly pulled up his horse's reins and rode out of the column. He stayed a moment by the roadside, then disappeared into the trees, in what direction Quintus could not see. And Quintus was miserable.

Soon, on the march, they forded the little Fleet River and passed the ruins of London—acres of black rubble and ashes, a devastation even worse than Colchester had been.

The faces of the legionaries grew pale and set as they remembered the thriving little town as it had been so short a time before, and remembered the thousands of wretched people who had stayed there to be slaughtered.

The legions turned north and marched some miles along the ancient British trackway until, in the heart of Epping Forest, they reached the strategic spot which had been previously picked by Suetonius. It was a funnel-shaped ravine, with just room enough for the disposal of the Roman forces at the narrow end, which was backed by dense underbrush and forest. The steep-sided funnel opened out on to a gravelly plain, also enclosed by rolling banks and forest.

Quintus at first did not understand the special advantages of this site, until the Governor ordered his whole force into battle formation, and they practised over and over throughout the remaining hours of daylight, and on into the night, until every man knew his place and exact part. The foot soldiers, each armed with two javelins or pila, a light one and a heavy one, were wedged in the centre, thick and deep, for a thin, strung-out line could not hope to hold against Boadicea's immensely superior force. The cavalry were placed on the flanks, which meant riding the lower rises of the ravine. The legions were not to move as the Britons came into view. They were to wait with their shields above their heads to form a roof, until Suetonius gave the signal to throw the first barrage of the deadly Roman javelins. Suetonius himself enacted the part of Boadicea's force in these grim rehearsals, galloping from the north, along the trackway into the plain in front of the ravine, judging the exact distance necessary to be kept between the two armies, scrutinizing the placement of all his troops, and finally watching the exact effect as he gave the signal for action.

At midnight the troops were permitted to rest. Each man munched the dried beef he had brought with him and drank brook water. Quintus did the same and, after presenting Ferox with a small bag of oats, went to find General Petillius.

The generals and tribunes were in conference with Suetonius beside a small camp fire on the edge of the ravine. The army had travelled unencumbered; not even the Governor had a tent. Quintus had to wait some time before Petillius, with a grave nod of agreement to the Governor, walked away from the fire, and saw him.

'Well, Centurion, what's the matter? Trouble with your new command?'

'Oh, no, sir. They're a fine bunch. Forgive me for disturbing you, but—did Lucius Claudius Drusus find you today?'

'Lucius Claudius Drusus?' Petillius frowned. 'You mean that Optio who deserted? Certainly not. What do you mean?'

'This, sir,' said Quintus unhappily, and told the story of his meeting with Lucius, though he did not say where it had happened or reveal Lucius' hiding-place. 'I don't know if I did right. He—I think now that he was desperately ashamed—underneath. I think he wanted to fight, and we need every man we can get—but——'

'But he has a rotten streak. It's the curse of aristocratic Rome nowadays and even our Emperor Nero——' Petillius checked himself. 'No, you did right, Quintus. If he had come, I wouldn't have been too hard on him. Forget it, and go and get some rest.'

CHAPTER X

*Memory restored—the sound of a trumpet—a problem of
loyalty—the defeat of Boadicea—dreams and fever—hopes for
the future*

SOME OF THE SEASONED LEGIONARIES slept a little that night
of waiting in the ravine, but Quintus was amongst those who
did not. He sat down near Ferox with his back against a rock;
and, staring into the night, thought long thoughts. He thought
about his mother and his sister in Rome, and about the quest
which had brought him to Britain in the first place and which
had once seemed the most important thing in the world. Then
he thought of Regan. He wore her brooch still, pinned now to
his white linen tunic beneath the centurion's shining breastplate
—Regan, far away on the other side of Britain in the Arch-
Druid's weird house of the living tree. It was there by the tree
that he had kissed her, there they had both admitted the love
between them.

'You won't remember this, Quintus—or I couldn't have let it
happen . . .' But he *did* remember now! Suddenly, as he sat there
in the ravine waiting for the battle, the last mists lifted. The herb
of forgetfulness had ceased to cloud that strange day's memory.

'Regan,' he whispered, sending her a prayer of longing so
strong that he felt it must reach her. Then he got up abruptly,
for the soft, pink dawn was breaking through the trees. He
examined Ferox in detail—his hoofs, his saddle, bit, and bridle
—before he moved amongst his men, rousing those that were
asleep, telling them all to check their own horses and weapons
again.

He said good morning to Rufus, who saluted and said, 'Looks
like a fine day, sir.'

'It does indeed,' answered Quintus, turning to see Dio and
Fabian behind him.

'Fine day for walloping queens?' chuckled Dio. 'We came to
breakfast with you, a sentimental gesture. *Viva* the wheat cake!'
He crunched one between strong, white teeth.

Fabian gave Quintus his slow smile and said, 'Dio's only con-
cern is his stomach, as you may remember.'

'I remember,' Quintus grinned back, deeply glad to see them, knowing, though neither of them gave any indication of it, that they had wanted to say good-bye—in case. 'Where've you two been placed?'

'In the middle of the Fourteenth, fifth cohort, just behind the shock troops,' said Fabian. Both young messengers were dressed in full legionary armour today, carrying the light and heavy javelins and the short sword. Their oblong shields hung ready on their backs.

'I, in fact, am in a superb position,' announced Dio airily. 'It's a handy thing to be somewhat small—by stooping a little I find I can keep myself thoroughly hidden behind the enormous Gaul in front of me—most convenient.'

Quintus and Fabian, who both knew Dio's courage, ignored this nonsense, and Quintus said, 'I wonder what time we may expect to be honoured by Boadicea's arrival?'

'Not long after sunrise, I should think,' answered Fabian. 'One of the Cantii spies was sure she camped this night at Braughing.'

As he finished speaking a trumpeted 'alert' sounded through the ravine.

'Well, here we go on our merry way,' said Dio, clapping Quintus on the shoulder. 'Good hunting!'

'And to you,' answered Quintus.

They shook hands all round. As Fabian and Dio sped back down the sides of the ravine towards their posts, they each paused at a rude little stone altar to Jupiter that the men had set up. They touched it reverently in passing.

Yes, thought Quintus, who had made vows at that altar earlier. May the great supreme god have Rome in his keeping this day. . . . He turned to make sure that each of his men had mounted.

The sun rose brick-red over the forest top. Its rays slanted briefly into the ravine where the legions waited, but then clouds gathered and the sky turned pearl-grey. A cool breeze began to blow from the north. Still nothing happened. The horses moved uneasily, now and then nibbling at the sparse grass. The men murmured to each other in subdued tones. There was a break in the tension when the Governor rode up on his huge bay horse, while Quintus and his company snapped smartly to attention.

Suetonius ran his eyes over the men's positions and their equipment.

'Repeat your orders, Centurion,' he said to Quintus.

'Wait. . . . Don't move while the legions make the first on-slaught after your signal, Excellency. Then charge here'—Quintus pointed right along the slope—'following General Petillius Cerealis round our own men below and veer down amongst the enemy to meet our left cavalry wing behind enemy lines.'

The Governor nodded. 'A pincer action. General Petillius will decide when to veer.' He jerked his bridle and rode off to inspect the next centurion and company behind Quintus. In two hours Suetonius had checked all his troops and returned to a place in the centre rear of the foot-soldiers.

This is a dream, and nothing is ever going to happen, Quintus thought after a while, when, like all of them, he had repeatedly strained his eyes towards the far end of the gravelly plain outside the ravine. There was no hint of sun now, nor any rain either, only the murky grey sky and the fitful breeze.

It was the breeze that brought them the first warning, just as Quintus had tested for the twentieth time the sharpness of his lance's nine-inch iron point and shifted the weight of the heavy shield on his forearm.

A quiver ran through the silent, massed legions as they heard a distant hullabaloo, a confusion of rumblings and shoutings from the north. The Governor's trumpeter let out a low, pulsating blast.

As one man, the legions behind the front row raised their shields and clanked them into place above their heads to form the famous Roman 'testudo', a metal roof impervious to falling spears, arrows, or stones. And they waited. The sounds to the north grew louder, but there was still nothing to be seen.

Quintus, concentrating on watching the plain ahead, did not hear rolling pebbles and stumbling hoofs behind him, until Ferox shied as another horse's nose hit his croup. Quintus turned sharply and saw Lucius looking at him with the same expression of uncertain bravado he had had when he appeared by the Isle of Thorns.

'What in Hades——?' breathed Quintus. 'How'd *you* get here?'

'Followed the legions, waited through the night—came along the trail—down the side of the ravine.'

'Well, get over there, out of that man's way! Don't raise your lance or move, until you see me move. Watch General Petillius up ahead on the white stallion for the signal, d'you understand?

Lucius swallowed. 'You despise me, Quintus—don't you?—I mean, "Yes, sir, my Centurion, I understand," ' he added bitterly, but, obeying, he moved up the slope to the place indicated by Quintus.

Then Quintus forgot Lucius, forgot everything but the far end of the plain, as thousands of howling British warriors galloped into sight through the trees.

The plain rapidly blackened with advancing figures brandishing clubs and spears and small, round, bronze shields. Here and there Quintus discerned an archer, and then he saw, thundering behind the mounted warriors, a line of war-chariots, the murderous, curved knives flashing round on the hubs of the wooden wheels.

The Romans did not move. They made no sound. The Britons could have no idea of their numbers, because the funnel-shaped site disclosed only the point of the legionary wedge.

The Britons, gazing down the plain towards the ravine, let out yells of triumph and paused well out of range, apparently waiting for something. Quintus had a good view from the slope and soon saw what they were waiting for—when a large war chariot lumbered into view.

There was no mistaking its occupants.

Boadicea, tall as any of the chiefs in the chariots near her, was shouting and brandishing a spear. Her masses of tawny yellow hair whipped in the wind. On her head was a bronze helmet; on her chest the gleam of the royal golden gorget. Behind her crouched the two red-headed Princesses, clinging to the chariot's high sides as their mother lashed the horses and drove frenziedly amongst her suddenly quietened forces.

Quintus could see that she was shouting to her troops, and he caught isolated phrases, 'Avenge!' 'Rid our land of the hated tyrants!' 'Kill them all—no mercy!' As she shouted this she reined in her horses and shook back a fold of her streaming mantle. A small animal jumped out and leaped to the ground.

Quintus saw long ears on the little beast. Their sacred hare, he thought, as the Britons let out a wild tumult of exultation, for the hare had turned and darted away to the east.

'Victory! Andraste! Andraste! The hare runs towards the sun for victory!' The Queen's harsh cry of triumph could be heard over all the rest.

They were drunk, Quintus thought, drunk with confidence as well as the heather ale they had undoubtedly been swilling all night. They seemed unaware that the Roman forces might have charged, by now, so absolutely certain of invincibility had the Britons become through their recent unchecked conquests. No doubt they thought the Romans held back from fear. But they were advancing now, the Britons, in a great, disorderly mass, pushed forward by arrivals at their rear. There were wagons, hundreds of them, wagons apparently filled with women and even children; Quintus could see long, flying hair.

By Mars, and are they as sure as *that*! he thought with dismay that changed to anger. They had brought their families as spectators to watch the massacre of the Romans, as one might go to the Circus Maximus to watch the punishment of slaves.

And there were so many of them! It was true then that half the British tribes had joined Boadicea, for there were many thousands of warriors in that packed, advancing horde, not counting the civilians drawn up in wagons on the far side of the plain.

Now it's coming, Quintus thought, and a thrill ran through him, though he felt no fear, only a cold, calculating expectation. Boadicea's chariot had disappeared into her ranks, while mounted tribal chiefs took her place. Towards the right, opposite Quintus' position, he recognized Navin by the Trinovante helmet. 'And so the time you prophesied is here, Navin, and we meet as enemies,' Quintus murmured grimly to himself.

The British front line was quickly forming. It was composed of archers, as the Romans had expected, and stone-throwers. Quintus glanced at Petillius' erect back on the white stallion and then involuntarily behind at Lucius. The young man's face was glistening, putty grey, sweat was pouring down it into his chin strap.

'Good luck,' said Quintus softly, with a prick of pity, and never knew whether Lucius heard him or not, for the air exploded into a pandemonium of war-whoops and battle-cries, of twanging bows and the hiss of slingshots, followed by the harmless clatter and thump of the arrows and stones on the roof of shields above the legions.

The instant after, came the Roman trumpet blast and Suetonius' shout, 'Legions, *charge*!'

The shields came down again as in one motion, the flying wedge ran forward, and, as it ran, discharged the light pilum, the snake-thin, razor-sharp javelin that could fly as far as an arrow.

The oversure Britons were taken by surprise. The archers and slingers, with no chance to rearm, staggered back under the onslaught and went down beneath the javelins. The Roman wedge broadened, the heavy javelins followed the light ones. They penetrated to the line of wildly plunging horses. At this moment General Petillius shouted and put his stallion to the gallop. The right-wing cavalry streamed after him along the edge of the tumult. A spear whistled past Quintus' ear, but he ducked his head unnoticing, watching the General, who raised his lance in signal and veered left, straight down into the middle of the enemy amongst the milling horde of British chariots and foot-soldiers.

The left-wing cavalry met them there, and the Britons, utterly bewildered, found themselves battling enemies on all sides—enemies whose management of the lance, the short, slicing sword, the bossed shield, far surpassed the Britons' skill with cruder weapons. The heavy Roman armour turned blows for which the British had no protection.

Quintus had lost all awareness of himself. He had become a machine that cut, thrust, sliced, parried, and that yet managed Ferox, wheeling him between the swirling knives on the chariot hubs, spurring him into a momentary space away from a brandished club, and twisting to plunge his lance at a tartan-covered chest.

The world had turned blue—the blue of woad stripes and circles on the savage faces, and now it had turned to the red of blood.

At one time he felt a streak of fire run through his thigh and then forgot it. A wild Parisii lunged at Ferox's bridle, Quintus leaned over and bashed his face in with the sharp boss of his shield. The Parisii fell across the corpses of British horses, isolating Quintus behind a momentary bulwark; the fighting had surged forward and beyond him, as the Roman legions advanced with disciplined and murderous precision.

Quintus found that he was panting, and forcibly quietened his breath while he soothed the trembling Ferox. Then he stiffened, paralyzed at a sight not far from him, but across a barricade of overturned chariots and thrashing horses.

He saw General Petillius on foot, the white stallion dead beside him, fighting desperately with Navin, the Trinovante chief, who was still mounted. Navin's mouth was lifted in a snarl beneath the stripes of woad, his spear had knocked away the General's lance. Petillius was parrying the continual spear-thrusts with his shield and short sword, but the Briton was backing him steadily into a corner formed by overturned chariots. Navin's spear darted down again and again; Quintus with horror saw that Petillius was tiring. He lifted his own lance and aimed it at Navin's constantly whirling back, praying that it would carry that far, and not hit Petillius.

But while he still aimed and hunted for a chance to throw, a horseman streaked up to the fighting pair. Quintus saw the lightning gleam of a Roman lance plunging into Navin. He saw the spurt of blood from Navin's breast, then saw the chief in a reflex action hurl his spear straight at the Roman, who was knocked sideways by the impact and slid slowly off his horse and fell to the ground.

Quintus spurred Ferox, galloped to a better spot, then jumped the barrier and reached the three he had been watching. Petillius was standing, staring at the two men on the ground. The General was still dazed from the blows he had received, from the shock of nearly fatal combat.

He looked up at Quintus without surprise.

'The chief of the Trinovantes is dead,' he said, 'and it seems this lad has saved my life.'

'Lucius!' cried Quintus, gaping at the crumpled figure lying beside the dead chief.

'Ay—Lucius Claudius—so he came to fight, after all,' the General said in a wondering voice. 'But he's still breathing!' Petillius gave himself a shake and became his usual brisk self. He glanced down the plain where the fighting now was—a plain strewn high with mangled corpses of men and animals. British corpses. 'Here,' he said to Quintus, 'help me carry him under that tree.'

Navin's spear had cut deep through Lucius' armpit into the lung. Quintus and Petillius stopped the bleeding by binding the wound tight with Lucius' under-tunic, after laying him carefully down. He breathed in wheezing gasps as they left him, but his heart was beating well.

'Your horse is dead, sir,' said Quintus. 'Here's mine.'

The General nodded and mounted Ferox.

'Follow as quickly as you can,' he cried, and galloped along the side of the carnage.

When Quintus arrived on foot at the scene of battle, it was nearly over. The Britons' confidence had at last turned to terror.

They had tried to flee, though the Queen herself hoarsely begged them to fight on. But blind panic had seized them, and they had surged back in mad confusion, only to be stopped by their own cumbersome wagons, which now blocked the retreat. The wagons were full of women who had come to watch the sport.

The legions' work from then on had been easy, and they had carried it out with merciless thoroughness.

Thousands of Britons had been slaughtered by twilight of that day when the groans and shrieks of the dying lapsed to a silence broken only by long drawn-out wailings—the Celtic keening for the dead.

For Boadicea lay there too among her people, on the ground. Her shield was beneath her head, her spear beside her, the golden hair outspread. The terrible face of fury was calm now and white, and still. When she had seen the last of her people fall, she had not waited for the Roman capture, which she knew would come. There had been a tiny vial of poison hidden in her bosom, and she had swallowed the contents.

She had died on the British trackway at the north end of the battlefield with no one near her but her daughters and four old Icenian noblemen, her relatives. It was the dirge of the two Princesses that wailed through the evening of the Roman victory.

The Romans did not disturb them. This forbearance was General Petillius' doing. Suetonius would not have been so merciful. Even in the midst of his great triumph, he had been infuriated that Boadicea had eluded capture. He wished to seize the Princesses, at least, and drag the corpse of the rebel Queen throughout the land as an example.

Petillius had had the courage to combat his Governor, pointing out that such a course would make a martyr of Boadicea and keep the British flame of hatred so hot that never could the Romans hope to rule here peacefully.

'Show them that Romans can be merciful, Excellency,' he pleaded.

Suetonius consented grudgingly to let them mourn the Queen until he decided what to do with the Princesses. But before he had decided, they had gone. The six had taken their Queen with them and rolled away in a wagon along a secret path through the forest to bury her with their own rites.

While the dreadful keening of the Princesses could still be heard down the plain, Quintus and General Petillius had gone to Lucius, taking stretcher-bearers with them.

Lucius lay beneath the tree where they had put him. There was bloody froth on his mouth, but he looked up at them with a faint smile, and said, 'We won?'

'We won,' said Petillius. 'The most glorious triumph against the worst odds Rome has ever had. Thanks be to the gods. I believe we've not lost over four hundred men, while all the British forces are wiped out—and Boadicea dead.'

'Good,' gasped Lucius painfully. He turned towards Quintus. 'I surprised you, didn't I? You never thought to see *me* die a hero's death!'

His weak voice still had an edge of bitter mockery.

Petillius made a sign to the bearers, who carefully moved Lucius to the stretcher. 'I believe you will *not* die, Lucius Claudius,' said the General gently. 'You'll live to find that your brave act on the battlefield today has wiped out all that's gone before. It is forgotten.'

Lucius sighed and shut his eyes. The stretcher swayed as the bearers picked their way amongst the scattered corpses. Petillius and Quintus walked on either side. Suddenly Lucius spoke again in the dream voice of half consciousness. 'And yet I did not fight today either. I waited on the hillside watching, until the moment that I saw the General in danger—it was then only I forgot my fear.'

'I know,' said Petillius. '*All* that came before your slaying of the Trinovante chief is forgotten.'

'I'm a patrician. I'm the blood of our divine Emperor Claudius,' the voice went on, unheeding. 'I wasn't made to be a common soldier in a barbarian land. I've been miserable—full of hate and fear—hate and fear——'

'Hush!' said Petillius sternly, and the rambling voice stopped, though the laboured breathing continued.

Quintus' eyes stung, he swallowed hard against the dread that Lucius might die. He didn't try to understand the complex misery that Lucius had suffered—from self-indulgence, from cowardice, and arrogance combined—the rotten streak which had been redeemed by one selfless, gallant action. He felt only pity and the old affection, purged now of contempt.

They put Lucius down on a bed of leaves at the back of the ravine, amongst the other wounded, and the Fourteenth's skilful surgeon examined his injury by firelight and gave the young man a powerful medicine to drink. 'I think he may pull through, sir,' said the surgeon to Petillius. 'Too soon to tell—— Hello,' the surgeon added, looking at Quintus, 'you seem to have quite a bit of gore yourself, Centurion. Is it yours or some Briton's?'

Quintus looked down in astonishment and saw that his left thigh and upper leg were a shiny mass of clotted blood. 'I hadn't noticed,' he said ruefully, though now he remembered the streak of fire he had felt in his thigh.

'You *will*,' said the surgeon grimly, while he washed the leg in warm water. 'Stiff as a log this'll be tomorrow! You'll have something to remember the battle by for quite a bit.' He drew together the edges of a great, jagged spear-gash. 'Lie down there beside your friend while I bandage this.'

So Quintus lay down on the leaves beside the sleeping Lucius, and found that he was very glad to do so. But he was happy. An exultation shared by all the exhausted troops, too deep for loud rejoicing, almost too strong for realization; and yet some, like Quintus, suspected that this was a moment the world would not forget.

Roman rule was once again established in Britain.

The next three weeks were a haze to Quintus, whose wound festered as almost all wounds did. He developed a high fever and was only dimly aware when he was taken back to base camp on the other side of the Thames and put in the tent hospital there. Various impressions penetrated the jumble of battle dreams, home dreams, and love dreams that chased each other through his confused brain.

He knew that Dio and Fabian had both escaped injury, beyond a few cuts and bruises, and that they came to see him. He knew that of his own company only one auxiliary had been killed, that the over-all fatalities had been miraculously few and almost entirely suffered by the infantry's shock troops.

He knew that Lucius, who lay in a different hospital tent, still lived, though he was not out of danger.

At last there came a day when Quintus awoke without fever, felt an interest in breakfast, and managed to sit up shakily to consume it. While he was eating, Dio trotted into the tent bearing a plate on which reposed a bunch of fragrant, purple grapes. 'Aha! So we're much better, I see!' said Dio, squatting down by Quintus' pallet, and shoving the grapes under his nose. 'Look what I've brought you!'

'Jupiter Maximus!' whispered Quintus, sniffing. 'I haven't seen anything like those since I left Rome. How in the world . . .?'

'A ship, loaded with provisions for us, arrived yesterday from Gaul. It's tied up at London, which, by the way, we've already started to rebuild!'

'A cargo of *grapes*?' exclaimed Quintus, with the first real smile he had produced since the battle.

'Well—no. There were a few bunches destined for His Excellency. I happened to be around when they were unpacked—and so——' Dio shrugged expressively, pulled off a grape, and popped it in his mouth. 'I doubt whether the Governor's much interested in grapes right now, anyway.'

'Oh?' Quintus leaned back on the straw pillow. 'Not trouble?'

Dio looked around quickly before replying. Quintus, as an officer, had been given a corner of the tent, slightly isolated, and the patient nearest him was asleep. 'The trouble is of Suetonius' own making,' said Dio seriously and very low. 'We've got a new procurator, Julius Classicianus, sent direct from Rome. A really good fellow, not like that fat scoundrel of a Catus who started the whole Icenian mess. I've been back and forth a lot with messages to Classicianus, so I know what he's like.'

'But what's the trouble, then?' asked Quintus. 'Unless Suetonius doesn't like sharing the rule of Britain again with a civilian.'

'Exactly. Suetonius is a superb general and man of war, and he's puffed up over his extraordinary victory. Can't blame him. But, the trouble is, he won't stop fighting. He wants to go on slaughtering Britons and making examples and crushing what's left of a people who are thoroughly beaten already. He's even beginning to anger our allies, like the Regni. Classicianus wants all this stopped.'

'I believe General Petillius feels that way too,' said Quintus after a thoughtful moment. 'That Rome has always managed to make friends with conquered nations—once they're subdued. Look at the Gauls, the Spaniards, the Germans—and all the rest of them; they're as loyally Roman now as we are.'

'As a matter of fact, *I'm* mostly Greek,' said Dio, with his little chuckle. 'Which clinches the argument. That's enough deep talk for a dashing young centurion who's been as balmy as a butterfly for weeks. You scared me one day when you took me for an Icenian and tried to throttle me, but you terrified Fabian another time when you called him "Regan" and tried to *kiss* him!'

'Great gods——' said Quintus, reddening. 'Did I?'

'You did, my lad. . . . Well, I'd better be going. Got to report in a few minutes. Hope I get sent to London again. It's unbelievable how quickly it's being cleaned up. Of course, we got all those troops in from Germany.'

'Troops?'

'To be sure; you don't know. Replacements for the Ninth. Your legion's being built up fast. They landed last week. Suetonius announced he was glad they didn't get here for the battle; more glory the way it was.'

Dio grinned affectionately and turned to go, but Quintus stopped him.

'Wait a minute, Dio—I've been wondering—in my lucid moments—what about the Second? Did it ever come at all?'

Dio sobered and leaned over Quintus' pallet. 'Three days after the battle, Suetonius sent the General of the Fourteenth and a vexillation of a thousand men to Gloucester. They found the situation much as we left it; Valerianus still mad, Postumus still shut up by himself in an agony of pig-headed dumbness. But this time . . .' Dio paused with a shrug, letting his hands fall open. 'This time the Prefect, Postumus, was *forced* to face the truth. When they finally got it through that ox-brain of his how he had dishonoured his legion, made it a laughing-stock, and shamefully disobeyed his Governor and his Emperor . . . well . . . he ran himself through with his sword.'

There was a silence, while both young men thought of the strange experiences in Gloucester's fortress. Then Dio added, 'They've got a new General now. Promoted one of the tribunes. . . . So long, Quintus; I've got to run.'

After Dio had gone, Quintus ate his grapes and stared up at the tent roof. His thigh-wound ached, and he was weak, but his mind was quite clear and capable of thinking through certain personal problems.

His thoughts started with Postumus' suicide and travelled back to the Arch-Druid's house at Stonehenge. Now that every detail of that lost day was vivid to him, he remembered the surprise he had felt that Conn Lear had let him proceed to Gloucester, and suddenly he saw the old man's sad, stern face as he had said, 'And you—young Roman soldier—will go to summon the Second Legion as it is your destiny to do, *but*——' And there had been the peculiar smile in his eyes, as he added, 'No matter, you'll find out for yourself. . . .'

And Quintus guessed now what he had meant. The Arch-Druid had foreseen that Quintus' mission would be a failure. As everyone knew, there were some people who could tell the future.

The augurs and the sybils could, and the prophets. And Conn Lear had said another thing. 'There will be blood and yet more blood, anguish for my people—and in the end——' *Disaster for them*—those were surely the words Conn Lear had not spoken, and the reason for his dreadful sadness. He had foreseen that Rome would conquer, had seen the coming of twilight to the Celts.

In his ears now Quintus heard again the agonized wailing of the Princesses by their mother's body on the battlefield. He had scarcely noticed it then, had felt nothing but exultation that the fierce, terrifying Queen was dead. But now there was no more cause for hatred and much cause for anxious uncertainty— because of Regan. She had said, 'Your people and mine . . . killing each other . . . it's no use, Quintus . . . there can never be a future for us . . . '

But she had given him the brooch.

I must get back to her, Quintus thought, I must find out. . . . But how? He was a centurion responsible for a company. As soon as he was on his feet, he knew what his orders would be: either work detail in London or return to their own garrison at Lincoln. The life of a Roman soldier did not allow for romantic excursions.

Nor were these things the only barriers to his love for Regan. Roman soldiers were forbidden to marry Britons. He had managed to forget that fact in the vague, rosy dreams he had had in the past. Impractical fantasies they were, he saw now with the clarity of convalescence and of the new maturity the violent experiences of the last months had given him.

It was a grave and quiet Quintus that Petillius found when he entered the tent that afternoon.   'Surgeon says you're out of the wood now,' said the General, smiling and accepting a camp chair from a bowing orderly, to sit down by Quintus. 'That leg had us worried for a while. But you're a tough young sprout. You'll soon be riding Ferox as recklessly as ever. A very good horse that.'

'Yes, sir,' said Quintus, with a faint smile.

Petillius looked at him keenly. 'I've been sent a good many replacements, and more're coming. When you're able, you'll have your own proper century in the Ninth, instead of those auxiliaries. We'll pull out for Lincoln pretty soon, and after that we're probably going to be stationed at York to keep order in the north.'

'Yes, sir,' said Quintus. 'Thank you for telling me. . . . How's Lucius today, sir? Do you know?'

The General nodded. 'I've been to see him. He's not been doing well. The lung's almost healed, the surgeon thinks, but he's been very difficult—wouldn't speak or eat unless forced. But he's better now, since I saw him.' The twinkle appeared in Petillius' eyes. '*Much* better. Quintus, I'm invaliding Lucius Claudius out of the army and sending him back to Rome. You should have seen his face when I told him!'

'That's wonderful for Lucius, sir!' Quintus cried.

'Yes. He was always a misfit, and I owe him that much, poor fellow. He wants to see you, Quintus. Have yourself carried into his tent.'

'I will, sir.'

And Quintus thought that Petillius would certainly leave now, but he did not. He scratched his chin a minute, while gazing down thoughtfully at Quintus.

'His Excellency,' the General said at last, 'is having trouble believing that the rebellion is over, except of course for scattered demonstrations which *I* feel should be dealt with firmly but without bloodshed. . . . In fact most of the remaining north-east Britons are starving, since they were so sure of getting our provisions, they didn't bother to sow any crops. The new Procurator, Classicianus, is trying to help them out, which infuriates Suetonius. . . . I'm speaking very frankly to you, Quintus. You'll see why in a moment.'

Petillius frowned as though remembering an unpleasant incident.

And then he went on, 'Classicianus has unlimited civilian administrative powers from Nero and has managed to curb the Governor so far, but now Suetonius has started the Druid persecution again. If he can't fight Britons in general, he wants to at least exterminate Druidism—ah, I thought that would interest you,' said Petillius, smiling, as Quintus raised himself on his elbow and began to breathe faster.

'Classicianus, being a typical Roman senator with tolerant religious views, isn't at all interested in wiping out Druids, unless they're definitely hostile to us. However, he's compromised with Suetonius to the extent of permitting an investigation—a peaceful mission to that mysterious land of the western plain to confer with the Arch-Druid and ask his co-operation. The Governor and Procurator finally agreed on me as leader of this expedition, chiefly because I seemed to have special knowledge of Stonehenge and the Arch-Druid.'

The General paused and gave a dry chuckle. 'I did not mention that my knowledge came mostly from an impetuous young centurion, who had got himself romantically involved with the Druids and, moreover, has managed to forget the most important day of his whole experience with them!'

'Not any more, sir!' Quintus cried. It's *all* come back!'

'Fine,' said Petillius, rising. 'Then you'll be useful, I hope. I'm taking a full cohort, by Suetonius' orders, and we'll leave to-morrow.'

'Tomorrow . . .' Quintus whispered, glancing at his leg. 'Then you're not taking me, sir . . .' The disappointment was so black that he could not hide it and he bit his lip.

'Tomorrow, because I'm urgently needed in Lincoln and can't waste much time down here, and yes, I *am* taking you. You'll travel by litter until you're able to ride. And those are your orders.'

'Oh, thank you, sir,' said Quintus, his face transfigured.

'Not thanks, Quintus,' said the General sternly. 'It's neither from favouritism nor a sentimental desire to please you that you're included in this expedition. You're going because you can help Rome. Any romantic hopes you may be nourishing are entirely irrelevant. More than that—they are *forbidden*. You understand that?'

'Yes, sir. I understand.' Quintus meant it with all his heart. His loyalty to his General, his legion, and to Rome had become the most important thing in life to him—and yet he could not prevent himself from thinking that at least he would almost certainly *see* Regan again.

In a little while Quintus had himself carried into the tent where Lucius lay, and deposited beside that young man, who greeted him warmly.

'By Mercury, Quintus, I'm glad to see you. Heard you had a bad time with that leg. . . . Quintus, did the General tell you . . . ?'

Lucius, though he was pale, hollow-eyed, and had lost much weight, gave forth an eagerness that Quintus had never seen in him.

'Did the General tell me he was sending you home?' Quintus asked, smiling. 'Yes, he did. It's what you want, isn't it?'

'What I *want*,' repeated Lucius, his eyes shining. 'How could anybody help but want it?'

'Well, I don't,' said Quintus temperately, 'which is lucky, since I'm in for plenty more years' service here. But, as a matter of fact, I'm getting fond of the country. It has a lot of beauty when you get used to it.'

Lucius snorted almost in the old way. 'You're welcome to it, AND to the army. I'm through with that forever. Petillius said he'd write a letter to my father that would make it all right.' He paused, and Quintus, who had been about to offer congratulations, did not speak, for Lucius reddened and looked away, and moistened his lips in obvious embarrassment. He murmured after a moment, 'I hope you'll forget all—all the things I—I mean what happened here—Quintus, I'm awfully fond of you—I admire you. I always have.'

Quintus reddened in his turn. He gripped Lucius' thin arm in a quick clasp. 'Don't be a fool,' he said gruffly. 'We've both done a lot of floundering since we got here. I'll miss you.' He cleared his throat and said, 'Lucius, there's something I want you to do for me when you get to Rome. Will you?'

'Of course.'

'Deliver a letter to my mother, Julia Tullia. I'll get it ready tonight, because I'm going west with Petillius tomorrow. And also I've got a lot of army pay saved up. I want you to take a purse.'

Lucius nodded. 'I'll be glad to, and keep an eye on them too. You know my father—is not without influence,' he added with a trace of the old arrogance.

'I know,' said Quintus, chuckling. 'Some day I may write to ask you to use that influence to get Mother and Livia sent here to join me.'

'Great Jupiter! You wouldn't do that to them!'

'Some day—perhaps,' said Quintus softly. 'If there's peace. I think they'd like it. But no use talking of that now. And mind you, don't tell them about my wound, or anything to worry them.'

'I won't,' said Lucius. 'I'll just tell them you've become a puff-headed centurion and gone completely native as well!'

They grinned at each other, and Quintus signalled the orderlies to carry him back to his own tent. When he got there, he lay for a while and wondered what his mother would think if he mentioned Regan in the letter, and knew that he could make her understand, but what was the use? He sighed heavily. Nor could he report the slightest success in the quest. Well, but Julia had never expected success, anyway. She was a sensible woman. Quintus sighed again and set about composing a thoroughly cheerful letter that could in no way disturb his family.

CHAPTER XI

One hundred miles by litter—lost in a mist—Bran reappears—Stonehenge again—Conn Lear speaks—the quest is ended—Regan gives her love

EAGER AS HE WAS to get back to Stonehenge, Quintus was glad that the hundred-mile journey took them over five days, because he felt foolish in his horse-drawn litter and was extremely anxious not to appear before Regan in such a subdued, undashing way.

He had looked ridiculous enough last time she had seen him as a fake Silure, anyway. So he gritted his teeth over the first sharp pains in his thigh, ignored his spinning head, and daily mounted Ferox for brief periods. And his strength came back fast.

Their marching time was below standard for several reasons. As far as Calleva, the Atrebate capital, they were accompanied by several cohorts of the Fourteenth who were bound for their own garrison at Wroxeter. And they all paused overnight at Calleva, while Petillius and the General of the Fourteenth inspected the former Roman camp there and drew up plans for its rehabilitation.

Calleva itself was a city of mourning; doors were shut and barred, the streets were empty; but now and then at a window a woman's face would look out and gaze at the legions with a listless despair. In some of the isolated farms, where the news of defeat had taken longer to penetrate, they were still keening for their dead.

At one place an old woman with matted grey hair rushed out of a hut and spat directly at General Petillius, while she waved her skinny arms and screamed curses. The General rode on, apparently unnoticing.

But another time on the outskirts of Calleva they passed two well-dressed little girls with neat, blonde pigtails and bright tartan tunics fastened by rich brooches. The children were huddled under a tree, sobbing. They clung to each other frantically as the legions marched by, too frightened and bewildered to run away.

This time Petillius reined in his horse and spoke to the Regni interpreter who rode behind him. 'Ask the children why they are crying.'

Quintus heard the children's answer, when the interpreter had finally soothed their fear enough so they could speak. 'Because we're so hungry, and our father was killed, and we can't find our mother.'

Petillius smiled sadly down at the little girls and said to the interpreter, 'Take them back into Calleva, put them with some kind, trustworthy woman who can search for their mother. Tell them that the Romans are sending food to their town, and they need not go hungry any more, but give them some now.' He gestured to his orderly, who took a packet of marching rations from the General's own supply and handed it to the awe-struck children.

See, children, Quintus thought, all Romans aren't cruel monsters, as no doubt you've believed. And he hoped there would come a time when the beaten people might look on the Romans with something besides hatred, or the apathy of despair.

But as they left the land of the Atrebates and approached the great sacred plain, the feeling of the country changed. Here the war had brought no desolation or famine. The little farms looked prosperous; the natives watched the Romans pass with startled curiosity and drew together murmuring and wondering, for this country was apart from all previous Roman military travel, and the trackway they followed would have been hard to find without their Regni guide.

As it was, on the last day's march, when they had reached the edge of the great plain, they got lost. The Regni could not find a way amongst the myriads of tumuli and barrows that dotted the plain.

These strange grass-covered mounds—the burial places of the ancient people of long ago—made a landscape so weird and yet monotonous that the Romans marched in circles amongst them. All that day there was no sun to help them get their bearings— nothing but a fine, foggy drizzle through which they could not see more than a hundred yards.

When night had fallen, they gave it up and pitched camp. Soon afterwards the General sent for Quintus.

Quintus, who had seen little of the busy General since they left the Thames, limped hastily to Petillius' tent and presented himself.

The General greeted him with his quick smile, and said, 'Sit down—I'm glad to see you're getting around so well. . . . Now, have you *any* idea where we are?'

Quintus shook his head. 'I'm afraid not, sir. I came into the plain from the south, you know, and left it to the west, also I had a guide.'

'I thought I did too,' said Petillius dryly. 'That Regni said he knew this country like the back of his hand, but he obviously doesn't. What's more, I think he's frightened. He keeps saying the spirits of the dead are haunting him, and that the Druids have raised this mist so that we can't find Stonehenge.'

Quintus had a sneaking sympathy for the Regni. There was a strange atmosphere in the spot where they were. The dark, silent mounds of the dead seemed to press around them, as though they were watching.

'It's ridiculous,' said Petillius impatiently, 'that six hundred men should be lost like this. We must hope that the weather will clear.'

'I know we have to cross a big river—the Avon,' said Quintus hesitatingly. 'It would be west of us—if we knew where west was —I'm sorry I'm not more useful, sir.'

'I'll send scouts out at dawn to see if they can locate that river somehow,' said Petillius. Then he answered Quintus' rueful apology with his usual crisp justice. 'You can't help our being lost. I didn't expect you to be a guide. I've brought you along because the Arch-Druid knows you. WHEN we finally get to him, I hope he'll be more willing to negotiate because you're with us.'

'I don't really know if the Arch-Druid likes me or not, sir,' said Quintus frankly. 'There was a moment when he certainly didn't.'

He thought of Conn Lear's fury when he, Quintus, had mentioned Gaius Tullius.

'Well—but his granddaughter likes you, I gather,' said Petillius with the sly twinkle,' 'and it's amazing what women can accomplish when they want to.'

Quintus stiffened. His tone was cold as he said sharply, 'I'll not take advantage of Regan, sir, or any feeling she may have for me, since there can be nothing—no future—between us.'

The General raised his eyebrows, surveying the stern, handsome young face, the resolute set to the mouth. 'Indeed . . .' he said without any expression at all. 'So. . . . Good night, Centurion; that'll be all at present.'

Quintus went back to his tent, wondering uncomfortably if he had annoyed the General, and was startled at his own anger at the suggestion that Regan's love might be made a tool of. Calmer thoughts later showed him that the General's remark had been reasonable enough, viewed from the Roman side. But it was almost impossible for Quintus to use reason when it came to Regan, and one part of him actually began to hope that they never would get to Stonehenge.

It looked for a time next morning as though that hope were on the way to being granted. The drizzling mist continued. Petillius' scouts, who had orders not to go out of shouting distance lest they too get lost, came back from various sorties to report that they saw no sign of a river, or indeed of anything but more mounds and rolling downs.

The General had just given orders to march, anyway, in a direction the nervous Regni had guessed at, when the last scout returned with a captive. Quintus saw the commotion in front of the General's tent and heard loud, gobbling noises, so he rode over on Ferox to see what was happening.

The captive was Bran—the Arch-Druid's ape man. He was standing in front of the General, thumping his chest and pointing over his shoulder into the distance.

'He was watching us from a mound over there, sir,' the scout was explaining to Petillius. 'I can't make out what he is, sir.'

Quintus rode forward and saluting, said, 'I know who he is, General Petillius. It's the tongueless servant of the Arch-Druid that I told you about.'

As he spoke, Bran turned, and, upon seeing Quintus, broke into a wide grin; ducking out from under his captor's grip, he ran to Quintus.

'I see he knows you, all right,' said Petillius. 'Can you make out what he's trying to express?'

Quintus, relieved to find that his General's tone and expression were exactly as usual towards him, answered that he would try.

He questioned Bran slowly in Celtic, and the familiarity he had learned earlier with the stocky little man's sign language helped him to understand.

'I think, sir,' said Quintus at last, 'that he's been sent out by Conn Lear to look us over.' As he spoke the Arch-Druid's name, Bran nodded violently and flapped his hands like wings beside his head, to represent the high priest's ceremonial crown.

Petillius nodded.

'That seems likely, though how would Conn Lear know we were on the way?'

'Grape-vine, sir,' said Quintus. 'Some secret runner from the farms we passed. We've probably been watched all the time. I think Bran wants to guide us to Conn Lear—at least he wants to take us somewhere.'

Again Bran thumped his chest and pointed repeatedly.

'So it would seem.' Petillius studied the beetle-browed cave-man face, the long, brawny arms, the garment of mangy otter skins.

'But can we trust him? He might lead us into a bog—any kind of trap.'

'Bran would never've let himself be captured like that, sir, if he weren't friendly. As for where he's taking us, I'm sure——'

Quintus stopped. He was nearly sure of Bran, but there was a way to make certain, a way that cost Quintus a moment of sharp struggle.

His finer sense of duty and loyalty won, of course, reinforced as they were by shame because he had snapped at his General last night.

But Quintus could not prevent himself turning brick-red, as, under the startled eyes of Petillius, the scout, and several other officers, he fumbled inside his breastplate and pulled out Regan's brooch—the brooch no Roman had ever seen except Dio and Fabian.

A snicker from one of the other officers was sharply suppressed by the General as Quintus, holding the brooch under Bran's eyes, said solemnly, 'Do you swear by this Druid sign of the ruby snake that you are leading us in peace to Conn Lear?'

Bran stared at the brooch in obvious awe. He nodded slowly. Then he leaned over and placed his forehead on the brooch in token of submission.

'Bran has sworn by this Druid emblem, sir,' said Quintus. 'We can trust him.'

'Good,' said Petillius. 'Then we'll march at once.'

Bran led them in quite a different direction from that the Regni would have chosen, and in less than an hour they came to the river.

Soon after they had forded it, Quintus' heart began to beat fast. The mist lifted, a watery sun came out, and he recognized many features that he remembered; rows of grass-covered earth rings, a particularly long barrow, shaped like a crouching lion. And then they saw ahead the long avenue of upright stones that led to the great temple.

When Quintus had seen the avenue before, it had been thronged with Britons going to the festival of Lugh. Today it was deserted as the Roman cohort marched along it.

When they entered the avenue behind Bran, Petillius had motioned Quintus to ride up near him, but the General did not speak until they topped a rise of ground and saw ahead of them Stonehenge, huge and mysterious, its great up-ended stones looming dark against the green down and forest grove behind.

'That's most impressive,' murmured the General, in surprise and half to himself, as he stared. 'I'd no idea.'

They rode on slowly, and even the tough legionaries in the cohort behind them let out murmurs of wonder as each in turn came to their first sight of Stonehenge.

Quintus, who had been on the watch, saw how they were to be met.

'There's Conn Lear, sir,' he said, pointing.

The Arch-Druid stood on a mound against the 'Heel', or Holy Stone that guarded the entrance to the temple. They saw the grey beard, the long white robe, the winged crown, and the golden sickle of office in his hand. Around him, densely packed, were a thousand Druids of all the orders; the Bards in green, the Ovates in blue, the priesthood in white. They were unarmed, except that, ranged on either side of Conn Lear, were twelve Druids-of-Justice with their golden spears. The spears were raised and lowered once, as the Romans approached, while from all the Druids there came a high, weird chanting. Again the twelve golden spears were raised, and this time remained poised, aiming in the direction of the Romans.

'Is this a *friendly* reception, Quintus?' said Petillius with a dry laugh, staring at the spears. 'It looks as though if we get nearer there may be one general the less in Britain—possibly no great loss. But it might be wise to alert the cohort.' He turned to give the command, 'Javelins up.'

Quintus called sharply to Bran ahead. 'What are you leading us to? You swore there was no danger!'

Bran gesticulated frantically and pointed.

'He wants us to go forward ahead of the cohort, I think,' said Quintus. 'And see, Conn Lear is motioning.'

'Very well,' said Petillius after a moment. He spoke to a centurion behind him. 'If they cast those spears at Quintus Tullius and me, you'll know what command to give the cohort!'

The centurion saluted grimly and went back to the men. The General and Quintus continued to advance in tense silence, watching the golden spears in the Druids-of-Justice's hands. The Druids' strange, formless humming pulsated through the air. It was like the rush of water, yet there was menace in it too, like the buzz of angry bees, an eerie sound, and frightening. Quintus felt the palms of his hands go moist on the bridle and sighed with relief when the sound suddenly stopped at a signal from Conn Lear.

The Arch-Druid descended majestically from beside the Holy Stone and took three steps towards the General and Quintus, who were now two hundred yards ahead of their cohort.

'What brings you here—Romans?' called the Arch-Druid in Latin, his stern, resonant voice echoing amongst the great stones of the temple.

'Peace! Conn Lear. Peace for your people and mine!' Petillius called back.

'Why then do you bring soldiers with you?'

'It was the command of Governor Suetonius that we bring a cohort. But would the centurion, Quintus Tullius, and I have dared advance alone in the face of your spears if we did not come in peace?'

'The Romans dare many things,' said Conn Lear coldly. 'Advance farther!'

The General and Quintus obeyed. The Arch-Druid also moved forward a few steps.

'Now dismount!' he commanded.

They obeyed this too, and Quintus, while he tried to hide the stiffness of his leg, knew that Petillius must be much impressed by the Arch-Druid or he never would have acceded to this request.

Conn Lear walked yet three more steps until he stood before the General.

'Now,' he said, 'we are equal. You have come to meet me,

and I have come to meet you. It is so that it must be, if you wish peace in Britain.'

'That is true, Arch-Druid,' said Petillius gravely. 'We shall understand each other.'

Conn Lear turned and signalled to his guard. The Druids-of-Justice slowly lowered their spears.

'Leave your cohort there to camp on the plain,' said the Arch-Druid to Petillius. 'You have no need of it. Then come with me and we will talk together.'

'Shall the centurion, Quintus Tullius, stay with the cohort?' asked Petillius.

The Arch-Druid looked at Quintus directly for the first time—a veiled, considering look, neither hostile nor friendly. 'The centurion may come with us,' he said. 'There is a foolish girl in my house who will be glad to see him.'

Quintus' heart jumped. It took all his will-power to keep his face impassive as he walked behind the General and the Arch-Druid on the road to the sacred grove. The Druid company followed at a distance. Quintus stared hard at the outside of the Arch-Druid's strange house, and the enormous tree that grew up through its centre. The oak's leaves and gnarled branches cast a canopy of shade, not only over the roof but all the palisaded enclosure round the house.

Conn Lear's door and windows stood open. It was light inside when they entered the circular room with the painted hangings on the walls.

As Quintus stepped in, he heard a sound, half gasp, half cry, and he whispered, 'Regan'. The girl ran forward round the tree-trunk, with her hands outstretched. Quintus bounded towards her, but the Arch-Druid quickly barred the way between them, as he had when they had parted here before.

'No, daughter of my daughter, you shall not speak to the Roman centurion until I have decided many things,' said Conn Lear. 'Sit down where you were, and you'—he pointed at Quintus —'over there.'

The girl gave Quintus a quick, involuntary look. Biting her lips, she raised her chin proudly and obeyed her grandfather. Then she returned to a stool near the small fire, picked up the distaff she had dropped, and began to twirl yarn round it slowly.

Quintus, from the bench indicated by the Arch-Druid, could just see her. She wore a new violet-and-yellow tartan, her lovely hair rippled with chestnut lights down to her waist. Round her neck there was a crescent of beaten gold, beautifully carved, that lent a sparkle to her charming, down-bent face.

She did not look at him again, and he gazed at her until he knew just how the tendrils sprang from her white forehead, the way a mole accented the corner of her full, red mouth, and the way her long lashes shadowed her cheeks.

He paid no heed to the Arch-Druid and Petillius, who were conversing at the other side of the room, until he was jolted from his absorption in Regan by the Arch-Druid's suddenly raised voice.

'Ay, General—it surprises you that I am willing to make peace with our conquerors? It was not always so. Once I hated the Romans as fiercely as ever Boadicea did. I hated as did the Arch-Druids before me, back through the years to the invasion of your Julius Cæsar. But I am old now, and of what use is it to hate that which *is*—and will be!'

'Who can tell what WILL be—Conn Lear?' said Petillius in a grave, thoughtful tone.

'*I* can,' said the Arch-Druid. 'Because Lugh has granted me the vision I have made the sacrifice of the bull. I have lit the sacred fire at midnight in the great stone temple out there. And I have seen.'

'What have you seen.' Conn Lear?' said the General softly.

The old man rose, turned his head towards the east window, and gazed at Stonehenge. Then he raised the hand which still clasped the golden sickle and spoke in the chanting voice of power. 'Blood I have seen, and defeat. I have seen the coming of darkness to the Celts in Britain—to my people. I have seen the Roman legions marching into every corner of this land. But more than that . . .' He paused. 'Ay, more than that. I've seen that the blood of Briton and Roman will some day mingle here, and they shall become one race and for hundreds of years this shall endure.'

'You are wise, Conn Lear,' said Petillius very low. 'I believe that you have seen the true sight of what will come.'

'The gods will mingle too,' went on the resonant voice, unheeding. 'Our own gods, our Celtic gods that you Romans will adopt and call by Latin names, just as you would dilute and Romanize our Druid lore in time—if we permitted it.'

'Permit?' cried Petillius sharply. 'Now you speak as though you would resist!'

The Arch-Druid lowered his head and looked at the Roman, a sad smile coming to his lips. 'We shall not resist. For if we did, it would be slaughter for us, as it was for Druids on the isle of Anglesey. I know your Governor Suetonius' nature. No—you must give us a little time, a month will do—then we shall leave this land to its own destiny.'

'Where will the Druids go, Conn Lear?' Petillius leaned forward earnestly.

'To the Islands of the West across the Irish Sea. There no Roman will pursue us.'

So the Druids were planning to leave Britain, thought Quintus in sudden panic—and what of Regan? He saw that she too had heard; her mouth was tight. Suddenly she threw her shoulders back and got up. 'Grandfather,' she said, walking towards him. Her voice trembled. 'I am frightened of your anger, but I must speak.'

'Speak then,' said the Arch-Druid, sitting down and looking at her steadily.

'You know what is in my heart, Conn Lear,' said Regan, 'and I know the condition you have made. Put it now to the test, I implore you. Tell Quintus Tullius.'

'You are impatient, child—you interrupt me,' said Conn Lear sternly, but his eyes were not unkind. 'Yet because I love you, daughter of my daughter, it shall be as you wish. Come here, Centurion!'

Quintus rose and walked to stand before the Arch-Druid, wondering much and worried because he saw that something portentous was coming.

'The Druids will go to the Islands of the West without me,' said the Arch-Druid, 'for I am old and sick and very soon shall die. When I die I would be laid here in this room beside the tree, and burned—my spirit to mingle with the spirit of this oak in fire, as in the ancient rites of long ago. I would that nothing here should be disturbed until the ashes of my body, and the oak, and my house shall all sink down and mingle with the quiet earth beneath . . . *undisturbed*,' he repeated solemnly, 'by any mortal hands forever.'

What has this to do with me? Quintus thought, profoundly uneasy, for the piercing gaze seemed to be searching his soul. Petillius too looked puzzled, as he sat a little withdrawn, watching. Regan's hands were tight-gripped, her breath came rapidly. Her eyes moved from her grandfather to Quintus.

'When you first came to Britain, what was it that you wished to find, Quintus Tullius?' asked the Arch-Druid quietly.

'The body of my ancestor Gaius,' murmured Quintus after a moment.

The Arch-Druid rose and pointed with the golden sickle.

'The body of your ancestor lies here amongst the roots beneath this tree.'

Quintus gasped. He stared at the great trunk in the centre of the room. Petillius made a sharp motion, but Regan held still—waiting.

'That Roman, Gaius Tullius, profaned our holiest things. It was for this that the Arch-Druid of that time built the stronghold of our religion here, to counteract the evil. Now that you know, Centurion, what will you do?'

Quintus breathed deeply, and looked into Conn Lear's eyes. 'I don't quite understand, Arch-Druid, but I've changed since I came to this land. *I* will not profane your holy things, as Gaius did, unknowing, nor disturb that which you wish left untouched.'

The old man's face quivered, the biting coldness vanished from his gaze, but he said inflexibly, 'There is Druid gold buried with your ancestor, Centurion—much gold. You wanted that, did you not?'

'Yes,' said Quintus slowly. 'I wanted that, but there are things now that I want far more.'

He looked at Regan and saw joy shining in her eyes.

'You have chosen well,' said Conn Lear. 'And I will tell you this. If the spirit of your ancestor has been unquiet, it will be so no longer. For in the fire that will consume us both, all differences shall be resolved—the Roman invader and the Celtic high priest shall both pass together into the paradise where there is always peace.'

The old man stopped and bowed his head. He walked to his chair and sat down wearily. There was a throbbing silence in the room of the living tree. Tears rolled down Regan's cheeks. She knelt by her grandfather and kissed his hand.

Petillius stirred at last and spoke; in the roughness of his voice, Quintus recognized the strong emotion that he felt in himself.

'It shall be done, Conn Lear, all as you wish it. Quintus has spoken and I have spoken.'

The Arch-Druid nodded slowly. 'You are good men. *You* are of the stuff that shall build up the new Britain.' He sighed, then his mouth lifted in a faint smile. He put his hand on the girl's bowed head. 'Ay—Regan,' he said tenderly, 'you may speak to your Roman now. Take him outside, for the General and I have still many things to talk of.'

Quintus caught his breath, as the girl rose from her knees and came towards him, but he turned to look at Petillius.

The General answered his look with a softness Quintus had never seen, and he smiled as he said, 'Yes, go with her, Quintus. And speak to her as you wish, for the Arch-Druid is right. From such as you and Regan will come the new race in Britain. You must have patience till the law is changed, but I'll see that it won't be long before permission will be granted.'

'Thank you, my General,' said Quintus very low. He took Regan's hand and they went out into the grove of trees, both silent, feeling only the clasp of their hands together, so deep in wondering happiness that they could not speak.

They stopped together, as of one accord, beneath an ash tree in the grove, and looked into each other's eyes.

'Regan,' Quintus whispered, 'did you understand what the General meant?'

'Not quite,' she whispered back. 'Oh, Quintus, I've prayed for this—I didn't know how much I—I—until you were gone, ah —but you're wounded—what has happened to your leg . . .?'

He put his hands on her shoulders and held her thus, looking down into her candid, beautiful eyes. 'I was wounded by a spear thrown by one of your own countrymen, and I killed many of them, Regan, in the battle that wiped out half of Britain. The battle in which Queen Boadicea died. You must know and face this.'

Her lids drooped for an instant, then lifted. Her pupils were dark and steady as she gazed up at him. 'I know. I have mourned bitterly for my people who are dead, for the Iceni and my foster-mother, who once was good to me. But it is past. Soon the snows will fall, then spring will come, and grass will grow again—even on the battlefield.'

'Yes, my Regan,' he said on a long breath. 'So now I will tell you what the General meant. There's still a law, a barrier between us for a little while, but when the grass has grown again upon that battlefield, then I ask you to become a Roman soldier's wife. And will you, Regan?'

She did not answer in words. She lowly raised her arms and put them about his neck. He caught her to him, and they stood clasped together beneath the tree. The slanting sun filtered through the leaves and glinted on the girl's bright, flowing hair and it glinted on the breastplate of the young Roman centurion, who had found in this land not the thing he had once searched for, but instead a new home, and love, and his destiny.

The
Suckling

Geraldine Symons

About the Author

Geraldine Symons is the author of four novels and three children's books. Educated at Godolphin School, she has had many jobs ranging from secretary, and cook, to acting as a guide to visitors at Wilton House. She is fond of gardening and playing golf, and she lives with her cats and Yorkshire terrier in Salisbury.

THE SUCKLING (© Geraldine Symons 1969) is published by special arrangement with Macmillan and Co. Ltd.

CHAPTER I

'NEVER forget you're English,' Mother said.

'No,' said Hattie. 'And my frock's English too, because you made it out of yours which was, but my petticoat and drawers are French because you made them out of French stuff, and my bodice and——'

'Stop it, you are going to extremes.'

Hattie stopped out loud, but her mind chewed on in silence —vest, stockings, boots . . . and the sand was French, and the sea, which had almost disappeared, leaving a great stretch of shining grey mud spiked with black sticks. 'What are those black sticks for?'

'I told you, they're to do with oysters, I expect.'

'And so's what we're leaning against.' Hattie shifted a little to escape a piece of slate that was digging into her neck.

'So's what—for goodness sake, Hattie, try to speak properly; so is the thing we're leaning against, not so's what.'

'So is the thing we're leaning against,' repeated Hattie, 'and I know what it is, it's a pile of oyster houses. Tell me again——'

'I've just told you.'

'*Please.*'

'Then listen. There are two bits of slate with an empty oyster shell between them like a sandwich with a bit of ham, and a whole lot of these sandwiches are strung together like beads in a necklace. The fishermen take the necklaces out and drop them in the sea, and baby oysters go into the empty shells and make another shell themselves, and when they are ready they are brought back to be eaten.'

'How do they die before they're eaten.'

'They don't. If you ate a dead oyster you'd be poisoned. Never, never eat a dead oyster, whatever else you do.'

'They're eaten *alive*?' Hattie turned to look at Mother.

'*Mon Dieu,*' thought the Wren—because French, in spite of her English backbone, had taken a grip on her brain—brooding for a moment on the solitary confinement of an oyster, she had forgotten how the child would mind. Staring back into those wide, horrified eyes, she said, 'Oysters don't *feel,* so don't start fussing about them for goodness sake. Some things have to be fussed about but oysters don't.'

'What things?'

'Forgetting you're English, copying Catholics, pretending things aren't true, letting your imagination run away with you.'

Hattie, staring ahead, saw her imagination running away with her—like her and not like her, because it was pale grey and made of jelly—running with her across the shining mud. 'Why don't we go back to England?'

'You know why—because Father hasn't finished his book and never will at this rate, because he wants to stay here, being like a chameleon.'

'What's that?'

'A lizard that changes its colour to suit its surroundings. Your father is being a Frenchman,' the Wren's eyes snapped with disdain. Thrusting the heels of her button boots impatiently into the sand, her fingers clawed up a pebble without looking at it and threw it down again.

'There's Madame!' cried Hattie.

'She's ready to go.'

But Madame, who had driven to the village to see her niece, descended from the cart and came over to look at the sea. 'There's the Ile d'Aix!—see—that smudge in the distance. It was there Napoleon stayed for three days.'

'While he was deciding whether to surrender to the English,' said the Wren.

'Surrender—he was treated by the English like a dog, he, the greatest soldier the world has ever seen!' cried Madame shrilly.

'If that was true, why was he beaten at Waterloo by Wellington?'

'*Him*——' jerking her head, Madame made to spit. The spittle should have carried down wind, but Hattie, looking for it saw nothing.

'You have no answer so you——' the Wren's voice that had risen in scorn, stopped; she had forgotten the French for 'spit'. She made use of *dégoûtante*, dubbing her disgusting instead.

'You English, you think you own the earth!' Madame squawked.

'We do—most of it.' The Wren's hat blew off her proud head, laying bare her golden crest. 'My hat! Run, Hattie, and catch it.'

Hattie tore off, mad to get back to the fight and be English with Mother. But the English boater, browned by a French sun, tore along the edge of the beach before banking in a cross scud of wind and wheeling over the mud. Hattie caught it, her boots covered with slime, but when she turned to go back to them, Mother and Madame were kneeling on the ground—two lumps, a grey and a black. They couldn't be saying their prayers. Mother would never pray near a Catholic. They must be looking for something. As Hattie got near she heard their voices low again as if they had finished fighting. She reached them, panting. 'I've got it.'

'Good——' said Mother, 'thank you.'

'What are you looking for?'

'My kingpin.' Hattie saw then that the golden crest had flopped.

'*Voilà!*' cried Madame. 'I 'ave it.' The three English words were part of her triumph. Her eyes, her whole face, radiated eagerness as she held up the big brown pin.

'Oh, how splendid! Thank you so much,' the Wren spoke in English, adding '*Merci, merci.*'

Madame seemed to have forgotten all about Napoleon, but as Mother pinned up her hair Hattie knew by her face that *she* hadn't.

Driving home, Madame spoke nothing but French; she had aired her English. She talked about the products of the sea—lobsters and scallops and soles and mussels, and a dead man that had come out of it too, washed overboard from a fishing boat. He had been in the sea for a long time. His fingers were dropping off.

'Why?' asked Hattie, wanting and not wanting to hear. Now she understood French she couldn't not understand.

'Swollen, sodden with water, bigger than sausages.' Madame let go the reins with her left hand, sketching a sausage shape in the air. 'He was——'

'Hattie, your *boots*——' exclaimed Mother as if she hadn't remarked on them already.

Saying that in front of the child—thought the Wren. Really, the French with their details were as coarse as their drains.

'They'll dry,' said Madame, relinquishing the corpse as easily as she had Napoleon.

The fingers were still in Mother's mind, Hattie knew, as she knew too that Mother wouldn't have interrupted about the boots if she hadn't wanted to stop Madame. Stretching out her hand to scratch a bite on her knee, she saw with fascinated loathing her fingers drop off and roll on the bottom of the cart.

Being out in the country, driving in the cart, was such a treat that Hattie could hardly bear to see the roofs coming nearer.

The Wren saw the country as flat, dull and wild, a hopeless substitute for the rolling downs and lush countryside of England.

Madame saw the country with an eye to food: crops, cows, pasture. The daughter of a chef, the widow of a restaurant proprietor and now its owner, food was the core of her life.

Le port, with its three great basins, was almost in the town itself. Coming out of the streets that first time, Hattie had thought the masts of the boats were bristling out of the ground. She knew better now. She knew too that although Father had said *le port* was the bowels of the town, she couldn't. 'Don't ever let me hear you say that again,' Mother had said. 'A bowel is one thing and one thing only, and you never mention it unless absolutely necessary.' When Hattie had asked when it would be necessary, Mother had said only when you're ill. 'Is Father ill?' 'No. Father——' Mother had shut her mouth in a way that meant she was cross with Father.

'Bowel,' whispered Hattie to herself as the cart creaked past *le port*, 'bowel, bowel.'

There was a frigate in that hadn't been there this morning.

'It's German,' Madame said in her spitting voice.

'We can do without them,' said Mother. About Germans the Wren and Madame were *en rapport*. Madame had never forgiven the Prussians for reducing her mother to skin and bone in the Siege of Paris and bestowing rickets on her baby born on the day of liberation. For over twenty years now Madame's skirts had hidden her affliction, but as a child her bow legs had been the butt of all the guttersnipes in Montparnasse. The Wren had never forgiven a German music mistress for boxing her ears for failing to strike a right chord. She was aware that one shouldn't hate a whole nation for breeding one woman with a vile temper, but there it was.

Whereas Germans united those two in a common loathing, the Eglise Saint-Sauveur, topped with its old calm tower, was as bad as a squib between them. Huguenots and Roman Catholics, protestants and popery; one up to the Huguenots who had destroyed the ancient Eglise Saint-Sauveur and taken the stones to build Fort du Gabut, two up to them for throwing the priests into the sea from the top of the tower. One up to the papists who had rebuilt the church. Sebastian could not forgive the Huguenots for destroying the *mise en tombeau* and the Wren could not forgive him for saying he would rather have had the Roman Catholics top dogs and preserved the *mise en tombeau*. And Madame and the Wren could not forgive each other on any religious score, but the Wren had no intention now of putting a match to the fuse, and whatever Madame's intentions might have been as the cart creaked past this sacred bone of contention had she thought about it, her mind had suddenly become engrossed in the price of fish.

Hattie sat stiff as a poker, her head held high, her hands in her lap, her face solemn, but as the Wren's glance fell on her daughter, she saw her turn and smile at the urinary where the head and feet of the occupant were disgustingly visible. 'Hattie, look this way.'

Hattie, who was riding in a tumbril to the guillotine, obeyed like a sleep walker; then came to her senses. What was there to look at? Looking back to see what she mustn't see, she saw one of those familiar nasty places on the pavement, with a black cap poking out at the top and brown boots at the bottom. As she stared, the occupant came out, buttoning his trousers.

'*Hattie!* Did you hear what I said?'

Just then Madame looked back. 'Henri! How are you?'

'*Ça va.*'

Shocked, Hattie knew without looking that Mother's lips were shut.

They passed the house where the wren had been, in a little cage hanging on the wall in the boiling heat of the midday sun. 'It's a golden-crested wren,' Father had said. Hattie, thinking it so beautiful, had looked with pleasure. 'Devils——' without glancing up or down the street, Father had opened the door of the cage and let out the bird. Hattie had seen it fly away with a dreadful sense of loss. 'Why did you let it go? It was so lovely.'

'Lovely—you're as bad as *them*,' said Father furiously. 'Have I sired a brat with no imagination?' Without waiting for an answer, he had strode off.

Hattie, hurrying after him, said, 'Mother says I've got too much.'

'You haven't any if you don't know what it would be like to be a wild bird in a cage.'

'I *do* know——' thinking and feeling the feeling of being a wild bird in a cage had made her miserable and ashamed. 'It was so lovely I forgot.'

'Well don't forget again. Always let wild birds out of cages.'

'Yes,' Hattie had promised. 'Will they mind—the people they belong to?'

'I hope so.'

Hattie had seen herself opening cage doors on and on till she died and all the people minding. 'What shall I do if they see me?'

'Tell them what you think of them.'

How dreadful it was going to be. Weighed down with foreboding, she had followed Father in silence. 'It was like Mother,' she had said then.

'What?'

'The bird.'

'Why?'

'Because of her hair.'

'The gold-crested wren—you're right, Hat.' Then Father had said, 'But your mother's still in her cage.'

'She isn't *in a cage*!'

'She is, b'gad, and she's made it herself—every damn' wicker rod of it.'

'Then why don't you let her out if you let out wild birds?' Mystified, Hattie had pretended he was talking sense.

'She's not wild. She's been tamed from her cradle, fed on slops.'

The vision of Mother feeding on slops in a wicker cage was horrible. And then Father had said what made it better, 'But you couldn't find a wren with a better crest than your mother's in the whole of France, Hat.'

When the cart stopped for them in the Rue St-Yen, the Wren thanked Madame, '*Merci mille fois.*' Silly, to thank a thousand times for a lift in an unsprung cart when Madame had been going anyway, but the French fed on exaggeration, thought the Wren impatiently, her spirit shrugging but not her shoulders. 'My husband will be glad to see us after writing all day—that is if he has finished.'

'M'sieur is a great fisherman as well as a great writer.' Madame's farewell smile, which had been merely over-effusive, now seemed veined with mockery.

'The two go well together,' asserted the Wren, forcing herself into an assumption of Saxon phlegm. '*Au revoir.* Come along, Hattie.'

When Madame's good-byes were finished, the cart did not start at once. The Wren could feel the eyes of its occupant watching them, dark and sharp and merry, as they crossed the empty vegetable market to the house on the other side. Shutting the door behind her, she told Hattie to go and find her father.

Hattie ran upstairs to Father's room. It was empty of Father but full of everything else.

'Is he there?' Mother called.

'No.'

'Has he been there?'

Hattie knew what Mother meant and she knew that Father hadn't been. She could tell quite easily. There was not the strong smell of tobacco for one thing—only the faint one which was always there. And although the room was very untidy, it wasn't untidy enough. 'Yes!' Hattie called. Shouting out a story seemed so much worse than whispering it, but he had been there yesterday and perhaps for a minute or two this morning. If only she could keep Mother from being cross. But Mother was coming upstairs. Hattie came out, shutting the door with a bang.

Mother opened it. 'He hasn't.' She looked at Hattie, 'You knew he hadn't. Go upstairs to bed.'

'I——'

'*Go*——' Mother's voice rose.

Hattie went, stumping, furious and humiliated, her throat sore with the unfairness of it when she had been trying to help Father. Sent to bed like a baby . . . Shutting herself into her room, she went to the window. She couldn't fall out; Mother had had bars put. 'What on earth for?' Father had asked, and when Mother had said, 'Why do you think?' he'd said, 'Have I sired an idiot?' and when Hattie had asked what 'sired' meant, Mother had told her to run upstairs and get a hanky. 'That's right!—teach her to run away from life!' Father's bellow had come after her as she tore up the stairs chased by life. Now, thrusting her head through the bars, she stared out across the roofs.

The tiles, like half flower-pots, were the colour of carrots—unwashed ones. The tower behind the cathedral was old and yellowish. It looked older when you got close and then you saw the birds wheeling and swooping around it. Six struck. She knew it was six, but she counted the dongs to be sure there was no surprise. The market place was empty, all the stalls taken away. Down in the 'Bar la Basquaise' there was quiet too. It was too early for the drinkers. Presently, when it filled up, their voices would go on and on with sudden shouts. Sometimes Pierre, the baker, would play his mouth-organ. Mother hated living opposite it. When Father went and drank there too she hated him.

Father was coming now across the empty market. He had been fishing. He was walking springily, whistling 'Cockles and Mussels.' He must have caught something. Hattie's face burned with anger and her eyes filled with tears. Why should he be happy when she was so miserable and because of him? Suddenly he broke into song: '*Light she was and like a fairy and her shoes were number nine, herring boxes without topses sandals were for Clementine.*' He was bigger than anyone else anywhere. Now, instead of feeling proud of his bigness, that and his bellowing made her crosser still. Gathering up her saliva, sucking it up from everywhere, holding her breath and waiting for more, Hattie got ready to spit. The postman could spit within ten millimetres of his target on a still day and fifteen on a windy day. The wind had dropped. She couldn't spit like the postman of course, but if she waited till Father was underneath by the door, hers would drop straight. '*Oh my darling,*' roared Father. Hattie spat. What had seemed so much in her mouth seemed so little when it was launched. The wind, which hadn't dropped after all, took it and sprayed it. It never reached its target. '*Oh my darling—*' Down below the door slammed.

Hattie burst into tears.

CHAPTER II

'MON DIEU, Rose, you'd think the sun was the plague.' Opening the window, Sebastian Suckling thrust back the shutters, letting in a tide of light. 'If you want to live like a corpse in a morgue you might think of the brat. You don't want her to grow up like a weed, do you?—' he glared at his daughter, 'if she *does* grow up —she's stunted enough already.'

'She's nothing of the kind!' said the Wren furiously. 'Run upstairs, Hattie, and get——'

'You've got it; the damn' thing's there in your pocket. What's wrong with the sun? Tell me that.'

The Wren's eyes were blazing, but for the sake of the child, and with the self-control ploughed into her in the Puritan nursery of an English vicarage, she not only answered the question but spoke quietly. 'It's hot.'

'Of course it's hot, good healthy heat slogging down through the flesh into the marrow of the bones—what's wrong with that?'

'Our bones are English and we are half-way down France; that's what's wrong. It's too much. It's shrivelling, desiccating.'

'Balderdash. What would you do in the Sahara?'

'Die,' said Hattie. She wasn't taking Mother's part, she wasn't taking anyone's. It had simply come to her that that's what she would do—die.

'You'd do nothing of the sort! Given a bottle of water, a topee and your winter coat—you'd need coverage in that heat—you'd have a hundred per cent chance, unless the Arabs saw you, and then you'd be wiser to shoot yourself.'

'*Shoot* myself?' Hattie stared at him aghast.

'Stop it,' said the Wren.

'Would I have a gun?'

'If you had any sense. If they got you——'

'What would they do?' Hattie whispered. She had to ask, but she didn't want to know, she didn't, she didn't. Her mouth had dried up, her heart was pounding.

'Sebbie, don't, please don't.' The Wren had humiliated herself to the point of entreaty, desperate in her dismay.

'There you go again. Every time I try to educate her—and by heaven she needs it—you tell me to stop.' Plunging bread into his coffee, Father slopped it up into his mouth and golopped it. Mother loathed this disgusting French habit, Hattie knew, but when Hattie looked to see if she was loathing it badly while she cut the bread, she didn't look so disgusted after all. That was because she was glad about not knowing about the Arabs. So was Hattie. She would shoot herself like Father said without knowing —*shoot herself*. She saw herself in the middle of sand, sand everywhere, in her blue reefer coat and a topee, with a bottle of water and a gun, with the Arabs coming and coming, riding on—'What do Arabs ride on?—camels or horses?'

'Be quiet,' said Mother. 'Don't start that again. Eat your bread.'

'Both,' said Father. 'You'll see a scuffle of sand in the distance and they'll be on you in a trice—nothing like a decent camel or an Arab stallion for speed. You'll have to be damn quick on the trigger—but not too quick, mind. Don't go and shoot yourself just because you see some dust. It might be the beginnings of a dust storm.'

'No, I won't,' Hattie promised.

'Good girl.'

Father worked that morning. When Father worked the Wren kept the house as quiet as if he were ill. 'This afternoon I'll take you to the beach,' she told Hattie. 'This morning Françoise invited you to play, you say?'

'Yes.' Hattie knew that Mother didn't really like her playing with Françoise because her father and grandfather kept a restaurant in Paris—although it was a much better one than Madame's who Mother wouldn't have dreamt of going out in a cart with in England, but in this French wilderness one did extraordinary things. But Mother would be fairly glad now for her to go to Françoise because of Father.

'You are quite sure you didn't invite yourself?'

No, Hattie hadn't. She had simply said that today she would teach Françoise to skip double-through. It was a pity Françoise couldn't come to *her* garden but she couldn't come to what she hadn't got.

Françoise's grandfather's house was in the Place du Musée. It had a big iron gate leading into a courtyard where there was a tree with huge flat leaves. Father said it was a catalpa and Mother said it wasn't, that whatever it was it wasn't a catalpa. Françoise didn't know what it was; no one seemed to. The garden behind had grass and sandy paths which were raked every day, two flower beds and an acacia tree. When Hattie rang the bell, Céleste opened the door. She was old and fat with a mud-coloured face, and she had a black moustache. She told Hattie in French that Françoise was ill, and then Françoise's mother came across the hall carrying a bunch of roses and aired her English. 'Françoise ees not well. She feel seek and 'as a—*mal de tête*—'ow do you say eet?'

'Headache,' supplied Hattie, feeling uppish.

Madame Delon said ''eadache' three times and laughed. It was a gay sound, soaring up to quite a high note, and pushing out the little pink buttons on the tucked bodice of her frock as her bosom heaved up inside it. Laughing too, Hattie gazed at her. She thought her beautiful with her fat red lips and her dark merry eyes and her crinkly fringe. Once, Françoise had taken her up to Maman's bedroom to ask something. Françoise had burst in without knocking and Maman had been sitting on a chair by the dressing-table in black stays and black drawers and black stockings, her feet in high-heeled white shoes, curling her fringe with a pair of tongs which she heated in the flame of a little lamp. Hattie had hung back, appalled, expecting Maman to be very cross at being seen undressed like that and curling her fringe which she must want to be a secret, but Maman hadn't minded a bit. She had gone on with her fringe, heating the tongs, trying them out on a piece of paper, and blowing on them and swishing them about in the air when they were too hot. Hattie had stared like mad with no one to tell her not to, drinking in her fill. Afterwards, playing in the garden, Hattie had asked Françoise why her mother wore black things. She hadn't liked to say 'stays and drawers'. When Françoise said, 'What things?', Hattie had said, 'Sitting at her dressing-table just now.' Françoise hadn't minded about stays and drawers at all, and in French they had sounded better. She had said that sometimes Maman wore pink and sometimes white. 'Mother always wears white,' Hattie had told her, and Françoise had said it was because she was English. Hattie, who hadn't been sure whether she was being rude or not had said, 'Why?' to find out. 'Because she wears white and she *is* English,' Françoise had said.

Now, when Maman had stopped laughing, she said that Françoise had gone back to bed and she hoped she would sleep. After a bit more conversation, Hattie had to come away. She felt cross and flat. If she went home she would be made to draw or sew. She would go to the cathedral for a little first. It was forbidden fruit. Mother had said she wasn't to go there any more. Father had said, 'If you forced her there, forced her on to her knees and made her rattle some of those confounded beads, you'd finish by having to drag her there by the hairs of her head.' Mother had pretended not to hear.

The Place de Verdun was blazing hot, the shadows black. 'If I had to cross it I ought to wear my coat and topee,' Hattie thought, but as she came out of the Rue Gargoulleau she only had to run across the corner, up the steps and through the door, and the cool dim stillness gulped her up. She went straight to where she was going first—the chapel with the ships.

All the ships were being wrecked. Father had been excited by them too when they had come that first time. They had stared at them together and Father had explained what was happening, why the Virgin with Jesus in her arms was sitting on a cloud in the sky while the *Suzanne Marguerite* was wrecked, with the sea washing right through the middle of her. The Virgin had saved the Captain, Mr Hardy. 'Didn't she save the crew too?' Hattie had asked, and Father had said, yes, some, he expected, but in

1768 all crews were scum and not worth saving, although the Virgin, presumably, was not a respecter of persons.

Stella Maris had been wrecked in 1696. There was a good deal going on there; six men were chopping off the masts, another was praying with his arms held up, and six were in the sea and didn't look at all like being saved.

Great curling waves were breaking right over the bows of another ship, Capitaine Knell's ship, June 1799. Hattie could feel the terror of it. Making herself into a little person standing on the sloping deck with those awful great waves coming crashing down, her whole backbone seemed to shiver.

The Demoiselle was a different matter; she had fallen down a well and got out miraculously without anyone's help but through the intercession of the Virgin. She did it in 1741.

Mother, who had been looking at something else, had arrived in the chapel just as Father was translating about the Demoiselle to Hattie who hadn't been able to understand French then. Mother had said, 'Why through the Virgin?', and when Father had told her how she had saved the captains of the ships too, Mother said she hadn't, God had. Father had said what did it matter who'd saved them as long as they'd been saved, and if they wanted to attribute it to the Virgin why shouldn't they? 'Because they shouldn't,' Mother had said, 'it's not right.' Father had said it was the *intercession* of the Virgin, and Mother had said, 'Nonsense,' and she wasn't going to argue in a church whosoever it was, and had made Hattie go on round with her, and after that she had told her not to come to the cathedral again. But Hattie had.

When she had finished looking at the pictures, Hattie went as near to the High Altar as was reverent even if she wasn't a Roman Catholic. Next she went into a confessional box. After a good look round to make certain there was nobody about, she crept inside, closing the door very quietly behind her, and knelt down in the stuffy dusty boxiness. It was stuffed with sin, it must be. No, it wasn't; it was empty. The sins had all puffed away into nothingness when Monsieur le Curé had forgiven them.

Father said Monsieur le Curé had the face of a cultured donkey. Mother said he had a voracious look. Voracious meant hungry. 'Perhaps he is hungry,' Father had said, and Mother had said, 'Not he.' It struck Mother he was greedy for sins, to listen to other people's.

Folding her hands, squeezing her eyes shut, Hattie saw him

with her mind's eye, waiting voraciously on the other side of the grille. 'I'm a murderer,' she whispered. There was no sound in the silent stuffiness. It was so much worse than any sin he had ever heard before that he was too horrified to say anything. 'I was in the Sahara,' she whispered, 'and I saw the Arabs coming and I shot someone.' She stopped, listening to the silence. 'It wasn't Arabs after all; it was a dust storm.' He said, 'You weren't careful enough. You made a mistake. It wasn't really murder.' He wasn't horrified. He was disappointed. 'I murdered someone with Madame's onion-knife. I murdered Madame.' She saw it quite clearly—the sharp thin knife that Madame used for cutting onions. She had shown it to her when she had taken her into the restaurant kitchen one day. 'I have had it for ten years, see—the edge is as thin as paper,' and she had held it up for Hattie to see. And now Hattie saw it in her own hand. She saw her stab Madame with it. She saw Madame fall across the chopping board, her blood spurting out and soaking the onions. Terrified by what she saw, she got up, and bursting out of the confessional ran through the cathedral. Thrusting open the heavy door, she collided with Monsieur le Curé. Gasping, she tried to push on, but he seized her. Holding her in an iron grip, he pulled her back with him into the cathedral.

'Ah—it's you, the little English one.' Tilting up her chin, his brown donkey face bent towards her. 'What have you been doing that you shouldn't?'

'I didn't; I only thought it!' Clutching black serge, Hattie fought free. Crashing out of the door, she tore down the steps into the blazing sun.

Out here in the heat, with people and the noises of the town, she was safe and she wasn't. She ran out of the Place and down the street. Suppose she had stabbed Madame? She hadn't, she hadn't. Suppose . . . the awful thing she had seen was still inside her. It came with her as she ran.

CHAPTER III

THERE WAS NO BREEZE even on the sea-wall. Sitting beside Father while he fished, Hattie felt her legs cooking like bacon on the hot stones.

'Why didn't you bring something to sit on?' Father said.

'You didn't tell me to.'

'Great Scott, Hattie, can't you use your own brain! What would happen if the Wren and I died?'

'I don't know.'

Father gave her a bit of newspaper that wrapped the bait. 'Here—put this over them.'

Sitting with her legs under the paper, Hattie thought about what would happen if the Wren and Father died. She felt sick with misery. 'It would be awful,' she whispered.

Father didn't answer; he was busy.

'What *would* I do?' she wailed.

'When?'

'If you and Mother died?'

'Fend for yourself. When I was your age I ran away.'

'Ran *away*?' Hattie stared at him incredulously. 'You never told me.'

'I'm telling you now.'

'Where did you run to?'

'Into the mountains.'

They sounded as desperate, or almost, as the desert. 'What happened? What did you eat? Where did you sleep?'

'In a haystack, a cave, and a hedge, bread and cheese, turnips and bilberries.'

'Oh——' Hattie gaped at the sea in an effort at absorption. 'Where did you get the bread and cheese? Did you beg for it?'

'No, certainly not. I stole it from the larder and took it with me.'

'When did you go home?'

'When I was starving. I showed initiative and common sense. If I'd been my father I'd have been proud of me, but I got a flogging instead.'

Speechless with admiration and effort, Hattie gazed at Father, trying to see it all. It wasn't easy. It had been easier to see herself stabbing Madame with the onion-knife than to see Father, sitting enormous on a camp-stool smoking a pipe, as a boy of nine eating turnips and being flogged. Striving after this vision, she didn't remember at once how different it would be for her. 'If you and Mother were dead I couldn't go home when I was starving,' she said presently. The awful sadness of it made her throat ache.

'Neither could you,' said Father cheerfully. 'Then you'd have to hitch up your belt a notch and go on.'

'Where to?'

But Father had started to whistle 'Auld Lang Syne'. He had finished with running away, Hattie knew. She knew, too, that when she went she'd have to be even braver than he'd been. She would rather hitch up her belt a notch than shoot herself; she would rather take to the mountains than the desert.

Presently the sky turned yellow and the sun went in.

'The storm's coming and I haven't caught a damn thing. I'll bet my boots that little brute's got them all again ' Sebastian Suckling glared towards the end of the wall, but the French fisherman was hidden as usual behind the small concrete maritime building 'Go and push him in, Hat.'

'I can't.'

'Don't say "can't" to me. If I tell you to push him in, push him in you are to.'

'He'll drown and then I'll be a murderer.' Staring ahead of her, blinkered by the sides of her sun-bonnet, Hattie saw herself in the box again. *I pushed a man into the sea.*

'No, he won't; he can swim. I saw him the other day, swimming like one of his own beastly fish. No mistaking that face; it's like a bearded cod's. A ducking'll do him good. Don't let him see you mind. Stalk him from behind and catch him bending.'

'I ca—how can I?' Hattie put down her hands on the hot stones each side of her, but there was nothing to cling to.

'So I've spawned a coward, have I?'

'What's *spawn* mean?'

'The same as *sired*, and it's not pleasant to sire a coward.'

The disgust and disappointment in Father's voice stopped Hattie from asking 'What's *sired*?'

'It's bad enough not to have a son,' Father went on, 'but to have a daughter afraid of everything is enough to make one puke.'

'What's puke?' it came out of Hattie by mistake.

'Vomit—don't you know anything?'

'Yes,' said Hattie meekly, 'and I'm not afraid of *everything*.' She wished she was a son. She longed for it more than anything else. She wished she was as splendid as Father had been at nine. She felt ashamed and sorry for him. She would do anything in the world to be more like he wanted. 'You needn't puke—' turning to look up at Father, she said, 'I'll push him in.'

As the words died on his daughter's lips, Sebastian Suckling felt a pull on the line and instantly became oblivious to everything but the business in hand.

Scrambling up, Hattie had no time for fish; she was immersed in the stalking of her own prey. Going quickly along the wall to the little stone house, she crept round it far enough to see him. She knew what he had on; they had followed him along the wall today. Besides, he always looked the same. He had grey trousers with thin black stripes, a shabby brown coat, and a black cap. He was bending down, messing about with his bait. 'Get him while he's bending,' Father had said. She saw herself pushing him, saw him fall over the side, saw the space where he had been with the rod fixed, fishing by itself, and the paper with the bait, and the bag and the wine bottle still lying there, and—she suddenly saw it—a big fish half hidden by the bag, that Father might have got if he hadn't. *Now* . . . but she didn't move, she couldn't.

He stood up. He went nearer the edge. Now was the time. Father would have when he was nine. A furious envy of the boy who had run away and eaten turnips prodded Hattie on. She inched a step forward, soundless in her sand-shoes. Just then he started to whistle. It was a puffing blowing noise. He blew out *Sur le pont d'Avignon*. Hattie waited. 'When he gets to the end I'll do it,' she thought. But while he was still blowing his music, he took a bag out of his pocket and dropped it. It burst. Orange balls fell out and rolled about on the wall. Sweets. Bending down, he picked one up and pushed it into his mouth above his black beard. Grovelling, snatching, he went after one that was rolling towards the sea.

She stood quite still, watching him. When he had picked up the last one, she crept away. She couldn't push him into the sea. The sweets had made it impossible. She didn't know why—that it was because he had become human.

Father wasn't looking out for her; he was packing up. His unconcern galled her. Thunder rumbled over the sea. Everything was exciting and unreal. She was beside him before he saw her. 'Pack up the bait,' he ordered. 'The storm's coming. Where've you been?'

'Pushing him in.'

'Good—well hurry up.'

'I pushed him in.' The black awfulness of the story seemed to belong to the thunder.

'The devil you did. Get the basket and hurry.'

While Hattie was scrabbling up newspaper, Father said, 'Lightning,' but she missed it. 'Do you still think I'm a coward?'

'You're as brave as a lion. Go on, run to the shed hell for leather. I'll come when I'm ready.'

'What have you got to do?'

'Don't ask questions. Go *on*!'

Thunder crashed over their heads. 'Is it the end of the world?' shrieked Hattie.

'Yes—run!' roared Father.

Hattie ran as if the demons of hell were after her. It began to rain as she went. She stopped at last in the doorway of the big shed at the beginning of the wall. If it was the end of the world she would be sucked up wicked, she thought wildly. The rain splashed down, bouncing up off the stones. She couldn't see Father. He must have finished packing up. *Don't ask questions.* He'd said that because he wanted her to go, she thought, not because of a secret. Lightning—she saw it! She shut her eyes when the thunder came. When she opened them and wasn't dead, she saw Father coming down the wall from beyond where they'd been, from further up towards the house. He'd been to the house and round it, that's why she hadn't been able to see him. He'd been to see if she'd pushed the fisherman in. She felt her face, which had been cooling off a little after running, get scarlet again with dismay. He'd know now she hadn't. She saw him stoop and pick up the things. He began to run. She looked to see if the man was coming, but there was no sign of him. Father ran slowly, heaving along; then he stopped and walked. When he reached Hattie after running again, he was panting and sopping.

She would say something first. If he had seen the fisherman she would pretend she'd been only playing, having a joke. 'Did you—go behind the little house, Father, to see the fisherman pushed in?' She grinned, ready for the joke.

Father didn't answer; he went on panting. His face was running with water or perhaps some of it was sweat. 'Did you?' Hattie asked anxiously.

'Is it likely I'd go messing about round there in this rain!' Father said.

He hadn't! He hadn't seen the fisherman! The relief was tremendous. Everything became different at once, so that Hattie thought, 'Suppose I did push him in?' She saw it as clearly as she'd seen herself stabbing Madame with the onion-knife, clearer. Suppose she had and he hadn't got out, that's why he wasn't coming although it was pouring. The thought frightened her. She hadn't! And Father thought her brave.

There was another crash of thunder. It seemed to crack the sky in half above them. Hattie bent her head. It had hit her, she would be killed, they both would. When it was over and again they hadn't been, she said, 'It's not really the end of the world, is it?'

'For God's sake, Hattie, stop asking such senseless questions.' Father pushed his hanky back into his pocket.

She saw the lightning zigzagging across the sky, just before Father pulled her behind him. Her nose rubbed his coat. She smelt the smell of wet flannel. 'Do you still wish you had a son? Won't I do, Father?' she called up the great spaciousness of back.

'You'll do, suckling.'

Putting her arms round him, she nuzzled the flannel.

That evening they had dinner at the *Coq d'Or*. First there was a quarrel. Hattie heard it through the *salon* door. Mother said they couldn't go when Father said they would.

'Why not? You always say you can't do it about everything,' Father roared.

'Don't roar at me; I won't have it. Nor will I have any child of mine sitting up eating late in a restaurant, as I've told you before.'

'Oh, *please*—' the *please* made a little hissing noise in Hattie's teeth.

'If French children of two can, surely an English child of five times their age can?'

'Four and a half times,' whispered Hattie when she had finished the multiplication.

'If French children are brought up in an atrocious way there is no need for the English to follow suit.'

'Balderdash!' shouted Father. 'Then leave her behind.'

'How *could* Father—' thought Hattie furiously, 'after I pushed in that man!'

'How can we leave her behind?' and now Mother was talking very slowly in her 'imbecile' talk. 'You know perfectly well that Marie always goes to her mother's on Tuesday evening, and you also know because I told you that I promised Berthe that after she had served dinner she should go to Benediction.'

'Ha—so you're an accessory to poking the heretic bonfire.'

Mother went on as if Father hadn't spoken, 'Hattie can hardly be left in an empty house.'

'No!' Hattie clenched her hands together. 'Take me, please take me,' she hissed.

'Why not? She's not a lunatic, thank God—though I sometimes have my doubts, and it wouldn't be all her fault if she was.'

'And sometimes I wonder why you ever married,' Mother's voice had changed from the 'imbecile' one to low fury. 'You are unfit to have a child; you don't care a button for its own good—if it interferes in any way with your own wishes—or for mine either. You drag us out here on the pretext of writing a book which you make little or no attempt to do, and you are quite content for your child to sit up half the night in a—French restaurant.' Mother's voice rose and cracked on those two dreadful sounding words.

'You make it sound like a brothel.'

'How can you say that word to me!'

'Don't be silly, Rose. It's high time you stopped being your father's daughter. You know perfectly well what a brothel is and what goes on in them—or some of it,' added Sebastian with unaccustomed accuracy.

The slam of the door shook the house. Hattie, who had been sitting on the stairs threading beads until she had stopped to listen, dropped a red one which rolled through the banisters. She waited to go after it until the Wren had gone downstairs, her golden crest flung high.

'What will you have, suckling?' Father held the menu in front of Hattie's nose. He was being specially nice because mother was cross. She didn't think it was because of the man.

Sebastian and Hattie ate fruits of the sea. Madame prided herself on her *fruits de mer*. Father had oysters; Hattie, mussels. Although oysters didn't feel and hadn't got to be fussed about, Mother said, Hattie didn't look much as they slid down Father's neck. She was occupied with her mussels for one thing. The great steaming purple pile was all hers. She ate as she had learnt to know how—without the fork, poking out the fish with the point of an empty shell, drinking the salty, parsley-flavoured water from the shells too.

'Don't be so disgusting, Hattie!—use the fork, and don't suck down the water like that. I've told you before.'

Yes, Mother had. 'French people do.'

'You are not French.'

'She is in France. Let her do as the French do.' Sebastian golloped an oyster. Confound Rosie's insularity. If it had been affectation he'd have put an end to it long ago, but it wasn't. She was honest, he would say that for her. The honesty of her beliefs gave them such damnable roots, and her obstinacy. Hackles up over one nonsensical thing after another. Upbringing—hadn't rescued her in time. Starting work on the next oyster, he said, 'How ever many more times have I got to tell you that *when in Rome*——'

'None,' said the Wren. 'I've heard that saying till I'm sick and tired of it, and to apply it to any country you visit is childish and ridiculous. If you went to Africa would you eat like cannibals?' she asked tartly.

Sebastian laughed. It was a rumbling sound, and it seemed to Hattie to begin down in the pile of oysters inside him.

The Wren, lifting a piece of onion omelette, suddenly laughed too. It seemed to Hattie, who had seen the sudden break-up of her face, that she hadn't wanted to but couldn't help it.

Hattie laughed uproariously. Everyone was happy again, she thought; everything was all right.

Madame came in wearing her black satin blouse which was too tight. When Hattie had asked Mother why she didn't let it out, Mother had said, 'She lacks modesty,' and then, in a different voice as if she were explaining it to herself, she'd said, 'She has no breeding and the mind of a whore.' 'What's a whore?' Hattie had asked. 'Hattie,' said Mother, 'never under any circumstances are you to say that word or that you heard me say what I did— promise.' Mother had looked quite red. Hattie had promised. 'I was talking to myself.' Mother had explained more gently.

'*La petite*—' putting her hands on the back of Hattie's chair, Madame bent over her. 'You are all very happy, yes?'

Hattie said, 'Yes, we are!' She knew it was there without looking up, black and solid and smooth. Mixing with the warm, salty, fishiness of the mussels was Madame's smell. She smelled of scent.

'What are you laughing about?' Madame enquired.

'An absurdity,' said the Wren, trying to catch Sebastian's eye.

But Sebastian said, 'Cannibals.'

Transferring her left hand from Hattie's shoulder, Madame laid it for a moment on his. 'What of cannibals?' she laughed as though it were a splendid joke.

'An absurdity of Rosie's as she told you.' Chuckling, Sebastian glanced up at Madame.

Hattie joining in Madame's laughter, looked at Mother to see if she was enjoying herself too. She wasn't laughing. She was scattering salt on her omelette, her face flushed and stiff-looking.

'How could you call me that?' Mother hissed at Father when Madame had gone.

'What?'

'Rosie.'

'It's your name, isn't it?' Father dropped vinegar on to an oyster. 'What should I call you?'

' "My wife" to a woman of her class—especially when she has so little breeding.'

'And yet you accepted a seat in her cart?'

'One can accept that from the humblest servant provided one knows how to behave. Eat up, Hattie, it's getting late.'

Mother wouldn't let her have anything more but custard.

'Let her have some meat—' said Father, 'she's out to dinner, isn't she?'

'Yes,' said Hattie, 'I want some pork.' She didn't. She suddenly felt sick, but she wanted to want some. Her eyes filled with tears.

'Pork at this time of night! At your age I went to bed at seven with biscuits and milk.'

'I wonder what a good plate of pork would have done for you,' said Father.

Monsieur Claveau, the bank manager, and his family came crowding in and sat at the long table at the end of the room. A cushion was put on a chair for the youngest and he was swung into place by Madame. His mother tied a napkin round his neck and he was ready.

'That brat won't be in bed till eleven after a good square meal, I'll wager,' said Father.

'He's only three.' Hattie burst into tears.

Sebastian stayed on after the departure of his wife and daughter, the course of his eating undeflected. He had a *crème de menthe* with his coffee which Madame brought herself while Émilie, the waitress, cleared the soup-plates from the family table.

Sitting down in Hattie's chair, Madame said, 'Rosie should have stayed. There was no need to take *la petite* home so early.'

'My wife thinks children should get to bed early. In England they do. Hat would be in the nursery there.' These observations so frequently on Rose's lips would have astonished her had she heard them on Sebastian's.

Madame ignored the gist of them. ' "My wife"? How long has Rosie been your wife?' she asked tartly.

'Eleven years,' said Sebastian coolly. Taking a gulp of coffee, he put down the cup with a clatter.

'She is only "Rosie" to your friends, eh?—not to Félicie Delon?' Putting her hand on his arm, Madame pinched it too hard for comfort.

'Don't be foolish.' Detaching the hand like a clinging bat, he examined it idly; small, smaller than one would expect from a worker, strong, blunt-fingered with long pointed nails, and the thick, clumsy wedding ring of the husband who had died of dropsy. He knew all about that, the loathsome details poured out one day as she had stood, chopping vegetables and throwing them into the soup pot. Nauseated, he had tried to stop her. 'Don't rake it all up; it's over.' But she had refused to be deterred. 'It doesn't hurt to "rake" it as you call it. It was a marriage of business convenience. Love—' she had smiled up at him, 'love is a very different thing.' He had just laid the hand on its owner's lap, when Jacques from the *boulangerie* came in with the news. Jean Picard had been drowned. He had been fishing from the sea-wall. They had found his body in the water.

'*Incroyable!*' cried Madame, rising. 'He was an excellent swimmer.'

Corroboration of the dead man's swimming powers came from Monsieur Claveau. He was an accomplished swimmer, yes. Émilie, who had just supplied the Claveau table with pork and beans stood transfixed, clutching an empty dish. The man at the table by the door, who had been swallowing his soup like a dog, napkin tucked into his collar, suddenly lifted his head. 'Why did he fall in?'

'Precisely—' said Madame, 'why?'

'When?' asked Sebastian. 'I was fishing there this afternoon. I saw nothing. There was only the usual chap at the end fishing past the building. That wasn't Picard, was it?'

When the descriptions were over, it seemed it was.

'Was he still there when you left?' Madame asked.

Sebastian shrugged. As far as he knew, but he couldn't have seen if he had been.

Coming to a dead end on that point, they returned to the question of what he was doing in the water.

'Perhaps he had a heart attack,' Madame suggested, demonstrating a struggle for breath that almost burst her bodice.

'Perhaps he was struck by lightning.' Sebastian asked Jacques if there were any marks on the body, but the baker, who hadn't seen it, didn't know.

It was all supposition, and when no one came along with any concrete facts, and Madame had regaled her audience with a melodramatic description of her brother-in-law's suction into quicksand, Sebastian, after an absinthe, left them.

Strolling through the hot, moon-filtered darkness, he had lost interest in the dead man, till the sight of Monsieur le Curé started a fresh train of thought. There was no mistaking that black pole, picked out in the moonlight, as it steered an even course ahead down the centre of the street. Then it swung left round a corner and was gone. A pity. Sebastian felt ripe for his company, in the mood to argue the hind legs off a donkey. He must be slightly drunk after all, he thought, to find amusement in that old donkey joke. Where had the fellow been? How should he know? There was hardly a pie the old fox hadn't got his finger in, and then he thought of Jean Picard again. Priests went to the dying, like vultures, to administer extreme unction, but that fellow had died without it, damned in the eyes of Rome—or wasn't he? How could he have helped it if he hadn't drowned on purpose?—and he'd yet to meet a suicide who'd have the will-power not to swim. Suppose it were murder? No one seemed to have thought of that. *I pushed him in.* Sebastian stopped dead in his tracks. Wasn't that what Hat had said? Good God! She'd been joking—must have been; she couldn't have been such a fool. She must have known he was only teasing her. Said something about being brave, he remembered now, about his wanting a son—that's why she'd done it, hell take it!

You never could tell with brats, he thought, moving on down the empty street again. It was one damn' fool thing after another. Give him an animal any time—instinct, and a small percentage of brain, and you knew what they'd do. Children had too little instinct and just enough brain to be dangerous. Rosie spent her time guarding Hat from things that didn't matter—seemed to think she was the suckling's sole protector. Didn't she know that if anyone touched a hair of the suckling's head he'd kill them? But it was Hat who'd done the killing now—though she hadn't meant to, poor little beast.

The man could swim—he'd told her that; then why hadn't he? It wasn't Hat's fault that he hadn't, but it wouldn't do for it to get around for her sake or his—God, no! It was his fault, the whole damn' thing. There'd be the deuce of a row if Rosie knew. Suppose Hat had already told her? Unlikely, he thought. She'd got enough gumption to know what line the Wren would take.

But he must speak to Hat at once—no, she'd be asleep now; first thing in the morning then. She didn't know the man was dead —a good thing. Dashed lucky they went home when they did. It would have been a rare old kettle of fish if Hat had realized what was up. She mustn't know—ever, if he could help it. She didn't want a lump like that on her conscience. It was enough for him to have it, he thought wryly. Wouldn't be easy to keep it from her. He'd have to say something to Rosie about it—tell her a man had been drowned and he thought it would upset Hat to know. That would surprise the Wren, to find the boot on the other foot, when it was she who was for ever trying to stop him saying the most innocuous things in front of the brat, trying to guard her from things she must learn to face—dark, ghosts, death, life— dashed ticklish business, life. But not this, the suckling must never face this.

Hattie's face swam before him, pale, in spite of the sun; it was those confounded shutters, the big blue-green eyes that could look as scared as a cat's, and the freckles over the bridge of her snub nose—his freckles, he'd had them as a boy, bone of his bone, and the small round obstinate chin—that was her mother's—and the long straight mousy hair; not like either of them in the long run— a changeling, that's what she was, a changeling. God, how he loved her. His eyes blurred with tears which he was sufficiently sober to know were maudlin.

Rose was in bed, reading the Bible, when Sebastian got home. She read it every night. When they first married he had accused her of using it as a façade to baulk him. She hadn't, he had known it really. She found pleasure in love. He had accused her of keeping him waiting on purpose. She hadn't; such nonsense was alien to her character. One night, in a fury, he had snatched the Bible from her and hurled it across the room. It had landed in the basin of water on the wash-stand, smashing the tooth tumbler. She had seen him as Beelzebub ranged against God and herself, he knew. Before he had done with her, she had given herself, body and soul, to Satan. Waking up in the early hours of the morning, he had seen her sitting on the chair by the wash-stand drying the Bible with her towel. She had accused him of sacrilege, and he had accused her of behaving like a witch-doctor and investing the Bible, which was only a book when all was said and done, with voodoo. He was not a heathen, but he liked to invest the Almighty with more broadmindedness than Rose did. He read the Bible but not from any religious compulsion. He read it for the beauty of its language, slowly savouring it like wine off the wood, or gulping it down in great draughts, according to his mood, seeing it as a yard-stick, measuring his own poverty and the poverty of others. And sometimes, taking the Bible from Rose, he would read to her, because he wanted to please her, because he liked reading aloud if he felt like it, or simply to put an end to the business quickly.

She glanced at him now, then went on reading, saying nothing. Hat hadn't told her, couldn't have, thought Sebastian with relief. He hoped she wasn't still put out about this evening. He wanted her on an even keel. Hunched towards the candle in the familiar attitude, her pigtail, dull in the half-light, dropping down the white night-dress with the thick hairiness of a dog's tail, gave her a peculiar air of defencelessness. That she wasn't defenceless he knew well enough. It was partly for her spirit that he had married her—milk and water was no good to him. Without it, her beauty would have had the incompleteness of unsalted food.

Her hackles had risen that first time when, bowling for a pig at the village fête, he'd sent five skittles flying with his first ball. 'I'm afraid that doesn't count,' she'd said. Didn't count? What on earth did she mean? He'd recognized her as the girl he'd just seen wiping the snot off a bawling baby and saying, 'Blow'. When he'd asked her what the devil she meant, she'd said as cool as a cucumber, 'Your toe was over the line.' He'd looked her straight in the face, 'What of it?' and she'd returned the look without a flicker. 'It's cheating, that's all.' Recognizing the 'that's all' as an understatement of what she apparently regarded as a bona fide crime, he'd said, 'What damn' nonsense!' Her chin had gone up then. 'It's just as bad to cheat at skittles as it is to forge a cheque. Do you always use such horrible language?' 'Worse, sometimes.' Tossing sixpence at her, accusing her of a put-up job to get money for the church, he'd got some more balls from the sexton and sending down three absolute snorters, had won the pig.

He had married her a month later. He had refused to wait as her disapproving stick of a father had wanted. The sooner he rescued her from that puritanical setting, the better.

Now, taking off his jacket, he asked her what she was reading. 'Habakkuk.' She didn't look up and her voice gave nothing away.

'He's so damn' gloomy—like all the prophets.'

'So would you have been if you'd been Habakkuk. The Chaldeans were insatiable, covetous, cruel, drunken, and idolaters—if you'd cared enough.'

Drawing odious comparisons? Insatiable for what? Covetous? —not particularly, cruel?—no, drunken?—he was not a drunkard, nor an idolater. If I'd been Habakkuk I would have.' Undoing his braces, he chuckled.

The Wren gave a small snort like a horse in its nosebag. Laughter. Her mood would do. 'Finish,' said Sebastian, 'I've got something to tell you.'

'I have finished.' Shutting the Bible, she put it on the table by the candle and turning, lay back. 'What?'

'After you'd left the *Coq d'Or* Jacques came in with the news that a man—Jean Picard—had been drowned fishing off the sea-wall.'

'How awful. When?'

'This afternoon—or this evening; they found his body in the water.'

'You and Hattie were there this afternoon. Did you see him?'

'If you mean did we stand and watch him drown, no we didn't.' For the first time it occurred to Sebastian to wonder if Hattie had. Great heavens, no, of course she hadn't!—simply given him a shove and run back to him. 'We saw him go along. He always fished at the end, beyond the maritime building—the one I told you about who took all my fish.'

'Doesn't anyone know what happened? I suppose he fell in and couldn't swim.'

'Yes, he could; he was a very good swimmer.' Stepping out of his trousers, leaving them on the floor, Sebastian dragged off his vest. 'Nobody knows what happened—at least Jacques didn't. He might have been struck by lightning, or had a heart attack.'

'Poor man—Hattie mustn't know,' Rose said. 'Madame went into quite unnecessary details about the fingers of a drowned man dropping off that day we went out with her. Hattie looks for fingers no whewnever she goes into the sea.'

Rosie had done what he'd hoped she would. Relieved, Sebastian agreed that Hattie mustn't know. 'But I bet Madame tells her—with fingers thrown in—if she gets the chance.'

'She won't; I'll see she doesn't,' said Rose firmly.

'*Or* the maids.' What a subscription to Rosie's wet-nursing, Sebastian thought drily. Buttoning up his pyjamas he put the second button in the top hole. He didn't notice, he never did—

and wouldn't have cared if he had—even when he came to the
end and his groping fingers found a hole without a button.

'I'll tell them they're not to, and she can keep away from
Françoise for a bit. That child is an inveterate gossip and hears
everything.'

'Trust a brat to spill the beans. While you're at it, you'd better
keep Hat from all the other tittle-tattlers too. Nothing like the
Latin predilection for morbid drama.'

'Nothing.' After a little pause Rose said, 'She'll toughen up
presently.' Her voice was kind. The kindness, the promise of
potential backbone was for him, Sebastian knew, for conniving
at her cotton-wool policy. The effect of the absinthe that had
brought tears to his eyes for Hattie had worn off during his
efforts at diplomacy. But in spite of sobriety, he felt a sudden
unqualified urge to please. Bending down, he picked up his
trousers and flung them over the back of a chair. Rosie hated
them to lie on the floor all night. It was another of her foibles.

CHAPTER IV

WHEN HATTIE DREAMED she had pushed the fisherman into
the sea, she saw his face when it bobbed up through the surface
of the water with immense clarity. It was like a lard bladder, a
hard shiny white, with a little black beard on the point. His
glaring eyes had pink sagging rims like Berthe's grandfather's.
He shouted, but his voice was drowned by thunder. Then his
beard turned into seaweed floating on the water and that was all
that was left of him—or should have been, but with a dream's
absurd disregard for logic he reappeared on the wall, a wet
menacing figure rushing to kill her. Gunless, shrieking, Hattie
ran; but she was as hopelessly outclassed as if he had been an
Arab stallion. When the hands grabbed her, they were Monsieur
le Curé's. 'Down you go and the Virgin'll get you up.' As Hattie
shrieked, 'Mother says she won't!' she went over and dropped.
She hit the water and sank; it poured into her mouth, choking
her. She came up again and spat. There was no sign of the Virgin;
Mother had been right. Monsieur le Curé had gone too. When
she tried to swim a great weight of seaweed pressed her down. It
was the fisherman's beard. He was dead on the end of it, and she

was alone in the sea with him. Struggling to free herself, she woke up trembling violently, hot and wet.

It was a tremendous relief to find it had been a dream, till she became aware of the weight on her chest. The seaweed. What should have stayed a dream was on her bed. How *awful*! It was the most awful thing that had ever happened to her, Hattie thought, terrified. Screwing up her courage, clenching her teeth, she lifted her head to look.

It was not seaweed. In the grey morning light she saw that it was—*sick*. She gazed in disbelieving amazement. Then sliding very carefully out from underneath it, she stood by the bed and gazed again. Mussels. She had sicked up mussels. Turning away in revulsion, she began to whimper, then to cry as she felt the warm heavy dampness cooling on her nightie. Going over to the wash-stand, she sponged it with the water she had washed in at bed-time. She didn't remember till she had almost finished that she had spat into it when she brushed her teeth. It was too much to bear alone.

She went out on to the silent landing and down the creaking stairs, the matting ribbing the soles of her bare feet. Father mustn't see her cry. When her hand clenched on the white enamel door-knob she was only sniffing. Turning it slowly, she opened the door and went in.

They hadn't heard her. Mother was asleep, lying in a flat ridge. Father was a huge mound.

'Mother——' as she said it, the odour of sick-drenched cotton rose up her nose and her lip trembled.

'Hattie—what is it?' Mother sat up, crestless, her hair in a pigtail.

'I've been sick.'

'Sick—where?'

'In my bed. I woke up and found it after an awful dream,' Hattie's voice shook.

'It was those mussels, at that time of night. Have you got a pain?'

'Like a bruise.'

'Sit down while I put on my dressing-gown. Where's yours?— you mustn't get cold.'

'I'm boiling.' Hattie sat down on top of Mother's stays, feeling the bones under her like sticks. 'I had an awful dream. I dreamt the fisherman pushed me into the sea.'

Father sat up suddenly. His hair was like a dog's. The collar

of his pyjamas was turned up behind as if he were going out in
the rain. His sleeves were rolled up. 'First things first. Don't
bother about your dream now. I'll see to her, Rose.'

Mother, who was just reaching for her dressing-gown, turned
to look at him. In her long white nightie with the bishop's sleeves,
she might have looked like a ghost, thought Hattie, if she hadn't
known she wasn't. 'You?' Mother sounded surprised.

'Yes, you get back into bed.'

'Oh, no, Sebbie, I'll go—' Mother's voice sounded soft and
pleased.

'Tell you what—you come and get into bed, Hat, while Mother
goes up to see what's what,' Father said.

'Yes, that's a good idea.' Mother was almost in her dressing-
gown. 'Do you feel sick now?'

'Yes.'

'Come on.' Mother helped Hattie on to her bit of the bed and
telling her to lie down, covered her up. Then she went to the
wash-stand, emptied the water out of the basin into the tin slop-
pail, and bringing the basin to the bed put it in a safe place
between Hattie and Father. 'Lie still. I'll be back in a minute.'

'Poor, disgusting little beast,' said Father.

Hattie's eyes filled suddenly and the tears rolled down her
cheeks. Everything was spoilt; now he'd think her a cry-baby.

'What's up? What's there to cry about?'

'I'm not.'

'I didn't think you could be. Don't think of being sick. You
dreamt the fisherman pushed *you* in, did you? That was turning
the tables, Hattie—or wasn't it?'

'Yes, it was such an *awful* dream. I dreamt——'

'Never mind your dream. It's what really happens that counts.'
Heeling over, Father dropped on his elbow. 'Did you really push
that man in this afternoon, Hat—or were you joking?'

'No.'

'No, you didn't push him in?—or no, you weren't joking?'

Licking up a tear with the tip of her tongue, Hattie thought of
Father when he was nine. 'I pushed him in.'

'The devil you did, but how? How did you manage it?'

'He was bending down picking up sweets—you said get him
bending. I ran at him suddenly and pushed him in.' She saw it
quite clearly with her mind's eye, like it had been in the dream
too.

'Good lord! Did he swim?'

'I didn't look over the edge, not really, but I did in the dream. In the dream——'

'We are not talking about the dream, we are talking about the truth. 'So you don't know what happened, if he got out?'

'No, I didn't wait.' Hattie was feeling more and more sick. 'If he drowned, though he didn't in the—I'd be a murderer,' her voice shook.

'He could swim,' said Father, 'like a fish. I told you. If he hadn't been able to I wouldn't have told you to push him in. You haven't killed him and you aren't a murderer. You just had a little bit of fun at his expense.'

'I feel sick.'

'Listen, Hat—we'll have it a secret that you pushed the blighter in. Don't tell anyone, not even the Wren. It can be our private joke—you'd like that, wouldn't you? And don't tell her or anyone else about your dream, either. It's all part of the secret.'

Hattie turned over and back again at once. 'I'm going to be sick.'

'Promise not to tell anyone, shake on it, Hat—' Father stretched out his hand and took hers. He crushed it till it felt like a bundle of twigs. 'Promise, suckling.'

'Promise.' Hattie sprang bolt upright as her mouth filled. Clawing at the basin with her free hand, dragging the one in Father's, she threw her head over the basin just in time.

Hattie was sick at intervals all day. Her bedroom was very hot. With the windows and shutters closed against the sun, even with the door wide open, there was little air. She never got used to the sickness. The terrible drag up seemed to be going to tear her to bits each time. The relief of survival bred no faith. 'If I die, Mother, you'll have no children.'

'Don't joke about death.'

'I'm not joking. I shall die, I'm sure I shall.'

'No you won't.' In the small pause that followed this assertion a fly buzzed across the room. 'Please God,' added Mother, and Hattie knew why; it was the same as touching wood.

When Mother had gone downstairs to see about barley-water, Hattie thought about death. Mother wouldn't want her to die in France. Father might like her to. Mother would hate France more if she died in it. What would she do without her? Would she go on the beach alone? At the picture in her mind's eye, Hattie's naked eyes filled with tears. Father could go on doing what he did now—if he had the spirit for it—fishing and reading and writing and drinking and playing bowls under the trees in the *Place*. The sun was burning out there beyond the shutters. Noises came up, voices from the vegetable market. She could see it without looking, the oranges and artichokes and cabbages and cheeses, roses and carnations . . .

Father came. He towered above her. 'How are you?'

'Dying.'

'You don't deserve to. Death is a treat.'

'A *treat*? It's dreadful, not something you want.'

'Sometimes it is.' Father sat down on the side of the bed and it slewed over like a raft. 'Sometimes it's an escape from a tired, worn out, rotten old body that has become nothing but a confounded nuisance.'

'Is yours rotten?' Anxiety made Hattie stiff.

'No, Hat.' Father took her hand and turned it into twigs. 'Not rotten enough to die—and neither is yours.'

Hattie gave a great sigh. 'Is Mother all right?'

'Your mother has the most beautiful body I have ever seen.'

'Oh—' Everything was all right, they were all safe. Savouring safety, Hattie's contentment suddenly snapped. She wanted to be dying, she wanted pity. But if death was a treat no one would pity her. 'Would you be sorry if I died?'

'One misses something one has seen about for nine years.'

'Like your pipe?' suggested Hattie crossly.

Father nodded.

'What would you do?'

'Pack up my own bait.'

'Would you go on fishing?'

'Why not?'

'And playing bowls?' Hating him almost, Hattie turned her head on the hot pillow and looked away. 'Mother would mind.' Gulping against the lump in her throat, she said, 'She'd sit on the beach alone and cry.'

'No, she wouldn't. I'd sit with her.'

'You wouldn't,' Hattie turned to look at him again. He wasn't smiling. 'Would you?' she said incredulously.

Father nodded.

She tried to see him there, sitting on the beach by Mother. She couldn't. 'You wouldn't.'

'Don't contradict. I tell you I would.'

The relief, if she could have seen him, would have been

tremendous. Shutting her eyes, she tried again. She saw the Wren in her—no, she'd be all in black. Father, in a black suit, sitting beside her. What would he do? 'I can't see you,' she opened her eyes.

'Can't help that. I tell you I would,' said Father obstinately. 'D'you think I'd let her sit alone?' He smiled suddenly. 'What a little fool you are, Hattie.'

Mother said, 'The doctor is coming to see you presently. He has been called to someone who is having a baby.'

'Having one?' said Hattie wonderingly. 'Hasn't she found it? Is she ill?'

In her anxiety the Wren had forgotten that the child knew nothing of birth. 'Found under bushes' was enough for her, as it had been for herself and her mother before her. It was only a matter of time, she supposed crossly, before Françoise or some other precocious French child told her what she was still too young to know. But if Madame did, she would never forgive her. The memory of that day in Madame's cart still rankled. 'Why is Marthe so fat?' Hattie had asked at the sight of the laundress crawling heavily like an enormous black gourd on spindle legs across the Rue de la Reine. 'Some people are fat and some are thin, and Marthe is fat, fatter than ever,' the Wren had answered. Madame, whose inadequate grasp of the English language was nevertheless sufficient to interpret this collection of simple, slightly repetitive words, shot up her eyebrows in amazement. 'She doesn't know that babies are carried in the womb?' The Wren, who had never heard the French for womb, managed also to collect its meaning. 'No. In England,' her back had straightened, 'children are brought up differently. They are not told things that they cannot understand.' 'But why cannot they understand? It is all quite simple. *Maintenant*—' lifting a hand from the reins, Madame, undaunted by the Wren's frown, had been about to launch out on a well gesticulated description of the whole business, when the cart, lurching over a stone and nearly upsetting, had diverted her attention from the womb.

Now the Wren said, 'Perhaps she isn't well.'

Monsieur le Docteur did not come till late afternoon. By then the sun was off the house and the shutters pushed back and the windows opened wide to the hot air from the town which was a little better than the stuffiness in Hattie's room. Monsieur le Docteur had big sad brown eyes. 'Always looks as though all his patients have died—' Father had said. 'Shouldn't wonder if they have.' Hattie had laughed loudly then, but now, as Monsieur le Docteur stood beside her bed, she was afraid. Her fear was terrible. Pulling the sheet up to her neck, she held it there with clenched fists. Although she was very hot, she began to shudder.

'And so you are sick, my little one?' He laid his hand on her forehead.

Everyone he touched died. Mother had forgotten and now it was too late. She and Father would never forgive themselves, thought Hattie. When he took away his hand it was too late to matter. She could see Father now on the beach with Mother.

'Why are you afraid?' he asked.

Hattie did not answer.

'You aren't afraid, Hattie, are you?' Mother spoke in French; it was bad manners to speak in English when there was someone there who couldn't understand.

'*Non*,' lied Hattie.

When he put the thermometer under her arm it was too late for that to matter, either. When he poked her to find the pain, he stared at her sadly because she was dying. A bite on her arm began to tickle. She didn't scratch it, she was dying.

Monsieur le Docteur went away with Mother discussing apricots. They didn't want to talk about apricots really, Hattie knew. They wanted to talk about her when she couldn't hear. Their feet went downstairs with their voices.

Outside, a dog barked. The sharp staccato sound brought gutters and dust and shadows under walls and sun on stones. Seeing those things with her mind's eye made her feel better. She wouldn't die. Scratching her bite, she sat up. The room whirled round. Lying down, she felt sick and afraid again.

Mother came back. She looked at Hattie and then smiled. 'He's gone. You weren't afraid of him, Hattie, surely?'

'He touched me and I'll die. All his patients die. Father said that's why his eyes are sad.'

'Don't be silly. It was a joke, you know it was—we all laughed.'

'It's true. I'm dying.'

'Hattie, stop talking such rubbish—I won't have it. You are not dying and you are not to keep on saying you are.' In the silence after this, Mother's lips moved. She was saying, 'Please God,' not tempting Providence. She went over to the window and looked out. 'It's very hot still.' She sighed. Propping her elbow in her hand she held her face with her fingers and put her little finger in her mouth. Mother was thinking. She came back then, and sat down on the chair by the bed. 'Have you ever thought about what's inside you?' Mother spoke quietly as though she were in church.

'Mussels.'

'No,' Mother winced. 'I don't think there can be any of those left now, darling.'

'Then there's nothing.'

'I don't mean in the way of food. I mean—well, how you're made, Hattie—bones, and blood vessels, and muscles, *muscles*, sinews, not fish and——' Mother was trying to think of something else.

'Heart,' contributed Hattie.

'Yes, heart of course, but I mean lower down. Lower down there's an appendix. It's a funny little thing—like a worm, I believe,' Mother smiled.

'Does it squirm?' Hattie wriggled.

'No, it wouldn't do that, ever,' Mother seemed to be sticking up for it. 'It stays there quite quietly, doing nothing in particular —at least I don't think it does,' Mother added conscientiously, 'until suddenly one day it may become inflamed with—food, I suppose.'

'Mussels?'

'Perhaps, I don't know—no, too soon I should think—and then it is best to take it out, and the doctor is going to remove yours—which is very kind of him,' Mother licked her lips.

'*Mine?*'

'Yes, that's why you're sick and have got a pain,' Mother said slowly.

'How will he get it out?' Hattie's face had got crimson. She felt crimson all over.

There was a flush on Mother's cheeks, too. 'He'll make a little slit, like slitting a——' the Wren paused in search of a simile, herring, sardine, no, certainly not; she could find none. 'You won't feel anything,' she went on hurriedly. 'He'll give you a whiff of chloroform and you'll float away on a cloud. There's nothing to worry about,' her lips trembled over 'Please God'.

Father came. He was whistling the 'Eton Boating Song'. He came without trying to be quiet, as though Hattie wasn't dying. 'What's all this I hear?'

'I don't know what you've heard,' the Wren said. 'You weren't in the house when the doctor came.'

Mother was blaming him and Hattie wished she wasn't, but Father took no notice. 'Berthe says he's going to cut Hat open.'

'Don't talk such rubbish!' exclaimed the Wren fiercely. 'How can you repeat servants' gossip?'

'Out with it!'

'He's going to make a small slit like a——' suddenly the Wren had got it, 'button-hole, and take out her appendix.'

'The deuce he is.'

'He's going to slit me and button-hole me all round,' Hattie saw the stitching quite clearly.

Mother spoilt it. 'Of course he won't do that. He'll shut you up and stitch it safely over and over,' her lips went on in silence as if she were making the stitching firmer.

'He'll kill me,' Hattie wailed, 'like all his other patients.'

'He won't dare,' said Father. 'He knows I'll wring his neck if he does.'

'Stop it! Stop talking about dying, both of you!' Mother's voice shook. 'You know what I said, Hattie, now stop it. I'm going downstairs, but I'll be back soon.'

'I'm here,' said Father, 'there's no need.'

'Aren't you going fishing, or drinking?'

'Not to my knowledge.'

Mother went downstairs. Father slumped down on to the chair by the bed. Hattie could never remember him sitting beside her before because she was ill. It made her proud. She wanted it to be a success, to please him.

'You aren't really afraid, are you?' he asked.

'No. I wasn't afraid to push that man into the sea, either.'

'No, but look, Hat—' Father took her hand, 'you forget that. It's a secret between us, and if you go on thinking about it you may tell someone by mistake.'

'I wouldn't.'

'You might, you might blab about it coming round.'

'Coming round where?'

'From the operation. They'll give you some chloroform, didn't the Wren tell you?—and waking up you might forget and say something and then we won't have our secret any longer. Think of something that isn't a secret.'

'What?'

'Letting the wren free, seeing it fly into the sky.'

'Mother says it was someone else's and we hadn't any right.'

'Your mother says a lot of silly things.'

She ought to defend Mother, Hattie knew, but how could she annoy Father with him sitting beside her, holding her hand instead of drinking and fishing. 'If Mother had been there and seen it go, she'd have been glad like us.'

'I doubt it. The Wren sees things as right or wrong. She never smudges the dividing line.'

Hattie wasn't certain what he meant but she knew Father didn't like Mother to be like that. Instead of saying anything, she picked her nose with her free hand. Father never minded; Mother did. She stopped picking it for Mother's sake, to make up. But then she asked Father something that Mother would hate. 'If I die can I have extreme unction please?'

'Good God, no! No brat I've spawned is going out on the crest of popery.'

Hattie's lip trembled. She was beginning to feel sick again. 'You've never minded, you've never minded me going into the cathedral or talking to Monsieur le Curé.'

'That's quite a different kettle of fish from taking part in a bare-faced fraud, that's all it is—setting up to shrive murderers and villains at the eleventh hour as easy as washing a shirt before a party.'

'You said I wasn't a murderer.'

'Nor you are.'

'I *want* unction. How can you refuse when I'm dying?' Hattie's voice rose and cracked.

'Easily—if you were,' said Father, 'but you aren't.'

Hattie looked to see if his lips moved in 'Please God' and they didn't. Dragging her hand free, she sat up and retched.

Monsieur le Docteur operated on the English child on the kitchen table. He was a precise little man and liked everything just so. His wife, a native of Montmartre, was an untidy, easy-going creature whose gods were stomachs—her own, her husband's, and the stomachs of her friends. Monsieur le Docteur hated his stomach and his wife's savoury meats that would have turned it into a gaseous balloon, had he permitted them to do so. The kitchens and bedrooms in which he operated were never just so either. Either there was no gas, or the bracket was over the cooking range, or in some equally inconvenient spot in a bedroom. Lamps and candles at night, flies in the day-time, ignorance, hysteria, and a maddening disregard for germs perpetually outraged his orderly soul. The Englishwoman was particular. She had a regard for cleanliness and orderliness, but she did not trust him. He was accustomed to that. In a practice in which the ignorant and suspicious far outnumbered those with a belief in himself and his profession, he was used to being avoided as a poisoner and a murderer. But it was not so with the English-woman. She did not distrust his profession, and her distrust of him stemmed from his nationality, he knew. He was neither annoyed nor amused; he saw it as a part of her orderliness, a tributary of the qualities that made her the kind of woman he should have married. The Englishman, on the other hand, had no orderliness, while possessing the characteristics that he himself lacked; physical strength, bull-necked obstinacy, and a dislike of blood drawn by a surgeon's knife; slaughter by shooting, bleeding pigs, gutting fish—those he would enjoy.

Sebastian Suckling, bending over the kitchen table, held his child's hands until she was unconscious. Hattie, who had lived through most of the day with Mother so that they had seemed to belong to each other entirely till Father came and sat beside her bed, now at the eleventh hour seemed his. It was Father who carried her downstairs and laid her on the kitchen table 'like a damn' piece of steak'. 'Shush,' the Wren hissed at him, but Sebastian ignored her. Hattie smiled to please Father and because she was being courageous to please him too. She did not shriek when the doctor's assistant planted something like the crown of a little hat on her face followed by dampness and a sweet disgusting smell. When she realized what was happening, that she was going to be killed with the onion-knife, she tried to shriek but could only choke. Trying to pull away her hands she fought for a moment with the savage feebleness of a dying kitten.

CHAPTER V

HATTIE could hardly believe her eyes when she woke up to see Father in the chair by the window *writing*. Lying still, she exam-ined him. He looked stern without being cross; he was thinking. 'Never go near Father when he's writing,' Mother said. It was one of Mother's rules of life, like never go near a dog-fight, or the back legs of a horse, or one of those things on the pavement, never lean out of a top window or speak to strangers. God's rules were the Ten Commandments. And now, without being able to help it, she was in the room while Father was doing it. Lifting her head from the pillow, she waited for him to look. When he took no notice, she lifted her shoulders. If she didn't lie still the stitches would burst. He still didn't notice. She'd got a pain. 'I've burst my stitches!' she had tried to sound ordinary but she squawked.

'Balderdash,' said Father as if he'd known she was awake.

'Mother said I would if I didn't lie still and I haven't.'

'Your mother knows nothing about it,' Father sounded as though Mother didn't belong to him at all. 'You couldn't burst one if you hauled a roller; they're catgut.'

'What's catgut?'

'The gut of a cat of course. You've seen a fish gutted, you know what gut is.'

Sickened by what she saw, Hattie said, 'It's *slimy*.'

'For God's sake use your brain, Hat. Never heard of drying things? Catgut looks like thread, at least yours does, not streams of entrails. Haven't you seen it?'

No, Hattie hadn't. When Monsieur le Docteur had peered at the awful thing under the bandages she hadn't been allowed to look. She hadn't wanted to, she had been afraid. 'I don't want catgut!' Her eyes filled with tears. She flopped back on the pillow so that Father shouldn't see them.

'You'd be in the deuce of a mess without it.'

There was the sound of wheels outside and the tramp of feet. The shutters and windows were open; there was no sun to keep out, only the air to let in, cooled by a drizzle and smelling of wet dust.

'What's that?' Hattie asked. 'Is it a procession?' She sniffed quietly.

Getting up with a great screech of basket-work, Father stood at the window blotting out the light. Now that his back was to her, Hattie wiped her eyes on the sheet. 'Yes, it's a funeral.'

'Whose?'

'A stranger's.' Black hearse, black mourners—all the macabre trappings accompanying the corpse to the worms. It was a good fishing day. The fellow inside the box should have been on the wall, master of the worms, Sebastian reflected, if he—damn it all, how could he have known? Drowned during a heart attack brought on by shock—the shock of the lightning, they said. They said he must have fallen off the wall during the attack, but he

knew better. He'd made it his business to be up here with the
brat when it passed. Rosie wouldn't have let the cat out of the
bag, not she, but he wasn't taking any chances for once. If something had happened and she'd had to go downstairs, she might
have sent up Berthe who couldn't be trusted to hold her tongue
if Hat badgered, who couldn't be trusted to hold it at all faced
with the sob-producing melodrama of a funeral. But Hat's illness
had saved the day so far—no doubt about that; it was the only
bright side to it. Had she been up and about just now what's the
betting she'd have got hold of the truth and raised the deuce of
an uproar about being a murderer or some such nonsense and
the whole damn' thing would have been in the stew-pot. What
was the matter with the brat—why didn't she speak?

Sebastian went over to the bed and looked down at his
daughter. Hattie was lying flat, her eyes staring like a cornered
animal's. 'What the devil's the matter?'

'I don't want to die. I don't want to be buried.'

'You'll have to be; you can't lie about.'

'I can't bear it,' her voice rose with hysteria.

'Stop it! I'm sick of the sound of death! Die, die, die—that's
all you can talk about,' roared Sebastian. Clutching at a mos-
quito, he displayed the body triumphantly. 'The brute would
have bitten you to ribbons, you're a sitting target.' Flipping it on
the floor he went back to the business in hand. 'You've got to live
before you die, and you'll make a pretty mess of it if you don't
stop puking about death and learn something. How d'you think
you're going to manage if you don't even know what catgut is?'

'I do,' Hattie whispered.

'How can you hope to write a decent book if you don't know
anything, tell me that.'

Hattie couldn't. Flushing with excitement, she could only stare
at him with gaping awe.

'You've got to accumulate some knowledge.'

'Accumulate?'

'Yes, pile it up, grain by grain like a pyramid of rice.'

'Oh—Will I write a book, really?'

'Why not? You're bone of my bone—though God knows you
don't look it. Lying there you look like a weed.'

Hattie didn't mind looking like a weed; she didn't mind anything if she could write a book. 'What shall I write about?'

'How the devil should I know! But it won't be about sailing
before the mast, or diving for a wreck, or medieval butchery in

a French port I do know, and if your mother goes on trying to turn France into Bloomsbury you'll never write a decent word about it—butchery or not.'

'When shall I start?' asked Hattie eagerly.

'When you've got your pile of rice and not before.'

When Father had gone stamping downstairs whistling 'Land of Hope and Glory', Hattie lay staring at the ceiling, swollen with this new splendid excitement.

The Wren came stealing, with rustling and mouse's creaks. 'Are you awake?' she whispered.

Hattie said, 'Yes', loudly.

'I'm not surprised after the noise Father made.'

'I was awake before he made it.'

'I've brought you some barley-water.' Mother put down the jug of thick white water on the table beside the bed, standing where Father had stood, looking little and thin after him. She had on her white nun's veiling blouse with the pearl buttons and her gold watch pinned on, and her white *piqué* skirt. 'How flushed you look, darling.' She laid her hand, cool and light as a leaf, on Hattie's forehead.

'Father said I looked like a weed—I'm a flushed weed.' Hattie laughed. The laugh careered up hysterically. Listening to it, Hattie felt almost as though it didn't belong to her. When it was over she said, 'Laughing hurts.'

'Then you mustn't laugh.'

'I can't help it.'

'Yes, you can. Whenever you feel like laughing think of something else, something that isn't funny.'

'Something sad?—like the funeral?'

'No, nothing like that—' Mother poured barley-water into the wine-glass.

'Did you see it?'

'I didn't stare if that's what you mean. Now, Hattie, drink some of this—' Mother put her hand under Hattie's head to lift it, but it reared up on its own.

'I can manage.'

'Hattie, lie *down*! Do you want to burst your stitches?'

'I couldn't if I pulled a roller, Father says, they're cat-gut.'

'Lie down at once and do what you're told,' the Wren's voice quivered with anger. Your father knows nothing about illness. He's never been ill himself.' Furiously, reluctantly, the Wren's lips framed 'touch wood'. Swiftly, she drew back her hand with the glass till her arm just flicked the wooden table. 'But he thinks he can lay down the law about that, like everything else. Drink, Hattie.'

Swallowing obediently, Hattie wished she hadn't said what Father said. 'Perhaps he was exaggerating,' she suggested.

'His life is one long hyperbole.'

'What's that?'

'Exaggeration—drink.'

'*Hyperbole*—how could she remember that for her pyramid of rice?' Something that rhymed. 'What does hyperbole rhyme with?'

In the silence when Mother might be thinking or might still be too cross to, Hattie drank with a sucking noise and outside a child shouted.

'Nothing,' said Mother.

CHAPTER VI

'YOU ARE WELL ENOUGH to learn the collect today.'

'I'm not well enough to get out of bed.'

'Don't argue, Hattie. You can learn it while Father and I are in church.' The Wren brought Hattie's Prayer Book and laid it open on the bed. 'It's that one—the eleventh Sunday after Trinity.'

Mother had on her blue frock and her leghorn hat swathed in blue tulle. When she bent over Hattie to point out the collect her hat brushed Hattie's cheek; she smelt of lavender water.

'Rosie!—Rosie!— Where the hell are you?'

'Oh—' Mother caught her breath. It sounded as though she were collecting spit to spit, but Hattie knew she wasn't; Mother never spat except when she was cleaning her teeth or had swallowed a fly. It was a cross sucking-up. She was cross with Father. 'Here,' she said sharply, but Father who was downstairs couldn't possibly hear, Hattie knew, and she knew that Mother knew it too. '*O God, who declarest thy almighty power most chiefly in shewing mercy and pity;*' Mother's voice rose a little as Father's feet pounded up the stairs, '*Mercifully grant unto us such a measure of thy grace,*'

'Rosie!'

'*that we, running——*' breaking off, Mother straightened up as Father arrived.

'Why the devil can't you answer, Rosie?'

'I did.' Mother stood very straight. 'Sometimes when you speak to me in the horrible language you do, I feel tempted not to.' Turning, she picked up her white kid gloves from the table with Hattie's lemonade on it.

'What's wrong with a language that's been good enough for the English for over a thousand years?'

'You know what I mean perfectly well—' Mother was pushing her right hand down the arm of her glove, 'and in front of the child too.'

'The sooner the brat gets to grips with life the better. How's the catgut, Hat?'

Hattie seemed to come back again from being an invisible stranger to herself. Why should they talk like that as if she wasn't there, she thought crossly, and then expect her to come back again directly they were ready? 'All right, thank you.'

Mother, stooping to kiss her good-bye, felt stiff inside. They were alone for a minute, she and Mother under Mother's hat, secret and shut away from Father as Mother's lips moved on her cheek.

'We'd better go if we want to get there before the sermon—' Father said, 'though I could preach better than that fellow, and I dare say you could too, Rosie, if you put your mind to it.'

Mother didn't answer. Hattie didn't know whether she was pleased or sorry, but Father had started downstairs without waiting to know.

'Begin the collect now,' Mother said as she hurried after him.

'*O God, who declarest thy almighty power most chiefly in shewing mercy and pity;*' Hattie's voice, repeating the words out loud, was the only sound in the room. Mother had let her have the shutters a little bit open. The sun came through the slit and ran across the floor in a golden stick. '*Mercifully grant unto us such a measure of thy grace, that we, running the way of thy commandments,* please God, let me have a vision.' But God didn't. He only sent a fly to sit on the counterpane. The marble top of the wash-stand was grey. It looked horrid on top of the brown wood. When she had asked Mother why it was grey like that she had said because it was cheap and she would have to endure it till Father had finished his book. 'Stuff and nonsense!' Father had said. 'That Louis Quatorze commode that took your fancy in Paris had a grey top'. Mother said that was different. 'You said when you'd written your book you would give it to me. It was a safe enough

promise. Father had said she ought to have married someone in
a sausage factory, and had gone out fishing. Mother had been
cross all day. Hattie looked away from the wash-stand to think
of something else.

The cathedral clock struck eleven '. . . *may obtain thy gracious
promises, and be made partakers of thy heavenly treasure.*'

Berthe came up with Hattie's milk. Berthe wasn't a virgin.
Father said he'd eat his hat if she was. How *could* she be the
Virgin, Hattie had wanted to know, and Mother had said of
course she couldn't. He didn't mean the Virgin Mary, he meant
a virgin, and she had reminded Hattie of the parable of the ten
virgins with their lamps and explained that although Berthe
trimmed the lamps like they had, they were all much younger
than Berthe who was too old to be a virgin. The milk had bits of
boiled skin in it; it looked beastly. Berthe smelt of sweat and
garlic. Father called it 'sweat' and Mother called it 'perspiration'.
Father didn't mind because he hadn't got to sleep with her.
Hattie liked it. Sniffing it up now as Berthe stood by her bed, it
came to her that it was the same kind of smell and not the same
as the smell of horses and manure and wet dogs and seaweed.

'Tomorrow I'm going to sit up in a chair,' Hattie said.

Berthe said it was a miracle, that after all that had happened
to her she should ever be able to get out of bed again. She beamed
at Hattie and Hattie beamed back, and everything seemed happy
and wonderful and strong.

'Sing, Berthe, please.'

Berthe sang 'Au clair de la lune' in a soft voice that didn't seem
to belong to the solid fatness of her, and Hattie sang too, squeak-
ing and soaring and crackling.

Mother heard the collect after tea. Hattie read the Epistle and
Gospel, and then they went on to the Catechism.

'What is your name?' asked Mother.

'Harriet Georgina Louise.'

'Who gave you this name?'

'My Godfathers and Godmothers in my baptism.' She only
had one Godmother left. Aunt Lulu, Father's sister, had been
drowned skating. Hattie couldn't remember her at all; she had
only been two when it happened, but she had given her a silver
porridge-bowl and a hobby-horse first.

Before Hattie had time to go on, Mother interrupted, 'I have
something to tell you, Hattie. I have been waiting till you were

better. It's about Godmother Adelaide. I had a letter the day
after your operation to say that she had caught typhoid fever
from one of the poor people she was so good to in the slums.'

'Oh—' Staring at Mother and not staring at her, Hattie saw
with her mind's eye Godmother Adelaide in a brown felt hat
and a macintosh with mud on her skirt and brown galoshes over
black boots. 'Is she better?'

'I'm afraid not, darling; she's dead.' Mother spoke in her
hushed church voice.

'*Dead?*'

Mother nodded.

'They're *both* dead! I haven't got a Godmother,' said Hattie,
amazed and injured. It wasn't fair. She was different. She suddenly felt excited at being different, like an orphan.

'You seem to be thinking only of yourself, Hattie. Aren't you
sorry about Godmother Adelaide for her own sake?' asked
Mother, shocked.

Hattie was shocked that Mother was shocked, and shocked at
herself that she didn't want to cry, that she even felt glad suddenly
that she would never have to kiss that soft, cold, yellow cheek
again. Appalled by her wickedness, she got wickeder still by
saying 'Yes'.

The Wren pushed back a strand of hair with impatient fingers.
She, who was for ever trying to shield Hattie from the knowledge
of sorrow and suffering, like the tragedy of that wretched man
found drowned off the sea-wall, was now trying to force her into
it.

'She'll be happy in heaven, won't she?—casting down her
golden crown around the glassy sea.' Putting her hand up to her
mouth, Hattie bit her thumb-nail, trying hard to see this happening properly.

Looking at her, the Wren could detect no irony; the child's
face was wrapped in thought. There was silence in the room
while she, too, struggled to replace that dreadful hat of Adelaide's
like a boiled chocolate pudding, with a celestial crown . . .

Sebastian Suckling's mind was not occupied by Adelaide
Boyle. He had wasted all the thought he ever intended to on his
wife's rag-bag of a cousin twice removed and now totally removed, thank God, for ever. Seated at one of Madame's small
iron tables on the pavement outside the *Coq d'Or*, he was drinking
the Ten Commandments out of his system, writer's paralysis, and
the nagging thought of the wretched Picard. When the waitress,

taking the place of Émilie who had gone home to nurse her mother, brought a fresh drink at Madame's instructions, he did not bother to glance at her.

CHAPTER VII

'AREN'T YOU asleep yet, Hattie?'

No, Hattie wasn't. 'Why hasn't Father been to say good night?'

'He came in late from fishing and after dinner it was too late for you. You should have been asleep by then.'

'I'm not. Please can he come now?'

'He's gone out.'

'Where?'

'For a stroll, I suppose.' Mother went over to the window and stood looking out as though she could see where Father was strolling. Hattie didn't believe her. 'Has he gone drinking?'

Mother turned round. 'Hattie, you are *not* to talk like that! *Gone drinking*—apart from the atrocious English, how dare you talk like that about your father?'

'I only meant—'

'It doesn't matter what you meant. You're old enough now to think before you speak. Suppose you had said that to anyone but me, what would they have thought?'

'I wouldn't.'

'I should hope not.' Lifting Hattie's dressing-gown off the back of the chair, Mother put it down again. 'He may be going to have an aperitif, he probably is—and there's no reason why he shouldn't,' she said slowly.

'At the *Coq d'Or*?'

'Perhaps.' Mother looked out of the window again. Her white frock was shadowy and all the gold had gone from her hair; it was a soft, dark blur.

In the morning Madame came. Mother brought her up to Hattie's room. 'Here's someone to see you, Hattie,' Mother said, in the brisk cheerful kind of voice that meant she didn't want Madame. Hattie did. Madame brought with her the same kind of outside feeling that Father did.

H

'Well, my little cabbage—what have you been up to?' cried Madame gaily.

Mother wouldn't like 'my little cabbage', Hattie knew, but she did. She saw a little green cabbage and then a red pickling one. 'I'm going to dress tomorrow,' she said, staring at the melon in Madame's hands. She knew she oughtn't to stare at it as though she thought it was for her.

'*Bien, bien, bien!*' Madame reached the side of the bed. Swooping, she kissed Hattie. Hattie, who had never been kissed by Madame before, who had just dragged her eyes politely from the melon to Madame's face, caught the kiss full on her cheek and with it the smells—Madame's smell, and the delicate fruity pungency of warm ripe melon. 'I have brought you a melon, see——' Madame laid it in Hattie's lap.

'Oh, thank you!' Taking it in her hands, feeling the roughness of the mottled yellow and green skin, the cracks between the fat slices, Hattie lifted it and sniffed. Moving her lips against the rind, she kissed it, kissing Madame's face, she thought, laughter suddenly surging up in her and bursting out.

'It amuses you, *chérie*?'

Ashamed, blushing, Hattie laid her hot cheek against the melon. 'I've never had one of my own before. Thank you a thousand times.' It was not hyperbole like the Wren's thanks for their cart-ride.

'It was kind of you to bring it, but you shouldn't have,' Mother said.

'Why shouldn't I?' Madame expected an answer.

'Spoiling.'

'*Pouf?* The sick and the bereaved, they both need spoiling.' Laughing, Madame shrugged. 'M'sieu Sooklin thinks so anyway. He is so kind to poor Julie.'

The Wren's eyebrows lifted.

'The widow of M'sieur Picard. I have engaged her as a waitress since Émilie has gone to nurse her mother. But you have not been to *Le Coq d'Or* lately, naturally, and M'sieur has not thought to tell you, perhaps?'

'He may have——' Without so much as a shrug or a movement of her hands the Wren seemed to relegate the matter to the waste-paper-basket. 'I have had so much to think about lately.' Her eyes rested on Hattie.

'*Me*,' thought Hattie, filling with the importance of having been nearly dead.

'But Hattie is so much better now there is no need to worry,' Mother went on.

Chagrined, Hattie didn't look to see if Mother was whispering 'Please God'. She didn't want to be better, she thought resentfully. She would like to die. She wished she had. The importance of being dead filled her with envy and longing, spoilt then by the reflection that she wouldn't be there to enjoy it. The Roman Catholics thought dead people went to purgatory. Mother said they didn't; they went straight to where they were going for good, heaven or hell.

'*Absolument.*' Madame smiled on Hattie. 'And that is what I say to M'sieur about Julie; that there is no need to worry about her now she has work, and as to being a widow—' Madame's voice sharpened, 'she is not the only widow in all France.'

'She needs time,' said Mother. 'Don't dig your nail into it, Hattie, you'll spoil it.'

Obediently, Hattie drew her thumb-nail out of the melon skin, leaving a crescent. If she could have made a smaller one inside there would have been a sickle moon. She ran her finger down a crack instead.

Father came up when she was eating mince. He threw the melon up almost to the ceiling and caught it. The room seemed full of strength and adventure.

'Where have you been?' Hattie asked.

'Aboard an English yacht. It put in last night.'

How pleased Mother would be, thought Hattie excitedly. 'Can Mother go aboard and see the English?'

'No. It's gone now.'

Father gave the melon another toss.

'Why didn't you come and fetch her?' The violence of Hattie's dismay made her shriek a little.

'There wasn't time. She wouldn't have approved of the owner anyway.'

'Why?'

'He was *nouveau riche.*'

'Do you mean he had just got rich?'

Father nodded.

'Did he *steal* it?'

'If you mean did he creep into a bank in the middle of the night with a mask and a jemmy and a sack—no,' said Father.

'Oh—' Hattie's spirits, which had lifted a little with this promise of fresh excitement, fell again. 'Then how did he get it?'

'Candles.' Father threw the melon from one hand to the other. 'He is a manufacturer.'

'Is it wrong to make candles?'

'Of course not, but people who do shouldn't have yachts, so your mother thinks. Everyone should stay in their own pigeon-hole and not try to escape.'

'Are we in our hole?'

'She says not, that I'm dragging us out of the damn' thing.'

There was silence for a moment as Hattie chewed over the extraordinary picture that Father's words had produced. Thrusting her fingers through her fringe, she asked 'Where to?'

'Down into a proletarian quagmire of Bohemian debauchery.'

'What's a quagmire?'

'A quaking bog.' Dropping the melon on Hattie's wound, Father went downstairs to *déjeuner*, which Mother called 'dinner'.

Messing about with the rest of her mince which she didn't want, Hattie saw Father dragging her and Mother down into a quaking bog which shook and bubbled like boiling chocolate.

That night she dreamt they were being wrecked. She saw Mother clinging to something, and then a roaring great wave came and washed her away. 'Father, Father, Mother's drowning!' she shrieked, but Father was hacking down a mast and didn't hear. She could see Mother's head and then she couldn't. Mother had gone.

She woke up then, but the fear and desolation were still with her. She must go to Mother. Befogged with sleep still, she forgot that she was ill. When she remembered that she had only walked across her bedroom holding Mother's arm, she flumped down on the stairs. Because the stitches had been taken out, it didn't mean she could be rumbustical and silly. 'The wound has only just healed, and if you burst it open now where will you be?' Mother had said, and she'd said, 'Dead' and it hadn't mattered then because she hadn't been rumbustical and burst them. Now, hugging her knees, feeling the pain, feeling burst, terrified, dying, the panic of Mother's drowning ebbed. She was there in bed and when she called her and she came she would scold her. Father wouldn't think it mattered. He'd put the melon on it. 'Burst?—of course you haven't.' She had. She and Mother *knew*. In the faint light coming through the landing window she could see their shut bedroom door. She would have to call loudly to wake Mother, and at the thought of how she must shout, slumped here unable to move—a target for ghosts, fresh panic seized her.

Then she heard it; down below in the hall a door opened. Then it shut. A burglar! Her heart thumped and the roots of her hair prickled. 'You'll have to be damn' quick on the trigger.' But the gun was for Arabs. Footsteps and voices and a light coming up the stairs. Petrified, Hattie waited.

'Why the devil aren't you in bed, Rose?' Sebastian said.

'Because I'm sick of lying there waiting for you to come.'

'Why wait?' Being waited for like a child or a rake, he thought angrily. Surely Rosie knew better than that?

'Because I can't sleep while you're making a fool of yourself and me running after that—*waitress*.'

In the face of her scorn, his anger dwindled. The red flag of her hackles was hoisted. If she had puked he would have given her short shrift, but his spirit applauded her for coming out into the open fair and square—more than he could do. 'Don't be nonsensical, Rosie. I'm not running after her. I'm sorry for her, that's all—as I hope someone would be for you and the brat if I went off like Picard.' Though he was dashed if he'd be such a fool as to let a chit of nine push *him* into the sea.

'Rubbish! Do you expect me to believe that?'

'That's why I said it.'

'And so you take her home at night?'

'She comes this way. She lives in the Rue des Founderies.'

'And you find it necessary to take her the whole way?'

'It's the least I can do at this hour.'

'Fiddlesticks! You've never had any qualms over Marie coming back alone at night from her mother's.'

'Marie?' Sebastian rumbled with laughter. With a face like that Marie would be safe on the Shanghai waterfront.' He hoped for Rosie's horse-bag snort but her hackles were too high.

'It may not be beautiful but at least it's honest.'

'Julie's is not beautiful either, and as for that I dare say it's honest. Her mouth is too large and her eyes too small, but she has an air of *je ne sais quoi* like your kid and patent leather boots.'

'Oh, stop joking!' the Wren said furiously.

Even in the dim light he could see the scorn in her eyes and again his spirit applauded it. 'Why should I?' Taking the lamp from her, Sebastian put it on the table. 'Don't make mountains out of molehills, Rosie.' He wanted to crush out her suspicion and disbelief and nonsense till there was nothing left but flesh and bone and spirit and love.

Staring through the banisters, Hattie saw Father put his arms round Mother. Mother didn't want him to, she fought him, trying to get away. 'Leave me alone, you're drunk,' her voice was low and hissing.

Father said, 'I'm no more drunk than you are.' He let her go suddenly and she fell against the wall. 'If that's how you feel I damn' well will!' Opening the door of the spare room, he went in and banged it. The house shook.

Taking the lamp, Mother went into their room and banged the door to.

Presently, in the dark silence, stunned and disbelieving, Hattie crawled up the stairs to her room.

CHAPTER VIII

ROSE SUCKLING pushed her daughter to the sea in a Bath chair that had travelled to Le Touquet with an arthritic English general twenty years before. From there it had moved to Paris as the mainstay of an anaemic English widow. Falling eventually into French hands, it had gone to the west coast with the consumptive mother of the Protestant priest, and passing from one predecessor to another had become as much a part of the living as the priest's house.'

'Look where you're going!'

Oh, yes, Hattie would. Gripping the wooden handle, she steered a straight course down the centre of the pavement. It was shady in there under the arcade because it was early. Presently, the sun in the street would splash through the arches like the sea slopping up the slipway.

There was a black, alive lobster in a tank in a restaurant window. Putting herself in its place, Hattie implored comfort, 'Does it hate being there? Does it *know*?'

'Of course not. Look where you're going.'

There was a crowd outside the Hôtel de Ville.

'What's happening?'

'I don't know.' Mother tipped up the chair so that Hattie wasn't guiding. 'It's a wedding.' She plumped it down again. The bride was all in white. The bridesmaids' frocks were the colour of a pink blancmange.

On the sea front was the salt sea air that Hattie had been

brought to breathe, untainted by the streets, by flies and dust and rottenness and urinals.

'Gulp,' said Mother.

Hattie gulped.

The sea was shallow, lying like blue-white watered silk on the wet sand. Each morning it had slipped out further, like a sash being slowly pulled away. Each morning Hattie gulped.

On the fifth day, because it had rained in the morning, they went after tea. On the front Hattie got out of the chair and walked. There was a long drop from the wall of the front to the sand below. 'Don't go too near the edge and fall over,' Mother said again.

No, Hattie wouldn't. 'Father says I wouldn't break my neck. He says if I fell like a cat nothing would happen, and if I fell ordinarily it probably wouldn't either because of the sand.'

'Father doesn't know. He isn't God.'

Mother was cross. Hattie wished she hadn't said it. She didn't want to think of the other night. A sea-gull squawked, swooping over the beach; she thought of that now. 'Would you like to be a sea-gull, Mother?'

'Yes.'

'Where would you fly to?'

'England.'

Hattie knew that she had really known the answer already.

Mother went further. 'I'd go to London, to St James's Park and swim on the pond there,' she said dreamily, as though she were talking to herself. She had stopped, and holding the chair with one hand, had turned to look at the sea.

Hattie felt proud and pleased, almost as if she herself had already turned Mother into a gull. 'I'd come with you.'

Mother turned back to the chair again. 'No—your place would be here with Father.'

'Wouldn't you want me?' said Hattie, appalled.

'It wouldn't be a case of wanting or not wanting, if this is where you should be.'

How *could* Mother be like this? What had happened to her? Cut to the quick, Hattie hit back. 'You'd have to feed on garbage, Mother.' She saw Mother pecking at some sodden old bread in London while she and Father ate pork chops and peas. In spite of being hurt by Mother, her eyes began to fill with tears.

'I wouldn't mind.'

'But you don't like nastiness.'

'I'm not a gull.'

No, Mother wasn't. Turning her back on her, Hattie wiped her eyes with her hand.

Mother changed suddenly. 'Hattie, what nonsense we're talking! It's time you got back into the chair, darling.'

Everything was all right, thought Hattie happily. 'Can't I walk a little more?—as far as the groyne, *please*.'

'Only as far as that.'

While the Wren stooped to take a stone out of her shoe, Hattie went on the last few yards to the level of the groyne. Beyond this and the next groyne was a little beach. The wall was lower here. As she went to look over, she heard the sound of crying. Dismayed, she stopped. Then tiptoeing to the edge, she looked down, straight on to the top of Father's straw hat with the hole in it. Tipped against his shoulder was a black hat with a black veil—a widow's hat. It was the widow crying.

Hattie stood stock still, staring down, shocked and astonished. It was very shocking to see a grown-up cry, even if it was a widow crying for her husband, and it was astonishing to see her doing it like that with Father. She was still gaping when, without looking, she felt Mother beside her. Father said, 'I'll see you don't starve.' He didn't roar or even sound cross.

Mother took Hattie by the arm, holding it so tightly that it pinched, and drew her quietly away. She walked her to the Bath chair which she had left by itself, and said, 'Get in.'

Hattie obeyed.

Mother pushed her quickly, in silence. She didn't even say 'Look where you're going'. When Hattie almost guided into a seat, she tipped up the chair as she had outside the Hôtel de Ville.

Then suddenly Mother said in a cheerful voice, 'Would you like to go back by *le port*?'

Yes, Hattie would. She was so relieved to hear Mother sound like that, even if she was pretending, that she brightened up a little herself. 'Perhaps there'll be an English ship in,' she suggested, wanting to please Mother.

There wasn't. There was nothing special.

Mother stopped with the chair facing the harbour. She came round from behind the chair to the side while Hattie was watching a man bale out his sailing boat. She said, 'Listen, Hattie—I don't want you to tell Father we saw him on the beach. I don't think—' the Wren's gloved hand fingered the neck of her frock —'he'd like it. There was no reason why he shouldn't have been there' of course" she said slowly and distinctly, 'but—are you listening, Hattie?'

'Yes, Mother.'

'Good. Well, sometimes there are times in everyone's lives when they don't want to be seen—and it is better that they shouldn't be—even if what they are doing isn't wrong. It's—it's nicer for them to be private. Your father was being kind to that —woman.' With a sudden movement of her toe, shooting out like some small wild animal from under her skirt, the Wren kicked something into the harbour.

To Hattie it seemed as though Mother had kicked the widow into the water. Craning forward to look, she said, 'What did you kick?'

'Only a stone. Your father,' Mother began again, 'is sorry for her because she's poor.'

'Is she Julie, the waitress instead of Émilie at the *Coq d'Or*?' Hattie said.

'Yes. How did you know?' asked Mother sharply.

Not the other night, thought Hattie, she hadn't got to say about that, she'd got to say about Madame. 'Madame said when she brought the melon.'

'Yes, so she did.'

'Why is she so poor if she's paid for being a waitress?'

'She isn't.'

'But you said that's why Father's sorry for her.'

'It is, it is—and because she's a widow. Your father has a kind heart—sometimes,' added Mother. The 'sometimes' was so quiet that it was almost like a 'Please God'.

Hattie still didn't understand why Father was sorry for her being poor if she wasn't, but there were a good many other things she wanted to know. 'Has she got any children?'

'One.'

'Is it a boy or a girl?'

'A boy.'

'How old is he?'

'Oh, I don't know!—about ten or something. Stop asking so many questions,' Mother's voice rose.

'But I want to know so that I can think about him.'

'And weave one of your make-believes—No, Hattie,' Mother's voice was calm again, 'I want you to forget the whole thing. They're nothing to do with you, and if Father wishes to be kind he doesn't want other people to know about it.'

'*Let not your right hand know what your left hand doeth.*' Hattie felt pleased at saying it first. She longed to know where they lived and if she would ever see the boy, or had without knowing. She wanted to see him awfully, like looking at the man whose brother had been stung to death by bees. But it was difficult to ask Mother now.

'Exactly,' Mother said.

'Why did her husband die? Was he buried while I was in bed?' Hattie asked in a rush.

'Yes.'

'Why did he die?'

'He had a heart attack.'

'Was he in bed when he had it?'

'Hattie, be quiet. The whole subject is finished with, and I want you to promise not to mention it to your father or anyone else.'

As Hattie was promising, a fisherman threw a crab out of his boat into the water.

On the way home they met Monsieur le Curé. She was safe in the Bath chair; he couldn't grab her now. Hattie thought, unless he grabbed the Bath chair and pushed her into the sea in it, but while he was getting to the sea Mother or someone else would rescue her. It had only been a dream. The last time she had seen him really, was the day he had given her the carnation, the day after she had fought him in the cathedral. His hand had come down suddenly on her shoulder in the market. 'Ah—the little English one again.' Hiding under the brim of her straw cartwheel, her cheeks flaming, Hattie had stared down, seeing the dusty toes of his boots poking out from under his black skirts. Her shoulder, hard and stiff in his grasp, had felt like the scraped bone of a joint of meat. 'Now then—' With his other hand he had grasped the crown of her hat, and pinching her head through it had pulled it up. 'You are not afraid of Monsieur le Curé, surely?' She had mumbled 'No', and then, forced to look at him, seeing his donkey face, the corners of his long mouth, with the bottom lip that jutted out, curling in a smile, it had unexpectedly seemed true. 'Would you like a carnation?' he had asked. Yes, she had wanted one badly. Freeing her head, pushing her by the shoulder, he had taken her to Babet's stall. 'Choose one—only one. The ecstasy of a single flower is lost in a multitude.' The words had flowed over her, undigested, as she chose with great care one crimson bloom. 'Where did you get it?' Mother had

asked. 'You didn't *take* it, Hattie, did you?' No, she had been
given it, she had said, not wanting to say who by, knowing that
Mother wouldn't like Monsieur le Curé to have given it. 'By
Babet?' Mother had asked, and Hattie had said, 'Yes.' It was
true in a way. Taking it out of the bunch, Babet had handed it
to her.

Today, stopping to talk to them in the arcade, Monsieur le
Curé had a little piece of cotton wool sticking to his long upper
lip. Hattie watched it moving up and down while he said how
pleased he was to see her so well. Mother talked to him like she
talked to Françoise's grandmother whom she didn't want to get
any further with. Hattie smiled at him secretly because of the
carnation like one spy to another.

Next, they met Madame. She was carrying two loaves, one in
her armpit and one in her hand. Talk squirted out of her. She
was amazed and enchanted to see Hattie out of doors. With her
loafless hand she smoothed the side of the chair, then grasped it.
'Bring her to dinner with me. I have *sole meunière* and breast of
chicken—what better diet for an invalid?'

'*Please* can we?' Hattie slewed round to look at Mother.

'No, of course you can't, you must go to bed.'

Hattie kicked her heels against the chair.

'I should be so happy to fill these matchsticks with my chicken
and cream.' Madame tapped Hattie's knees with one of the loaves.

Stretching out her legs stiffly, Hattie looked at them, seeing
them without the black cotton stockings, filling with chicken and
cream till they were like long, fat, tight sausages.

'It's not chicken and cream she has lacked, but the desire to
eat,' the Wren said tartly.

'Naturally,' said Madame, as though the Englishwoman had
uttered a cliché. She was still holding the chair.

'We must go.' The Wren's knuckles whitened on the handle.

'I also. Émilie, silly girl, forgot the bread. Her head—never
very strong—' Madame hunched her shoulders, 'is still full of her
mother. You knew she was back, yes?'

'No.' The Wren tried to push the chair, but Madame held it
as though clamped.

'So Julie Picard is without work,' she continued. 'There is no
need for her to be, but she is a parasite. Your husband has been
very kind to her—too kind. When a man becomes kind to a
woman of that type—' Madame's shoulders seemed to throw up
the consequences into mid-air and leave them there.

The Wren unclenched her teeth. She was shaking a little, but her grip on the chair helped to control it. 'Please leave go of the chair, Madame. It's time the child was in bed.'

'*La! la!*—then of course you must go. *Au revoir, ma petite.*'

When they had left Madame and were on their way again, Hattie said, 'What's a parasite, Mother?' When the Wren didn't answer she asked again.

'Someone that feeds on someone else,' Mother said then.

'How can Julie Picard feed on someone? Is she—' in her horrified excitement, Hattie guided the chair off the pavement, 'a *cannibal*?' she shrieked as the chair jolted into the gutter.

'Hattie, *will* you look where you're going!' Tipping up the chair, the Wren righted it.

'I'm sorry. *Is* she?'

'Stop asking stupid questions,' Mother's voice shook. 'Stop talking and guide properly.' She let the chair down with a flump.

Hattie's eyes filled with tears. How could she get her pile of rice if Mother wouldn't answer?

CHAPTER IX

THE DAY Hattie went for a walk without the chair, Françoise came to tea. She had on white everything—white hat, white frock, white socks and white kid boots. Hattie would have hated to look like that on a weekday; she'd have hated to wear white kid boots even on Sunday, but although Françoise was eleven she didn't mind looking namby-pamby. If the Arabs chased *her* she wouldn't shoot—she'd shriek. Secure in the knowledge of her trigger-sense, smugly conscious of the black bow in front and the blue square of her sailor collar behind, Hattie allowed Françoise to pick up her hand as though it belonged to *her*. Shaking it, Françoise said politely how happy she was to see her better.

They had tea in what Father called the *salle à manger* and Mother called the dining-room. French people didn't have tea; it was an English custom. Françoise was being made to *when in Rome do as the Romans do*. She did it very well. She had one of everything and two of some. While she was having the *patisserie* with an apricot that Hattie wanted, Mother said, 'What a pretty frock you have on, Françoise; it is so beautifully tucked.'

Françoise smiled at her from under her long dark lashes. 'Thank you, Madame,' she said, speaking in English, slowly and carefully. 'Madame Picard made it,' she explained in French. Gasping, she clapped her hand to her mouth, dropping her eyes to her plate.

The Wren's backbone tautened. Her ribs became a framework of armour holding in the vulnerable core of her heart and stomach that cried out with disgust. 'Did she? She is an excellent needlewoman.' The level calm of her voice acted like a wet flannel on the flushed disorder of the French child, as she had intended that it should.

'*Oui.*' Glancing up at her, Françoise looked down at her plate again. There had been relief not chagrin in the look. It had not been slyness but a genuine gaffe, the Wren decided.

'Will you have one?' Hattie was holding out the plate of *patisseries* to her mother. Was it for comfort or just a spurt of good manners? the Wren wondered. That a child should have to comfort for such a reason—curling up her toes in her shoes as an alternative to hurling a plate through the window, Rose Suckling asked which Hattie wanted.

'You say.'

Taking the plainest, distastefully forcing her tongue round the name, the Wren said, 'Does Madame Picard make many clothes for you, Françoise?'

'Never before.' Reassured by the matter of fact continuation of the conversation, Françoise elaborated further. 'She has gone to Neuilly to stay with her cousin. When she returns she will make me a blouse.'

'And when will that be?' Was it possible to bamboozle with a pretence of lightness this recipient of adult conversation and odious gossip? Unlikely, decided the Wren.

Françoise shrugged. 'Ten days perhaps—she doesn't know.'

Ten days for reclamation. A small, fierce flame of determination licked up in the Wren's brain. Her eyes met Hattie's which were alight with pleasure. If only it were food; to be pleased because your father——

'Here's Father!' Hattie cried.

A distant rollicking rendering of 'John Brown's Body' grew lustier and lustier as Sebastian strode nearer. How glorious! thought Hattie. Father was coming, Madame Picard had gone away, and the *patisserie* with cherries was still uneaten. Deep down inside her, delight squiggled like a worm.

Sebastian arrived. 'Rosie!' he bellowed.

'We're here!' shrieked Hattie.

'Not such a noise.' The Wren's fingers closed on the handle of the teapot.

Sebastian burst open the door. 'What's going on here?'

'We're having tea.' The Wren spoke in her polite imbecile voice, but in French because of Françoise. 'We have it every day.'

'Not to this extent.' Sebastian's eyes surveyed the plates, then rested on Françoise. 'Who's this?'

'Father, you *know*!' Hattie said.

Françoise, who had been gazing at him with fascinated awe as though, at last, unprotected by either Monsieur le Curé or the Virgin, she had come face to face with the devil who was rather to her liking, swallowed a piece of pastry and prepared to be social. If she had hoped that Monsieur would raise her proffered hand to his lips, she was disappointed. Ignoring her hand, he pinched her ear. There was a gathering underneath the lobe and she gave a little gasp of pain. He slapped Hattie on the back. The sudden impact sent a crumb down her windpipe and she choked. Sitting down, he took the *patisserie* with the cherries. Hattie didn't mind. With the coughing over, looking through streaming eyes, everything seemed big and disorderly and not to matter.

'They've got that Brie woman's murderer,' Sebastian said.

'*Bon!*' Françoise clapped her hands excitedly. 'Where did they find him, M'sieur?'

'Not now.' Frowning at Sebastian, picking up the plate of biscuits, the Wren held it out to Françoise. 'Would you like another biscuit, Françoise?'

'*Murderer?*' Hattie's mouth, which had some jam sandwich in it, stayed slightly open.

Françoise's eyes turned to Rose as good manners demanded. Almost snatching a biscuit, she swiftly thanked her. 'Where did they find him?' she repeated, turning back eagerly to Sebastian.

'In the forest of Fontainebleau. They got the dogs on to him.'

'What dogs?' asked Hattie.

'Bloodhounds—they sniff 'em out. They give them something of the murderer's to smell—clothing, socks or something, and then they pick up the scent like hounds do a fox,' Sebastian explained obligingly. 'He'd have done better to have gone to Paris. He might have hidden there.'

'Where?'

'In the sewers.'

'*Sewers?*'

'Drains for filth, Hat—don't you know anything?'

'How could you hide in a drain?' Hattie saw a drain-pipe; she couldn't fit a murderer into it, she couldn't even fit a baby.

'Damn' easy,' said Father. 'The Paris sewers are like passages, with steps and sewer rats and everything—they run for miles underground. That's where I'd go,' he said triumphantly. 'Never make for a port, Hat—you'll put yourself straight into the bag if you do.'

'What bag?'

'Great heavens!—talk about dolts!'

'Who was murdered?' Hattie thrust on, wanting and not wanting to know.

'Never mind, Hattie. It's over and done with now. Let's talk of something more pleasant.' The Wren's look was wasted on Sebastian who was stretching for a sandwich.

'You know!' Françoise shot across at Hattie, 'Marie Bric who was found stabbed in a wardrobe!'

'That's enough, Françoise. We don't want to hear anything more about it. We don't discuss horrible murders in this house.' That ought to shut her up, thought Rose.

'*Never?*' Françoise looked at her in astonishment. Dampened by Madame's expression, she formally begged her pardon. Feeling unfair, furious with Sebastian for not backing her up, Rose reassured the child.

'Who found her in the wardrobe?' Hattie, who had swallowed the piece of sandwich without knowing it, was now opening the wardrobe door as she stared at Françoise.

Françoise hesitated. Her lips moved. She glanced at Rose, shut her mouth regretfully, and looked at her plate.

'Françoise can tell you, I expect,' said Sebastian.

Françoise, almost unable to contain herself, looked at him like a pomeranian sighting a bone. Emboldened by what she found in the rosy, weather-beaten face of the Englishman whose skin was so different from the pallid brown smoothness of her father's, risking the enragement of Madame, she enlightened Hattie. 'The housekeeper—she had once been Jean Brie's lover.'

Horrible, precocious little wretch! Hardly knowing that it did, the hand of the Wren flattened out ready for the good hard slap that the laws of etiquette, of class and race, made it impossible

for it to administer. Ignoring the child, she attacked Sebastian.
'How can you encourage her?' she said furiously in English. 'Stop
it, for goodness sake!'

'Why should I?'

'You know why.'

He'd be damned if he would. Françoise was too good to waste.
Hat looked like a hare, but it was high time she stopped looking
like that when there was anything squeamish on the stocks.

'Was it a big wardrobe?' Hattie whispered hoarsely.

Meeting that hare stare, compunction stirred in Sebastian.
'She wasn't in a wardrobe, I remember now.'

'But M'sieur——'

Silencing Françoise with a gesture, Sebastian held course. 'It
was a tent—one of those big brown ones with flaps.'

'Oh—' Hattie's eyes got smaller.

'Now finish your sandwich,' said the Wren. 'More tea, Sebbie?'
her voice was soft.

'Thanks.' Pushing over his cup, pity satisfied, Sebastian turned
his attention to Françoise. 'Why did he do it?' he demanded.

'You don't know, M'sieur?' Françoise was incredulous. 'But
it was *un crime passionnel*.'

Sloshing tea into the saucer with a sudden jolt of her hand,
Rose bit her lip in her wrath.

'What's that?' asked Sebastian.

Françoise stared at him. 'But you know?'

Sebastian shook his head. 'The English—' he spread his hands,
'in England we have different customs, we call things differently.
You must explain.'

'*Un crime passionnel*—it is a crime of love. One lover kills
another.'

'*Mon Dieu*, but why?'

Françoise shrugged. 'Because one doesn't love the other.'

'And yet they are lovers?'

'How can you be so abominable! Hattie, pass your father's tea,
please.'

Hattie obeyed her mother mutely.

'One stops,' Françoise said. 'Maman says passion is a dangerous thing.'

'The devil it must be! But this passion—how would you
describe it, Françoise?'

'Sebbie, stop it, please.' Rose had sunk to the ignominy of
entreaty.

'Be quiet, Rose. *Out of the mouths of babes and sucklings*—not yours, suckling, and for God's sake shut your mouth.'

'Maman says that love without passion has weakness, like wine and water, but passion intoxicates like absinthe.'

'The devil she does!'

Outraged, her face flushed, her eyes snapping, the Wren rose. 'Come along, children, we'll go into the drawing-room and play spillikins.' A child, that's all Françoise was, repeating her mother's nauseating conversation like a parrot without understanding. Or did she understand? No. Once she believed she did, that there had been any calculation in the glance that had passed from Sebbie to herself, she could not bring herself to play spillikins with her, thought Rose Suckling violently.

Two days later, Hattie paddled for the first time since her illness. The sea was half-way, neither out nor in; it was smooth and flat and warm. Hattie, her frock tucked into her drawers, gazed down at the water round her ankles. Her feet, on the solid soakiness of sand, were pale flaps.

'It's so friendly being *in* it again.'

'Like coming home.' The Wren sighed in her spirit.

'Yes, that's what it was. How did you know?' Hattie asked wonderingly.

'I just did.'

The shade from Mother's white parasol covered the top of her. It reached to the fattest part of her chest and then stopped. Hattie looked down again at the sea. 'It only just turns over at the edge. It looks as though it can't and then it does.'

'Thin like the hem of a hanky,' the Wren said dreamily.

'With lace—the foamy part's the lace!' cried Hattie, clapping her hands with joy. The clap parted the Wren's dreams. French. At the memory of Françoise clapping her hands at the capture of the murderer, she felt renewed disgust—not that she held any brief for the murder, naturally. She didn't want her child to clap. She saw it as proof of a further injection of French influence. A surge of anger against Sebastian was followed by a wave of love at the sight of the child's lighted face. It wasn't her fault. Because of the love, as though too she were making amends for the unfairness of a mythical scolding, she said gently, 'Yes, exactly. How clever of you to think of it, darling.'

That was the day that Sebastian said he was going to Paris. He said it at *déjeuner* over the globe artichokes.

To Hattie, he sounded as though he was going to do nothing more exciting than fishing. 'To *Paris*?' she stared at him.

'That's what I said.' Tearing off a leaf, pushing it carelessly into the butter, he put it in his mouth and pulled it out again almost at once stripped to a shred. Hattie sucked and bit hers and brought them out and dipped them a second time to get more butter. Mother never dipped a second time, but she was slower and less thorough than Father.

Mother said nothing. 'Aren't Mother and I coming?' Hattie asked.

'Not this time. I'm going to do some research for my book.'

'Oh—' Hattie's lips suddenly trembled. Appalled, she seized a leaf and pushed it into her mouth without waiting for butter.

Still Mother said nothing. Glancing at her, Hattie knew that she wasn't pleased.

Sebastian had stripped the heart of his artichoke clean now. Out of the corner of her eye Hattie saw it grey and naked as he dug in his spoon. 'Nobody here knows anything worth knowing when it comes to history; they're all a pack of illiterates—little wonder when there's not a decent library in the place.'

'Have you only just discovered that after two years? Hattie, wipe your chin,' said the Wren, 'it's covered in butter.'

'Of course not, but now's the time to check up on a few facts.'

'Do you expect me to believe that?' Lifting her glass, the Wren sipped wine.

'Yes.' Raising his eyes from his artichoke, Sebastian looked down the table at her. 'Why not?'

Rose put down her glass and in silence jerked off a leaf.

'Why not? You tell me that, damn it, if it's the last thing you ever do.'

'We are not alone.'

'Hattie, go upstairs,' ordered Father.

'I haven't finished.'

'Take it with you and do what you're told,' he roared.

'I don't want it!' Bursting into tears, Hattie tore out of the room and rushed upstairs. Throwing herself face down on the bed, she cried into the cotton counterpane till the wet warmth of it smelled of washing.

The crying made her ashamed as she waited that evening for Father to come and say good night. It had made her ashamed for the rest of the day when she thought of him. He would wish he'd got a son again. That's why he didn't come, but she knew it wasn't that he wouldn't come because of that. He would rather come and tell her she was a cry-baby. When the cathedral clock struck nine, she thought, 'He won't come now.' He *would*. He wouldn't go away without seeing her, he wouldn't, he wouldn't.

She had asked Mother when Father was going on the way to the *boulangerie* this afternoon. She had to ask although she knew Mother was cross. She could hardly believe it when she'd said he was going tonight, on the eleven o'clock train. 'How can he suddenly go?' It wasn't like going to Napoleon's island. Paris was so far. 'When he wishes to do something your father does it.' Mother had sounded as though he was nothing to do with herself. 'Won't he go to bed at all?' He would sleep in the train, Mother supposed. She had sounded as though she didn't care whether he did or not. 'Don't scuff, Hattie.' When Mother said that Hattie knew that she didn't want to talk about Father any more.

Why didn't he come? Where was he? He couldn't be with Madame Picard—she had gone to Neuilly, wherever that was. He had gone drinking. But he would have to come back before he went to the station to get his luggage and say good-bye. He wouldn't go without saying good-bye to Mother—not to Paris— even if they were cross—or to her. He'd come then even though he knew she ought to be asleep. He wouldn't creep like Mother, making little mouse noises. If he tried to creep, which he mightn't, he would still squash the stairs.

Straining her ears, lying on her back stiff as a ramrod, she turned into a dead body. Terrified, she turned over on her side. She was all bent up now, stabbed, in a wardrobe. No, she'd been in a tent—she had, she had!—Father hadn't made it up. Sitting up, she stared hare-eyed at her wardrobe, having to, not wanting to. She'd looked in before she'd got into bed. There was nothing there, there couldn't be, she'd been here all the time, awake. Suppose there was? There wasn't!—there wasn't! Lying down again, she scratched an old bite that was really finished, raw. There was sand between her toes. Her scar hurt. Father said it was a sign of rain. It was as useful as a piece of seaweed hung outside the door.

She went to sleep and dreamed she was going to Paris with Father. As they hurried down the platform she looked for Mother. When she asked Father if she wasn't coming, he said, 'No, she doesn't like Paris, she'd rather go to London.' Father heaved himself up the high steps into the rain. He had his fishing-rod. 'Come on.' He stood at the top, not trying to help.

'I could have got up when I was nine,' he said. 'So can I,' Hattie said, but it wasn't easy. Clinging, struggling, she tried not to look as though it was difficult, so that Father wouldn't want a son. 'Hurry up!' Father roared. 'The train's just going.' Hattie woke up knowing she hadn't hurried enough.

Had Father been while she was asleep and not woken her? Sitting up, Hattie looked for signs. The door was still wide open like it had been. He would have woken her. He'd have made a noise, and if she hadn't woken he'd have wanted her to, which Mother never did, because he'd come to say good night. He hadn't come. He might have. The thought of having missed him made her feel frantic and deserted, wanting him wildly with panic. What was the time? The house was quiet, but there were noises outside from the *Bar La Basquaise*.

Getting out of bed, Hattie crept to the window and looked down. If only she could hear 'Cockles and mussels', see him coming, she could call softly so that Mother didn't hear, or spit —no, he wouldn't see spit—drop something, her hanky.

A man came out of the Bar. He crossed over to their house and stood close up facing it. Hattie knew what he was doing; he was being disgusting on their wall. Pig, beast. 'Don't look, don't look,' Mother seemed to be crying it in the room behind her. Her face went scarlet as she did look, outraged and furious—her head thrust through the bars—but seeing nothing, nothing awful. '*Cochon!*' the forbidden word sounded louder than she dared. Glaring down, immobile with panic, she waited to see if he had heard. He hadn't. He went on, head bent, with what he was doing. When he had finished and turned back into the street, another man came out of the Bar. He wasn't Father either. He was quite little. He started talking to the other man; they stood talking, far down underneath her window.

The little man looked like the fisherman from the end of the wall that she'd pushed into the sea. She hadn't really pushed him, she hadn't, had she? If Father saw the fisherman he'd know she hadn't. She'd forgotten that as she hadn't pushed him in, he might see him again. Father had fished a lot since, but he'd never said he'd seen him. Suppose she had pushed him in? If the man looked up and she saw his face and it wasn't the fisherman, 'It'll mean I have,' she thought. She must see his face; she would never know if she didn't. It mattered dreadfully. Suppose she shouted something? Not *cochon!—bon soir*. She couldn't, in her nightie, to a stranger when she was supposed to be asleep.

Dragging her head back through the bars, Hattie fetched her soap. It was a purple cake of violet only just begun. When she threw it down it landed on the little man's head. She gave a gasp of pride and fright. Got the bull's-eye! If only Father could have seen. The man looked up. She could see his face in the gaslight. It was thin and he hadn't got a beard. She didn't know him; he was a stranger. She sped across the floor and leapt into bed.

Sitting bolt upright, she listened. He must have seen her. Would he ring the door-bell and bring back the soap? 'Please God make him not to.' Mother would be furious.

There was no bell, no sound in the house. The men stopped talking and went away. Hattie heard their footsteps. The cathedral clock began to strike. It was twelve. Father had been gone for the last hour. How *could* he not come, if he hadn't? Because he'd gone drinking, that's what. 'Gone drinking.' She said it louder and much more clearly than '*cochon*'. Lying down, she bit the sheet in furious despair.

CHAPTER X

IN THE ABSENCE of Sebastian, the shutters of the *salle à manger* remained closed during *déjeuner*. Hattie felt herself getting weedier and weedier. She saw the sun trying to get in to save her, beating against the grey wall of the house with cracks on it like rivers and islands where the plaster had fallen off, and the places where the dry scuffed-up paint fluffed like dust. Mother didn't care if she was a stunted weed. Father didn't love her enough to say good-bye. She didn't care either if Mother was still cross with him. 'Has Father got there?' she asked truculently.

The Wren, snatched back from the chaos of her thoughts missed the truculence. 'To Paris?—yes—in the early hours.'

'What early hour?'

'Five—half-past, I think the night train gets there.' Owl-eyed with rings, the child looked like a starveling this morning, thought the Wren, just when her conscience wanted reassurance about the racket of a journey. 'Did you go to sleep early?'

'No, I stayed awake for hours.'

'You were asleep when I came up about half-past ten.'

'I woke up again. I waited—' Hattie's throat began to clog,

'for Father, and he never came.' She swallowed. 'He didn't, did he?'

The Wren didn't know. Shut away in the *salon*, stitching an insertion into a petticoat, she had washed her hands of Sebastian. Better to let Hattie believe he hadn't. Braced by resentment, the going without him would be easier perhaps. No, not that, her spirit rejected the thought with distaste. 'I expect he came when you were asleep.' He didn't deserve it.

'You don't *know* he came.'

'That doesn't mean he didn't. I was sewing in the drawing-room and I heard him go upstairs.'

'You don't know he came to me,' said Hattie stubbornly. 'Can we have the shutters open?'

'No. The sun's full on them.'

'Father says——'

'I know what he says.' The Wren's fingers did a small dance of exasperation on the table-cloth. 'Your father is a man.' This plain truth, both simple and bizarre, in her opinion answered every-thing, but for the child it was not enough. Lowering her voice which had a tendency to soar this morning, she patiently ex-plained the qualities of man. 'Some things that are good for your father are not so good for you and me. Men's skins are thicker——' her voice rose a note but she levelled it again, 'your father doesn't always realize this.' *And if he did he wouldn't't care*, her brain snapped.

'He says I'll be stunted,' Hattie pursued obstinately.

But he's quite ready to stunt your whole existence by a squalid affair, the Wren's nostrils quivered. 'It would take more than some closed shutters to stunt you, and I don't want to hear anything more about stunting; it's silly. Your father still doesn't realize that the sun can be too hot.'

'He does.'

'Don't contradict, Hattie.'

'He said in the Sahara I'd have to wear my winter coat and a topee.'

How irritating children were! Hattie's mood was impossible. The Wren, bending her head, kneaded her forehead with her fingers where it ached. 'No one—man, woman, or child—could fail to acknowledge the heat of the equatorial sun. Now eat up your bread.' *And no French man, woman, or child should say that the English Madame and her daughter had skulked away.* Head lifted, smiling, the Wren said, 'I've got a surprise for you Hattie. We're going to England tomorrow.'

'To *England*?' There was some apricot jam on Hattie's upper lip and bread in her cheek. Taking advantage of her gaping to say what had to be said, the Wren spoke calmly.

'People generally go away when they've been ill and the change of air will do you good. English air is best for the English just as African air is best for Hottentots.'

'Hottentots?'

Ignoring Hattie's ignorance, the Wren proceeded, skating firmly on the cat-ice. 'Father isn't coming with us. He came here to write his book and it's got to be finished. He'll join us when he's ready in his own good time,' *if ever*. The Wren curled her toes. The tautening of the muscles served like the clenching of a fist.

'How can we go alone?' Riddled with amazement, Hattie picked on the question nearest to hand.

'It will be quite easy. It isn't like going to a foreign country; we shall be going home.' With hardly any money and nowhere to go, thought the Wren. Hattie had what Sebbie called 'her questing cat look' wanting to get things straight before she pounced on something. The Wren understood; she got it from her but there was a wariness too and she saw this with dismay.

'Does Father know we're going? He never said.'

'He was busy.'

'Does he know?'

'Not yet,' said the Wren, cornered. 'But he won't mind,' she went on lightly. 'We'll leave a letter for him. He can come and join us when he's ready. He won't be lonely, he's got too many friends—' *a parasite and a whore*. Her fingers tapped a small tattoo on the table.

'Why don't we wait for him?'

'Because the sooner you get the air the better. Don't worry, darling—he'll understand. He always does things on the spur of the moment himself—like going to Paris. He didn't tell us till the day he was going, and he always says I make too many plans and he likes surprises.' The Wren smiled. 'You can leave a letter for him too, and when we get to London you can send him a postcard of the Houses of Parliament.'

Hattie beamed. 'London?—are we going to London?'

The Wren nodded her crest.

'Can we go to Westminster Abbey and the Tower and the pond where you want to be a seagull?'

'Yes, I expect so. But before we go there's a lot to be done—

packing and saying good-bye to our friends. I think—' the Wren drained her coffee '—we won't say that Father doesn't know we're going yet. We won't tell an untruth if we're asked, naturally,' she went on slowly, 'but there's no need to proclaim it unnecessarily. French people mightn't understand that the English make quick decisions. Father should be proud of this one. He's always saying I take too long to prepare for everything.'

'It is a very sudden plan, no?' said Madame. Leaning against the restaurant counter, she looked what she was, a well-fed business woman of flexible virtue on whom there were no flies.

'Yes,' said the Wren, 'very. The Sucklings have always been a family of quick decisions. My husband's grandfather decided to sail to China on a tea clipper one day and embarked the next.'

Madame showed no interest in Grandfather Suckling or the tea clipper. Flicking them away with her hand, she said, 'Your husband made this sudden plan, yes?'

The Wren's head gave an almost imperceptible nod, scarcely a movement. 'We both think Hattie is still too pale. It is still very hot here and the weather shows no sign of breaking. She needs English air for a bit.'

'Father's coming when he's finished his book,' Hattie cut in.

The look in Madame's eyes which had made mincemeat of the Wren's utterances, was hidden from her now, as she lowered them to the child. 'And when will that be, *chérie?*—not for a long time?'

'He'll come when he's ready.' Excitement and fear, the fear of Madame's words, made Hattie's voice shrill. 'He'll join us in his own good time.'

'But naturally, *ma chérie.*'

Françoise's mother seemed quite to understand the need of air for Hattie. 'Françoise's face becomes the colour of—' Madame Delon lifted her merry eyes rapidly to heaven in search of a simile '—white marble. Then we know that it is time for her to leave Paris.'

The Wren knew this to be nonsense. Nothing could make that brown Gallic skin look like marble, not even death—proof, surely, that Françoise never grew pale languishing for change of air or a simile would have been ready. But the brightness of the woman's eyes was without malice as she turned her attention to the English climate. 'Would all that fog and damp be good for the little one?'

'There is no fog in September,' the Wren explained. 'It is a lovely, still, warm, golden month as a rule.'

Madame Delon was very interested in England. She did not mention Sebastian. Gossip of his visit to Paris might not yet have reached her, the Wren thought. Whether it had or not, she felt grateful to her for her silence—*grateful*; the humiliating irony of feeling gratitude, because a Frenchwoman socially her inferior had made no mention of her husband, hit her like a slap.

Down by the canna lily bed, Françoise suffered no scruples. 'Why are you going in such a hurry? You can't have suddenly got pale.'

'I've suddenly got to where I ought to be rosy, I s'pose.' Hattie laughed. The laugh spurted up a bit. The coo of a dove in the acacia tree sounded lower and more comfortable.

'Is your papa going with you?'

'No, he's in Paris, finding out things for his book. He'll join us when he's ready.' Hattie made a squiggle on the path with her toe. When the gardener came to rake, he'd rake it.

'In *Paris*?' Françoise's mouth made the shape of an open cod's through which her breath sieved with a slight whistling noise. 'Has he,' her voice lowered, 'gone to see Madame Picard?'

'No, of course he hasn't! He's gone to Paris.'

'Madame Picard is in Neuilly.'

'Neuilly isn't Paris.'

'It's a part of it. He's gone to see her.'

The blood which had rushed up into Hattie's face made it feel like a burning coal. 'He *hasn't*!' With bent head, she swung her foot, making a half circle on the path.

'He wouldn't have told you if he had.'

'He would.'

'Does he know you're going to England?'

Moving a little away from Françoise to get a fresh place on the path, Hattie marked an H. 'H for Hattie, look. H for Harriet really. My name's really Harriet.'

'Does he?' Françoise, who had moved towards her, stood waiting.

'Yes, naturally,' said Hattie, 'yes, yes, yes.' Defiantly, with colours flying she flouted hell-fire.

CHAPTER XI

'ARE WE REALLY going to England because I'm pale, Mother?'

'I've told you, Hattie.'

'Françoise said——'

'What?' What had that horrible child said?

'She said had Father gone to—to see Madame Picard.' Hattie, who had been unable to contain it inside any longer, didn't look at the Wren's face; she stared down her own face to where the rug began.

'What did she mean?' But without waiting for an answer, Mother said, 'I hope you said, no, that he had gone to Paris about his book.' The effort to control her fury made her words slow and very distinct.

Yes, Hattie had.

'Why should he go to Paris to see a *waitress*?'

'I don't know.' Why had he let her sit on the beach and cry with her head on his shoulder when he hated crying people? 'He let her cry on the beach,' said Hattie slowly.

'He couldn't stop her.'

'He wasn't cross.'

'He had to be polite. People have to be polite to strangers and acquaintances, when with the people they really love—' in spite of the web of nonsense she was weaving, the Wren's lip quivered '—they can be cross and the other one understands.'

'It doesn't matter?' Hattie asked.

'No.'

Hadn't it mattered that night on the landing? 'Do you and Father love each other like that?'

'Yes. Now stop talking and go to sleep.'

It was as though a parcel of worry had been lifted out of her, Hattie thought; at least that was how Mother meant her to feel and how she wanted to.

The Wren lay down on the other seat. She wouldn't sleep, but it was the thing one did at night, even in a train, and it would keep her legs from swelling. They had been like sausages after that crowded, dreadful journey to Florence. It had been her fault for refusing a *couchette*—if you could call it a fault to try to bank up a financial reserve. How she had hated Catherine de Medici who had led them trailing to Florence and from Florence to France—an existence completely unsuitable for a small child and one that she loathed. When it came to his books Sebastian wouldn't leave a stone unturned, but for weeks sometimes he was too lazy to turn one. After Catherine it had been Toulouse-Lautrec, and then, as if there was nobody and nothing to write about in England, it was Protestants and Huguenots in a French port. And now—Rose shifted her body on the hard seat—she was leaving him to go back to England where she and the child belonged. Lying there, vulnerable in her inactivity, there was no escape, no burying her head in a trunk or arranging with Marie for a meal when the thought of eating it sickened her. Their trains would pass if Sebbie did what he said he was going to. He would arrive at six and take a *fiacre*. He would find her letter on the hall table, and Hattie's too, with a stamp chalked on the envelope. She would send him their address, she had said, when she knew it. It wouldn't be a hotel in Bloomsbury, she did know that. She couldn't have borne it for one thing, or risked being recognized by anyone; she had had her fill of subterfuge.

'Brains and talent mean nothing to you. It's a carriage you want, five storeys in Kensington with butlers and nurses and nursemaids galore,' Sebastian had said. Not galore; one of each would do, she had told him. Her joke, which had been flat before it was uttered had fallen flatter still. 'That's not true. You know I don't set store by riches.'

'*Where moth and rust doth corrupt*, say it, go on.'

She had never had any desire for a carriage or a butler or anything absurd like that. She had simply wanted for Hattie the safe, organized nursery life of the babies pushed by their nannies in canopied perambulators to Kensington Gardens. It wasn't very much; it was only the natural order of things for her own town cousins, for any normal middle-class family—a version, on a more enlivened plane, of her own country upbringing. She had never been able to accept the differences in Hattie's existence, that mouse-infested house in Bloomsbury where she had been born. 'Set a trap,' Sebbie had said, as if that was the end of it all. What good did he think one mouse a night would do? she had asked him. 'Breeding, are they?' 'They've bred.' 'Get more traps.' And what was to be done with them all when they were caught? she had demanded furiously, knowing the revolting answer. 'Drown them.' It had been their first frightful quarrel. Now, with something that really mattered, she remembered her anger with shame and contrition. Her spirit reared up in self-defence. It wasn't rational to take all the blame. There had been greater provocation—plenty. You followed your husband to the ends of the earth, if he was sent there, but when it was his own choice and he was lazy, when he couldn't or wouldn't see that life in a remote French port left much to be desired not only for his daughter but for his wife as well . . . And now there was this . . . how much did Hattie know? 'Damn and blast that bloody little Françoise,' the words, pouring out of her in silent violence, seemed more malevolent than if they had been bellowed. Searching for something worse, she could find nothing. Sebbie, who could have, had never said them in her hearing. Appalled by her hypocrisy, loathing herself, her spirit writhed.

She hadn't said her prayers. She would say them lying down. Father had knelt to say his in the train to Switzerland with Mother. 'Aren't you going to kneel down, Mary? Surely God is more important than a little dust on your skirt?' Mother had knelt. She had told Rose about it in a shelter on the parade at Bournemouth on a wet summer's evening when Rose, with spots and a pain, had suggested hanging herself. 'No, Rosie, I shouldn't do that. Think,' Mother had always been telling her to think, 'how inconvenient it would be for your father and me.' Rose had been sixteen then, and she was thirty-three now. Her mother had died when she was twenty, and her father three years later, a year after her marriage. She still missed her mother. With Father it was different. When you had married and left home . . . she always tried to make excuses even to herself, because even inside her the decency of her feelings mattered. She had been fond of him, she had, but he should have been a Roundhead. Love stripped you to the bone. There was no call for decency or excuses. Grossness—a spark of humour flickered in her—didn't matter; what she had said to Hattie was true, but for the rest, the things that did, love turned them into hell. When you loved—oh, don't, for God's sake! She was at it again.

She prayed demandingly, as though God were simply a producer, a grocer, a postman. She was ashamed, but she went on lying there not even asking, she thought, but ordering without so much as a please, and then she began to cry quietly, seeing herself doing it as though even her tears were all wrong. The train rocked and squeaked and bumped, swinging out sometimes —or so it seemed—like a swing-boat at the fair. The railways never seemed to get any better, reflecting the emotional and casual inefficiency of the French temperament. There were such dreadful accidents. If anything happened to Hattie she would never forgive herself. She didn't think Sebbie would forgive her either. And if anything happened to him—it would be his own fault, she thought violently, but she couldn't sustain the violence. She began to pray wildly, beseeching God on the knees of her spirit . . .

'I think we had better stay at the Grosvenor tonight,' the Wren said. She didn't want to, it was much too expensive, but Hattie, owl-eyed with tiredness, had had enough for today. The Russell would be cheaper, but although she was unlikely to meet anyone she knew or who knew her after seven years in so short a time as a night, she couldn't face home ground. Tomorrow, without fail, she must find somewhere inexpensive. If only she could remember the name of that small hotel, somewhere off the Cromwell Road, where she and her mother had once had bed and breakfast.

Following the porter, her hand in its white cotton glove grasped in Mother's kid, Hattie said, 'The station's not different.'

'All stations are the same more or less. The trains here are lower and the porters are dressed differently.' It wasn't enough to stem disillusionment, the Wren knew, even if the child hadn't already seen these things, which of course she had. Heaven knows what she had expected—something fantastic. 'A harbourer of extraordinary visions,' Sebbie had once said with the pride of production. 'Without me—' the Wren bit off the memory like a rabbit biting off its leg in a trap.

The hotel astonished Hattie, from the enormous solid black walls outside, through the hall like a palace, up the great staircase to the bedroom on the fourth floor with the window overlooking rows of slopes.

'What are those things?'

'The station roofs,' the Wren supposed.

'I'd rather look out on the vegetable market—I think, really,' said Hattie slowly. She didn't think, she knew. She didn't want to disappoint Mother. Suddenly she wanted to cry.

'This is a change. Without change, life would be like a stagnant pond.' The Wren dragged the hat-pin swiftly out of her hat. The action braced her. Her words braced her child as they were meant to do, implying no necessity for happiness, simply a state of affairs to be accepted and endured like a dose of tonic.

Jean Mailly, the carpenter who made coffins, had a stagnant pond with mosquitoes on it in the yard behind his workshop. Mother said it had germs and he shouldn't have it. Father said, 'Germs are animals the same as we are. If we can't tame them we ought to be able to get the better of them like lions and tigers, and if we don't, it's grist to the coffin mill.' When Hattie had asked what grist to the coffin mill was, Father had said, 'Bodies in the bag.'

'Father's life isn't a stagnant pond, is it?' Hattie asked.

'Of course, it isn't. If it had been more stagnant—' Mother didn't finish. Sighing, she took off her hat. 'Which side of the bed would you like, darling?'

When they had washed and tidied, they went downstairs to find some tea. Hattie saw them hunting for it like hidden treasure, sniffing it out like pigs sniffing out truffles like the snuffling pig on Father's cheese plate.

'They may serve it in the lounge,' said Mother.

'Or the *salle à manger*,' suggested Hattie.

'Dining-room. We are not in France now,' Mother said, although in France she had called the *salle à manger* 'dining-room' too. It didn't seem fair on France.

'*When in Rome*—' Hattie began, but Mother cut her short. 'We are not foreigners trying to fit in with aliens in a foreign country; we are English in our own country. Try to remember that, Hattie.'

Hattie jumped the last stair, remembering.

There were slices of currant cake for tea. Father would have loved it.

Rose Suckling lay in bed that night seeing London about her: the orderly squares of smooth paper-white houses, blotched in the sun, as she remembered them, with the shadows of plane leaves; the tall Regency houses in Kensington, so despised by Sebbie for their respectability, and in particular the Queen Anne one where Uncle George and Aunt Emma and the cousins had lived, sold after Uncle George's death when Aunt Emma had emigrated with Fanny, the only unmarried daughter of her brood, to Hove. If they had been in London now?—no, she couldn't have gone to them however much she had been tempted. She saw the shabby Georgian house in Bloomsbury of course, and the pond in St James's Park where Sebbie had kissed—her mind shied, her thoughts rushing wildly to the Round Pond and the great stretches of grass in Kensington Gardens. How she had missed grass abroad, grass that you could walk on. Hattie should walk on grass; it was her birthright.

CHAPTER XII

THERE WERE PRUNES and porridge and kippers and eggs and bacon and kidney and ham and rolls and toast and butter-balls and marmalade and honey and tea and coffee for breakfast. Hattie read the menu with mounting amazement. When she had finished, she searched back in it for the butter-balls already on the table in a silver plate like a scallop shell. They were not mentioned. 'They haven't put the butter-balls on the menu, Mother. Did they forget them?'

Mother thought no, that they'd taken them for granted.

Hattie hardly listened to the answer. 'How can we eat prunes and porridge and kippers and eggs and bacon and kid—'

'We can't,' Mother broke in. 'We aren't meant to—any more than you were meant to eat everything on the menu at the *Coq d'Or.*'

'Kippers,' Hattie's voice rose as she went on tackling the list.

'Hush,' said Mother, 'people will think you've never seen food before.'

'I haven't—not like this for *petit déjeuner.*'

'Not *petit déjeuner*; it's an English breakfast.'

'What are kippers? Why didn't we have them in France?'

'Because the French prefer soles and mus—' Mother didn't finish mussels and Hattie knew why; she didn't want to remember. *She* didn't mind remembering although it was she who'd been sick.

'Do you catch kippers?' and suddenly Hattie was on the sea-wall again with Father in the boiling sun on the day she'd pushed —she hadn't, she knew she hadn't really. Shying away from the thought, she was possessed by a tremendous longing to be sitting on the wall beside Father with a newspaper over her legs. She didn't want the longing.

'No. Kippers are smoked—' Mother paused '—herrings, I suppose.'

Hattie wanted to be here with mother too. '*Smoked?*'

Mother nodded, and just then the waiter came. Mother chose porridge and bacon and egg, and Hattie chose porridge and kipper.

This afternoon, if there was time, or tomorrow morning without fail, she would go to that agency in Knightsbridge if it still existed, thought the Wren again. She had gone there with Aunt Emma to find a parlourmaid and had never forgotten it. She could see the woman's face now, fat, rouged, and with a fuzzy ruche of hair. 'It's a toupée,' Aunt Emma had said, 'I'm sure of it. It has looked exactly the same for twenty years.' She had every kind of servant on her books from scullery-maids to companions and governesses, the woman had told them. It had surprised Aunt Emma and herself that governesses and companions should be classed as servants. 'They serve,' had been the reply to Aunt Emma's remark, and the woman had gone on to say that satisfactory temporary servants were not always easy. 'Temporary spells fishy more often than not.' 'I shall be fishy,' thought the Wren, 'if Sebbie comes.' If he didn't—the prospect was unbearable. Turning her thoughts, focusing her gaze, the Wren was conscious of a man's eyes fixed upon her, staring as though he had a right to, as though she had been staring at him. He must have thought she had. Flushing, confused and angry, she looked back at the table and lifted her cup. 'Don't dream, Hattie, get on with your kipper.' The business of drinking brought relief.

'Mother?'

'Yes.'

'You know the sea-wall—'

'Yes.' The Wren was sure he was doing it still.

'Suppose someone had pushed a fisherman off it—'

'He wasn't pushed. He had a heart attack and fell in.'

'*Fell in?*' Hattie gaped.

If Sebbie had been here he wouldn't have dared. Sebbie liked her in this blouse too. He'd said—

'What fisherman, when?'

'The Picard woman's husband. That's why Father's sorry for her.'

'Did he—fish off the end, past the little house—the one that took Father's fish?'

'Yes.' He *was* still looking at her, thought the Wren distractedly.

'How—do they know he wasn't pushed in?'

'Why should anyone want to push a fisherman into the sea?' He must have realized by now she hadn't been staring. Why shouldn't someone look at her if they wished to? She was not ugly. The Wren stiffened her neck the fraction of an inch.

'S'pose someone had?'

'Had what?'

'Pushed him in.'

'I tell you they didn't.'

'I didn't!—I didn't!' thought Hattie wildly. 'Was that the funeral that passed when I was ill?'

'Yes, I expect so.' The Wren saw him out of the corner of her eye get up and thread his way towards the door, assured, conceited. Relieved, her whole body seemed to relax, followed by a degrading sensation of void. Hattie looked like a hare. Oh, heavens, that wretched Picard! She oughtn't to have told her; she hadn't been thinking. But it was over now. There were plenty of other things for her to think about. 'There's no need to think about that fisherman any more, Hattie. He had a heart attack brought on by the thunderstorm and fell in. It didn't hurt him, he wouldn't have known anything about it,' lied the Wren staunchly.

'Did Father know?'

'Yes.'

He knew she'd told a story, thought Hattie. All this time he'd known and he hadn't said.

'Eat,' said Mother.

Why hadn't he? Why hadn't he scolded her? Because she was ill. But he knew she hadn't been brave.

'Is Father unhappy because I'm not a son?'

'No—you know what he said,' conscientiously the Wren went on, 'that he wouldn't change you now any more than he'd change his fishing-rod.' Feeling like that, surely he'd come, but he must come for her too, she thought bleakly.

They went in a bus to find a smaller hotel. The well-fed horses spanked along. Hattie, all agog, sat with her eyes glued to the window. When they had found the hotel they would move at once, and this afternoon, if there was time Mother said, they would go and see Westminster Abbey or something famous. 'I shall leave the agency till tomorrow.' And then she said, 'How would you like to share your lessons with some other children? After having them alone with me for so long, it would make a nice change for you.'

'What children?' Suddenly, terrifyingly, Hattie saw Struwwelpeter, the dreadful picture on the cover of the book, that beastly face, the long hair standing out all round his head, and the long claw nails that he wouldn't have cut.

'I don't know,' Mother said. 'You may not share with any, we must wait and see, but if you do they will be nice English children.' Well-brought-up by an English nanny in an English nursery in Kensington, thought the Wren obstinately; not like Françoise, feeding on grown-ups' gossip and eating—heaven knows what that child ate—till all hours of the night.

'Was Struwwelpeter German?'

'Yes.'

Hattie sighed with relief.

'Hattie,' said the Wren, 'if you are weaving nonsense, stop it.'

'Yes, Mother.' There was an English child on the seat in front of them in a lovely hat trimmed with buttercups, daisies and forget-me-nots and tiny little pink rosebuds. She had ringlets like Françoise. Françoise had hers done up with bits of rag at night. Mother said she was never going to have hair like that and she never had. Hattie wondered if the English child knew a great deal more than she did. Father said, 'Don't you remember anything?' but she did. She couldn't know everything. Mother said she'd never get anything into her head, leave alone keep it there, if she didn't listen and try to remember things. She did, but she was afraid that the head under the hat in front might have more in it—a bigger pile of rice. No—the rice was hers. 'Do English children know more than me?' she whispered.

'Why should they? You've had a good grounding and speak fluent French which should be of value to you all your life, which is more than most—or any of them—can do, I expect.' Mother sounded now as though French was a splendid thing to speak. 'If you marry a diplomat and he becomes British Ambassador to France, think what a blessing your French will be. You must never forget it, Hattie, ever.'

'You said never to forget I'm English.'

'Neither must you. I said never forget your French, not never forget you *are* French which you aren't, and for goodness sake try not to talk about the English as though they're foreigners,' Mother whispered.

The hotel was still there where Mother had thought it might be, and directly she saw it she remembered its name. It was less like a palace and more like a home, which was what she had wanted, although it was not in the least like their proper home, naturally. There was a vacant double room. The manageress had

not got a face like an oyster really; it was not crinkly grey, it was
smooth, the colour of cold fat, but there was something about it
that reminded Hattie of one. There was an aspidistra on a bamboo stand. Father hated them. The first thing he'd do if he got
into Parliament, he'd said, would be to ban every aspidistra in
the country. 'And spoil the pleasure of thousands of people,'
Mother had said. 'If they set store on anything as hideous as that
they deserve all they get.' Hattie had reminded him that the first
thing he'd said he was going to do was something else. He'd said
—she'd remembered it quite well because he'd said it the morning
he'd read the piece of newspaper Mother had used for cutting
out the pattern of her bodice—he'd said he'd shoot down anyone
with the same blasted leaning as that swine Oscar Wilde. Hattie
had seen Father shooting a pig under a tree blasted sideways by
the wind, but when she had reminded him there had been a
dreadful scene. Mother had sent her out of the room and the
quarrel had floated in roars and shrills up the stairs. Presently,
Mother had come up. 'Hattie, never ever as long as you live
mention Oscar Wilde again.' It had seemed a long time for not
mentioning. 'Not till I die?' Hattie had asked. 'Not even dying
—well, not till you are much older,' Mother had relented unwillingly, 'and then only if you have to to someone—oh, it's in-
sufferable!' Mother had suddenly broken off, and Hattie had
seen that her chin was trembling and been afraid that she was
going to cry, but she hadn't. She had said in an ordinary voice,
'Put on your hat, we're going to the beach.'

The bedroom had a black iron double bed with brass knobs
and a paisley bedspread. The washstand jug and basin and soap-
dish and chamber had blue tulips on them. The wallpaper had
blue bows and rosebuds all over it. The bows weren't tying the
roses so they were silly.

'Yes, this will do nicely,' Mother said.

Out on the pavement, Mother said, 'It's less than half the price
of the Grosvenor with full *pension*.'

'What's full *pension*?' Hattie poked with her toe a paper-bag
in the gutter which looked puffed up and full of something but
wasn't.

'All food—breakfast, luncheon, tea, and dinner in the evening,
but as you won't be having the evening meal they'll make a
reduction I expect.'

'If I was a French child of three—'

'Don't start that, Hattie.' Even so, it was going to cost quite

enough, thought the Wren anxiously. She couldn't have come if
it hadn't been for that small nest-egg of money paid into the bank
by her father's executors after she had gone abroad, an unexpected final winding-up. She had kept it there for an emergency,
seeing it as a foothold on her native soil, but one to be shared with
Sebbie. Never had she dreamed that she would use it in circumstances such as these. This afternoon she would go to the bank,
and to the agency directly after breakfast tomorrow. She would
lay special emphasis on her ability to teach French. A parent mad
on French would, she hoped, disregard algebra. 'We'll fetch our
luggage now and bring it back in a cab, and then,' she gave
Hattie's hand a little jiggle, 'we'll go and have lunch in a shop
as I said we wouldn't want it in the hotel today, and then when
I've just been to the bank, we'll go and see Westminster Abbey.
That'll be enough for one day, and we'll go back to the hotel then
and have a quiet tea.'

Hattie didn't want a quiet tea in the hotel; she wanted a noisy
one in a shop.

Getting the luggage took quite a time. 'I shan't unpack now,'
said Mother, stooping to unlock their trunk in their new abode.
'I'll just hang up the things that matter like I did last night.'
When she had finished, she locked their papers in the trunk for
safety. 'There's no point in carrying it around with us.' To Hattie
it seemed as though she was locking up France.

After roast beef and Yorkshire pudding and cabbage and baked
potatoes and boiled potatoes and horseradish sauce and apple
tart and custard at Gorringes, they found the bank shut. They
went straight to Westminster Abbey.

All those statues astonished Hattie. There had been none like
that in the French cathedral, only the holy ones. 'Who was
Pitt?'

'You *know*, Hattie—Prime Minister.'

'If Father was the Prime Minister—'

'He never will be. You must try and think about sensible things
that *do* happen,' Mother said.

Hattie felt a sad aching pity for Father. Why shouldn't he be?
'Oscar Wilde,' she said it inside. Her lips moved but made no
sound. She felt on Father's side. But she wasn't against Mother.
Why shouldn't Father have a statue? 'Do you have to be very
famous to be here?'

'Very.'

'Do you think Father will be?'

No, the Wren said, she was afraid he wouldn't. She looked down on the crown of her daughter's hat. She knew, without seeing it, that it had worked up again, sliding up on the smooth hair because it was a little too small. In this great company of the dead a too small hat didn't matter. Life was what mattered—the life of the child who was greater than any of them now because she lived, while they—eternal life . . . no, she was not greater, but she mattered more. Their vicissitudes were over, while Hattie— she was missing Sebbie. It was natural that she should. 'I ought to be glad she's normal,' mused Rose wretchedly, knowing she couldn't bear the child to be wanting what it was her right to have, knowing too, she thought, that she wasn't normal, that no solid normal child wove such webs of fantasy or thought such thoughts. None of them were normal, Hattie, herself, or Sebbie. Sebbie's attitude as a father wasn't normal, saying such frightful things, using such awful language in front of the child, being so hopelessly irresponsible. And yet, she thought grudgingly but with a flicker of superiority as though it were to her own credit, Hattie adored her father while she—this strange company that she was keeping seemed to incite honesty—hadn't loved hers, not really, though he had had the qualities that Sebbie lacked. Heaven forbid that Sebbie—His handling of this miserable affair wasn't normal either, the lack of furtiveness. Heaven knows, she didn't want him furtive, but this 'kings can do no wrong' attitude was almost as bad, she thought ambiguously. 'And I—what am I?' Would anyone else have left as she had done?—with very little money, and a convalescent child, and no concrete hope of a post, especially with the damning factor of an absent husband, and all with no proof that Sebbie hadn't been telling the truth about Paris. Anyone else would have said they'd seen him on the beach that day. It was she that was furtive. No, not really—that woman's head, that black widow's hat on his shoulder had given her such a spiritual sickness whenever she thought of it. Could she expect him never to have a peccadillo? Was it reasonable? Reason, reason—she was sick of reasoning. Yes, she could expect it, and certainly not with a woman like that. It was easier with one's hackles up, till that awful fairness to the absent enemy took hold. 'Hattie, your father has a very good brain, but it is given only to the very few to be famous. Fame isn't everything. The writers and poets are together, in Poets' Corner; we'll go and find them.'

It pleased the Wren to find the bust of Tennyson. Her pleasure

pleased Hattie. Father would hate his long hair. He had called
Byron a 'long-haired incestuous little rotter'. When Hattie had
asked what 'incestuous' meant, he had said, 'Loving your sister.'
Mother had been angry and told him to be quiet. 'What's the
matter now, Rosie?' Putting down his coffee-cup, he had got up.
'You haven't got a sister, suckling.' He'd patted her head as he
passed. 'Keep it in your rice for a *bonne bouche* when you're older.'
Looking at Tennyson, Mother said softly,

> 'Break, break, break,
> On thy cold grey stones, O Sea!
> And I would that my tongue could utter
> The thoughts that arise in me.'

Hattie didn't want her thoughts. She didn't want to see the sea
breaking on the cold grey stones of the sea-wall. She didn't want
to see what she saw in the sea. Walking on, she came face to face
with the big flat face of Thackeray. Then she saw someone like
Father. It was Walter Scott. Although Father knew she had lied,
she felt better and stronger.

The likeness to Sebbie disturbed the Wren. Moving away, she
caught sight of the names of Keats and Shelley. Where was
Byron? Looking about, she could see no sign. One would have
thought . . . no, of course not.

'What will happen when there's no room left here?' Hattie
asked.

'There are other ways of honouring the famous. Statues—' said
the Wren dreamily, 'in the streets and squares of London.'

'Oh—' Hattie's breath sucked up, 'how lovely if Father could
be there!'

'He would have to be dead, Hattie, for that to happen, so don't
let's think about it now.'

Hattie's pride and happiness crumbled into dust. 'If Father
died I'd die too.'

Conscience-stricken, the Wren said gently, 'No, you wouldn't
—please God. And what about me?' she added, chagrined.

'We could all die!' Hattie's voice shrilled with hysterical
excitement.

'Shush, we're in church.' Taking Hattie to a chair, the Wren
pressed her into it. 'Sit down and be still.' Then the Wren knelt
down to pray.

Hattie saw Father standing on a monument in the middle of
the street. 'Who's that?' someone would ask. 'It's Sebastian

Suckling, the famous writer,' someone in the know would say. 'Has he got a son to carry on his name?' 'No, only a daughter who's a coward and a liar.' Hattie sat very still. 'I'm not really,' it came out loud by mistake but Mother, whose head was bent down on her hands, didn't move. Poking her finger up the back of her neck under her hair, Hattie felt her spot. It had the makings of a boil but wasn't one. Mother had told her to leave it alone. If Father knew she'd told a story it was funny he hadn't said something when she was better from being ill. He gave lies no quarter. Suppose he still thought she had pushed the fisherman in, that he really knew he hadn't had a heart attack, that he'd drowned because of her?—then—he'd think she was a murderer —that's why he hadn't said anything: it was too awful to mention. He hadn't said anything to anyone. He didn't want her guillotined. Hattie's breath sucked up in a sound like a sob. She wasn't crying, but her chest had filled with fear and horror. 'I didn't!' It was all right, she hadn't. She wished she'd known before she came away so that she could have told Father. He'd rather she was a story-teller than a murderer. 'I didn't, I didn't.'

It was Father's fault if she had; he'd told her to do it, but she hadn't. He'd said the fisherman could swim, why hadn't he? He was too ill with his heart attack, that's why. Sitting there in the gathering gloom while the Wren prayed, Hattie's mind chewed on. She saw the sea-wall, the man stooping to pick up the sweets. She saw herself telling Father she'd done it. He'd told her to run to the shed and he would come when he was ready and when she'd asked him what he'd got to do, he'd said, 'Don't ask questions.' She'd run to the shed and waited for Father, looking up the wall and not seeing him, and then seeing him coming, looking as though he'd been behind the little house. He hadn't though. When she'd asked him he hadn't said 'no' which she'd awfully wanted him to, but he'd said was it likely he'd mess about there in the rain. Suppose Father *had* gone there? Suppose—*Father had pushed him in.* Everything inside Hattie seemed to stop. She didn't seem to be breathing at all. *Father was a murderer* . . .

The Wren rose from her knees. 'We'll go now, Hattie. What's the matter? You look as though you'd seen a ghost. Do you feel all right, darling?'

'Yes, thank you.' Hattie got up. The choked feeling was still in her chest.

They took a bus to Hyde Park Corner. 'We get out here,' the Wren said. 'Come on, Hattie, we've got to get out.'

Out on the pavement Mother said, 'I'm not sure which bus we take now. I'll ask that woman.' She went up to someone waiting by a post. Hattie stood where she was. That's why Father had gone to Paris, to hide in the sewers like he'd said he would. He didn't want to be sniffed by dogs.

'Come along, Hattie,' Mother called.

In a daze, Hattie started to cross the street, following someone in a blue coat and skirt, who suddenly darted forward in front of a dray. Why didn't Mother wait for her? When she tried to catch her up the dray blocked Hattie's way. Left alone in the middle of the street, she looked round, bewildered. A cab swerved past her. 'Hattie!' Mother was calling. She was still there on the pavement, she was starting to cross. 'Hattie! Stand still, stay where you are!' Hattie saw a fire-engine with clanging bells and galloping horses sweeping down on her. With a shriek of terror, she started to dash back towards the Wren. Seconds later she landed with a cracking thud on the ground. Bemused with shock and pain, she lay still for a moment making no sound. Then someone picked her up and held her in a smothering embrace. 'There, there—you'll be all right, lovey.' Twisting her head free as she was pushed back, Hattie saw the sprawled body of the Wren.

CHAPTER XIII

SHRIEKING, Hattie fought like a wild animal in the hold of the fat woman whose hands, in white cotton gloves, gripped her arms with a strength derived from thirty years of elbow-grease and handle-pulling in the Bear and Elephant. ' 'Ush, dearie—'

The doctor, stooping over the body on the ground, raised his head for a moment, 'Stop that child screaming, someone.'

The occupant of the hackney, catapulted into a disaster as inescapable as it was unwelcome, turned, and pushing his way through a crowd collecting like seagulls round a dead fish, reached the screaming child and the woman. Putting his hand on Hattie's shoulder, John St Aubrey said, 'Stop screaming,' in the voice he reserved for hysteria, gun-dogs, and his youngest son.

Hattie stopped. The silence, after the noise, surprised her. It seemed no more of her own making than the shrieking had been.

'Your mother's not dead, only unconscious,' he said it slowly and plainly.

To Hattie, looking up hare-eyed, the shock of hearing 'dead' said aloud in connection with the Wren, accepted by this man as an obvious possibility and not a fear of her own making, was so terrible it bludgeoned her speechless.

'Praises be,' said the woman, though she wasn't leaving go of the poor little thing, not to go and see *that*.

'Not dead,' repeated John St Aubrey.

'Let me go!' Hattie's voice shrilled to a crack.

'I'll take her to look,' St Aubrey told the woman. 'It will be better for her to see.'

'No, don't, sir. It'll be enough to 'aunt the poor little mite for the rest of 'er life.'

'It's the things we don't see, madam, that do the haunting sometimes. Do you know her?' he asked.

'Never set eyes on 'er before, but *someone* 'ad to look to the child.'

Hattie butted and bit. Instead of flesh, her teeth clenched on the slack top of a button glove.

'Go it!' shouted a paper-boy, and swerving round a horse, plunged through the crowd to see the fun.

'Stop it, you naughty girl! Trying to bite me and me only acting for 'er good.'

'Let her go.' As St Aubrey pulled Hattie back, the hands unclutched. 'I'll take care of her. I had the misfortune to be in the cab that knocked her mother down, and although it was no fault of the cabby's, I feel responsible for her till we've got some facts and found out who she is.' Looking down on Hattie to see if she was in a condition to divulge something, the crown of her hat told him nothing. 'The accident could hardly have happened in a more convenient place—in front of a hospital,' he added dryly, 'with a doctor in a brougham thrown in.'

Freed from the fat woman at last, tensed to jerk away from the man's grasp, Hattie's mind blotted up his last sentence. 'Monsieur le Docteur.' For a moment of flickering excitement, she saw the thin dark body, the big sad eyes in the sallow face, hungering after the familiarity. Then the hope was snuffed out by a grain of sense: it wouldn't be him. He mustn't touch Mother, he killed his patients.

'Come along—' clasping Hattie's hand tightly, the man took her through the crowd to her mother.

The shock of the Wren's ignominy was terrifying. She lay at Hattie's feet on her face in the street with her hat off. If Hattie had wanted to, she could have touched Mother's ear with her boot. The horror of it turned her face brick red.

The English doctor had finished his brief examination, and risen to his feet. No good moving the woman till the stretcher came. Standing there bare-headed—he had left his silk hat on the seat of the brougham—he was the complete antithesis, physically and mentally, of Monsieur le Docteur. He loved his stomach for one thing. He could fill it with anything from pork dripping to oysters and it never retaliated. His eyes had the bright snapping sharpness of a small dog's. They snapped now with impatience as he waited, his Gladstone bag in his hands. 'Go away, all of you,' he said to the crowd. 'Never seen anyone knocked down before?'

'Scores of 'em, mister,' said the barrel-organ man.

'Then have the grace to go away.'

Over the body of the woman, the doctor addressed the new arrival, 'Is this your mother, child?'

Hattie's drooping head jerked.

'Poor li'le nipper! Bloomin' shime,' said the barrel-organ man.

A murmur of agreement rumbled round the crowd.

'Stand back.' said the policeman, who had just taken a statement from the cabby.

'Your mother's not dead and she's not going to be. Look at me, child.' The doctor's voice held a faint trace of thunder. 'Do I look like a humbug?'

Lifting her head, Hattie's eyes fastened in miserable wonder on the flowing white beard and hair and whiskers.

'Well?'

Hattie's lips moved in soundless denial. He looked like Moses on the top of Mount Sinai being given the Ten Commandments by God.

The policeman was coming towards Hattie when he was diverted by the arrival of the stretcher, and the business of pushing back the crowd to make way. The men laid the stretcher on the ground beside the Wren. Hattie couldn't bear to watch; she looked straight down the buttons on her coat. She knew when they had finished lifting Mother; and when they took up the stretcher, she looked. They had covered her with a blanket. All Hattie saw was a bit of her crest as she was carried away.

The policeman handed Hattie Mother's hat. 'You carry that

missie, and I'll take care of the bag. You're bringing 'er along to
the 'ospital, aren't you, sir?' Hattie's companion said he most
certainly was.

The crown of the hat was pushed right in behind the lavish
watered-silk bow. Someone—or perhaps the cab-horse—must
have trodden on it. The policeman hadn't tried to push it out.
With one hand held, Hattie couldn't either. It was Mother's
Paris hat. She had bought it when they lived there. Father had
forbidden her to throw it away. It was the best hat she'd ever had,
he said. Mother said it was simply because he knew it had come
from Paris, he'd have said that about her pancake which he
hated if he'd thought it was Parisian. Father had never heard
such balderdash. If he had woken up alone in an igloo with it,
even in that cold beastly twilight, he'd have known at a glance
that it had Paris stamped all over it. When Hattie had asked what
an igloo was he had refused to tell her. 'Go and look it up in the
dictionary. You get all your education too easily by a long chalk.
If you got it through your own exertions by sweat and blood
you'd damn' well lay some store by it.'

As they followed the stretcher to the hospital, tears trickled
out of Hattie's eyes and her throat hurt worse than her knees
which had been so scraped on the stones.

After some preliminaries, the motionless body of Rose Suckling
was pushed away on a trolley on its way to a ward. The hat and
bag went too. She was going to be put to bed till she regained
consciousness, the Sister told Hattie. But with a kick like that
you couldn't tell, she thought. The sense of desertion terrified
Hattie. Stricken, unbelieving, she stood with her hand still in the
man's.

'What's your name, dear?' the Sister asked.

Hattie couldn't speak. Her neck was blocked.

The Sister looked at the man; lean, legal, attractive, a wife
with jewellery in a house in one of the Squares, she thought. She
summed up and docketed people as methodically as she summed
up constipation, hypochondriacs and approaching death. More
often than not she was right, but this time she slipped up on the
Square; it was Vicarage Gate.

John St Aubrey shook his head. 'It's been a bit of a shock.'
Looking down on top of the child's head, he had no idea that her
hat had risen up a bit.

Sister bristled. She didn't require to be told the child had had
a shock. Who did he think he was, talking to her as though she

were an untrained idiot? Then he smiled at her. It was brief,
scarcely perceptible, a flicker in his eyes, a slight lifting of the
corners of his mouth. Her bristles went down like the hairs on a
cat's back. 'Naturally she has.' It sounded almost pleasant.

There had been no means of identification in the bag, that's
why P.C. Futcher had let it go up to the ward. 'I'll 'ave to ask
the kid again,' he said now. 'Got to get something out of 'er.' It
sounded like an operation. The kid was her, thought Hattie wildly.

The policeman stooped, putting his hands on his knees. It was
unnecessary to bend quite so much to look under Hattie's hat-
brim, but it was the technique he adopted when dealing with
dumb children. Hattie gazed, unwillingly, point-blank into his
fat face. He had a large soft lower lip that looked as if it had been
stuck on after. His chin had a deep crease down the middle
dividing it into two separate cushions. 'Come on, Lizzie—tell me
your other name.' It nearly always worked with shy or gormless
children. 'My name's not Lizzie.' After that it was generally plain
sailing. But Hattie, her aching neck stuffed tight as a chicken's
crop, still felt incapable of speech.

'Leave her to us and call back later if you want to.' Sister was
in no awe of the Law as represented by P.C. Futcher. It wasn't
the first time he'd been in with an accident and it wasn't likely
to be the last.

Letting go of Hattie's hand, John St Aubrey went off with the
policeman with the assurance that he would ring up later. He
was already half an hour late for his appointment.

Sister stooped to look at Hattie's knees. 'They're not cut, only
scraped. Come along and we'll get Nurse to clean them up.'
Sister put her hand on Hattie's shoulder and pushed.

Nurse had her sleeves rolled up. Her arms were thick and solid
like Berthe's. She smelt of carbolic instead of sweat and garlic.
Hattie didn't know if she was a virgin, she thought dully without
caring. She sat on a chair and Nurse knelt at her feet with a basin
beside her like Jesus washing the disciples' feet. Hattie wished she
was Jesus. He'd have told her what to do. He'd have taken
Mother's hand and she'd have got up quite well again off the
stretcher, and when they had thanked Jesus, Mother would have
put on her hat and taken her bag and they'd have gone back to
the hotel for tea. She wanted to cry so dreadfully.

When Nurse had finished dabbing with wet cotton wool, she
said, 'We'll put some iodine on them; they won't need to be
bandaged.'

The iodine hurt frightfully. Clenching her teeth and hands, Hattie stiffened like a poker. Her inside drew up and her scar hurt too. Then she began to tremble and couldn't stop. Nurse took her back to Sister who was in a little room having her tea.

'We can have tea together,' Sister said to Hattie. Nurse went away; she hadn't been asked to have any. Sister put a cup of tea to Hattie's lips. 'Drink up.' Hattie didn't want it and could hardly swallow. Her mouth filled and she swallowed twice. She knew she couldn't swallow a biscuit when Sister gave her one. Biting off a corner, she put it in her mouth and pushed it about with her tongue till it was soggy. Mother was ravenous; she'd said so in the bus. 'I can't think why I should be after that enormous lunch,' she'd said, 'or why when I'm so—' she had broken off. 'What?' Hattie had asked. She hadn't really minded about knowing, she had been too worried about Father, and Mother hadn't answered.

'Mother's ravenous,' Hattie said and started to bawl. She heard the noise she was making with shame.

'Is she?' said Sister as though she hadn't noticed that Hattie was crying. There was a time for comfort as there was for everything else. A good cry acted as an emotional purge. 'Well, that's splendid. When she comes round she'll be able to have a nice cup of tea.' Tea was about all she would be fit for. Was she really hungry?—another of those undernourished cases? Clothes didn't go for anything; misers, cranks, Spartans, martyrs, and grinding poverty, concealed under a fur coat—she'd met the lot of them. Pouring out a second cup for herself, Sister cast a calculating glance at the child; thinner than she should be but not hungry enough to eat the biscuit. If she'd been really hungry she'd have eaten it willy-nilly. Highly strung all right, and she'd got something to fidget about now, poor little soul, but even so, if she'd been hungry she'd have had it down her by now. Something a bit queer about her coat, but it wasn't shabby exactly. Boots poor leather, but not stubbed at the toes or down at heel as far as she could see. Sister looked away, and lifted her cup. 'You'll feel better after a good cry, dear.'

How could she be? Father wouldn't think so. He'd think Sister a fool. This thought was like a passing fish in the wretchedness of Hattie's mind, but in spite of its transience it made her cry less. Then she stopped and was simply heaving.

While she was reading the off-duty list, Sister saw out of the corner of her eye the child put the biscuit into her pocket.

Keeping it for her mother, was she?—or for her own supper?
'Directly your mother is ready for it, she will be able to have as
much food here as she can eat—meat and vegetables and good
nourishing milk puddings, and bovril and cocoa.'

'Mother doesn't like cocoa,' said Hattie huskily. She had
dabbed her eyes with her hanky and now set to on her nose.

'Beggars can't be choosers,' thought Sister tartly, resenting the
rejection of a single item in her horn of plenty. 'There are worse
things than cocoa,' she said.

'Oysters,' whispered Hattie.

What did she know of oysters? *They* weren't beggars' fare.
'Nobody in this hospital eats oysters; they're too expensive.'
Sister did not pursue the subject. Holding out the plate, she said,
'Have another biscuit, more than one, take as many as you like.'

'No thank you, I'm not hungry,' said Hattie politely.

Good manners, registered Sister. Ignoring food, she came
straight to the knuckle-bone. 'What's your name?'

'Hattie.'

'Hattie what?'

'Hattie Suckling.'

'Where do you live?'

She wouldn't say 'France' because of Father. If she did they
might find him. 'Nowhere in particular,' Hattie said slowly.
Burying her nose in her hanky, she blew it again.

'Do you mean you wander?'

Hattie nodded.

'You're gypsies?' Sister smiled gaily.

Hattie nodded again.

'Where's your caravan now?'

She was teasing her. 'We don't live in a caravan.' Hattie was
too miserable to be stiff about being teased; besides, she would
have loved to live in one.

'Oh, I see—' Sister drained her teacup. 'If you don't sleep in a
caravan where do you sleep? Where were you last night?'

'In a hotel.'

'Which?'

'By the station.'

'Which station? There's more than one in London, dear.'

'Victoria.'

Sister made a long shot. 'Was it the Grosvenor?'

'Yes.'

'Are you sure?' Sister was looking at Hattie very closely.

'Yes.'

'Oh—' chagrined, taking the couple out of the undernourished pigeon-hole in which she had so nearly placed them, turning back to the duty list, Sister said, 'You didn't starve there, *I* know.'

'No, we had a *tremendous* breakfast.' It seemed so long ago—like another day. Remembering it, Hattie's lip trembled.

Sister didn't see the lip. 'What did you have?' she asked, partly to draw the child out and partly to know how the rich fed—not like the hospital staff, she did know that.

Hattie told her, painstakingly. The business of remembering everything steadied her.

'And what did you have?'

'A kipper.'

'Holy Mother of God!—out of all that collection,' thought Sister, and put Nurse Gill down for a half-day on Monday. Aloud, she said, 'And where did you have dinner?'

'In a shop.'

'Then I don't know why your mother should be ravenous,' she said bluntly.

'Mother didn't either.' Hattie's voice shook.

'Never mind—she'll have plenty here.' Sister tipped up the teapot but only a trickle came out of it, not worth drinking. 'Is your father at the Grosvenor?'

'No, we've moved. It was too expensive.'

Sister nodded. Ignorant?—feckless?—first port in a storm? 'Where have you moved to?'

'A little cheaper one.'

'What's its name?'

'I don't know.'

'Where is it? What's the name of the street?'

'I don't know!' Hattie's voice which had been quite low suddenly shrilled.

'Never mind,' said Sister, 'you'll remember soon.' And what would happen if the child didn't, heaven alone knew. 'Is your father waiting for you there, dear?'

'No.'

'Where is he?'

'He's dead.' Frightened by the awful lie, feeling as though she had killed him, Hattie began to cry again.

CHAPTER XIV

'AS YOU'RE COMING to stay I'd better tell you something about us.'

'You needn't if you don't want to,' said Hattie being fair.

'I don't mind. You're bound to find out when you do see us,' said John St Aubrey dryly.

'I shan't pry,' Hattie told him. If there was anything Father couldn't stand it was prying women poking and fussing.

'Good. *Whatsoever ye would that men should do to you do ye even so to them.* Are you conversant with the Bible?'

'Yes.'

So she'd lived with grown-ups had she?—knew what conversant meant. Baby wouldn't have had the foggiest notion. 'There's Baby; she's about your age.'

'Why is she called Baby?'

'Because she's the baby of the family; there's never been another one to oust her.'

Hattie's mouth hung open for a moment. 'What's her proper name?'

'Angela.'

'Will she always be called Baby?' How could she be? A silly question deserved a silly answer, Hattie knew, but although his answer was astonishing, it wasn't silly. He hadn't considered the matter, he said. He didn't seem to mind. If *she* was called Baby —which Father would never have allowed, but if she was—what would Father do? 'Puke,' thought Hattie.

'Her mother likes to have a baby still, it makes her feel young.'

Mother didn't want to grow old, either. When she had said she was getting on, Father had said she ought to be damned grateful, that she'd got the hell of a trudge if she lived to be a hundred and each year ticked off was a blessing in the bag.

'But she isn't a baby if she's *my* age,' Hattie pointed out. 'I'm nine.'

'So is she. No, of course she isn't a baby really, although she sometimes behaves rather like one, I'm afraid.' The three boys had just gone back to school, he told her.

In happier circumstances these details about a strange English family would have been meat and drink to Hattie, but in her misery and role of potential guest, their fascination for her had some of the hypnotism of a mouse about to be fed to a snake.

'What time do they come back from school? Will they be back when we get there?'

'No, they're boarders. They won't be home till a week or so before Christmas.'

How awful for them, weeks and weeks! Shuttldg her lips, Hattie sucked up. But it was a great relief they wouṛun't be there. 'Do they mind?'

'Eddie was a bit homesick his first term, but he was not quite eight when he went, a bit earlier than the other two.'

Younger than she was. Chagrined and appalled, Hattie saw him crying in a playground—or had he managed not to?—in a black pinafore like the French boys wore. 'How old is he now?'

'Eleven and naughty. Ethel's the eldest of the family; she's seventeen and just gone to Paris.'

Hattie, who had just been going to ask why Eddie was naughty, switched suddenly away and said 'Paris!' before she could stop.

'Does it surprise you? It's quite usual to go to a finishing school there, but perhaps you know Paris?'

Hattie shook her head, shaking a lie.

'My wife has gone with her to settle her in and won't be back for a week or so, but Nana will look after you. Fräulein, who's new, comes for lessons in the morning which Prissy shares—she's a friend of Baby's.' After a little silence he said: 'Do you have a governess?'

'No.'

'Do you go to school?'

'No. Mother gives me lessons. She doesn't like Mam'selle Sévigné; she says she'd try to make me a Catholic. Françoise says she's always fasting which makes her cross. Father hates people who fast, he loves—'

Ignoring the present tense, he asked, 'What does he love?'

'Food,' her voice quivered. What would he do for food down there? Desperately trying not to cry, Hattie turned further round towards the window to hide the tears in her eyes.

'Combien de temps as-tu habité Paris?'

The familiar sound of French further weakened her strategy. Mourning over Father's food, it caught her unprepared. Pushing out her tongue as far as it would go, Hattie licked up a tear. Then she told him in French that they didn't live in Paris.

'But you've lived in France,' he thought. She hadn't acquired that accent in an English schoolroom. And they had stayed at the Grosvenor, she and her mother, last night—Victoria, boat train. What was she up to? She had slewed round, revealing nothing but hair and hat.

'I'm English,' Hattie heard her voice shrill. 'Mother says never to forget I'm English and Father says *When in Rome do as the Romans do.*'

'Father? I thought—' recrossing his legs, he left the sentence unfinished.

He didn't have to finish; Hattie knew what he was thinking. The blood poured up into her face and down her neck. 'He said it before he died.' She had killed Father again, she thought wildly. Her vest was wet.

It was a tremendous relief when he changed the subject. Pointing out of the window at a railing, he said, 'Kensington Gardens, as you probably know. Do you know your London well?'

Her London? He had given it to her and she didn't want it, in spite of being English, in spite of Mother wanting her to want to be. 'We left when I was three,' she whispered.

'Six years ago—quite a slice out of a lifetime of nine, but one doesn't want to spend all one's time in one place, naturally,' he said pleasantly

'Life would be like a stagnant pond,' said Hattie dully. She wanted to be a pond.

He said that would depend, he thought, on where you lived, whether you lived in Paris or London, or in a one-horse place in the back of beyond. 'Have you travelled much, or have you spent the last six years in the same place, I wonder?'

He was waiting for an answer, Hattie knew. She could *feel* him waiting, looking at her. 'There was more than one horse,' she said, her mind ranging from the dappled grey that had pulled the cart when she and Mother had gone out that day with Madame, to the *fiacre* horse with the straw hat. Father had said, 'To blazes with the hat, what it needs is a full belly.' When Hattie, dreading the answer, had asked if it didn't get enough to eat, Father had said, couldn't she see it was a bag of bones? but Mother had said, 'It's old, the old get thin.' Father had been cross. 'Why always try to pretend life's one long rollicking picnic whenever the brat gets a chance to smell out the truth? It isn't a picnic and never has been for that scraggy little brute.' When Hattie had suggested giving it a picnic, Mother had said that

Jacques, the owner, was a nasty man and wouldn't like it. Hattie had bought a secret picnic with her pocket-money—a bit of one of those huge round loaves like lifebelts. She had crept downstairs when she was supposed to be resting to look for the horse and *fiacre* in the Place de la Ville. When it wasn't there, she had gone on through the boiling heat to the sea front, where she had found it in a puddle of shade under an acacia tree; there had been no sign of Jacques. '*Ici*—' she had held out a piece of bread, but although she had stroked the horse and pleaded with it, it had refused to eat. She had just been putting the bread on the ground in case it was shy, when hands had wrenched her up, 'Leave my horse alone,' and she'd been swung round face to face with Jacques. 'Ah—the child of the English *m'sieur*—' His eyes had red sagging wet rims and were horrible, his face was covered with black hairs like the prickles on a sea-urchin, his teeth were yellow and broken and his breath was *dégoûtant*. 'How would you like to come for a little drive in my *fiacre* and hide from your father? How many francs are you worth, *mon enfant, hein*?' Terrified, Hattie had tugged back, and with a cackle of laughter he had let her go. She had run like a cat, streaking for cover.

'Our house is round the next corner,' St Aubrey said, plumping Hattie back from the Rue sur les Murs into an English cab in Kensington. To Hattie this was worse than that scorching flight in France; she had been running home then. The prospect of somebody else's home, of strangers in strange rooms, appalled her. She wanted the cab to go on, anywhere, so long as it didn't stop.

It stopped outside a tall solid house in a row of solid houses that looked as if they would never flake or crack or crumble. It was not a secret-looking house; there were no high railings to be peered through. Below the low railings on the pavement were the bottom windows, underground and not underground. She wasn't near enough to peer through them.

John St Aubrey led Hattie up the steps to the front door. Each side of it were shiny ginger-coloured pillars with speckles on them. Letting go her hand, he took a key from his pocket and opened the door. She could run away now, she thought, but there was nowhere to run to except the hospital where they wouldn't let her stay and he would be sure to find her. She allowed herself to be pushed inside and the door to shut behind her. In the hall he took her hand again, 'Come along up.'

Their feet made no squeaks as they went upstairs on the thick soft red carpet. The banisters and the bottom part of the walls were the colour of *chocolat*, the top had red paper with curly leaves. When they came to the second landing, the carpet stopped and green matting began; the familiar bare homeliness of it, like and not like the matting on the stairs to her bedroom in France, made Hattie's lips tremble. There was a dull thudding like far-away guns.

'Baby's rocking—that's what the noise is,' he said.

The picture Hattie saw stopped her from crying. She saw Baby rocking in a wooden crib like the one in Mother's Dutch painting; Nana was rocking her. She wasn't a baby, she was nine. 'She's an idiot,' thought Hattie, like the *gendarme*'s son who was taken for walks in a long flat basket spinal carriage. 'Don't look,' Mother had said. Hattie had. It had been so dreadful she had had to have a night-light.

On the third landing, John St Aubrey threw open the nursery door. 'I've brought you a visitor.'

Hattie saw a child on a rocking-horse. Staring at the horse, she forgot almost at once that she had expected an idiot in a cradle.

'Papa!' Flinging herself off the horse, Baby rushed at her father, hurling herself with dramatic emotion into his arms. Abandoned, feeling very separate, Hattie looked from the horse to Nana sitting at a table with a sewing-machine. She had stopped machining with one hand on the handle and the other lying still amongst the bunched up white cotton she had been smoothing under the needle. She was smiling at Hattie as if they were old friends. It warmed Hattie's core a bit but she wasn't bamboozled. They weren't old friends and Nana would want to know things. Nana did; she wanted to know what the child had been through to look like that. She said, 'It will be nice for Baby to have you,' making Hattie feel valuable.

John St Aubrey detached his daughter's clinging arms. 'Aren't you going to say how do you do to Hattie?'

Baby obliged, pouting, then her face changed as she shook hands. Smiling, she gave Hattie a knuckle jelly. It wasn't as bad as the one that Father had given her when he'd ground her knuckles till they felt like loose tortured lumps and she'd shrieked. 'Great Scot, Hattie!—if you can't bear torture better than that what in heaven's name will you do if you let the Arabs get you?' She didn't shriek now. Grinding her side teeth together she behaved as though nothing was happening. Baby had big blue eyes, her fair curls flopped almost into them and her lips were fat.

'Come outside a minute, Nana, will you?' John St Aubrey turned, jingling the money in his pocket.

Taking off her steel spectacles, Nana rose. 'Ask Hattie if she would like to rock, dear.'

They were going to talk about her, Hattie thought with satisfaction, feeling again the pleasing importance of her illness. They didn't know where she came from; it was like being a spy.

Directly the door shut Baby rushed at the horse, and getting on it, rocked violently till the ends banged the floor.

Showing off, thought Hattie. 'She wouldn't if she knew how mysterious I am.' Feeling old and dignified, she went over to the window and looked out. There was not much to see, except the houses opposite. A light went up in a window, the yellow showing a big yellow patch in the grey smudginess that was the beginning of darkness. The hospital was over there somewhere, and at the end of a train journey the white cliffs of Dover and the sea. Standing on deck, holding the rail, her chiffon scarf tying on her hat, Mother had told Hattie that if she skinned her eyes she could just see them. It was the sight that homesick English dreamed of while they roasted on the Gold Coast or ate out their hearts on lonely tea estates for years. 'Did you in France?' Hattie asked. Not like that, Mother said. 'I was not lonely or homesick—not to that extent of course, with your father and you.' Seeing the faraway pale blur, Hattie had said, 'Would you have been if you hadn't had us?' Without Father and Hattie, Mother wouldn't have lived abroad. 'Where would you have lived?' Mother had answered slowly, 'After your grandfather died?—I don't know —how can I tell? Life drags you on, and if you break away, you don't know . . .' Mother's voice had dwindled into nothingness as she went on gazing. Hattie, gazing too into the golden shimmery breeziness, had imagined herself with a hole where she had eaten her heart clean out in the awful loneliness of nothing but tea.

She *was* eating her heart out now. She felt it crying inside her —but not for the white cliffs of Dover. She wanted to go home and be stagnant, she couldn't go without Mother, she—

'Do you want a rock?' called Baby.

'No, thank you.' Hattie went on staring at London.

'Are you cross because I gave you a knuckle jelly?' The rocking had almost stopped.

'You didn't—' Hattie turned, 'not a proper one. If you'd ever had one of my father's, you'd know what a proper jelly was.'

'I do know; mine was proper. Where's your father?'

'Dead.'

Baby stared.

Bending her head a little, Hattie moved her finger up the hard stalk of her neck till it could poke her spot. Poking, she drew comfort from the secret possession of it.

'Is your mother dead too?'

'No.' Hattie stopped poking. 'She's not going to die, please God.' The 'please God' came unexpectedly. It was more than a lip movement, or a whisper; Hattie's voice shrilled.

'What's the matter with her?' Baby demanded.

'She was knocked down by the cab your father was in.'

'Why?'

'She ran into the street to rescue me.' It was the first time Hattie had said it. Saying it made it seem all her fault. 'It was a mistake. It wasn't really my fault, I followed someone across I thought was Mother, and it wasn't.' She was explaining to herself more than to Baby. It hadn't been her fault, it hadn't!

'Where do you live?'

'Nowhere.'

'You must live somewhere.'

'Why should I?'

'You haven't come to live *here*, have you?'

Outraged by this deplorable frankness, repelled by the suggestion, Hattie had a sudden hunger to spit bang into the middle of the fat pink and white face. She couldn't do it; she knew her limits. She couldn't project her spittle, she could only drop it. It was a disgusting vision, and the thought of Mother's displeasure sapped her desire. But Father—— 'Good God, brat, what in heaven's name put that damn' fool idea into your head? Live with you! Great Scot, d'you think I'd want to?'

Baby's expression changed to one of astonishment. Her emotions washed across her face with a transparency far exceeding Hattie's. Laughing suddenly, she clapped her hands. 'If Nana heard you you'd be sent to bed or made to stand in the corner. When Eddie said "damn" Father thrashed him.'

Hattie, who had often been sent to bed or put to stand in the corner, felt on home ground. She had never been thrashed, but she knew who ought to be. Father was for thrashing all sorts of people—some to within an inch of their lives and some to the bone: cheats, and bullies, and people who kept dogs tied up and beat lame donkeys, and Hot Gospellers, and scores more.

Nana returned alone. 'Doesn't Hattie want a rock?'

'She won't, she's afraid,' Baby said.

'I'm not!' Hattie's lips moved in a gibber of fury.

'Of course you aren't. Baby shouldn't say such silly things; don't take any notice of her,' Nana came hook, line and sinker on to Hattie's side. 'Let's take off your hat and coat. Have you had any tea?'

'Yes, thank you.'

'Not much, I expect. We must see what we can get for your supper.' She spoke as though they would have to fish for it. Hattie didn't care if they didn't catch anything; she wasn't hungry.

'I often have soup,' Baby said. 'Do you always have milk and biscuits?'

'No, soup and mussels and—pork,' Hattie's voice rose, cracking a little on 'pork'. How angry Mother would be. All the violence ebbed out of her, leaving her dull and wretched.

'What are mussels?'

'Fish.'

Pouncing on the table, Baby grabbed a comb and a piece of tissue-paper. Wrapping the comb in the paper, she put it to her mouth and began to hum 'God save the King'. As she reached the middle of the first verse, there was a sudden shrill burst of song. Hattie, her lips parting in astonishment, looked round. In a cage, standing on a round table in the corner, was a yellow bird.

Breaking off, Baby stamped her foot. '*Stop it!* You always spoil it every time I play.' Going over to the cage, she smacked the side of it. The bird stopped singing.

'How *can* you?' Hattie's face was crimson.

'I didn't hit him, it was only the cage, silly.'

'How *can* you keep a wild bird in a cage?' Hattie cried.

'He's a canary, surely you know that? Canaries aren't wild.'

'They aren't meant to be in cages. How would you like—' Hattie's voice cracked, 'to spend your life alone in prison?'

'It's his house, it isn't prison.'

'It is!—I tell you it is!'

'Hush,' said Nana. 'There's no need to get worked up over Twittie; he's quite happy.'

'He isn't,' Hattie wailed. 'Father says all wild birds ought to be let out of cages.'

'He isn't wild, I tell you! And how can your father say anything if he's dead?' Baby yelled triumphantly.

'Be quiet, Baby, *at once*!' said Nana. 'As for you, you're tired out, child, and no wonder.'

Weakened by this sympathy and at the thought of her exhaustion, Hattie's lips trembled.

'What about a game of something before you go to bed?' Nana suggested. 'What shall we have, Baby?'

Baby said she didn't care.

They played snakes and ladders. Hattie would have been happy if she hadn't been so miserable.

Before they went to bed Baby put a black cloth over Twittie's cage. Hattie pretended not to see. Now he was in a dungeon—like Father, she thought wretchedly. Were the sewers dark in the day-time as well as at night?—down underground in a pitch dark drain for filth . . . what she saw was so awful and terrifying, she didn't know how to bear it. It comforted her a little when she remembered how cheerful Father had sounded when he'd said the sewers were where he'd go.

Tonight they could use the big bath. It had cold and hot taps and was in a bathroom on the landing below. In France they had had a tin tub which had been used before that as a cow trough. Mother said if you gave the French a nice bathroom, they'd rather die than have a bath. 'Die?—would they really rather?' Hattie had asked, and Mother had said when it came to the point she supposed they'd rather get into the bath, but they wouldn't like it, they didn't know what proper washing meant and didn't want to.

'There was a bath in the hotel last night,' Hattie said. 'I didn't see it, but Mother said there was. She said—' she broke off because she wanted to cry.

'What?' Baby demanded. 'What did she say?'

'I was too tired for—the paraphernalia involved.' The pride of remembering, picking this morsel from her pile of rice, gave Hattie a momentary comfort.

'I have to have the beastly little hip-bath in the nursery if Mama wants a bath before dinner,' Baby said. 'She doesn't like me much,' she added complacently.

'Not like you?' Hattie gaped.

'Now then, don't talk rubbish!' said Nana sharply.

'She doesn't like me as much as the boys.'

Aghast, filled with pity, Hattie saw great tears flopping out of Baby's eyes like water out of blocked gutters.

'Enough of that! You know what I said last time. Now stop crying *at once*,' Nana ordered.

Hattie had second bath.

'There!' Nana turned off the tap. 'Off with your vest, dear.'

Hattie dragged it off obediently.

'Snakes alive!' gasped Nana. 'What has happened to your tummy, child?'

'It's my scar.' *Mine*, thought Hattie. No one could take it from her. Now, homeless and without luggage, it seemed excessively precious. She gazed lovingly at its familiar lines. If there had been another vertical scar with the horizontal bars of the stitches running between the two, it would have made a ladder or a railway line.

'What was the operation for?' Nana's eyes were still glued to it.

'Appendicitis.'

Nana clucked. 'When was that?'

'August.' Hattie got into the bath.

'And now it's September—You're staying in bed tomorrow, child.'

'No!' Hattie's voice screeched, partly with indignation and partly with the pain of her knees which she shot up out of the water. 'I've stopped staying in bed ages ago. My knees hurt *awfully*!'

'For breakfast then.'

'No!'

'Put your knees down. They'll stop hurting in a minute and the water will do them good.' Nana handed Hattie the sponge. 'Where did you have the operation?' she asked.

'On the kitchen table.'

Nana had hoped for 'Paris'—that was what Mr St Aubrey had thought. There was some mystery here, he'd been right. She didn't like mysteries in the nursery, they were unwholesome. The child's nerves were all over the place, you could see that, and no wonder. She'd been brought up nicely; nice manners, clean, sensible clothes. She had folded them carefully when the child took them off. There was beautiful needlework in the smock, and the petticoat with all that tucking and insertion. Good lace on her drawers too. It was her boots that were different; you could see they were foreign, and now her vest—Nana folded the vest that the Wren had bought at the *boutique* in the arcade. The vest told Nana very little. The child must tell her more. 'Who operated on you?'

Hattie, her eyes shut, had been moving the sponge slowly up and down in the water imagining the sea sloshing seaweed hanging off the rocks at the bottom of the sea-wall, seeing a hand with fingers like sausages; one fell off, and a crab—with a gasp, she opened her eyes. He wasn't there now, he was buried——

'Who operated on you, dear?' Nana repeated. The child looked terrified.

'M'sieur le Docteur.' Hattie began lowering her knees. The pain helped to take away her thoughts.

A French doctor! Nana's inside recoiled in dismay. What had the man done to her? She wouldn't trust a Frenchman a single yard. They hadn't left her alone with him, surely to goodness? 'Was he a nice man?' she asked.

'All his patients died.'

'They couldn't have!' Nana said, horrified. '*You* didn't.'

'I'm the exception.' This dramatic conversation was putting back some stuffing into Hattie.

'I don't believe you.' It was not wholly true, but it was the state of disbelief in which Nana would have liked to have been, and the saying of it helped as a bastion against the appalling alternative. She could believe anything of the French, especially a French doctor, but she hoped that in this case she was mistaken. 'You mustn't fabricate, Hattie. If he was such a bad doctor that all his patients died, why did your parents let him operate on you, tell me that?'

'He was the only one and if he hadn't I'd have died for certain —I nearly did anyway.' The memory of the drama of her illness was like wine again. 'Someone who did die was buried while I was in bed.'

'One of the doctor's patients, you mean?' asked Nana slowly.

Hattie nodded, 'Yes.' Nana thought he'd killed him, but she hadn't said he had, she'd said he was one of the doctor's patients and as there wasn't another he must have been if he'd been ill, but Monsieur le Docteur hadn't killed him, he'd had a heart attack and fallen in and drowned. At the thought of it, Hattie felt the fright and the fingers coming back again.

The fear didn't escape Nana, but it was no good rushing children. Bending over the bath, she picked up the flannel. 'You lived in France, did you?—that must have been nice.'

What did it matter if Nana did know she'd lived there? thought Hattie. They couldn't find Father if she didn't say where she'd lived. Hattie nodded.

Nana was soaping the flannel. 'You lived in Paris, I expect?'

'No, we didn't. We've none of us been there.' The lie seemed less than it might have, wafting in the lovely hot steaminess, and she'd done it for Father.

'Would you rather soap yourself?' Nana handed Hattie the flannel. Children who were brought up by their mothers—and the child had never mentioned a nurse—were more used to fending for themselves: very often they were hopelessly neglected. She'd never forget that child of Lady Something or other with some high-falutin governess when she came to tea, pitch-black nails with the skin growing halfway up, and as for her ears— they'd been so full of dirty wax she was almost deaf. But this child's nails were well kept, you could see she'd been taught to rub down the skin. 'Let's have a look at your ears—London's such a dirty place.' With a practised movement, Nana plucked at the lobe of the nearest one. Clean as a whistle; nothing to complain of there. 'I expect France is lovely.' She didn't expect anything of the sort—French people, frogs, drains, excitability, not to mention doctors whose patients all died—long ago she'd put it in her black books and had never found any cause for altering her opinion. 'When I was sixteen,' she said, sitting down on the edge of the bath, 'I was nursemaid to the children of an Army officer. Then they went abroad and I left. I was sorry to see them go, I was very fond of them.'

'Couldn't you have gone with them?' Holding the flannel against her chest, bunched up like a bread poultice, Hattie gazed at Nana, her heart wrung for her disappointment.

'No, it wasn't possible.' Because although they had asked her to go, she had cried herself sick at the thought of it. It had been Egypt, not France, but there was no call to tell the child that. 'Tell me about France.'

Hattie told her. It was all right to start with, and then in the middle of telling her what the house was like, her voice cracked. Standing up, she soaped her scar. Nana watched, pursing her lips and grinding her teeth. Hattie started on Madame and the *Coq d'Or*, which led up to being sick—she didn't tell her about her dream; she didn't want to think about it—and the next day which led to the kitchen table.

The child's conversation was peppered with her father, the things he'd said and done. Nana conceived a vision of a coarse kind man who was no more dead than she was. Why wasn't the child in mourning, pray, tell her that, if he'd only just died? He'd been alive when she was ill in August and dead now in September. '*Where* was it you lived?' asked Nana, 'I forget.'

Hattie was brought up with a jar, the worse because she was standing naked and vulnerable. She sat down. 'I haven't told you.'

'Haven't you? Well if it wasn't Paris, where was it?'

She must say somewhere, Hattie thought wildly.

'Not that it makes much difference to me,' added Nana casually, 'seeing that I've never been to France and am never likely to go.'

'Chartres,' said Hattie.

'Well, what a nice place it sounds, to be sure.'

Hattie's backbone relaxed; she softened all over. It wasn't such a story as it might be. They hadn't exactly lived in Chartres, but they had gone there for a night just before they left Paris when she was six. She and Mother had talked about it the other day, sitting by the sea with the Bath chair. They'd talked about how lovely the glass in the cathedral was. Hattie had never forgotten the blue splashes it made on a pillar and the floor—like being splashed with the sea, she'd said, and Mother had said, no, not really, because if you took a bucket of sea it lost its colour. The glass had fed Mother's soul like hyacinths. '*If I had but two loaves, I should sell one and buy hyacinths for they would feed my soul,*' she had said. 'Would you?' Hattie had asked. 'Yes,' said Mother. 'Even if we were starving?' 'Yes—no, no I suppose not *then*.'

CHAPTER XV

THERE WAS PORRIDGE and boiled eggs for breakfast. Full of porridge, Hattie didn't want her egg.

'Eat it up,' Nana said, 'you look as though some food will do you good.'

'I've had food.' It wasn't fair to pretend that Mother hadn't fed her, although it would have been nice to have seemed starved, Hattie thought wistfully.

'Of course you've had food,' Nana agreed, 'but when you've been ill you need as much as you can eat.'

'I can't eat any more, I'm not hungry,' Hattie said. She was too unhappy to be hungry and she wanted Nana to be afraid she'd die. On the other hand, she wanted to take the top off the egg. Baby had bashed hers and picked off the shell in little bits. Hattie could slice off the top like Father did. 'Do it in one clean sweep as though you're cutting off someone's head,' he'd told her. When Nana said 'Try' and she'd waited for Baby to look, she did it with her knife. She was cutting off Madame Picard's head. A sudden feeling that perhaps she ought to be sorry for her spoilt it. She didn't want to feel sorry for her, she wouldn't.

'Papa says there's all the food you need in an egg.' There was a trickle of yolk streaming down Baby's chin.

'Then it would be just the thing for the desert,' said Hattie thoughtfully, adding a bag of eggs to the familiar picture of herself in her winter coat and a topee with a bottle of water and a gun in the sand.

'Never mind the desert—' Without even moving her hand, Nana seemed to sweep the whole desert away, sand, Arabs, mirages, 'Eat it up, there's a good girl.'

'You're going to do lessons to stop you thinking about your mother,' Baby said.

'She's going to do them to learn something, just as you are,' Nana said tartly.

'Nothing will stop me, they're my thoughts.' Hattie saw her thoughts like little fish swimming round and round inside the safety of her head. She saw Mother's thoughts quite still, as though they were dead; that was how they had been yesterday. What were they doing now? Was Mother conscious? Baby's father was going to enquire at the hospital on his way to his office. He had said so when he came up to say good night. 'I'll send word to you by a messenger boy,' he had promised. A messenger boy! Hattie had gaped with flabbergasted relish. How exciting it was! Then, remembering, her spirits had slumped in shame and misery.

'Fräulein will know if you aren't thinking about your lessons,' Baby said with satisfaction; 'she can see right through you.'

'Balderdash,' said Hattie, through skin, flesh, bone—'of course, she can't!'

'Fräulein's no different from any other person,' Nana said plainly and rather loudly as though she wasn't sure that she wasn't, 'even—'

'Even what?' Baby asked.

'Even nothing and blow your nose, please.'

By the time Prissy arrived, a green serge cloth had been laid on the table, Baby had been forced to get out the lesson books, and telling them to wait quietly, Nana had abandoned the nursery. Hattie, who had never been taught by anyone but the Wren, felt an excited tremor of sickening fear. Suppose she didn't know enough?—that her pile of rice was too little compared with those of the others? Glancing at Baby, swinging on her stomach on the back of the rocking-chair, her fat lips puckered in a breathy whistle, Hattie took heart. 'I'll be damned if her pile's bigger than a flea's—a nincompoop if ever there was one.' Striding over to the rocking-horse, she slapped him on his dappled quarters.

Prissy was a red-haired, stringy child, with large round steel spectacles through which she stared fixedly at Hattie. Hattie stared at the band pressing back Prissy's teeth which looked very much in the way.

'That's Hattie,' Baby said. 'She's staying with us because Papa's cab ran her mother over. It was *her* fault.'

'I made a mistake. I went across the street because I thought I was following Mother and then in the middle I found I was following someone in a blue coat and skirt like Mother's and it wasn't Mother. A fire-engine came and Mother ran out to rescue me and was run over.' Hattie tried to speak slowly and quietly in Mother's imbecile voice, but her own rose at 'fire-engine' and went on up without coming down.

'Is she dead?' Prissy's band *was* in the way.

'No, of course she isn't,' Baby said. 'Hattie wouldn't be going to do lessons if she was. She'd be crying in her bedroom in black.'

This matter of fact announcement of a vision that Hattie had already seen several times with horrifying clarity turned Hattie's face red. It came almost as a relief to be told that Fräulein was coming up the stairs. 'Papa says she walks like a coal-heaver,' Baby giggled.

Prissy giggled too. 'I hope she's in a good menper.'

When the footsteps stopped on the landing and there was a murmur of voices, Baby said, 'Nana's telling her about Hattie,' as though Hattie wasn't there, which made Hattie feel special and out of the ordinary again at once. 'Why do you call her Fräulein and not Miss Fräulein?' she asked.

'German governesses are always called fräuleins,' Prissy explained.

'Is she a *German*?'

'Of course she is, silly!' Baby said.

Hattie's mouth was still open when Fräulein entered the nursery.

'*Guten Morgen, Kinder,*' Fräulein said.

'*Gupem Morgem, Fräulein.*'

'*Guten Morgen, Fräulein.*'

'And you—' Fräulein looked at Hattie, 'you say to me good

morning not. It is perhaps because you German not understand?'

No, Hattie didn't. The Wren had no wish to go to Germany and had no intention of ever hobnobbing with the Germans. When Germans came into Madame's restaurant, Madame always saw to it that they were served last. Hattie saw Fräulein as the enemy who had boxed Mother's ears, who had starved Madame's mother in the siege of Paris and made Madame's legs bandy. She knew about Arabs, but no one had told her what to do when she had to be with a German. She was afraid. Father had sired a coward. No, he hadn't!—he hadn't! she thought wildly. Defiantly, she forced herself to stare back at the large heavy-boned face with pale grey eyes that could see right through her, skin, flesh . . . When Fräulein lifted her hand to push back a wisp of hair, Hattie ducked.

'Of what are you afraid? I am not going to eat you.'

Scarlet with shame, Hattie's eyes fell and stayed on an ink-spot on the table-cloth.

Lessons began with German. 'First,' said Fräulein, 'we shall see what you remember.' Rapping the table with a shiny black ruler, she said, 'What is this?'

'*Ber Pisch*,' said Prissy triumphantly.

'*Der Tisch, der Tisch*—because of your teeth you cannot properly speak.'

Baby giggled.

'It is not funny,' Fräulein said sharply, picking up a book. 'What is this?'

Baby knew. Out from her fat, pursed lips came '*Buch*.'

Twittie was *der Vogel*.

They learnt a verb. 'After me repeat—' ordered Fräulein, '*ich liebe*, I love.'

Hattie didn't love Fräulein. Mother wouldn't want her to love her, or to learn German. Then, as she reluctantly repeated, '*Du liebst*, you love,' she remembered about spies again. 'Spies are damn' brave,' Father had said, 'clever too—got to know the language of the country they're spying against inside out, idioms and the whole caboodle.' Inside out. '*Sie lieben*,' Hattie echoed with dawning eagerness; she would be a spy and Father would be proud of her. She'd be shot if she was caught, blindfolded, by a firing-squad. She would rather be shot than shoot herself. Bad spies who spied against their country were hanged. Hanging, Father had said, was too good for them. They needed squashing like slugs.

After German they did geography. Because she had no atlas, Hattie sat at the end of the table with Fräulein and shared hers. Fräulein's white cotton blouse was not as tight as Madame's black satin; when she lent forward the insides lay on the table like two heavy great bags. Hattie could see her face without looking up. There was a mole on her chin with two curly black hairs on it. She couldn't bear to be touched by it, even if it brushed the top of her head and she didn't know. She bent lower over the table; she couldn't bear to be touched by Fräulein at all. Crouching beneath her, she felt like someone in a stuffy tent. Fräulein's hand, holding a pencil, had big splashing freckles on the back.

'Look how small England is compared with Germany,' Fräulein said. 'Germany could gobble up England.' Fräulein gobbled 'gobble'.

'*You English, think you own the earth!*' Hattie was back again on the wet grey sand of France. Madame hadn't gobbled, she had shrieked. Mother had said, '*We do—most of it.*' Hattie would rather have been Mother saying that to Madame on the beach, than herself saying it crouched over by Fräulein who was an enemy; but Mother would expect her to. Fräulein would box her ears. She might strangle her. How would Mother bear it with her strangled and Father in the sewers? 'Please, I feel sick,' said Hattie.

'Sick?' Dropping the pencil, Fräulein's hand disappeared from the table and pouncing on Hattie's head swivelled it round; with the other she tilted her chin. Skin, flesh—Hattie didn't look.

'She's been ill,' said Baby importantly.

'*Ja*, but that is over now. You are hot. Go and stand by the window and breathe.'

Resting her chin on a bar at the open window, Hattie breathed. If only she were a bird and could fly away over the roofs and in at Mother's window. Twittie couldn't fly, he wasn't allowed to. The misery of it stiffened her, helping her with desperation to do what she had to do. Turning, Hattie faced them—Fräulein watching her with an expression on her face she didn't understand; Baby, turned round in her chair, picking her nose; Prissy sucking her plate and staring. 'We own the earth,' Hattie's voice, which had set out with defiance, rose on 'earth'. Unlike the Wren, she had forgotten to qualify her statement.

'We? Who is we?' Fräulein demanded.

'The English,' Hattie shrilled.

'*Du liebe Güte!*' Fräulein made no move to spit; she snorted, compressing her lips for a moment before denouncing a nation of undisciplined, lazy fools. Her chin trembled, her sallow face reddened with passion as she gave vent to an accumulation of hate engendered in nearly thirty years in English schoolrooms, triggered off by a pale-faced child in a blue smock who stared at her with wide shocked eyes. She was as unconscious of her audience as she was of the tears that invariably ran down her cheeks as she sat in one of the cheap seats at a concert. Now, as her anger petered out, she felt the humiliation of having permitted this child to rouse her. 'Come and sit down. You will not be sick,' she said coldly.

Hattie dreamt that Fräulein was strangling her. As her fingers closed round her neck, she screamed. She woke up as Nana came. 'What in the world is the matter, child?' Hattie could still feel the hands on her throat as she sat bolt upright, shaking with terror. Nana answered herself, 'You've been dreaming.'

'I dreamt Fräulein was throttling me.'

Nana clucked. 'She wouldn't want to do a thing like that.'

She would, Hattie knew—the Fräulein in her dream and the real Fräulein, both badly wanted to throttle her.

Nana's mind made a business-like inventory of the day's food; porridge, scrambled eggs: boiled mutton, beans, potatoes, bread and butter pudding: plum jam, seed-cake—her mind lingered for a moment on the seeds and then rejected them. Not food, overwrought nerves. There had been some trouble with that German woman. Baby had been bursting with it, but Nana wouldn't be a party to tale bearing and Hattie had said nothing. 'Was Fräulein cross with you today?'

'Yes—' Hattie still shook, 'I said the English owned the earth, but I forgot we only own part of it.'

'Well,' said Nana, 'I can't think *that's* anything to get into a taking over. Neither of you can make a mort of difference as to who owns it. I suppose,' she said, 'that woman—Fräulein wants it.'

Hattie nodded, 'Madame did too.'

'Well, you lie down and go to sleep again. I'm just going to bed myself.' Putting down the lamp on the dressing-table, Nana stooped to tuck Hattie up. 'Shut your eyes and think of something nice, think of a party.'

Shutting her eyes obediently, Hattie thought of Françoise's birthday party, when they had gone in a wagon to a faraway

K

beach and the bread had been wrapped in Françoise's father's bathing-suit. Mother had said it was horrible and she didn't want any bread and she didn't want Hattie to have any either, but as guests she supposed they would have to. Hattie, who hadn't minded a bit and was ravenous, had eaten two great hunks. They had dug a sand-castle and Marcel and Jean had been disgusting into the moat.

CHAPTER XVI

'YOU'RE STAYING IN BED this morning after that nightmare,' Nana said.

'Fräulein will think I'm afraid,' Hattie said slowly.

'Afraid of what?' Nana looked at her sharply. 'That dream was only a dream and she doesn't know anything about it.'

'Her being cross.'

'Not she! If you ask me, foreigners don't think the same as we do, and why should you be afraid?—tell me that.'

Hattie couldn't. She couldn't explain about Fräulein's chin shaking and the dark tide of blood that had swept up under her yellow tough-looking skin, and the fury and scorn in her eyes that could see through skin and flesh—'Damn' German scum.'

'*Hattie!*' said Nana. 'You naughty girl!—what are you saying?

Lifting her chin, squaring her shoulders in Baby's nightie which she hated, Hattie felt strong and sensible and brave. Then, remembering Mother, her spirit slumped.

After the nursery door had shut behind Nana, John St Aubrey came into Hattie's bedroom. 'Hullo, Hattie—so you're taking it easy and giving Fräulein a miss, I hear.'

Had he heard about everything? Hattie wondered in dismay. 'Nana made me. I'm not *afraid* of Fräulein.'

'Naturally not, though I dare say I would be.'

'Afraid?' Hattie knew he was joking, he was smiling. 'Is Mother better?' He wouldn't smile if she wasn't. At the thought her heart lifted. Then seeing the change in his face as the smile faded, she was filled with sudden terror.

He had seen the eyes of a trapped hare, its neck in a wire noose, look like that. He had put the hare out of its misery. It had been easily done, he had wanted nothing from the hare. 'Your mother was still unconscious last night I'm afraid. I have not heard this morning.'

'Oh—' Hattie's breath sucked up. The relief was tremendous. Then, as the terror ebbed, her wretchedness came back. 'It's like being *dead*,' she burst out. Her lips trembled.

'Nothing of the sort, it's not a bit the same.' Juggling the money in his pocket with a bracing fanfare, he drove his point home. 'When you faint you're unconscious, but you aren't dead. Even so, Hattie, it's imperative that your father should know what has happened to your mother, and the only person who can let him know, or tell me where he is so that I can, is you—' he paused. 'If you don't, he may never forgive you,' he said gravely. 'Where is he?'

In the sewers. She didn't know for certain, but she was pretty sure. *In the sewers.* Suppose she said it? They would go and look for him. Mother wouldn't want him caught because of her. Hattie looked down at the sheet, seeing the spot again where she had spilt some porridge at breakfast.

'He's dead. I told you.'

'What happened? Why did he die?'

'He was drowned, fishing. He had a heart attack and fell in. They think he was fri—' how furious Father would be if she said he'd been frightened by thunder. He would never forgive her for that.

'What do they think? Why don't you finish?'

'They think he was frightened by—something, but Father never was frightened by anything. He can't bear cowards.'

'He won't have to suffer them any more if he's dead,' said John St Aubrey brutally. 'And so you can't help us? If your mother regains consciousness and asks for your father, he won't be there.'

'*I* will. Please let me go,' Hattie pleaded, 'I'll explain to Mother.'

'What is there to explain, except that you refused to help?'

'I *can't* help,' Hattie wailed, her throat filling.

'And you can't go, I'm afraid,' his voice softened. 'They won't let children into the wards as I told you, and while your mother is unconscious there would be no point in your going.'

'But you want Father.'

'He doesn't know about it and you do.'

'Mother will die and I shan't be there,' the pain in her throat made Hattie croak.

'I promise you, Hattie,' he said slowly, 'that if your mother is going to die you shall see her, but she isn't, she is going to get better.'

Hattie got up in time for dinner. When Nana had finished dishing out shepherd's pie and carrots, she looked round the nursery. 'Where in the world has Twittie got to?'

'He's in the cupboard,' Baby giggled; 'I'd forgotten.'

'In the cupboard? Whatever for?'

'Fräulein told me to put him there: he was singing.'

Choking down a mouthful of mince, scarlet with outrage, Hattie said, 'How *could* you put him there?—shut up in the dark because,' her voice cracked, 'he was singing.'

'It's nothing to do with you, he's mine,' said Baby furiously, 'and I'll always keep him in the cupboard if I want to.'

'You wouldn't want to; no one would want to do a thing like that,' *except that German woman,* Nana would have liked to add.

Getting up, she went over to the cupboard and took out the cage.

Twittie wasn't on his perch and there was no sound from him.

'Is he dead?' Hattie was trembling.

'Good gracious, no! He's down in the corner, cleaning up under his wing,' said Nana cheerfully.

They went to Kensington Gardens that afternoon. Yesterday rain had baulked them. Hattie was astonished by the grass which seemed to stretch on for ever. 'Are you allowed to *walk* on it?' She supposed you must be; some children were playing and a couple of grown-ups strolling on it arm in arm.

'Of course you are!' Baby said.

'You aren't allowed to in France.'

'France must be a silly place.' Tossing her head, Baby tore off across the grass.

'Is she being a mad dog?' Hattie asked.

'I couldn't tell you,' said Nana. 'I know she's showing off.'

A thread of wisdom seemed to bind Nana and Hattie together. Hattie felt grown-up and sensible, seeing Baby, as Nana did, as silly and babyish. Then, suddenly, she felt a familiar wriggle in the pit of her stomach, a rapid twisting like the movement of a worm. Excitement shot up in her; kicking up her heels, she ran as she hadn't run since before she was ill, leaving the path, tearing across the grass like a mad dog into the sun. She stopped at the pond.

Panting, she stood and stared in wonder.

A man with a bamboo was threshing the water behind a lovely great toy yacht; there were other boats, and a boy was paddling; an old woman in a purple coat was throwing food to the ducks. Hattie had never seen so many ducks; there were pigeons waddling about on the edge, and sparrows, and there were children and prams and nurses. Suddenly there was a squawking screech and a gull swooped down on the flat shining water. Looking up, Hattie saw another and another. This familiar homely noise, the sight of them, filled her afresh with longing and homesickness. She remembered Mother. Mother wanting to be a gull on the pond in St James's Park. This must be the pond: there couldn't be two ponds with gulls in London. As she watched, one of the gulls came down and strutted on the water's edge. Mother. Mother was still unconscious. Suppose she had died and changed into a gull? For a moment Hattie's heart seemed to stop. No, she wouldn't do that if she was dead. She might have if she wasn't and could. Hattie stared huge-eyed as the old woman threw a piece of bread at Mother and she snatched it. Why should she feed her? Why didn't she come over here? 'I haven't any food, that's why.' '*Your place is with your father.*' Mother didn't want her. Father was in the sewers and hadn't a place for her either.

Filled with a wild despair, Hattie saw the gull take wing again and swoop up, shrieking. Tears flooded her eyes.

'Hattie, what a naughty girl you are tearing about like that after you've been ill!' Nana was beside her. 'What would your mother say if she knew?'

'She wouldn't care.' Hattie didn't say it out loud. Her lips trembled. Biting the bottom one, twisting one of the buttons of her coat, she said nothing for a moment. Then she asked, 'Is this the pond in St James's Park?'

'No, it's the Round Pond. We're in Kensington Gardens,' Nana told her.

It wasn't Mother, it was only a gull.

Relief poured into Hattie.

While her daughter stood by the Round Pond, Rose Suckling regained consciousness for the second time. The mystification of her initial resurrection six hours earlier had been profound. Where was she? What was this appalling pain in her head? Turning it a little, gazing with effort, she had recognized a hospital ward. Hattie!—where was Hattie? What in heaven's name had happened? Lifting her throbbing head, she had looked round wildly, seeing an old woman hunched in a shawl, someone else lying mummified with bandages, faces—no child anywhere. 'Nurse—' her voice had risen in a weak replica of one of Hattie's wails, but the figure down the ward had continued bending over a bed.

'Nurse!' the woman opposite, black-haired, beef-faced, shouted in the stentorian tones of a vendor, 'Nurse!—'er's woked!'

The Wren's head fell back. She had become aware of striped flannel in place of her cotton nightdress, but with Hattie missing, that and the outrage of a public ward tapped on her mind but never touched her spirit. She watched, squinting a little, with agonized impatience, the movements of the nurse. 'Where's Hattie?—where's my child?'

The nurse, near enough to hear then, came right to the bed before she said, 'Quite safe. There's nothing to worry about.'

'She hasn't had her tea.'

'It's morning now, Friday morning. She's had her tea—' the nurse paused for a moment's calculation '—two of them perhaps three, if she had tea on Tuesday—since you came in,' she smiled. She had the face of a tired, kindly old sheep, her cap perched on a ruche of fuzzy yellow-white hair.

'What do you mean? I don't understand,' the Wren's face puckered.

'You were knocked down by a cab on Tuesday, dear. The gentleman in the cab took your little girl home.'

'A *gentleman* took Hattie—' wild-eyed, the Wren reared up. 'How dared you let him—'

'She's perfectly all right. Lie down—' taking the Wren's shoulders in her broad, scrubbed hands, Nurse laid her back as if she were a child. 'And don't worry, there's no need.'

'No need? Of course there is.' The throbbing was like an iron bar being battered through her head. 'How can I not worry with Hattie—' lying vulnerable and powerless like an animal in a trap, her lips quivered.

Nurse straightened the sheet.

'Your little girl is with his own child in a nursery with a nanny, so Sister said.'

'A nanny, a nursery—' the Wren sighed gently, as realization filtered among the hammer strokes into her brain—what she had always wanted for Hattie, but now, among strangers? Better France, *better a dinner of herbs where love is*, but France, the thought of France, of Sebbie engulfed her with mounting agitation.

Drugged, Rose Suckling had slept for six hours. When she woke for the second time, it was nearly three. The throbbing in her head was better, less like boring iron and more like the slower rhythm of a steamer paddle.

Sister came. Brisk, impartial, she treated her as one with an equality of brain.

'Can you remember?'

'Yes,' said the Wren; the load of her memory was almost unbearable. 'I must see my child.'

'Your child is in clover.'

Hattie in a field of clover, purple-red on the other side of the hedge where the honeysuckle grew in the village at home.

'Nurse says she told you the circumstances.'

'Yes.'

'Mr St Aubrey and his wife have five children; the youngest, the same age as your little girl, is still in the nursery with the nanny. If someone had to run you over it couldn't have been more fortunate,' Sister stated the practical facts untouched by humour.

The Wren was not in the mood for humour, anyway. 'However safe she is, Hattie has been ill. She has never been away from me before, and she must have seen me knocked down, carried off—' her lips twisted in the face of Hattie's load.

'Children are adaptable. As regards her health, the nanny will have seen to that—if she's worth her salt.'

'She is highly strung—'

'So are many children,' said Sister, as if an over-excitable, unhinged collection could have an ameliorating effect on Hattie's condition. 'But you will hear how she is quite soon. Mr St Aubrey is coming to see you for a few minutes at four o'clock—only a few,' she said repressively. 'In your condition you should keep absolutely quiet, but although it is not visiting time we are stretching a point in view of your anxiety.'

'Thank you,' said the Wren humbly.

'Hattie cannot remember the name of the hotel where your luggage is.'

'Our luggage—' the brown trunk and her hat-box, 'it's at a small hotel called—' neither could she; the Wren's brain clogged. 'We went there from the Grosvenor—' shutting her eyes, she bit her lip '—Prince's,' she gave a little murmur of triumph.

Sister's orderly brain received the fact with satisfaction. 'Good.'

The Wren's mind, never so orderly and now further disordered by weakness, boggled at the realization of the disaster that Hattie's ignorance had meant. 'Hattie's got no clothes—'

'What she stands up in.'

What did she stand up in? Searching her momory, the Wren's brain was slowly, laboriously, dressing Hattie, when Sister diverted her thoughts almost as thoroughly as if she had pressed some button. 'Have you a next of kin?—someone you would like informed?'

Sebbie—the Wren's longing was unbearable. 'Informed? Am I dying?' Unexpectedly, before she had time to control herself, her eyes poured tears.

'Dying?—good gracious, no! You'll be as right as rain in next to no time. But it's customary to notify your next of kin when you're in hospital,' Sister's tone held a note of reproof at this ignorance of social etiquette.

'My husband,' whispered the Wren.

The screens parted and a young red face thrust through the opening. 'Please, Sister, can I speak to you?'

'What is it, Nurse?'

'Mrs Smith, Sister, I can't feel her pulse. I think she's—' the girl's eyes, round and blue like a baby's, focused on the Wren for a moment.

'She's too young,' thought the Wren, this maternal reflection helping to steady her.

'It helps to feel in the right place, Nurse.' There was no sarcasm; it was simply another of those pedestrian statements with which Sister damped down the first spark of agitation in her nurses. It was quite on the cards that Mrs Smith was dead. She was unlikely to last the night. Promising Mrs Suckling a cup of tea, leaving in abeyance her next of kin, Sister disappeared through the screens followed by the nurse.

Long after the Wren had drunk her tea, and passed from acute emotionalism to a daze that was almost sleep, Sister returned with a man. 'Here is Mr St Aubrey to see you, Mrs Suckling.'

CHAPTER XVII

WHAT WAS SAUCE for the goose was sauce for the gander and although, in Nana's opinion, Fräulein would do better to go back to her own country and good riddance to bad rubbish, since there seemed no hope of that happening just now, and Baby had to suffer her presence, Hattie must too. Hattie had had three days in which to recover from her nightmare, although there was no telling with a child like that, as Nana well knew. 'You were afraid Fräulein would think you were afraid: now you can show her that you aren't,' she told Hattie on Monday morning.

Hattie *was* afraid. Even fortified by a message of love from the Wren who, now that she was conscious, lived again, and the possession of her own clothes from the trunk whose locality the Wren had remembered, Hattie was still afraid. Fräulein was still Fräulein, twice over—fleshy Fräulein and nightmare Fräulein. The latter had been the worst, but now they had mingled in Hattie's mind to make one horrible whole.

'*Guten Morgen, Kinder.*'

'*Guten Morgen, Fräulein,*' Hattie joined in.

Fräulein behaved as though nothing had happened, but it had, and Hattie could feel a wall between them. During dictation, Twittie made little pecking noises. When Fräulein wasn't looking, Hattie glanced furtively at the cage which was full in the sun. 'Please God, don't let Twittie sing,' she prayed. After dictation they did French.

'Hattie knows French,' Baby said.

'That we will see, *nicht wahr.*' Rapping the table, Fräulein said to Hattie, 'What is this?'

'*Le table.*' How could she think she didn't know? thought Hattie indignantly.

When Fräulein said, '*Gut,*' it made it worse.

'*J'aime, tu aimes, il aime,*' they recited like sheep. Hattie didn't love Fräulein, she hated her. Roused by the chorus of voices, Twittie began to sing. Hattie spoke louder to try to drown him, but it was no good.

'*Du liebe Güte!*' Getting up, Fräulein strode to the cage. '*Schweig 'mal!*' she shouted, slapping the bars, then seizing his black cloth from the table, put it over the cage.

Beast, beast, *beast*! Scarlet, choking with fury, Hattie squeezed her hands together in her lap. The singing stopped. On her way back to her chair, Fräulein pulled back Hattie's head by the hair and pinched her nose, 'What is this?'

Hattie could not speak.

'Oh, you the French know, *nicht wahr*?'

'*Le mez*,' said Prissy proudly.

'*Nez*, not mez—*nez, nez, nez*.'

They were on the future tense of *aimer* when Twittie began to sing again. In silence, Fräulein rose. The silence, the knowledge of her pent-up fury, seemed worse to Hattie than an outburst. Snatching off the cloth, grabbing the cage, swinging it roughly so that Twittie, terrified, fluttered and clawed at the bars, Fräulein went straight to the cupboard and hurling the cage inside, shut and fastened the door.

Starting up, Hattie rushed at the cupboard, too angry to be afraid. 'Don't! Take him out! It's cruel!' she shrieked.

Fräulein's hands seized Hattie's upper arms. Her fingers squeezed, her nails bit into the sleeves of her Holland pinafore. '*Du unhöfliches, dummes Mädchen!*' Switching to English, the torrent of abuse above Hattie's head as she was shaken dizzy, before being pushed back and forced into the chair. 'Baby, get your skipping-rope,' Fräulein ordered.

Baby, on whose fat parted lips some neglected dribble had collected, stared blankly. It took a shout from Fräulein to blast her into action, sending her over to the corner to fumble with clumsy excitement to disentangle her skipping-rope from her hoop.

Struggling, Hattie tried to kick, but Fräulein was behind her chair, and when she tried to bite her hand she could not reach that either. Fräulein made swift work with the rope; tying Hattie to the back of the chair, she pushed her up against the table, wedging her like a sardine. Then she fetched Twittie's black cloth and put it over Hattie's head.

Shocked, shaken almost out of her wits, Hattie sat under the cloth as silent as Twittie. Tears trickled down her cheeks, tickling as they went. As the shock ebbed, the feeling of being blind or in a dungeon became worse. The folds of black cloth hung down as far as her chest. She was buried alive. She wanted to shriek, to yell for Nana, but if she did Fräulein would throttle her. Digging her teeth into her lower lip, she thought of Father. Just thinking of him made her braver. '*Brute, damn' German bullying brute*,' it was as though Father had spoken inside her. What would he do if he were her? Fräulein couldn't have done it to him. But what would he do if she had?—break the skipping-rope like Samson in the temple and bring the whole nursery down? No, he couldn't do that. He'd throttle Fräulein, wrench open the cupboard and take out Twittie. He would take the cage to the window, open the window wide, open Twittie's door and let him fly away up into the sun . . .

It was daylight when Hattie woke up. She did not know what time it was, but she had hit her head six times on the pillow last night. Sitting up, she listened. Hearing no sound, she got out of bed, and putting on her dressing-gown, crept barefoot along the passage to the nursery. The clock on the mantelpiece said six twenty. First she went to the window and opened it as quietly as she could, but it still made a noise. It was misty and rather cold; she did wish the sun was out. It would be later; that's what Mother loved about the autumn—the mistiness which made her think of pith and the hot midday sun. Hattie couldn't wait for the sun for Twittie. Nana said his cage must never be left in the nursery again during lessons, but when she had set him free he would be safe. 'That's what comes of having a German,' Nana had been so angry she had said it out loud, when before she had only thought it. Hattie wasn't going to lessons again. 'She's not your governess,' Nana told her, 'and I only wish she wasn't Baby's.' Baby had pretended not to wish it. 'She likes me,' she had said complacently. 'That remains to be seen. You wait till you cross her. She's only been here a fortnight, there's plenty of time.' Time for what? Hattie knew: time to throttle Baby. 'Skipping-rope, indeed! Either she goes or I do.' Fräulein would go, Nana wouldn't; Hattie knew that too.

Going over to the silent cage, Hattie took off his black cloth. Twittie was awake and cleaning under his wing again. '*Der Vogel*,' Hattie whispered, but even those two words seemed to bring back Fräulein, making her wobble inside. '*Le petit oiseau, bon jour, mon chéri*,' and that brought back France and her home-sickness and the longing for the flaking old house in the vegetable market so that she didn't care if she was being stagnant. There was a rattle in the road below. Taking the cage with her, she went to the window, and poking her head through the bars, saw the milk cart. She must hurry. Opening the door of the cage, quickly turning it towards the open air, she cried softly, 'Fly away,

Twittie.' But instead of bursting out, Twittie set to work on his other wing. He couldn't have seen the open door. Putting her hand into the cage to take him out frightened him into a flutter. 'It's all right, Twittie, I'm not Fräulein.' Her hand closed round him, pinioning his wings like Fräulein holding her arms. She could squeeze him till he died if she wanted to, but she didn't. Fräulein had wanted to kill her. Stroking Twittie's head with her finger, she bent and kissed it. Then, from somewhere down in the house, she heard a noise. 'Quick, Twittie! *Vas-y en toute vitesse*—' thrusting her arm out of the window, she let him go. '*Adieu, mon chérie.*' She watched the little lemon-coloured body swoop and be swallowed up by the pithy mistiness.

CHAPTER XVIII

SHUTTING HER EYES, pressing her neck sharply against the
top bar, Hattie pretended it was the knife of the guillotine. Her
head had dropped off into the basket below, brave, bloody and
unbowed, before the knitting jeering scum. Opening her eyes,
she saw the tortoiseshell cat down there, the only living creature
apparent in the sedate tidiness of Vicarage Gate. It had nine
lives. She wished Father had. It was so awfully dangerous to have
only one. She saw him with his life in his hands like a pale grey
jelly. If he lost it, he would die. It was like his soul which would
float to heaven when he died. Was it the same?—his life and his
soul? Cats had no souls, the Wren had said.

'Why shouldn't they have?' Sebastian had argued.

'How could they?—all the cats and kittens?'

'What about the Chinese and Indians and Hottentots and
Eskimos and cannibals?—where are they going? Tell me that.'

'There are many mansions.'

'There'll dashed well have to be.'

'Shush—'

'What d'you mean, shush?'

'You know what I mean.'

When Father had let out the golden-crested wren, nothing
had happened to him, no one knew who had done it. It seemed
very unfair to Hattie that when she had only done what he'd told
her to, she should be in such disgrace. It was not her bird and
she had had no right to let it out, Nana said; she said that to let
something that belonged to someone else out of the window was
almost as bad as stealing. If she was a thief, then Father was—a
thief as well as a murderer, Hattie thought. No, he *wasn't*! Nana
had said 'almost', and it wasn't a bit the same as stealing a gold
watch.

Baby had set on Hattie and Nana had dragged them apart. Then
Baby had had a screaming stamping tantrum. She had gone on
crying afterwards, trying to. 'There's no call for you to carry on
like that, now stop it,' Nana had told her exasperated. 'Hattie
had no right to do what she did; on the other hand it's not a mite
of good for you to pretend that you laid such store on Twittie.
Time and again I've had to remind you to feed him, and if I

hadn't taken the cloth off his cage, he'd as often as not been covered till bedtime.' After lessons, when Fräulein had gone, they would open the window wide and put the cage by it with the door open and Twittie might fly back to it, she'd said.

He wouldn't be so silly, of course he wouldn't, Hattie thought. By this time he might be at the Round Pond with the seagulls and ducks and sparrows and pigeons. Her heart warmed at the thought of his pleasure, while she looked about to make sure he wasn't anywhere.

Far down below a cab pulled up at the front door. Craning her head further through the bars, Hattie glared down. Perhaps it was Baby's mother?—come unexpectedly; no one had said she was coming today.

It wasn't. It was a man. He had no hat. His hair was thick and fairish and rough like a dog's.

'Father!' Hattie shrieked.

Sebastian looked up. Four storeys up, in the kind of house he'd always loathed, the face of his daughter, working with excitement, hung stork-necked through bars. 'Hullo, Hat! Come down, brat, and let me in!'

'Coming!'

The man's roar, the child's banshee shriek, had parted the air of respectable, residential Kensington.

Dragging back her head, Hattie rushed out of the room. Tearing downstairs, she collided with Bessie the housemaid. 'Father's come!' she shouted.

'Lawk-a-mussy, I thought 'e was dead.'

Dead—Hattie had forgotten. Tearing on, she tore to save him. If only he didn't ring, if she could get to him before anyone saw him. Pelting through the hall, fumbling with the lock, she opened the door and burst through, slamming it behind her.

She was in his arms, hanging on to him like a monkey to a tree-trunk. His arms squashed her till her bones seemed to crack. Nuzzling, she smelt the smell of his serge coat, stubbing her nose against the warm hard thickness of his neck, she heard his soothing rumble. Dragging her head away, she said, 'Quick!—we must go.'

'Why?'

'To hide.'

'Who from?'

'The police.' Struggling, she was on her feet again.

'What have you been up to, suckling?'

He was trying to hide it from her, pretending still. 'You, it's you. I know you've been hiding—in the sewers—' she whispered. 'Please come,' she dragged at his arm.

'In the sewers? Great Scot, Hat, what d'you think I am?—a damn' rat?' he let out a meaty chuckle which suddenly roared into laughter.

The baker's boy, with a hand-cart of cottage loaves and buns, stopped to stare. Hattie glared at him, horrified. 'That boy's seen you, he'll tell them.'

'What damn' bee have you got in your confounded bonnet now, Hat? What d'you think I've done?'

Hattie couldn't say it; although she had tried to do it herself she couldn't tell him. He hadn't meant to kill him, but she couldn't.

'Answer me,' his voice was almost a roar.

'I'll explain,' Hattie wailed.

'Well, you'd better come somewhere and do it.'

'The door's shut, we can't get in without ringing and they mustn't see us.'

'I don't want to get in, we'll go for a walk.'

'I haven't got my hat and coat.'

'Who cares—it's warm enough.'

She didn't, she didn't want them. She felt ashamed of mentioning them with Father in such danger. As she went after him, she felt the familiar glorious freedom for a moment. 'Let's go into Kensington Gardens, I'll show you the way,' she took his hand. 'Mother's in hospital—you know, don't you—that's why you've come. She came to save me because I went across the street. I thought I was following her but it was someone else, and a fire-engine came, and running away from that I went in front of a cab and Mother pushed me out of the way and was knocked down herself. I didn't mean to go across without her, it was a mistake,' Hattie finished breathlessly.

'I know, I've seen her.' The memory of it tugged at him.

'Everyone sees her but me! They won't let me in,' said Hattie furiously. 'They've shut me out!' her rising voice shook.

'She'll come out soon.'

'What'll we do then?'

'What the Wren wants.'

'Always?' asked Hattie with wonder.

'Not for ever,' said Sebastian with honesty.

'What would you like to do?'

'Eat, drink and be merry.

'I've eaten and drunk, but I haven't been merry.'

'Poor little beast—' he looked down on the top of her head, packed with rubbish again. It must be cleared out.

'I'm in disgrace for letting out Twittie—that's why I was in my bedroom. But I wasn't going to lessons anyhow, Fräulein wants to kill me.'

'The devil she does! What for?'

Hattie told him.

'Sounds like a sadist.'

'What's a sadist?'

'Someone who would rather pull the wings off a fly than kill it.'

Hattie tried to remember. 'I didn't see her doing anything to flies.'

'I dare say not.'

When Hattie told Father about letting out Twittie, he said, 'Damn' silly thing to do, letting it out like that.'

'But you *told* me to let wild birds out of cages.'

'Wild birds, yes, but I'll wager that one wasn't. What was it?'

'A canary,' said Hattie defiantly.

'Then it wasn't wild—might have been if you'd found it in a cage on the Canary Islands, but I'll bet you it was born in captivity.'

'But even if it wasn't wild, why should it live in a cage?'

'Got to live somewhere, doesn't miss what it's never had, and now you've let it out the wild birds—' *will peck the poor little brute to bits*, he had been about to say, but the absence of the Wren stopped him; better keep the boat on an even keel, 'won't know him.'

'They'll think he's lovely,' said Hattie with conviction. 'Nana's going to open the window in case he wants to come back, but how could he? Let's go to the Round Pond and see if he's there.'

The Gardens received them—the vast stretches of grass, the trees heavy and dark with the long summer behind them, splashed here and there prematurely with yellow. Prams, nurses, children.

'That's what the Wren wanted for you: a nurse and a pram in Kensington Gardens,' Sebastian said.

'Would it have made me different?'

'It would have coated you with an orthodox crust.'

Hattie, seeing herself coated in pastry, said, 'I like Nana, I like her awfully, but would I have been like Baby?' She knew it was a silly question deserving a silly answer, as she hadn't told him properly about her yet. 'She's nine and she's still called Baby.'

'What on earth for?'

'Because she's the youngest.'

'They're damn' lucky she's not an imbecile—or is she?'

'No—she's not mad, exactly,' said Hattie slowly, 'but she likes crying, and she says her mother doesn't like her much but I think she was pretending, and she wouldn't be any good with Arabs, she wouldn't shoot herself, she'd shriek, and her lips are fat.'

'Can't help those—though from all accounts I'm not surprised if her mother doesn't like her. Sounds as though she could do with a bit of a walloping—though it's their fault, bound to be I should think, for not calling her something sensible. Hasn't she got a name?'

'Yes, Angela.'

'Well, then—I should have thought St Aubrey would have had more sense, a damn' good fisherman like that. D'you know what he caught in Scotland?'

Hattie didn't. She didn't want to think about fishing either.

'A twenty pound salmon—takes a bit of landing a fish of that size, Hat.'

'How do you know?'

'He told me.'

'Have you seen him?'

'Of course I've seen him, been to his office. He telegraphed me about the Wren.'

'A telegram—all the way to France?' said Hattie, awed. France reminded her—'Baby's mother's gone to Paris; she's taken Ethel to be finished. They haven't quarrelled—her and Mr St Aubrey.'

'Why should they have?'

'They might have, but I don't know if they ever do.'

'Everyone quarrels sometimes—no spine if they don't. The Wren and I don't always see eye to eye.'

'It doesn't matter being cross when people love each other; they understand,' Hattie said.

He'd sailed too near the wind with Rosie—never thought she'd make off or he'd have come into the open before—saved her being knocked for six and prevented the whole footling caboodle all for the sake of a bit of nonsense. He'd have got her back though without the intervention of a cab. *It doesn't matter being cross when people love each other, they understand.* How the devil did the brat know that? Sebastian looked with attention at the top of his daughter's head. 'Who told you that?'

Father thought it was a good thing to have said, that's why he wanted to know. *No one. I thought of it myself.* Hattie rejected the story wistfully. 'Mother.'

'When?'

'In the train. She said you and her loved each other like that.'

Moved, he ignored the villainous grammar again. Rosie had said that, had she?—at as late a stage as in the train. Said it for Hat's sake? But she'd conceived it, hadn't she, whether she'd said it for the brat's sake or not. He saw it as the foundation for her gamble, the knowledge on which she'd staked her future, hers and Hat's, plunking down her fortune with her hackles up on a rank outsider. 'She was right,' said Sebastian. 'Your mother's got wisdom and courage—sound to the core; there's no rotten marrow in your mother's bones, Hat, never forget that.'

'Is my marrow rotten?'

'No, thanks to her, and if I ever find it is there'll be the devil to pay, suckling.'

Father's marrow? Hattie lost interest, they had reached the Round Pond. Gulls were over it again.

'If Mother had turned into a gull in France she'd have come to the pond in St James's Park.'

'No, she'd have come here. It was Kensington Gardens she was always on about,' Sebastian said.

'She wouldn't have, she said St James's Park, Father.'

'Why?'

'I don't know.'

'I do.' Raking in his mind, he'd raked it up; he'd kissed her there on a seat by the pond. It wasn't the first time, or the second, but she'd laid store by it, must have.

'Why?' Hattie asked, but Father didn't answer. 'Why did Mother want to go to St James's Park if she was a gull?'

He looked at her then, 'Because she'd been happy there, that's why, Hat. She deserves a better life than a gull's.'

'I told her she wouldn't want to eat nastiness. If you were a gull you'd be safe, you could swoop down and screech at the *gendarmes.*'

'Why the *gendarmes*?'

But Hattie, engrossed in this vision, scarcely heard; she was Father swooping—

'Why the *gendarmes*?'

'Because of them wanting you, and they couldn't get you,' she said triumphantly, 'however much you screeched.'

'They could shoot.'

'No!' What she saw was horrible. 'You mustn't swoop, say you won't!' her voice shrilled.

'Stop talking balderdash.'

'I can't see Twittie.'

When they sat down on a seat, Sebastian said, 'Now, Hat, let's get things straight. What in heaven's name made you think I was skulking in a sewer?'

'You said the sewers were the best place, better than Fontaine-bleau.'

'You think I'm a criminal, do you?'

Hattie picked at a scab on her knee.

'Do you?' said Sebastian inexorably.

'You didn't mean to do it.'

'I never do what I don't mean to.'

Hattie's inside went hollow. 'You didn't mean to—' she couldn't say it. She picked abstractedly at her scab, wasting the glory of it.

'To what? If there's one thing I won't stomach it's women who leave their sentences unfinished, and if you start growing up into one of those you'll go into an orphanage and do your growing there.'

'I'm not an orphan.'

'Don't argue. Finish.'

'Murder—' Hattie whispered, 'you didn't mean to murder him.'

'Oh, that's it, is it? If I'm hanged you *will* be an orphan,' said Sebastian triumphantly.

'Mother——'

'Your mother would die of shame.'

A couple of tears slid unexpectedly down Hattie's cheeks. Horrified, she went on staring straight ahead, letting them drip. Struggling for control, she picked harder. The scab was half off.

'Who d'you think I've murdered? Out with it.'

'You didn't!' said Hattie wildly. 'You thought he could swim.'

Sebastian's hand came down on his daughter's, grinding it into the scab, grinding the scab into the bone. 'Who?'

'The fisherman on the sea-wall.'

'Picard?—the one I told you to push in? You said you had.'

Hattie nodded silently. She left her head down at the end of the last nod, she hadn't the heart to lift it.

Sebastian lifted it. Transferring his hand from her knee, he lifted her head and twisted it to face him. 'Look at me, *look— d'you hear?*' his voice deepened to the makings of a roar.

Hattie looked, her eyes met his ashamed and wretched. He would know now that she was a liar and a coward, that instead of a son he'd got a——

'Did you push that man in, or didn't you?'

'No.'

'Will you swear that you didn't before Almighty God?'

Without looking, Hattie saw Almighty God standing on the grass waiting. She saw the fisherman grovelling for sweets. She hadn't. 'Yes.'

Sebastian searched her face. He would give no quarter for what he saw there; the time for fabrication was over. He'd be damned if she'd bamboozle him a second time. 'What do you mean "yes"?' he said awfully. 'D'you mean yes you'll swear you didn't, or yes you did push him in?'

'I mean yes I'll swear I didn't—before Almighty God had gone.'

'And so you let me believe you were culpable, forcing me to make retribution to a woman with an intelligence the size of a pea.'

'A pea?' In her wretchedness and ignorance Hattie clutched at the small familiar word. 'How big is a proper intelligence?'

'I shan't tell you.' Sebastian crossed his legs. 'For once we are going to stick to the point. What makes you think I murdered the wretched little brute?'

He had put the weight back again into Hattie's head. It lay in the middle of her brain like a stone. 'You disappeared.'

'Disappeared? What do you mean?'

'When I was sheltering by the shed I saw you on the wall and then you disappeared and I thought—I thought you'd gone behind the little house to push him in.'

'No, I hadn't.' Sebastian stared ahead of him—where had he gone? Scratching about in his mind again, he tried impatiently to uncover some small futile action. He'd got it! 'My hat fell in. I had to go down the steps and land the blithering thing with my rod—that's when you lost sight of me.'

'Your hat—' that brown familiar shape with a hole in it that Mother wanted to burn. 'Did it float?'

Yes, Father said it did. 'So that's that.'

'Yes—' Hattie sighed, the wind of relief sucked up her nose and blew slowly out again. There was no need to see Father in a sewer or worry about him any more. She saw the hat in the sea instead, not with terror and misery but with the excitement of savouring a tragedy that hadn't happened till her skin prickled. 'How awful if you hadn't saved it, if it had floated out to sea drifting farther and farther alone with its hole—'

'It would have swamped and sunk; the fishes would have had it.'

'Like people's eyes.'

'No, not like people's eyes—quite different.'

They sat in silence for a moment, each seeing what they saw.

'If you weren't fleeing,' Hattie said slowly, 'why did you go to Paris? Did you really go to find out things for your book?'

'Of course, I did! What d'you think I went for?'

Hattie didn't answer.

'Out with it, brat.'

'It's *my* thought, it belongs to me.' She saw her thought, with surprise at not having seen it like that before, as so much her own that nobody, not even Father, had a right to make her say it.

'It doesn't, when it concerns me. Out with it.' He knew, the Wren had told him, 'Françoise told Hattie you had gone to Paris to see *her*, but Hattie already knew there was something wrong. Children aren't so easily bamboozled as one hopes.' The choice of 'bamboozle' had arrested him; it wasn't one of Rosie's words. He had seen it with satisfaction as a further proof that she had missed him.

'Did you go to see Madame Picard?' Hattie glared in front of her.

'No, of course I didn't! Good God, Hat, why should I go to Paris to see her?'

'Françoise said you had.'

'Damn' little scandalmonger! She'll end up in a wardrobe if she's not careful.'

'Wardrobe?' Hattie looked up at him. 'Was the body really in a wardrobe?'

'A big brown tent with flaps, I told you.'

'I think you told a story,' said Hattie slowly. 'I think you told it because you didn't want me to be frightened of, not *frightened* —uncomfortable—looking in a wardrobe.'

As her eyes widened, her face seemed to shrink. A lifetime of wardrobes—poor idiotic little devil, thought Sebastian. 'It's immaterial what it was, a wardrobe or a tent,' he said. 'I'll bet you a hundred pounds you'll never find a body in a wardrobe or a tent.'

'A hundred pounds—' Hattie sucked up. 'When'll I have to find it by?'

'The bet will last till you die. I'll leave a clause in my will.'

She looked away from him towards the pond. The man thrashing the water was still there like he'd been on Saturday. Father had said he was a dolt. Why couldn't he set the sails? he'd said. Anyone could thrash the water, it was the same kind of rubbish as having an auxiliary motor on a yacht. Hattie's eyes saw the man, but her mind had no place for him. 'I wouldn't want a hundred pounds after you were dead,' she said.

'Balderdash. When you haven't got me sweating my guts out to get the money to feed you, you'll be glad of it.'

'I wouldn't,' said Hattie hoarsely.

'Don't contradict. But you won't get it whether I'm dead or alive. The odds are a hundred to one against your finding a body and it serves you right.'

'I don't want to.' She looked back at him, the misery of potential bereavement swamped in a flood of hope. 'Won't I ever find one, really?'

'I've told you the odds.'

With a sigh of relief she seemed to flop and swell. 'Would you rather not find one, or have the money and a body?'

'Money and body.'

'*Body!*' How could Father be so brave? He didn't seem to mind anything.

'Why should you believe what Françoise said—about your own father?' Sebastian went back like a dog to a bone.

'I said you hadn't gone to see Madame Picard, but—I knew about you and her myself,' said Hattie slowly.

'What did you know?' Someone other than Françoise had told her, must have. She was as green as grass when it came to that sort of thing, not precocious like that little French brute cottoning on to every bit of prattle; her head was too full of her own rubbish already. 'Who else has been tattling to you?'

'No one.'

'Madame?'

'No.'

'Out with it,' his voice deepened ominously.

'You sat on the beach with her,' Hattie picked abstractedly at her funny bone, 'with her head on your shoulder.'

'Not for long—I'd as soon be nuzzled by a polecat. How d'you know?'

'We saw you.'

'You and that little fiend, Françoise?'

'No—Mother and I saw you,' said Hattie slowly.

'The deuce you did!' No wonder Hat knew something was up. 'What were you doing on the groyne? Spying?' No, Rosie wouldn't spy, his mind threw that overboard at once.

'Gulping sea breezes.'

Plain, innocuous truth—digestible. Rosie hadn't told him. 'Your mother has pride and dignity, Hat.'

'I know.'

'How?' he looked at her challengingly.

'She'd stand in the tumbril like a ramrod.' Gazing in front of her, Hattie saw Mother standing in the cart, her golden crest held high.

'The devil she would! She'd mount the steps to the guillotine as though she were sweeping up a staircase to a *soirée*—wouldn't give those bloody gibbering hags of knitters one damn' ounce of pleasure.'

Hattie's breath came up in a sucking whisper, 'Yes.' Pride and excitement churned in her stomach, swelling up into her chest.

They looked in silence at what they saw, with admiration.

Sebastian heaved himself to his feet, 'Come on.'

Hattie sprang up, 'Where are we going?' She hurried after him as he strode off across the grass.

'To see the Wren.'

'They won't let me in!' her voice shrilled.

'They will, I'll make 'em. She's ours isn't she, suckling?' His hand closed round hers, crushing the bones like twigs.